CAMBION'S BLOOD

ERIN FULMER

ALSO BY ERIN FULMER

Cambion's Law
Cambion's Rise

PRAISE FOR THE CAMBION SERIES

"[*Cambion's Law*] sucks readers in with smoky tendrils of forbidden desires...a winning combination of paranormal passion and murderous mayhem."

– Tonya Mathenia, Ind'Tale Magazine

"Lily Knight is a force to be reckoned with! *Cambion's Blood* hooks the reader from the start and never lets go as tension and suspense ratchet up from one page to the next! Although this is book 2, enough backstory is given to situate the story...The action and obstacles Lily faces constantly raise the stakes. *Cambion's Blood* offers up a gripping paranormal tale that intrigues and captivates right from the get-go!"

– Tricia Hill, Ind'Tale Magazine

For the lost girls.

Author's Note

Cambion's Blood is a dark paranormal thriller which depicts on-the-page violence, blood, and abuse of authority. It references gendered violence to explore themes of feminine rage and recovery from trauma, including a scene in which a traumatic flashback disrupts an intimate moment. It features an established relationship which includes light elements of negotiated power exchange and bondage play, with open-door spice. The main character experiences same-gender as well as opposite-gender attraction, with reference to past religious trauma, including conversion therapy and parental estrangement.

The author has endeavored to depict her most challenging themes with nuance, sensitivity, and respect for the complexity of trauma, while telling a fast-paced tale of romantic suspense that flirts with the darker side of desire.

Soundtrack

Control – VNV Nation
Lilith – Halsey
You Want It Darker – Leonard Cohen
Lilian – Depeche Mode
To Your Love – Fiona Apple
Tell That Devil – Jill Andrews
No Light, No Light – Florence + the Machine
Kill Your Darlings (Aesthetic Perfection Remix) – Mesh
Boudica – Karliene
You are the Problem Here – First Aid Kit
East of Eden – Zella Day
Shake It Out – Florence + the Machine
Après Moi – Regina Spektor
Morrigan – Omnia
Blood of Eden – Peter Gabriel
Ireland – Tori Amos
From Eden – Hozier
Evening On the Ground (Lilith's Song) – Iron and Wine
Sacred Heart – The Civil Wars
The Tradition – Halsey
Couldn't Breathe – Lennon
Milk & Honey (Alt Version) – Billie Marten
Lose Control – Meduza, Becky Hill & Goodboys
When Another Midnight – Sarah Slean

The Morrigan – Heather Dale
Beautiful Hell – Adna
The Humbling River – Puscifer
Wreck of the Day – Anna Nalick
Lost It All – Jill Andrews
One More Murder – Better Than Ezra
Knock Me Out – Linda Perry
Devil In Me – Halsey
Love Your Demons – Terminus
Nightlight – ILLENIUM & Annika Wells
Vertigo – Sarah Slean
Widow's Peak – Odetta Hartman
Dust In the Wind – Sarah Brightman
The Other Side – David Gray
Wintersun – Brendan Perry
Capture – Edge of Dawn
Original Sensuality – Tori Amos
Clarity (feat. Foxes) – Zedd
Ne me quitte pas – Valeria Sattamini
Easier Than Lying – Halsey
No, I Don't Remember – Anna Ternheim
The Mercy of the Fallen – Dar Williams
11:11 – Ben Barnes

Contents

PART I.

BLOOD FEATHERS

I

TO CATCH A DEMON

I frowned at the twin bell towers soaring into the foggy San Francisco twilight. Either someone was punking me, or some damned fool was about to try to exorcise me again. No matter how many times I explained to people that religious iconography didn't work on cambions, they never seemed to take my word for it.

Under the circumstances, I supposed I couldn't blame them. It was true that I didn't care for houses of worship, but that had more to do with trauma from growing up in and around them while harboring a secret identity than some metaphysical susceptibility.

"Stop me if you've heard this one," I muttered to the incurious pigeon giving me side-eye from its cozy roost under the eaves. "A demon, a murderer, and a lawyer walk into a church. The priest looks up and says, what is this, some kind of joke?"

No one laughed, especially not me. The pigeon put its head back under its wing. I sighed, tucking back a dark strand of hair pulled loose by the cool Pacific breeze. The joke, of course, was that they were the same person, and all of them were Lily Knight: half-human, half-succubus, out-of-work attorney, and total hot mess, a.k.a me.

About six months ago, I blew up my life, and now I was living in the wreckage. Some of the shrapnel was probably still hanging out somewhere in the stratosphere waiting for its moment to come screaming down. I'd say I was waiting for the other shoe to drop, but quite a few boots of the steel-toed variety had already drop-kicked me right in the face since the initial explosion.

I hadn't slept much lately, either, and my trains of thought tended toward the runaway mixed metaphor kind.

As for the murderer part, I did what I had to that night in the desert. I kept telling myself that. And yet Ariel's last moments haunted me, my mentor and sometimes lover's handsome, angular face crowned with blond curls and creased with pain, his angelic beauty marred with smears of dark blood as the light went out of his fierce golden eyes.

But I couldn't afford to entertain those memories right now. I had to stay in the present. I had to move forward, if only somebody would give me the chance.

I checked the address the recruiter had sent me again, stabbing at my phone screen until it registered the touch of my gloved fingers. Unless someone had made a typo, I definitely had the right place.

The email didn't mention a church, but here it stood, glowering companionably at the soft-focus evening sky in high Roman Gothic fashion. My current situation may have sounded like a comedy set-up in terrible taste, but those cupolas took themselves very seriously.

Well, what did I expect? No one in their right mind would want to hire me, not since my fall from grace from up-and-coming assistant prosecutor to lightning rod of scandal last year. After my unceremonious firing from the D.A.'s office, not to mention the pending disciplinary action on my bar license, every resume I sent probably traveled the direct-to-trashcan pipeline. With no income, I had given up my little apartment near Civic Center. Now I lived in the garret over my best friend Danny's garage and paid rent when I could.

On the off chance this wasn't a cruel prank or some bizarre demon-napping plot, I needed this job. I squared my shoulders under my blue silk blouse, smoothed my black pencil skirt over my knees, and scaled the steps to the building's arched triple doors inlaid with ornate stained glass.

The leftmost swung open at my touch into a dim-lit vestibule decorated in rich gold, scarlet, and white. Someone with modern sensibilities and traditional tastes must have restored this place. The thick, pristine burgundy carpet absorbed my footsteps, and the soft lighting came from candle-like LEDs. A faint scent of incense tickled my nose.

"Hello?" I stretched out my demon senses for a hint of human energy, the synesthetic desiderata that allowed me to sample their needs and cravings. Whispers and scraps of energy from passersby drifted to me off the street, but inside the building, all lay silent and empty.

Maybe I did have the wrong address after all.

But in six months, only one potential employer had recruited me. I pushed open the inner wooden door into the nave.

Inside, it didn't look like the churches of my childhood at all, but a gallery, with large canvases displayed beside each pillar and the transept where the altar would have stood blocked off by a tall painted screen. Richly upholstered couches and chairs sat in small circles throughout the main space around round tables laden with florals and classical busts. Lantern-style lamps along balconies to either side of me cast their soft golden glow downward and bright white spotlights illuminated each painting.

"Hello," I called again, stepping further into the airy, high-ceilinged room.

"Lily Knight. Good, you came."

The deep male voice came from behind me and to my right, and I whirled around to face the speaker.

A tall Black man with a slight salt-and-pepper scruff along his square jawline nodded at me from mere feet away. He wore dark slacks and a black leather bomber jacket that stretched tight around his broad shoulders. His close-cropped hair showed some gray around the temples. He must have emerged from one of the curtained aisles, his movement soundless.

His energy should have registered with my demon senses regardless of his stealth, but he broadcast nothing at all.

A demon? I tensed and automatically shifted my weight to the balls of my feet, ready to run or fight, at least to the extent I could in my interview heels. "Who are you?" Maybe it wasn't the best way to start off an interview, but I didn't want to play games anymore.

He let out a low, rolling chuckle. "Sorry. I didn't intend to startle you."

The hell he didn't. "What is this place?"

"This is St. Joseph's. A former house of worship, now owned by an art society." He gestured toward the stairs leading upward to the balconies. "Won't you step into my office?"

He had only answered one of my questions. I stayed planted. "I'd like to know more about the opportunity, if you don't mind. Is this an attorney position?"

"Don't worry, Ms. Knight." The barest ghost of a smirk played around his mouth, but his dark eyes remained hard and unreadable. "I think you'll find the position an excellent fit for your singular talents."

"And what talents are those?" Adrenaline tingled along my limbs, leaving them cold. What did he know? Why did he look at me like that, as though we shared an uncomfortable secret?

In answer, he gestured again to the stairs and, without waiting for an acknowledgment, began to climb them. I bit back an unprofessional curse and hurried after him, my restrictive skirt curtailing my strides. I should have followed my instincts and worn slacks.

Despite the gray in his hair, he moved with the fluid power of a trained fighter. Could I take him if it came to that? I hadn't drawn any human life force for a few days, but I had a date on the books later tonight with my not-quite-boyfriend, the eligible tech bachelor Sebastian Ritter. Fingers crossed it would still double as a celebration after this, and I would get the weekly fix of energy I allowed myself from him.

My interviewer, if indeed I could call him that, opened a door on the near side of the balcony and headed up a second staircase, this one a steep, tight, echoing spiral.

I settled into a seemly pace for a human of average fitness, though my demon endurance meant I could keep up without breaking a sweat. The steepness of the staircase didn't bother me. I had looked down from higher heights. The isolation of the belfry that awaited us did worry me, though. Especially since he still hadn't given me a single useful piece of information about himself or the supposed job he would interview me for, and he still didn't betray a hint of aura.

Maybe there was no job. Maybe this really was a set-up, and death by silver awaited me at the end of this long climb.

But when he reached the small room at the top, he pulled out a chair and turned, expectant, to where I hesitated on the landing.

"Have a seat, Ms. Knight," he said. "I'm not going to throw you off the tower, if that's what concerns you."

It wasn't, but I wasn't about to tell him so. "Thank you." I stepped into the room, but I didn't sit.

After a moment, he shrugged and headed to an armchair in the corner, lowering himself into it and crossing long legs out in front of him. "You must have a lot of questions."

"You could say that." Wary, I finally followed suit, taking the chair he offered. "Why are you meeting applicants up here?"

"Security. We wouldn't want our conversation to be overheard."

A chill trickled up my spine. "There was no one else around downstairs."

"Even so."

"You still haven't told me your name." I frowned. He hadn't attempted a handshake, either. I wore gloves, so touch didn't present a risk to either of us, but everything about his behavior set off alarm bells in my head.

"Ira Delaney. You can call me Ira."

I leaned forward in my chair. "So, Ira. You're not a priest, because this isn't a church anymore. You don't strike me as a gallery curator, either. What are you? I'm guessing cop. Or active military, maybe."

"Good guesses," he said. "In a way, all of them are right. I'm employed by the gallery, but as a facilities manager. I was a Marine corps chaplain, but I'm no longer a man of the cloth or an officer."

The man did *not* like to give a straight answer, did he? "And now?"

"Now, I work for the U.S. government. They pay me to do a specific kind of job. And that brings me to you." He spoke in a near-pleasant tone, and he didn't move a muscle. But I still flinched, my hands tightening on the arms of my chair.

"I don't know what the U.S. government has to do with me." I had some guesses, though, and I didn't like them.

"Don't you?" His pointed look sliced through me. "Ms. Knight, you're an intelligent woman, or so I assume from your resume. Surely you didn't think that your actions last fall escaped notice at the highest levels."

"What are you saying?" I held onto my plausible deniability to the last. He wouldn't get me to admit to anything. I would make him put it into words.

He sighed. "Between the fact that you dispatched a very dangerous supernatural subject without any backup or formal training, and your growing influence over James Ritter's son, we didn't know what to think, or what to do with you."

Damn, but I wished I could get a read on him. "Back up. This is about Sebastian? Or about Tonepah?"

"It's about you, Ms. Knight. The government has decided that you represent an untapped asset."

I stared at him for a long moment. Then I started to laugh. I couldn't help it. "You're *recruiting* me?" I leaned back in my chair, breathless. "So that's what this is about. You want me to, what? Become some kind of super soldier? Fight your endless wars for you?"

"No." His face remained unmoved, without even a flicker of my mirth reflected in it. "Your assignments would be far more domestic."

"Domestic?" I grimaced. "I can't say housework is my forte."

"Very funny." Nice of him to acknowledge it, but he still didn't crack even the slightest of smiles. "Domestic as in local. Domestic as in defending the homeland."

"Spying, then."

"Not exactly." He rose from his seat. I stiffened, but he only strode across the room to stare out the round window of the belfry. "Have you ever seen the film *To Catch a Thief*?"

"Of course. Are you kidding me? Hitchcock, Grant, and Kelly? It may not be the master's best work, but it's iconic. Why would you... Oh."

"It takes a thief to catch a thief." Ira Delaney turned from the window, his grim expression engraved in dark stone. "And it takes a demon to catch a demon, Ms. Knight."

"I'm only half-demon." A concerted effort kept my voice steady. "You asked me here because you want me to hunt my own kind? I hope you understand why I might have mixed feelings about that."

"I hear you." He paced back to the chair and sat, leaning forward this time, his posture alert now, his tone urgent. "But I'm not talking about hunting just any demons. I'm talking about the bad ones."

"We're not that bad when you get to know us. We aren't killers." But the words turned to ash in my mouth. I was thinking of Ariel again.

Ira seemed to catch my drift. "Not all of you are. But could you vouch for every one of your kind?"

Ice filtered through my veins. I shook my head. "You think there's a demon killer out there. Another one."

"Yes."

"What's your evidence?"

"I'll show you," he said, "if you agree to help us. I've already told you more than enough."

I folded my arms. "And if I don't agree?"

"If you don't agree, our assessment of you will change from potential asset to potential liability. Our posture will change accordingly."

"That sounds like a threat."

"I like to tell it as it is."

"Which means it's not *not* a threat." My pulse sped up, an uneven thunder in my ears. If I didn't agree to help, what would they do to me?

Ariel had said the feds liked to use demons for terrible experiments, when they weren't keeping us in silver cages like they did in Tonepah. *They want to know what we are, how we tick, what we look like from the inside. How to hurt us better. How to destroy us once and for all.*

Ariel had also lied about a lot of things, but somehow, I didn't think he lied about that. I had some experience with the U.S. government myself after my own visit to Tonepah. According to Danny, they almost didn't let me go after they had me in their clutches. I couldn't remember much, but what I did remember chilled my blood: a white hallway, restraints, faces that looked down at me like I was something alien and dangerous.

"Listen to me, Ms. Knight." Ira Delaney's voice cut through my racing thoughts. "Do you have any idea what would happen if the public got wind that demons were out there murdering humans? They wouldn't care whether you're different. They wouldn't care that you're only, as you say, half-demon. They won't make the distinction between good and bad. They'll want blood."

"You're saying this is for our own protection."

"I'm saying I don't want to see a holy war on our streets."

The man didn't seem to like me much, but he did make good points. I scowled. "I don't want to seem selfish or uncivil-minded or anything, but I came here for a job. I have rent to pay. Not to mention bar dues."

He sat back in his chair, and for the first time a recognizable emotion flickered over his features. It looked like relief. "I think you will find our compensation package adequate. We'll provide an expense account and a commission fee. Half on acceptance and the other half on capture, plus other benefits. Not to mention a full support team, should you need one."

"Capture." The word fell flat from my lips as the enormity of what he'd said washed over me. It sounded dangerous. It sounded terrible. Even if Ira was right, and there was some killer demon on the loose, I didn't want to kill again myself, any more than I wanted to put one of my own kind on some black site's lab table. I opened my mouth again to say something more intelligent. What came out was, "Can I think about it?"

Another expression appeared, this time one that resembled surprise. Did he really think I would jump on the chance to become Lily Knight, Demon Bounty Hunter? "Of course, if you must. My people will be in touch."

Ominous, but at least he didn't seem inclined to bring out silver cuffs and black bag me out of there. I rose. What did one say at the end of such an interview? "Thank you for the opportunity, Mr. Delaney."

"Don't thank me," he said. "I'm just the messenger." A muscle in his jaw leaped, as if he'd bitten back something else on the tip of his tongue.

"I'll let you know what I decide," I said, in faint tones, and made my escape.

But Ira Delaney's voice floated after me. "Don't think too long, Ms. Knight."

2

FIRST WORLD SUCCUBUS PROBLEMS

Rather than pass through the main house and tell my friends I had a job offer that I hadn't decided to take yet, I let myself in by the side door to Danny's garage. I kicked off my interview heels at the bottom of the carpeted stairs and climbed with slow barefoot steps to my little garret room.

Ira Delaney's warning weighed on every step, as did his promises. If I agreed to work for him, I could pay Danny the back rent I owed her. Maybe I could even find a new place of my own. As much as I loved my best friend and her fiancée, Berry, sharing space with humans presented a daily challenge to my demon cravings. I had to guard my instincts and stay alert in case of accidental touches. I had freed Danny of my influence when she almost died, and I didn't care to repeat my past mistakes and put her soul at risk yet again.

My gray cat, Delilah, raised her head from her comfortable nest in my unmade double bed and chirruped in greeting at my entry, blinking green eyes at me.

"Must be nice, cat," I grumbled. "Don't let me disturb you."

She stretched with luxurious ease and returned to her nap, unbothered. She had adjusted to our move better than I had, since she didn't care about having to share a bathroom with me. I kept the litter box in the claw-foot tub and went downstairs when I needed a shower. We made it work, but she definitely got the better end of that deal.

Closing the door behind me, I took in the chaotic state of the cramped room. Its minimal floor space barely accommodated the baskets of laundry that didn't fit in my closet and boxes of law books still packed, evidence of my stubborn belief that I wouldn't live here forever. On the wall next to the door, a print of Audrey Hepburn as Holly Golightly gazed over the mess, cigarette holder in hand, with the wide doe eyes of an ingénue.

Holly made living in chaos look easy. Maybe I should take a cue from her.

I crossed the room to the bed and knelt, fishing around until I found the reinforced lockbox stowed beneath it. I pressed my thumb to the keypad, and the tumblers clicked softly. The box hissed open, and I sat back on my heels and took stock of its contents.

The custom pistol glinted up at me, bright steel on the outside, six silver bullets in its clip. My stomach clenched at the sight of it, the weapon that had shot Danny after I brought it to the desert out of some hazy idea of holding a rogue demon at gunpoint.

Sebastian had gifted me the fancy biometric lockbox after he took exception to me keeping the gun in an old shoe box. I probably should have given the thing back to Tobias Kaine, from whom I'd confiscated it, but I trusted the other cambion even less with firearms than I trusted myself.

I ran a finger along the smooth, cold metal of the barrel. If I took this job, I might need to use the gun after all, another thing I didn't like about it.

Under the weapon, the edge of a faded photograph showed beneath a sheaf of other papers. Frowning, I plucked it out.

Ariel and Nepenthe stared up at me from it, his arm snaked possessively around her neck, her dark eyes shadowed with pain or weariness. A barbed wire fence and desolate buildings formed a backdrop to the portrait.

Why did I hang onto this photo from Nepenthe's apartment? Her friend Theo and I had cleaned out the place together. She had kept an old daguerreotype of Nepenthe as Cleopatra, and I had kept this. It was the only image I had of the incubus who had first taught me to embrace my demon side, the person who had lied to me over and over about everything that mattered.

"Lily! Are you up there?" Danny's voice came faintly from downstairs.

Heart pounding foolishly loud, I dropped the photo, slammed the box shut, and pressed the lock button. Then I shoved it away from me, back under the bed.

It wasn't that Danny didn't know about its contents. Hell, she'd been there for the event itself. I just didn't want to talk about it, not right now, maybe not ever.

"Lily, oh Lily! Come down from your tower," Danny sang out from below. "You have a caller of the gentleman persuasion."

"Oh, crap." I scrambled up. Either Sebastian had arrived early, or I had lost track of time, and I should change out of my interview suit for my date, at least.

A brisk knocking commenced on the other side of the door. "I know you're home because you left your serious lawyer bitch shoes in the hall. How did the interview go?"

I groaned. "I don't want to talk about it."

"That well, huh?"

"It's complicated." I snagged a mostly clean pair of jeans from the floor but kept the blouse.

"Okay, but if you don't hit pause on the mega-brood and come out, I'm sending your Prince Charming up to administer the kiss of life."

"All right! Give a woman a minute to put on some pants." I hopped into the skin-tight jeans and shimmied until I could button them up. "No kiss of life needed. And I wasn't brooding," I added, yanking the door open.

Danny raised an eyebrow at me. "Sure you weren't, Sugarbean."

My best friend had deep tan skin and short, spiked hair currently dyed a faded aquamarine. She wore a black band t-shirt with a rainbow-colored butterfly embossed on it, with an apron haphazardly tied over the top that commanded, "Kiss the Cook." She folded her arms and leaned against the wall of the landing, her expression mock-stern, but a light of mischief danced in her warm brown eyes.

"Okay, fine," I said, and she laughed. "Maybe I was brooding a little."

Sometimes I lied badly to Danny because I could count on her to see through me. She called me on my bullshit and didn't get hung up on the whole half-demon thing. Maybe I leaned on her too much, but I didn't trust many other people with all my secrets, including the latest one haunting my sleepless nights.

She'd witnessed me do the thing that haunted me. She helped me. And she didn't seem to lose any sleep over it. But then again, things probably looked a lot simpler from her perspective. To her, we'd put down a murderer and kidnapper who would have killed us if we didn't kill him first.

But that was Danny. She didn't endure a lot of internal conflict, as a rule. She did a thing or didn't do it, and she usually picked right. I envied her so hard that it hurt sometimes.

To her, we'd slain a demon, nothing more. But to me, he *had* been more: my mentor, my tempter, my sometime lover, and ultimately, my worst enemy. It was a lot to unpack, and I wasn't ready to do more than I'd done just now with my portable gun safe: open it, look in, close it again, and shove it into a dusty corner to deal with at some unspecified later date.

I followed Danny back downstairs through the garage into the kitchen. Pots bubbled on the stove, and a delicious scent permeated the small space, cheese and chilis and cilantro. From the living room, Berry's peal of laughter mingled with the rumble of Sebastian Ritter's baritone.

"You're making enchiladas?" I lingered, reluctant for reasons that belonged in the lockbox of things I chose not to consider. "Maybe I should stay in tonight after all."

"I'll save you some leftovers." Danny frowned at me. "Are you worrying that he's too good for you again? These are first world succubus problems, Sugarbean. Quit feeling sorry for yourself and go enjoy a night out with your boyfriend."

"He's not my boyfriend."

"Whatever. Go say hello to your friend who also happens to be a man whomst you do the sex things with." She waved a slotted spoon at me. "Shoo. Go!"

I opened my mouth and then closed it again. True, "sex things" with Sebastian were nothing to sneeze at. The man had a natural talent and an engineer's determination to work around technical parameters, like the fact that touching him could knock him out like a light if we didn't both have our wits about us.

That first time with him had been literally life-changing, even magical. He blacked out afterward, and I grew some brand-new sparkling demon wings before flying away to fight my arch-nemesis, superhero style. Then I murdered said nemesis in cold blood, anti-hero style. Super fun happy times, right?

And therein lay the problem. I craved the heady sweetness of him like a junkie. How could I tell if I liked him for himself when I needed him for my power-ups? How could I tell if he liked me, or if I just had him in my succubus thrall? Ira's words about my "influence" over him had rekindled my doubts all over again.

I didn't want to have the kind of influence over Sebastian that made government agencies sit up and take notice. I didn't want to use him like that. I didn't want to use *anyone* like that.

"Hey." Danny poked me in the shoulder with the handle of her spoon. "He's not here to pick out color swatches with my fiancée, you know. He's waiting for you."

"I wouldn't be so sure," I said. The man had impeccable taste. Berry could do a lot worse than recruit him for her wedding planning efforts.

Danny rolled her eyes at me, and I sighed. Rather than digging in for another round of her "Lily get laid" pep talks, I pasted on a smile and dragged myself out to the living room to face the music.

She had it right about first world succubus problems, because he wasn't just music. Sebastian Ritter, the tech entrepreneur I'd snagged through some combination of sexy powers and being in the wrong place at the right time, was a veritable symphony in the key of tall, dark, and handsome. Deep in consultation with Berry over her and Danny's wedding planning binder, he leaned forward, his dark hair falling over his pale forehead, his narrow features serious and blue eyes intense. Then he glanced up with a sudden smile like a sunrise, his energy swelling with warm light, and my heart did a slow flip-flop in response.

"Hi," I said, displaying the stunning eloquence of a trained advocate.

Sebastian's smile slipped. Something in my tone or face must have given me away. "Rough day?"

"Let's just say I'm ready for that drink you promised me." Could I tell Sebastian about the offer? But Ira's words about my *influence* still nagged at me. No, better keep it to myself, at least until I decided to do something about it.

He unfolded his long legs from the couch. "I'm calling it now. It's a Midleton night."

"Hey, Lily?" Berry set her binder aside. "There's some mail for you on the hall table. It looks important. Something from the State Bar."

"Thanks." My gut knotting, I headed for the hall.

Sebastian followed, his desiderata extending little caressing flames of concern that licked at me and then withdrew. "Are you ok?"

"Fine." I hunched my shoulders against the weight of his worry. My numb fingers fumbled over the envelope that bore my name. After one look at the single sheet of paper it contained, I swore under my breath.

"That doesn't sound like fine."

"They set my disciplinary hearing." I dropped the notice like it burned me, like they had taken the trouble to dip it in silver before stuffing the envelope. "It's in three weeks. That's so soon." Maybe I should take a job that didn't require a law license, after all.

"I could call in a favor. My dad—"

"No!" My voice rang out too loud in the enclosed space and carried a hint of an intimidating demon Presence. At his startled look, I gritted my teeth and took a breath, counting back from ten as I eased off the gas. "I mean, I appreciate the offer, but I wouldn't feel right about it."

I had no intention of owing Senator Ritter any favors. I liked his son—I could admit that much—but I didn't count myself among the senator's biggest fans after the way he'd treated me last fall.

"There's no shame in accepting help, Lily." His hand fell on my shoulder, warm through the silk of my blouse. It wasn't a skin-to-skin touch, but heat surged through me in response.

I turned to meet his concerned gaze and pushed my misgivings back. That box of things I chose not to examine too closely kept filling up. "How about that drink, Mr. Ritter? Somewhere more private than last time, please. I don't want to end up on Page Six again." Not-dating one of San Francisco's most eligible bachelors had its downsides.

His desiderata shifted to a dark, rich, rough-textured velvet. "I thought you'd never ask."

At least there was one form of help I could accept from him, even if that connection scared me too, how deep it ran and the high it gave me. And tonight, as powerless as I felt over every aspect of my life, I needed the power he offered me.

I needed to taste his soul. I needed *him*.

I spent the ride through the city streets in Sebastian's shiny black muscle car preoccupied, mentally listing the pros and cons of accepting Ira's offer. When Sebastian opened the passenger side door for me, I frowned around at the vaguely familiar, mostly empty parking garage.

"Where are we going?"

He raised an eyebrow at me and hit the elevator up button. "You don't know? You've been here before."

"I have, haven't I?" The elevator opened, revealing an all-glass interior. "Wait. Why are we at your office?"

"You said you wanted somewhere private." The elevator soared upward, and the city dropped away beneath us.

"I thought we would go to your house."

His lips quirked upward at that, but then he sobered. "You seem so weighed down lately. I wanted to take you somewhere with a view, where you can be on top of the world for a little while."

"Your house has a view." Elevation didn't pose a problem for me. I could look down on the city anytime I wanted, as long as I touched Sebastian first.

"Not like this one," he said. "Besides, you didn't get a chance to really appreciate it on your last visit."

I grimaced. "I hope your dad isn't going to join us this time."

Last time we'd ridden to the top of his skyscraper—it still blew my mind that the man had a damn skyscraper with his name on it, and he wasn't even compensating for anything—only to find his father, the senator, waiting at the top. At that point, I made a break for it, and Sebastian and I almost never spoke again. It didn't stand out as one of my most shining moments, but then, it was also the week my life fell apart. Overall, it could have gone a lot worse.

"Definitely not." As if on cue, the elevator opened, and Sebastian gestured me out into the huge executive suite. As promised, it lay still and empty. Motion activated lights sprang to life at our entrance, but Sebastian said, "Dimmer," and they dipped low again.

"What do you think?" His desiderata glittered, proud as the towers of the Financial District sparkling below us, a forest of bright obelisks shining against the dark blanket of fog and water folded around the San Francisco Peninsula.

I joined him at the floor-to-ceiling glass window that wrapped around the suite. The last twilight faded above the Pacific on one side, while on the other, the peak of Mt. Diablo thrust its head over the fog, the moon rising huge and yellow above it like a paper lantern.

"It is a hell of a view," I conceded. "But you promised me a drink."

"Not to worry." He went to the big desk in the room's center and rifled through the bottom drawer, coming up with a three-quarters full bottle of amber liquid and two glasses. "I keep the good stuff on hand."

I accepted the glass he offered and took a long swallow, savoring its smooth heat. The alcohol would do nothing but fizz pleasantly in my veins unless I drank a staggering amount or became otherwise impaired. The contact high of Sebastian's proximity affected me more than the whiskey.

He hitched one hip up on the desk, glass in hand, watching me. His desiderata tingled at my senses, a complement to the whiskey heating my belly. "And your verdict, your honor?"

"I'll allow it."

"I thought you might. Midleton can tip the scales against a multitude of sins." He sipped his drink, his expression turning serious. "Lily, there's something I wanted to ask you."

Uh oh. I didn't like the sound of that, or the tremor in his energy when he said it. I took another fortifying sip. "What's that?"

He straightened from the desk. "My father is having a black-tie fundraiser this weekend in the North Bay. I want you to come with me."

I almost choked on my mouthful of Midleton, which would have been a sad waste of spectacular whiskey. Coughing, I set my glass down on the desktop with a louder-than-intended clunk. "You want me to *what*?"

"Be my date. I want to introduce you. He's been asking about you."

"We've met," I said, tone dry as a California summer. "It went swimmingly, if you recall. He tried to get me fired. And then I *was* fired."

His desiderata pulsed with the ultramarine salt-sting of distress. "He was trying to protect me."

"You don't even like your dad." I gulped the rest of my whiskey. Its burn lingered in the back of my throat, and my eyes watered. Sebastian and I had a distaste for our living family of origin in common, or so I'd thought.

"It's not that simple." He ran a hand through his dark hair, mussing it so it flopped over his forehead, a habit I usually found endearing. "He's expecting us to be there."

"*Us?*" I glared. "You accepted *for* me?"

"Please, Lily." He sat back, exhaling, his exasperation prickling the air. "It's out in wine country, on family property. We could make a weekend trip of it. We'd stay at the villa, so you could leave the gala as soon as you had enough."

I almost laughed. Of course, we'd stay at the villa, like a couple of movie stars on a carefree jaunt through wine country. "Sebastian, I can't." How had this become my life? "I don't have anything to wear."

His eyebrow arched. "Seriously? That's it?"

When I argued myself into a corner in the courtroom, I fell back on my last-ditch strategy of going for broke on my broken theory and hoping the jury missed the gaps in my logic. Now, I followed that strategy and doubled down.

"Seriously. This may be outside your frame of reference, but I'm poor. I have no job and no savings. And I can't have a do-over with your father in a second-hand cocktail dress from Out of the Closet."

"I promise you he wouldn't notice."

"And I promise you everyone else would."

"Come on, Lily. This is a surmountable problem." He reached across the gap between us, took my gloved hand in between his. "If it's just clothing you're worried about, I'd be happy to cover the cost of the dress."

I resisted his pull. "Classing me up now, Mr. Ritter? I didn't know you had a *Pretty Woman* kink."

His hurt didn't show in his face. He would have had a hell of a career as a poker player, but he couldn't bluff a succubus, or even a half-succubus like me. His energy shifted, drew into itself.

Damn, it got dark in there fast, like someone had him on a dimmer switch just like his office mood lighting. Not someone, me. I had my hand on that switch. Demons depended on the life force of human desire—their kether—to survive, and our senses and powers evolved to manipulate them.

The better to eat you with, my dear. Reading human emotions on instinct made it all too easy to target the weak spots in their armor without thinking, and I had unreasonably good aim.

His keen blue eyes caught and held me fast. "I don't have a *Pretty Woman* kink, whatever that is. I have a *you* kink. Is that really so hard for you to believe?"

Shit. Did we have to have this conversation now, tonight? I didn't want it to go like this. I didn't want to have it at all.

"It's a new one, that's for sure." I wouldn't tell him that what he called a Lily Knight kink was nothing more or less than a garden-variety succubus kink, and I happened to be the only living succubus in his orbit. I wouldn't tell him that I had no way to separate my desire for his kether from my desire for him, or how unfair this...*thing* between us could become when I relied on him to access my full powers. I wouldn't say I should stop seeing him, but couldn't stay away. I wouldn't put words to the hollow, vulnerable place that opened under my breastbone when I looked at him.

I couldn't tell him any of that. It would destroy him, and I needed him whole.

"That right there. That's what I don't understand." His voice went rough around the edges again. It sent goosebumps shivering down my spine. "Talk to me. Did I do something wrong?"

"No!" I forced myself to meet his eyes. They burned into mine, but his desiderata pleaded with me. Damn it, I couldn't afford to screw this up. "Of course not. The opposite, in fact." Maybe that was the problem, the way he said all the right things, what I wanted to hear and what I couldn't believe.

"Then explain it to me." The rough edges in his tone deepened, verging on a growl. "You're holding out on me again. But I'm a big boy, I can take it. Tell me the truth. Why do you keep pushing me away?"

He couldn't handle the truth, and I couldn't hold his gaze. I turned my head away. Outside our aerie, purple twilight had faded to full night, and the city glowed like a reef of jewels in a dark sea. "It's complicated."

"I like complicated." He sighed. "Come on. I didn't ask you to define our official social media status."

"You're not even on social media." I tried on a casual shrug and half a truth. "I'm just scared, I guess."

"Yeah, I got that much. You're not as hard to read as you think. Scared of what? That I'll hurt you, or that you'll lose control?"

"Yes."

"Yes, what?"

"Yes, all of it." I swallowed hard. "You can't understand what it's like for me. It's not just sex for me. If I let it, it could own me. And I...I could own *you*."

A certain incubus had told me once that a succubus couldn't have a sex addiction. But he also tried to convince me that demons were superior beings who deserved to rule over weak, inferior humans. And before that, he'd let me believe he meant well, that he respected consent, personal agency, the right to live and love as one pleased.

He'd told so many lies, and even though the liar had died, his lies still wove their tangled web around me like a shroud.

"I know you could," Sebastian said calmly. "I've known from the beginning. It's not so different for me as you think."

I had to look back at him, then. "You think you could...own me?" Heat flooded my cheeks at the words. They sounded much filthier out loud, especially when his desiderata pulsed in response.

"If you let me. If you wanted me to." His expression seared through me, and he drew me toward him. "My own desires run pretty dark and deep. If I give them free rein, they'd control me, too."

"It's not the same." I could break free with ease. My strength outmatched his by a factor of ten. But his need sang to me. It hammered at my resistance like thunder, like the beat of huge dark wings. "Sebastian, I—" But the words died on my lips.

I couldn't tell him the truth about what happened that night, our first night together. I couldn't tell him what I did with my power, his power, the alchemy of our pleasure.

I couldn't tell him that I killed someone with it.

"It's all right," he said, in that rippling velvet voice. "Come here."

I took a long breath and pushed the box of things I couldn't say back into the shadows. Then I stepped toward him of my own free will. Or at least, right now, I chose to believe I did.

"I have a confession, too," he murmured, his lips inches from mine, not touching me anywhere skin to skin.

My breath came short. "I'm not a nun, Mr. Ritter."

"Thank fuck for that." His desiderata enveloped me, deep, rich, and over-whelming. "Because I didn't just ask you here so we could take in the view."

"You lied to me," I whispered, but it didn't matter. I didn't need truths right now. I needed what he offered me.

"By omission only." He put his hands on my hips, turning me with gentle pressure and steering me backward until my ass hit the hard edge of the desk. "The truth is, I've been very distracted lately during my workday by thoughts about you, me, and this desk." His fingers worked under the band of my jeans, skimming my skin, and I moaned.

"Say ten Hail Marys and ten...oh, *fuck*."

"Now that's the kind of absolution I can live with," he said, and bent his head to claim my mouth with his. His kether flooded through me. It suffused my body with a rush of light. It made my head spin, driving all my doubts away.

I drank him in, drank him deep, and when he pressed me down against the hard, cold surface of the desk, I did beg in the end—but not for absolution.

3

DEMON ON A HOT TIN ROOF

I didn't truly appreciate the beauty of the San Francisco Bay until I learned to fly.

Tonight was the perfect night for flying, too. The overcast sky hid the moon and made it easy to travel unseen. I dipped low over the waves, my fingers skimming the water, my body arched to keep my boots dry, then rose again with a strong, swift downbeat of my wings.

"You take such time in your foolish games." My companion circled around toward me, her lightly accented words carried down to me on the brisk wind.

"You should try it." But I quickened my pace to catch up. "You might enjoy it."

"You think I have not?" Theo's voice floated back to me, reproving. "I was young once too, you know."

"So you say. How long ago was that?"

The other succubus's wings had the deep violet hue of a starless night, unlike my bluish black plumage studded with tiny star-like lights. When she turned in the air to glare at me, my kether-enhanced vision could just make out her disapproving expression and a hint of the ruddy hair working itself free of her coiled braids to whip around her face. I had pulled my own back in a tight bun at my crown, as I had no desire to eat a mouthful or two of it during the flight to Angel Island for our training session.

"You are young *and* rude." She executed a tight flip in the air, a dive and recovery that sent her hurtling on toward our destination.

"Show-off," I grumbled, following.

Theo landed near the old fort at the southwest tip of the island, and I touched down a few feet away. The deactivated military facility loomed over us, a hulking shadow in the dark. From the top, one could see the entire bay, bounded by the lighted orange span of the Golden Gate Bridge against the western horizon and the San Francisco-Oakland Bay Bridge to the south.

But we didn't come here for the view. Theo pulled off her gloves, theatrically and finger by finger, like a burlesque performer beginning a strip tease. I stripped my own off with less ceremony and shrugged off my heavy coat, folding it up and setting it aside on the concrete steps.

"You may want to keep your coat," Theo said. "Today, we do not fight. I have another lesson for you."

"What lesson?"

She didn't answer but jerked her head toward the path that led downhill through a dark thicket of oaks. We headed down in silence. The rich smell of chapparal and earthy tannins filled my nostrils, and the underbrush rustled with the soft sounds of small, busy animal lives. The quiet here welled up in my soul, not silence but the deeper peace of distance from human desires. Not many people lived here, and the ones that did dwelled miles away on the north shore of the island, near the ferry landing.

I met Theo last year when everything went down with Ariel. She didn't much care for me or my human heritage. But afterwards, when I told her what I'd done, she softened enough that I dared ask her if she would take over the role Ariel had vacated and teach me more about my father's kind.

To my surprise, she agreed. "I owe you a debt," she had said when I asked why. "For Nepenthe. For Astarte. You have avenged them."

I didn't have anything to say to that. I didn't tell her that Nepenthe and Astarte died because of me. Ariel killed them to reel me in, to bring me back into his fold, to make me afraid so I would buy into his twisted worldview of cubines and humans as enemies. He wanted me to set my humanity aside and help him build a new world order where demons reigned supreme. He literally put Astarte's body in my path so I would trip over her and get involved.

And now Ira Delaney wanted me to hunt my own kind. Murderer or no, what would Theo think of that?

"You are troubled," Theo said now. "Your energy stinks of it."

"Sorry." I struggled to tamp down my worries. Full cubines like Theo didn't project desiderata the way mortals did. While I got to enjoy the peace and quiet out here, she still had to put up with the psychic noise of my half-human emotions.

She shot a quick glance at me, her eyes shining gold in the darkness. "You have no discipline."

"I'm trying!"

"A human would say that speaking of it might help you calm your mind."

Caught off guard, I almost stumbled. Did she just invite me to confide in her? But she strode on a half-step ahead of me, her expression in profile betraying nothing.

Well, all right. Maybe Theo was trying, too.

I chose my words with care. "I was just wondering how many others are out there like us."

"This I do not know. Once, it was said that we are legion. Now..." She shrugged. "We are as scattered as the four winds. We are not a sociable people among ourselves. No one keeps track of us."

I made a silent bet with myself that Ira Delaney and his shadowy government agency did. He never said which agency, either. "And what if one of us...goes bad?"

"You mean like *him*." She meant Ariel, and I appreciated that she didn't say his name.

"No." I didn't want to talk about him, now or ever. I didn't want to think about him, even though I couldn't seem to help it.

"You are doing it again," Theo said.

"I'm not doing anything." I took a long breath in, let it out slow. "I'm talking about a cubine who hunts humans to kill, not feed. Is that even a thing?"

"It is not a *thing*. It is folly. We have no need to kill." Theo paused for a long moment. "It happens at rare times by accident when a fledgling is young, untrained. It is possible to take too much, too fast."

"Right." I had made that mistake, once. I had hurt a human in my haste and inexperience, another thing I didn't care to remember. I sucked in another long breath, exhaled. "But we don't kill on purpose."

"You are very noisy with your mouth," Theo said. "No. But who can say? We are like them in one way. We are individuals."

I quieted my breathing. "So, it is possible."

"Anything is possible." Her tone had turned curt. "Why all these questions?"

"I'm just curious, that's all. I feel like I don't know anything about us. Not one of us has ever studied our own kind?"

"We do not keep records of ourselves." Theo's pace sped up. "That too would be folly. What if some human found our writings?"

"Bullshit." I had to trot to keep up with her. Theo was tall, and her legs were longer than mine. "You've been around long enough, seen enough. Don't tell me we don't have any history!"

"Our history is their history," Theo said. "We have lived alongside them for time immemorial. We are different, but inseparable. It has always been that way."

"I can't believe that."

Theo didn't answer. The path opened in front of us, spilling us out of the woods and into a row of abandoned military housing.

Speaking of history. Humans had preserved this small settlement long after the troops that once lived here had moved on, had families, lived and died. It belonged to the state now, an exhibit for curious tourists to walk among, touch, and absorb some sense of those who came before them.

If demons had nothing like that, what did that mean for us? Could we know ourselves if we didn't know our own past? Did we have nothing of our own, no culture, no tradition, no history except that which we shared and stole from humankind?

Ariel had taught me the only demon history I knew, about the doomed holding facility in Tonepah Valley and its tragic end. But he had lied to me over and over about so many things, I hardly knew what to believe anymore.

I shivered. People had been caged here too, human people, in another part of the island. The dark windows of the old buildings stared out like empty eyes, reflecting nothing but the night, a little too much like the burned-out ruins where I...where Ariel...

No. I promised myself I wouldn't think any more about that.

"Come," Theo said. "You say you wish to know more about your father's kind. I will show you. Watch." She strode toward the nearest building.

"Look out!" I cried.

Theo didn't slow. She walked straight into the wall—*through* the wall—and disappeared. I blinked, chills crawling up my spine. I would never get used to that trick. The last time someone did it in front of me—

Pushing aside the memories of my last encounter with my mentor, I approached the wall with caution and placed my hand against the cool painted wood. It didn't budge when I pressed lightly against it. "Theo?"

Something flickered in my periphery. She stood in the window to my right, staring down at me in her haughty, queenlike way, like a ghost of the past she refused to acknowledge. She put a hand on the window, mimicking my own gesture, and once again faded through the solid wood and glass, returning to my side.

"Now you try," she commanded me.

"I don't think I can do that."

"That is why I must teach you. Try."

I tested the wooden slats again. When I pushed harder, the wood creaked. "I'll break it."

"No. Look." She placed her hand next to mine. A slight crease of concentration appeared between her eyebrows, and her hand melted into the wall. Then she withdrew it, shaking her fingers a little as if they tingled. "It is easy."

My neck prickled. "Easy for you to say. What's the trick?"

"There is no trick. Or one could say the wall is the trick."

"I don't get it. Is it like a kether push, or...?" I knew how to do a push, the technique of transferring energy out instead of taking it in. I had learned that from watching Theo and had used it in extremis to save my best friend Danny's life when she would have bled to death from a bullet in her gut.

"It does not even require kether. This is more fundamental to our nature. We are not like humans, bound to the flesh and its laws. We are masters of our matter."

"Okay, Yoda."

She scoffed. "I do not know this Yoda."

"It's a movie." I sighed at the look she shot me. "Come on. I thought everyone had seen that one. Human or otherwise."

"Oh. Their popular culture." She made it sound like an unspeakable horror. "No, I have not seen it. Moving pictures make my head ache."

"I thought you said we were masters of our matter. That doesn't include eye strain?"

"Now you are stalling."

She had me there. I could only postpone my inevitable failure so long. I pushed my fingers into the wood again, willing them to pass through.

To my complete lack of surprise, the wall persisted in its solid state. I dropped my hand, aware of Theo's uncompromising gaze on me. "I don't know. Maybe I'm too human for this."

"It is possible," she allowed. "However, Tobias has had some success. His technique is imperfect, yet serviceable. And he is as human as you."

Well, that stung. Tobias *was* as human as me, which was to say, half, and one of my least favorite people of either category.

Disappointing Theo shouldn't have bothered me as much as it did. After all, she didn't have a very high opinion of me to start with. But maybe that made it worse. She set a low bar, and I couldn't even clear that.

Maybe it was like target practice, and it would get easier if I didn't think about it. I drew back my hand with an indrawn breath, then exhaled as I drove my palm into the wall.

The crack of splitting timber echoed through the clearing, and my fingers came back full of splinters.

Well, that was one way to get through a wall, and destroy a painstakingly restored Civil War era building in the process.

I cradled my scraped-up hand to my chest. "I can't do it. I told you so."

"You cannot," Theo said, "because you believe you cannot."

I rolled my eyes, turning away from her to stare out at the smooth black surface of the bay. "Can I ask you something?"

"Yes?" She sounded impatient, frustrated with her dunce of a student.

"The government knows about me. They want me to work for them. Should I?"

She gave a sharp, indrawn gasp. A sudden breeze washed over me, whipping at my exposed nape.

"Theo, I don't know what to do."

She didn't answer.

"Theo?"

I turned back toward where she had stood, but she had disappeared. The windows of the empty houses glared down at me. Somewhere upslope, a long, mournful howl sounded. A coyote, perhaps? Whatever it was sounded lonely, and maybe hungry.

Damn it. I'd spooked Theo, and she'd left me to figure things out on my own. She always contacted me to set up our training nights from a throwaway phone number. Now, I might not hear from her again.

Chest heavy and tight, I unfurled my wings and took to the air to fly home.

Outside the converted Victorian that housed the Safe Haven Legal Clinic, a faint reddish hue spread across the western sky like blood sluicing down an industrial drain.

Five days had passed since Ira's offer, five days of distracting myself with volunteer shifts at the clinic and reliving the events of my night with Sebastian in more idle moments. The email with the offer details sat in my inbox unopened. If I didn't read it, I wouldn't know what I was giving up. Maybe Ira would give up on me in the meantime and make my decision for me.

Well, I had one more chance to take a different route. I couldn't put it off any longer.

I swung open the glass door of the clinic's office entrance and propped it ajar with my hip. Safe Haven crowned the top of one of San Francisco's breakneck hills and its porch faced downhill. The bristling, cramped, exuberant peninsula sparkled before me under a slow-breaking wave of evening fog that curled in from the ocean and swallowed the distant span of the Golden Gate Bridge.

One high heel inside, one braced on the weathered slats of the patio, I waited on the threshold. The clinic's rules required us to use the buddy system while locking up at night, and Rae McGuire, the advocacy director, had run back inside to do one last thing, as usual.

A sudden clamor of harsh cries broke out from the eaves. I craned my neck and squinted up through the twilight. A cloud of black birds swirled into the air from the building's gables, their windswept calls conveying some avian dispute I couldn't comprehend. Others winged up the hill to join the bickering flock. They gathered here each night at sunset in unnerving numbers, clustering along the roof line until some unknown signal flung them back into the sky in a swirling mob.

"Damn birds." I ducked back under the overhang and shielded my head with my purse in case one of them decided to take a dump on me. That would be just my luck. "Can't you go flock somewhere else?"

"It's called a murder." Rae's quiet, husky voice behind me made me jump.

I spun. "*What?*"

With her array of prominent body piercings and her bright scarlet hair swept back in a long, thick French braid to expose a sharp-angled undercut, Rae McGuire looked more like a punk rocker than the director of the city's biggest nonprofit survivors' shelter. Her desiderata bristled with enough sharp spikes to put my teenage goth phase to shame and shimmered with the copper-bright scent of new pennies.

She stepped out onto the porch, a tall, imposing, gray-eyed figure in a black denim jacket, torn jeans, and clunky steel-toed boots. "The crows." A slight smile quirked her lips. "When they flock like that, it's called a murder."

"Creepy."

"They have complex social structures, and they're quite smart." She turned to lock the door, her heavy braid dropping forward over her shoulder and shadowing her face. "If a human hurts one of their own, the rest of them never forget the culprit's face."

I shivered, though the chill of San Francisco's fogbound evening couldn't touch me. "I didn't know you were a bird expert."

"Once upon a time," Rae said, straightening, "I wanted to be a wildlife biologist." In the fading light, my night vision revealed her wry expression, and my demon side sensed the energetic pulse of the rest of the story, a weight she chose to hold back.

"Can I ask you something?"

"Shoot."

"I threw my application in the ring for the clinic attorney job last month." Her eyebrows went up, and I rushed through the rest of my rehearsed speech. "I haven't heard anything yet. Do you—"

"I have a question for you, Lily." Rae's desiderata shifted, became a fog-piercing searchlight bearing down on me. "You were a prosecutor. What would you do if you knew someone had committed a crime, and no one would do anything about it?"

"I—" What was this, some kind of test? The scent of ozone clogged my nose, the air charged as if with an oncoming storm. "Do you mean in a legal sense?"

"Legally. Morally. Whatever." She shrugged. "You're the lawyer. I'm just a layperson. I'm wondering what you would do."

"I'd advise you—advise anyone—to report the crime to the authorities." But I faltered under her keen gaze. I hadn't gone to the police last fall. I didn't trust them to help me. In the end, I'd made my own justice, but I couldn't make my own peace.

"But if you have no evidence, the authorities won't believe you. They'll say there's nothing they can do."

I frowned, catching her drift. Safe Haven's clients came to us with cases like that all the time, like the college student who wept in our meeting room earlier that day because her university found no credible evidence of her assault. Not so long ago, I prosecuted cases like that. But even then, I couldn't do much to hold abusers accountable if the cops didn't take a report.

"If the crime is ongoing, document everything," I said. "Build a case so strong they have to charge it. Get a restraining order, find other victims. Bad behavior is rarely a one-and-done. It's usually a pattern."

"Right," Rae said. "They get away with it and then they escalate. That's the cost. It could be someone's life."

Ariel had escalated, and I would kick myself for the rest of my life for not recognizing his patterns. He'd fooled me, and people had died because of it. Danny would have died if I hadn't brought her back. But I couldn't bring the rest of them back.

Their bodies had crumbled into glittering sand, vanished like they'd never existed at all. But I remembered them, though I never really knew them. Nepenthe and Astarte, goddesses among men, dust in the wind.

"I'm a lawyer," I said again, like it mattered. "I can't advise anyone to break the law, no matter how justified."

"Of course not." Rae tilted her head, looking me over for a long moment. Then she sighed and headed down the stairs toward the sidewalk.

"Rae! Wait. You never told me if I got the job."

"I'm sorry." She paused, turned at the foot of the porch steps. "We can't hire an attorney with an open disciplinary inquiry on her record, Lily."

"So that's it. I don't even get a chance?" Had I failed her strange test?

She shook her head. "The organization's board won't allow it. But you can always apply again once your license is clear."

I held her gaze, and she met it without giving an inch. Her energy swirled like the fog spilling over the city below us, darkening with the twilight.

I could use my powers to nudge and influence her with a persuasive Presence. Temptation gnawed at me, my succubus side accustomed to getting her way, but I pushed the demon back. I wanted Rae's respect the authentic way, not because I hypnotized her into it. She'd only resent me eventually if I countered her free will, unless I sustained the Presence for as long as she employed me. That sounded like an exhausting prospect.

"Thanks for letting me know," I said.

She nodded once, hesitated as if about to add something, then seemed to reconsider. "Well, good night," she said abruptly, and strode toward the cross street without glancing back.

I lingered on the porch, feigning a fascination with my phone screen until she turned the corner, but actually just cursing myself.

I shouldn't have bothered to ask. I'd made things awkward between us. With all my powers of charm and seduction, I should have had the natural ability to avoid awkwardness, but maybe my human blood got in the way and genetically predisposed me to social shame.

If only I had gained Ariel's social graces when the kether he stole from me flowed out on his dying breath and back into my soul. Quick-witted and silver-tongued, he always had the perfect quip for any situation.

But apparently it didn't work like that. Inside, I became a killer like him, but on the outside, I stayed the same old Lily Knight, only with fewer job prospects. And even a cambion couldn't live on the wages of sin alone.

"Oh, hell," I muttered, and thumbed open my phone. The red badge on my email application waited for me, daring me to look.

It came from "Recruiter"—probably Ira himself, come to think of it—and it more than fulfilled my expectations. The number in it made my breath come short. That would definitely solve some of my short-term problems. If I caught the bad guy, I might even be able to afford my own place again.

I swallowed my pride and hit the telephone number at the bottom of the email. The line rang only once before it picked up.

"Hello, Ms. Knight," said a deep, rumbling voice on the other end. "I was beginning to wonder if I'd misjudged you."

He did have a knack for those polite threats. But of course, he hadn't misjudged me, and he knew it.

"Hi, Ira." I clutched the phone tight to my ear, full darkness falling fast around me as the fog took hold and the city glowed to life. "Tell me about those *other benefits* you mentioned."

When it came right down to it, every demon had her price.

4

DELTA ALPHA MURDER

Downtown SF on a Friday night sounded like a terrible idea, but Ira didn't give me choice of venue. My new employer—or handler, perhaps—had rattled off the address of our meeting place and then hung up before I could lodge an objection.

The place was predictably packed. With a grimace, I wove my way through the crowded, bright, and noisy bar at the front of the cafe, then ducked into a darkened cave of a dining room, no less noisy and crowded. I found Ira at a table in the far corner, his back to the dark wood panels of the wall, flipping through an official-looking manila folder with one hand while tucking into a giant plate of pasta with the other.

He didn't seem to clock my entrance, but he didn't look surprised when I slid onto the red-leather booth seating across from him, either. He wore the same leather jacket, open this time to reveal a black cotton t-shirt beneath.

"What are we doing here, Ira?" I scowled at him over the table.

"Eating." He handed me a menu. "You should try the Bolognese."

"You don't have to buy me dinner." God, was this a date? Not that he wasn't attractive in an older guy kind of way, but I still couldn't get a bead on his energy, and that bothered me.

It bothered me a lot. It meant he might be a demon, or maybe something worse.

"I'm not paying. Uncle Sam is." He raised an eyebrow at me. "You do eat, don't you?"

"Of course I do." Full-blooded demons could live on kether alone if they had to. I could go without food or kether for a little while, getting by on one or the other, but I still got hungry like humans did, and I needed both for peak performance.

"Don't get huffy," Ira said. "I've never met one of you before. Half-demons aren't my specialty."

"Really?" That implied someone existed who did have that specialty. Nonplussed, I perused the menu to hide my unease. "I find it hard to believe that you don't have a single cambion specimen under the microscope in a black site somewhere."

"Black site? Microscope?" His forehead creased. "We're not monsters, Ms. Knight."

The jury was still out on that one, but for now, the only confirmed monster at this table was me. "No. You're the government."

Amusement flashed in his eyes. "And that's worse?"

"You said it, not me." Apparently, Uncle Sam didn't pay for meals like Sebastian did, at restaurants that considered it gauche to list the prices on the menu, but if left to my own devices, I would have ordered a fifteen-dollar salad. As it was, I took the path of least resistance and ordered the Bolognese like a good little junior agent of whatever the hell agency I'd gotten myself mixed up with.

"Besides," Ira said, when the server left, "you demons are notoriously hard to study. Dead or alive."

I almost choked on my ice water. Ira handed me a red cloth napkin in silence and waited for me to finish wheezing.

"Is that what this is? Are you studying me?"

"Sure I am." He sounded unconcerned. "And you're studying me, I have no doubt. Drawn any conclusions yet?"

"Yeah." I hadn't, or at least, nothing useful. "You're kind of a dick."

This got a bark of a laugh out of him. "They don't pay me to be Mr. Nice Guy."

"Right. *They* wouldn't. What *they* am I dealing with here, anyway? FBI? CIA? DHS? Any other three-letter acronym I should know about?"

He chewed, looked thoughtful, swallowed. "No."

"Of course. You could tell me, but then you'd have to kill me." I sighed. "Aren't you going to tell me why I'm here, Ira?"

He pushed his manila folder across the table to me. "Have at it. Tell me what sticks out to you."

I opened the folder and stopped at the first picture, one I vaguely recognized. "Wait. I thought this guy died of a drug overdose a couple of months back."

"We've kept it quiet. Wouldn't want the populace getting wind of this."

"Wind of what?" I shuffled through the next few reports. At first, the victims seemed unconnected and random, some old and some young: a stand-up comedian, a restaurateur, a newscaster, a doctor, even a district court judge. But as I turned the pages, a pattern began to unfold. My gut churned, and when my food came, I pushed it aside.

Each had held a prominent role in a professional field. Most were white. All were male. All had died in their beds, with no sign of struggle and no forced entry, a few without alerting private security outside. Video surveillance revealed shorts or outages around the time of death. No witnesses had seen anyone coming in or out, either.

And upon discovery, each had a bundle of black feathers stuffed down their throats and not a single drop of blood left in their bodies.

The news hadn't reported those facts, of course. Ira's nameless agency had done their job well. According to public record, they had died of natural causes: drugs, heart attacks, a stroke. The deaths had started late last fall, spaced out enough that no one in the media had thought to connect them.

I certainly hadn't heard about most of them, but late last fall, I had a lot on my plate, what with throwing away my career and all. I closed the folder, swallowing hard. "What happened to the blood?"

"Your guess is as good as mine. Forensics found no trace of spatter." Ira had finished his meal, unbothered by grisly crime scene details.

"Any marks on them?"

He shook his head. "No fang holes, if that's what you're thinking."

"I wasn't." I bristled. "Vampires aren't real."

"Would you stake your life on that?"

Was that a joke? But he looked dead serious, and my demon senses still gave me nothing to work with. I chose to ignore it. "A human could have done this, given enough time and the right equipment. What was the cause of death?"

"Inconclusive." Ira shrugged. "Without blood, forensics has a tough time making the call. Could be the blood loss. Could be they choked to death."

"Those feathers make me think you're looking for a very dramatic serial killer. Not...something else."

"It's possible." He didn't sound convinced. "But suppose it wasn't human. What kind of something else are we talking about here?"

"I don't know." I picked at my now-cold pasta. "But I do know a cubine didn't do this. We're good-time monsters. We like to bang. We don't suck people's blood."

But Ariel had killed. A full-body shiver came over me, and I let my fork fall to the plate.

It couldn't be, could it? I had kept my eyes locked with his as the light went out of them, as his energy left his body and grounded itself in me.

No, he couldn't have come back. Not even demons could cheat death, could they? And Ariel hadn't killed like this. He had left Nepenthe's blood to soak into the thick carpet of the Ritz Carlton's Presidential Suite. And he had targeted other demons, not humans.

Well, with one exception. He had tried to kill Danny.

"Goose walk over your grave, Ms. Knight?" Across the table, Ira watched me with a narrow gaze.

"I'm a demon." I forced a smile. "I don't get a grave, remember? No point in burying dust."

"Half-demons might get a little more than that." His focus shifted to my plate. "I suggest you eat something. You might need your strength later."

"Why? What are you planning?"

"I'm not planning anything." He pulled out his phone, checked it, and then set it aside.

I took another grudging bite. "I still don't know why you think I can help you solve these murders. There's no evidence, nothing to go on. I'm not some kind of demon-sniffing dog, you know."

"You'll act as a consultant." Ira sounded almost distracted. "And, if necessary, as muscle."

"You don't look like you need much of that," I mumbled through a mouthful of cold Bolognese.

He almost smiled at that. "Thank you, but you and I both know that even a well-trained human can't match a well-fed demon in a fight. Even if we're armed with silver."

My head snapped up, and I choked down my food. He knew our weaknesses. It woke a cold spot at the base of my spine. He might not match me in strength, but he could still kill me if he took me by surprise.

I couldn't relax around him. A mistake like that could cost me my life. "So, you *are* human."

"I didn't realize that was in doubt."

I hesitated. How much did Ira know about me—about cubines in general? He already had enough of a hold over me. I didn't want to admit my inability to read him.

I didn't have the chance. His phone vibrated on the table, and all at once he seemed to relax. He turned the device over, read the message, and his face changed. "Time to go."

"What is it?"

"There's been another murder." Ira swept the folder full of victims into a brown leather valise. "Or rather, murders. Five of them this time."

Five more humans dead, and he blamed a demon for it. The cold crept up my spine, expanded in my core. "You were waiting for this. You knew this would happen!"

"I thought it might." Ira stood and stretched. "You didn't look at the dates in the file, did you, Ms. Knight?"

"The dates?" I wracked my brain, but I couldn't come up with anything special about them. "What are you talking about?"

"All the murders happened on weekend nights." He took out his wallet and dropped a pile of bills on the table.

I stared at him, realization washing over me. "This was a test."

"Yes, and you passed."

"You thought *I* might be the killer."

"Are you coming or not?" He didn't wait for an answer but jerked his head at me and strode toward the entrance.

Did I really have a choice? I hurried after him through the crowded bar. I hadn't exactly dressed for a crime scene in my serious lawyer shoes and slacks, but at least I looked like a professional. My stomach twisted and the few bites of pasta I'd managed to swallow sat heavy as lead.

The last time I visited a crime scene, I had gone with Ariel. And I left it unconscious, drained to near-death by his deceptive seduction. On the balcony of the Ritz, he had leaned over me, dark wings spreading until they took up the whole sky and blotted out the lights of the city below.

In the present, I stumbled, and Ira caught my elbow, steadying me. His firm hand guided me from the restaurant and out into the night. The sudden cool breeze and the roar of traffic hit me like a slap and broke the memory's grip.

"All right there, Knight?" His deep brown eyes swept over me, an impersonal assessment. He might not like me, and I might not trust him, but he didn't seem like the trickster type.

"I'm fine." If I wanted to make this opportunity work out, I had to put the past behind me.

I closed the lid on my memories and shoved them into the dark where they belonged.

We sped up the hill from downtown toward Pacific Heights in Ira's black SUV, and my breath caught in my throat at a sudden thought. With all those well-known, wealthy men dying, what if Sebastian—? It seemed unlikely, but all the same, I pulled out my phone and tapped out a quick message to him.

Ira glanced over, eyebrow raised, and I hastily pocketed the device, like a teenager caught slipping notes to her not-boyfriend on a school trip.

"Do I have to remind you that everything I told you tonight, and everything you are about to see, is confidential?" Ira sounded dead serious.

Damn, this guy had zero chill. "Just checking on a friend. I didn't tell him anything." I shifted in my seat. "Where are we headed, anyway?"

"Out to the university." Ira's expression turned grim. "The victims were students this time. Five Delta Alpha Mu fraternity brothers living in a house off campus."

The growing tightness in my chest released with the snap of a broken rubber band, and I sat back, exhaling with mixed relief and guilt. Five people had died, but Sebastian was safe. "That doesn't fit the profile."

"We'll see." He turned the dials of the SUV's radio, seeking through channels until he found the one he wanted. The voices of police dispatch crackled through the speakers, calling out codes and asking for emergency personnel.

"10-55. That's a coroner's case." I leaned forward as if it would help me hear better. "I didn't know you could get police scanner traffic on the radio."

"Not on your radio, you can't." He turned left on Divisidero and hit the accelerator, taking us south at a speed that made me wince.

"You're going to get pulled over."

For answer, he hit a button on the dash, and blue and red lights flashed out from the windshield. "Government work does have some perks."

"Very fancy."

"Very necessary. We need to get there fast, before the locals fubar the crime scene. Or start asking too many awkward questions."

"Hey now! I know some of those locals." That included Danny, who worked for the medical examiner's office and took her crime scenes more seriously than anything else in her life.

My phone chimed with Sebastian's response to my impulsive text: *All good here. At dinner with my dad. What's up?*

I hovered my fingers over the keyboard for a moment, trying to decide how to answer. Finally, I settled for: *I got a new job.*

Congratulations! We should celebrate. What's the job?

I typed *secret agent.* No, that was too dramatic. I erased it. *Federal contractor.* No, too boring. I backspaced furiously. *It's complicated. Tell you later.*

Of course it is, came his response. I pictured his eyebrow arching in amusement. *I look forward to hearing all about it.*

What exactly could I tell him? I turned to Ira. "What's my job title?"

"Officially? Case consultant, limited appointment."

Well, that sounded ominous, and almost as boring as a contractor. "What about unofficially?"

"Unofficially, you're a big damn gamble."

I was probably lucky he didn't say *pain in my ass.* "Whose gamble? Yours?"

"That's not your concern, Knight." He jerked his chin at the windshield. Ahead of us, more red and blue lights flashed into view, with a cordon stretching past the sidewalk into the right lane. Ira screeched to a halt, double-parking between a cop car and the coroner's van. "This is."

Several news vehicles jockeyed for position around the perimeter, and a small crowd of looky-loos thronged the sidewalk across the street, where the lights of the city abruptly plunged into the darkness under the trees of the park. An SFPD truck blocked the driveway, and a grim-faced officer moved along the police tape, ordering people back from the cordon.

The house was a handsome brick building several stories tall, set back a bit from the street and screened by a mature cypress tree. Those students must have paid a bundle, even split five ways.

"What a mess." I swallowed hard. Even at a distance, the emotional miasma of the onlookers throbbed with an unsavory blend of morbid curiosity, borrowed grief, and fascinated horror, an oil slick sliding over darker undercurrents.

"Well, what are you waiting for?" Ira said. "Go do your demon thing. Take care of it."

I stared at him, shocked. "You want me to use a Presence on them."

"If that's what you call it, yeah, I do."

"And tell them, what? There's nothing to see here?"

"Sounds good to me."

"You're serious."

"I'm not known for my comedy skills."

That tracked. After a moment of hesitation, in which Ira drummed his fingers on the steering wheel in an impatient rhythm, I hopped out of the SUV and crossed to the knot of bystanders. Gathering the shreds of my composure, I steeled myself against their energy.

"You can all go home." I put the force of command behind the words. "We have this handled. Don't waste your time hanging around."

It worked. They didn't even grumble about it, but dispersed in less than a minute, hurrying down the street away from the house. No one glanced back.

Huh. I understood why Ira wanted my help a little better now.

I turned to rejoin my new boss, who had headed for the cordon to negotiate with the uniformed cop working security. Then I froze.

Two people in forensic unit jackets came out of the house, their heads bent together, and behind them came Tobias Kaine. The other cambion looked bad: gray-faced, white-lipped, his eyes staring and wide.

I wreathed myself in a don't-see-me Presence and ducked under the tape to intercept Tobias. When he came abreast of the police vehicle, I grabbed him by the arm and pulled him into the shadows under the trees.

He yelped in surprise and yanked his arm from my grip. "Lily Knight? What are you doing here?"

"Shh," I hissed. "I could ask you the same question."

"The cops called me out here. They wanted my expert opinion."

"Your expert opinion on what, exactly?" I cast a glance over my shoulder, but Ira seemed deep in conversation with the uniformed officer.

This new wrinkle would likely piss him off. The cops didn't know that Tobias was a cambion either, but he featured demons and other urban legends in his streaming online show and never failed to jump at a chance for notoriety. Since he'd leaked the story about Nepenthe's death, everyone took him a lot more seriously.

"This thing—" Tobias wiped beads of sweat from his brow. "Lily, I don't think we can stop this from blowing up. I don't know what this is. No one does."

That didn't sound good for anything except Ira's demon murderer theory. "Well, you better stop it," I snapped. "We're talking torches and mobs, Tobias! They won't suffer us to live. We'll be dissected, experimented on, and disappeared."

He didn't answer. His furtive gaze shifted to the house as if drawn by a magnet, and a sudden dizzy wave of his energy washed over me—his desiderata, momentarily out of control. He didn't want to think about what lay inside, but he couldn't stop himself, either.

"Geez." I leaned away. "Pull yourself together, man."

"You don't understand. Their blood...it's not inside them anymore. It's—" He waved an arm, vaguely, and staggered. "It's everywhere else."

My skin crawled at his queasy energy and the import of his words. "What do you mean?" Blood everywhere didn't fit with the other murders in Ira's file.

"I need to sit down," Tobias rasped. He leaned back against the nearest tree trunk, hand over his mouth and his face greenish white to the gills, like a fish rotting belly up on Stinson Beach.

"Knight. Who's this?" Ira's deep voice came from behind me.

I turned. My Presence should have hidden me from any nearby humans until I released it, but here my new boss stood, looking between me and Tobias with an eyebrow raised.

"It's no one important." I hated Tobias, but I had no intention of outing a fellow cambion if the government didn't already have a bead on him. "Just a damn fool."

"One of your locals?" Ira shrugged, looking bemused. "Let's go have a look inside."

Tobias made a choking sound. I winced. "I'm ready."

We left Tobias to breathe it out, or retch it out as it happened, and headed up the steps to the murder house.

Apparently, Ira's nameless government agency did have some clout, because no one gave us any trouble about our presence on an active crime scene. The cop guarding the door nodded to us, handed us disposable booties to cover our shoes, and lifted the tape without a word.

In the house's front room, the smell of old beer, patchouli incense, marijuana, and vomit mixed in an overpowering bouquet. I covered my mouth with my sleeve and took shallow breaths.

The two stained couches facing a big screen TV mounted on the wall had seen better days. A bar stool lay on its side next to the kitchen island, and another lay shattered into splintery chunks of wood beside the back door. Red plastic cups littered the kitchen counters, and more scattered the floor, wet stains seeping into the carpet. The screen leading to the back porch had a huge tear through it and the door hung askew, its frame broken at the hinges from the inside.

"Signs of a struggle," Ira murmured. "That's different."

I pointed. "That's not the only thing."

A single set of reddish-brown footprints led down the darkened staircase, across the filthy floor, and out through the ruined door to the back porch. I matched my steps to the prints, taking care not to disturb them. But in the doorway, I stopped, adrenaline tingling through me.

Someone had walked out of that house with their small bare feet covered in blood. But on the porch, their prints stopped, as if they had dematerialized.

Or perhaps they had leaped into the air and flown away.

5

BLOOD WILL OUT

Ira didn't comment on the footprints. He knelt to take snapshots with his phone, laying a pen alongside them for scale.

Two could play at that game. I kept my mouth shut. If he didn't know about cubine powers of flight, I wouldn't tell him. Not yet. Not until I had a better idea of who, or what, we were dealing with here.

Quiet voices filtered down the stairs. I focused my night vision and moved upward, keeping to the side of the steps to avoid the bloody tracks. Several closed doors led off from the darkened landing. I pushed the first one open with gloved fingers.

The dim room smelled worse than downstairs, unwashed young man and dirty laundry overlaid by a pervasive sour, coppery scent that didn't bear thinking about. Forensics had already passed through here, it seemed, taking with them any bodies or evidence the room had contained. The stripped bed exposed a bare mattress marred with ugly black stains.

I swallowed. In the half-light, the walls looked wrong, smeared with something dark. A rhythmic, ominous dripping noise echoed through the empty room, and I ventured a step inside. Up close, the near wall glistened, coated with a sticky-wet substance that looked and smelled like blood.

It's everywhere else, Tobias had said.

Maybe I should have gone easier on him.

I backed away into the hall and let the door swing shut, heading toward the hushed conversation emanating from the room at the end of the hall.

"I don't understand it." The familiar voice stopped me in my tracks.

"Crap," I whispered. Danny was here? That complicated things. I hadn't told her about my job offer yet, unsure if I wanted to take it. And of course, I didn't have time once I talked to Ira and he summoned me downtown to double check my innocence.

"There are no wounds on him anywhere," Danny continued. "No marks. Not even needle tracks. I checked all the usual spots."

"So where did all the blood go?"

"Do you have to ask?" Danny's tone turned acerbic, her dry gallows humor reasserting itself.

I paused in the doorway. Danny and her male colleague had their backs to me, bent over a still figure lying face up on the double bed under the window. The body's face had a sunken, pallid cast, skin pulled tight over his bones.

As in the last room, blood covered the walls, the occasional thick drip adding to congealing puddles on the floor with a skin-crawling plop, plop.

"I thought they called in that consultant on weird shit," the other medical examiner said. "And much as I hate to say it, we could definitely use a second opinion. What happened to him?"

"He's outside touching grass," I said. "Or vomiting in it."

Danny's head whipped around. "Lily? What are you doing here?"

"My weird shit spidey senses were tingling." Off her skeptical look, I added, "I'm consulting on this one, too. I didn't know you were working tonight."

"I got called in." Danny frowned at me, but she didn't question me further. "This is a multiple homicide, and it's all hands on deck."

"I can see why." I picked my way to the bedside. The boy—man—who had lived here didn't leave much evidence behind of an academic career. Sports posters hung on the walls and a tower of beer cans occupied the desk. A stack of uncracked kinesthesiology textbooks sat on the floor by the bed.

Danny moved aside, making way for me. The dead man's wide eyes stared up with fixed terror at the ceiling. He'd watched death coming for him.

"They all look like this," Danny said. "Found dead in their beds."

"What a horror show," the male M.E. muttered.

"Are you sure all the blood is theirs?"

"We'll test it, of course. But that's not the only weird thing. Look at this." Danny grabbed the dead guy by the jaw and stuck her gloved fingers into his mouth. "They all had *this* stuck up in there." She pulled a bundle of something black and bedraggled out of his throat.

"I'll take that." Ira appeared in the doorway, holding out a plastic evidence bag. Damn, but the man moved stealthily. Or maybe my inability to sense his energy dulled my subconscious awareness.

Danny eyed him. "Who are *you*?"

"I'm with her." Ira jerked his head at me. "This is now a federal investigation, Ms.—?"

"Rios. Did you say *federal*?" Danny turned back to me, mouthing something that looked a lot like *what the fuck?* Her energy spiked red with protective alarm.

"Tell you later," I said, then corrected myself. "If I'm allowed, that is. Can I see that? What is it?"

Her desiderata roiled with misgiving, but she spread the bundle out in her gloved hand. "Feathers," she said. "Their throats were full of black feathers."

I exchanged a glance with Ira. Despite the differences in this crime scene from the one in his file, the feathers matched the killer's modus operandi. I took the evidence bag from him, holding it out to Danny. She dropped the bundle in with a grimace, and I handed it over to my new boss.

"You better keep your chain of custody straight," she said to Ira.

"Don't worry about that, Miss Rios." He tucked the bag into his jacket pocket. "Who found the bodies?"

"An anonymous caller," the other M.E. said. "No one was alive in here by the time the first responders arrived. But given the state of the blood, the scene is under two hours old."

"The time it would take to bleed five grown men dry…It just doesn't add up." A question shadowed Danny's face and her desiderata, but she didn't voice it.

"All right if I start on the next room, Rios?" the junior medical examiner said. Danny waved him off, and he hurried away.

"It's weird shit, all right." Now I could answer her unspoken question. "But let's not jump to any conclusions."

Ira cleared his throat. "There is the matter of the footprints."

"About that." Danny's expression cleared. "We think there might have been a witness, maybe even the anonymous tipster. The police found a teenager's out-of-state ID in one of the rooms. They're looking for her now."

Ira's eyes widened. He pulled out his phone, turned, and strode from the room. His terse, low voice snapped out orders as he headed back downstairs. It was the first time I had really seen him look surprised.

"Wait," I said. "Someone walked out of here, and she's not a suspect?"

"From what the detective said, she's just a kid," Danny said. "Do you really think a kid could have done all this?"

"I don't know what could have done this." The corpse's staring eyes and the blood-coated walls reminded me too much of another gory scene I had walked into, the hotel room where Ariel killed a succubus with the goal of getting under my skin. I shifted on my feet. If I had expected a crime scene visit, I would have worn more sensible heels.

"Lily." Danny stepped between me and the dead man on the bed, breaking me out of my increasingly uneasy thoughts. "Are you in trouble? That guy—is he really with the feds?"

"I think so." I shook myself, dislodging the grip of bad memories. "And it's not trouble, it's a job. I help him find whoever—whatever—did this, and hopefully I get to pay you all that back rent I owe you."

"Okay," she said, but she didn't sound too sure. "I'm not worried about the rent. I hope you know that."

"I know. But it worries me." Danny would always have my back, but it seemed like everywhere I turned lately, I found myself beholden to someone. "I'll be fine, Dan. I promise."

But when I looked around once more at that bloodstained room in the house of the dead, my spine tingled with the creeping certainty that my promise would turn out to be a lie.

What kind of person, human or demon, could kill like this, and why? And why would they spare the witness who fled on bloody feet?

None of it made any sense. But then again, most murders seemed senseless from the outside. It only made sense from the inside, the moment of desperation or of cold knowledge, recognizing just how far a person could go. Most people didn't believe themselves capable of dealing a killing blow. But most people had something that would drive them to it.

After all, I knew that from experience. I found what drove me, and she stood by my side even now. I killed to protect the friend I loved and save myself. I killed to get myself free from the demon who controlled me.

And after all, maybe Ira was right.

Maybe it did take a demon, or a killer, or both, to catch one.

Midnight had come and gone by the time I padded up the back stairs to my narrow garret room under Danny's eaves, clad in pajama pants and an old She-Hulk t-shirt. The grinding hours spent at the murder scene left me wrung out and emotionally exhausted. But when I closed my eyes, images of blood and death swam across the inside of my lids. Sleep seemed unwise at best.

I didn't bother to turn on the light, but I did switch on my electric kettle and retrieve a mostly clean mug, along with my stash of instant cocoa, from my desk. A few minutes later, cocoa in hand, I ducked my head to avoid the ceiling's low slant and tucked myself into the dormer window seat for a first-rate brood.

I told Danny the truth. I didn't know what kind of monster could have killed those college students. Alone in my dark garret with my hot chocolate, fortified with a substantial spike of bourbon from the bottle I kept stashed in my bottom drawer, I could admit how much that scared me.

Cubines didn't do things like that—did we?

I shivered, lifted my cup to my lips—and froze. Outside my window, movement flickered in my periphery. Without turning my head, I slanted my gaze sideways.

Heavy darkness clustered the crook of the Queen Ann-style roof. Three stories up, the light from the street didn't reach all the nooks and crannies of the old Victorian. The ambient orange glow of the restless city obscured the darker corners further and hampered my night vision. But for a moment, a pair of golden pinpoints flashed out at me, reflective in the half-light.

Then they vanished. I waited motionless and breathless for a long, eye-watering minute, heart hammering in my chest.

There. A furtive shadow melted away into the deeper shadows among the Tudor chimney pots. It wasn't my imagination or a manifestation of the post-murder house willies. Something, or someone, lurked on my roof, watching me with eyes that shone yellow in the dark.

Had Delilah gotten out somehow? The glint of eyeshine seemed high up for a cat, but the roof's angle might explain it. With a soft curse, I set down my cooling cocoa. I ran my fingers along the dusty window jamb until I found the catch and cracked the window open.

"Delilah?" The chilly, slightly fetid air of the San Francisco night wafted in, tickling my throat with damp and an underlying sweet fragrance I couldn't quite place. "Here, kitty, kitty!"

Nothing moved. I shoved the window up further. It gave with a harsh, grudging scrape and rattle.

A quiet, trilling mew answered it—from behind me. I jumped and turned as a furry gray fluffball emerged from under a heap of blankets on my unmade bed. She blinked at me, sleepy and aggrieved at the disturbance. In the darkened room, her eyes shone green, not gold.

Whatever creature had looked back at me from the shadows outside, it wasn't Delilah.

Well, maybe another cat had gotten stuck on the roof. I propped the window all the way open and pulled myself up to perch, barefoot, on the sill.

"You stay right there." I addressed Delilah over my shoulder in a stern undertone. "No getting any ideas."

She folded her tail primly around her feet and favored me with a long, suspicious look: had her person finally lost it for good? I sighed and turned back to the thick-layered shadows outside.

"Hello?" I called softly to the listening night.

No one answered me. But the strange, sweet, familiar aroma came back stronger on the breeze. It smelled of incense, of sandalwood and smoke, and another tingle of *déjà vu* crawled down my spine. A memory rose unbidden of Ariel's yellow eyes laughing at me, pupils fierce and slitted, his voice smooth and laced with triumph as the scent of frankincense and myrrh hung thick in the air.

Hello, Lillian.

But Ariel was dead, and besides, he didn't smell of sandalwood at all. I shook off the memory of his voice and stepped out onto the slick tiles of the roof. A moment of human vertigo shuddered through me. But the latent kether in my blood flowed back in after it and balanced me. I stood light and sure-footed on the balls of my feet.

I lowered the window behind me, careful to leave it open a crack so I could get back in but not so far that Delilah could slip out after me. Then I turned my head, nostrils flaring, following the scent on the breeze.

So, I didn't get to save a cat, after all.

"I know you're there." I kept my tone light and conversational. "And I know what you are."

A faint gasp answered my words, followed by a scrabbling noise from behind the chimney pots. I squinted, and the shadows shifted into higher resolution, my demon sight piercing the glamour that thickened them. A small shape hunched there, silhouetted against the sky, an irregularity in the border between chimney stack and roof line that didn't fit with the rest of the architecture.

The succubus huddled on the knife's edge of the roof's peak with her head bowed and one small hand splayed across the brick of the chimney like a ragged, lost little gargoyle. Her shadowy figure had wings, dark, intangible pinions that ruffled and folded around her slender form as if warding off the night's chill. The half-transparent feathers drooped and dragged, shredded into torn ribbons at the tips. Where still intact, they appeared shot through with streaks of gold that glowed with an internal luminescence.

A tangled mat of light hair screened her face and hid the eyeshine that had caught my attention from the window seat. But it didn't hide the way she trembled with each long, shuddering breath.

"Hey, it's okay," I said. "I'm not going to hurt you."

She didn't respond. I took a tentative step up the slope of the roof toward her and offered her my hand.

Her head snapped up, face and body taut. For a split second, she teetered on the roof's ridge, arms flung out, ruined wings beating a futile, frantic tattoo against the sky. Her nails scraped along the chimney stack. She rose halfway onto her tiptoes, as if about to take flight.

Then she crumpled. Her wings tore and streamed off behind her, bleeding into the night. They dissipated like fog burning off the bay in the morning, but all in the negative. No light here, just a girl falling from a high place, and now she had no hint of wings at all.

I stretched out my arms, launched myself from the shingles, and snatched her plummeting body from midair. For a moment, my own wings flashed gauzy and transparent around me. They glittered with phantom starlight, as with one strong, steady beat, they lifted me and brought me down again.

The girl hung limp, a dead weight in my arms, her limbs loose and swinging. Demons didn't get sick, as a rule, but her skin burned hot and dry as though scalded by fever.

I shifted her over my shoulder in a fireman's hold. Thank...well, not God, who might not exist and certainly didn't care, nor goodness, which I couldn't claim. But thank Sebastian and as he would say, thank fuck, for the kether-strength it took to open the window one-armed from the outside and maneuver the succubus into the window seat without hitting her head or mine on the sill.

This time, I switched on the light, the better to study my uninvited guest, and brushed the matted snarl of dirty blond hair away from her face. She had dark crescents of dirt caked under her fingernails, and she looked incredibly young, with the willow-limbed, raw-boned build of a teenager still growing into their full height. Barefoot, she wore nothing but a skimpy, stained purple top and a scrap of vinyl skirt.

What kind of parent would let a child leave the house dressed like that? And did that question make me officially Old?

Did full-blooded demons even have parents to speak of?

Dark bruises marred her upper arms, livid and stark against her peaches and cream skin. I frowned. Cubines didn't usually bruise like that, or run a fever, or faint for that matter. But this one had done all those things.

What had happened to her? A possibility occurred to me, made more likely by the segmented patterns of the bruises like an imprint of grasping fingers. What if this succubus had fed on tainted kether?

We demons needed human desire and pleasure to feed us, but quality mattered. *What* a human wanted from us mattered. Kether could weaken rather than strengthen us if we drew from the wrong source.

The energy of a soul sick with violence or hatred could still fuel our powers, but the aftereffects of a tainted pull would roar through our bodies like the sum of the world's worst bender, a heroin overdose, and a thirty-two-ounce strychnine berry smoothie. It could leave a demon ill and incapacitated, or at its worst, destroy our health, our sanity, or our lives.

I had experience with that kind of mistake. The first man I kissed harbored a knot of sickness at his core, and the energy pull left me bedridden for a month. And the backlash of my reaction put him in a permanent coma.

But this girl had manifested her wings. She'd made it up on the roof somehow. She couldn't be that far gone.

I knelt by the window seat and sucked in a long, slow breath. Giving kether didn't require an intimate touch. A kether push from me via a forehead kiss had saved Danny's life and stopped her from bleeding out after Ariel put a bullet in her belly.

I had almost died instead, but this girl didn't need everything I had, not like Danny had. Assuming no silver contamination, her bruises would heal after the taint of the poison pull wore off. But I could speed things up. I had some questions to ask her, first and foremost how she ended up on my roof at all.

I took her limp hand in both of mine and closed my eyes, focusing the flow of my surplus kether on the simple touch, offering my strength to her.

It came on slow, like a change in polarities from my palms to hers, an ache in my throat of yearning or loss. A heavy sense of fatigue crept over me, leaving my body clumsy, weak, and weighted down by gravity.

Without my kether surplus, the last bit left over from my encounter with Sebastian days ago, I was normal. I was tired. I was...almost human.

I dropped the girl's hand and rubbed my palms over gritty eyes, souvenirs of my long day and sleepless nights of late. Leaning my shoulder against the wall, I folded my arms and waited for a sign of life.

For a moment, nothing happened. Had I done it wrong? But then she stirred, mascara-clumped lashes fluttering open. Her eyes darted back and forth, blank with palpable confusion.

"Hey, kid," I said. "Welcome back."

6

MIDNIGHT LEGAL CLINIC

The demon girl propped herself up on her elbows, eyes wide.

"You're safe here," I said. "Don't get up. You should rest."

Her throat jumped, swallowing. "What happened?"

"You fell off my roof." I rose, one hand pressed flat against the wall for support. My kether gift to her had taken it out of me. "I caught you. What were you doing up there, anyway?"

"Nothing." Her gaze skated away from mine, her expression clouded. "I don't remember."

Somehow, I doubted that. "What's your name, kid?"

"I'm not a kid," she said, with a flash of defiance.

Good. Maybe she was starting to feel better. "Sure, okay. How old are you? Fifteen?"

"Seventeen." She pouted. "Old enough to not be called 'kid' by a middle-aged hag."

"Thanks a lot." In all fairness, though, I probably did look haggard. I certainly felt older than thirty-one. "I'd happily call you by your name, if you have one."

She glanced at me sidelong. The stubborn set of her jaw suggested she wanted to argue further, but she said, "It's Eve."

"Pleased to meet you, Eve. I'm Lily Knight."

"I know who you are," Eve said softly.

Her quiet, unequivocal statement rocked me back on my heels. Of course, her presence on my roof was no accident. And I had brought this stray demon child into the home I shared with my friends without a single iota of knowledge about her or her intentions toward me and mine. Then I'd transferred over to her the only advantage I had over her, should she attack me: my kether strength.

Not my brightest move ever. Lily Knight, Esq.: proof positive that they didn't test for common sense and good judgment on the bar exam.

"You were watching me." I backed up, putting space between us. "That's why you were out there."

Eve gave a little half shrug and sat up. The power had shifted between us, from an adult caring for an injured child to two predators in close quarters with motives unknown to one another.

"I'll take that as a yes," I said. "How long have you been following me?" I'd come from a crime scene marked by the possibility of supernatural violence. Maybe her sudden appearance was a coincidence, but I didn't like those odds.

"That's not..." She trailed off. "I just didn't know where else to go."

"You'll have to give me more than that, Eve. Because I don't know you from Adam." *Ba dum tish.* I paused for effect, and she rolled her eyes. *Tough crowd.* "I hear that you felt low on options, but why did lurking outside my bedroom window in the middle of the night seem like the best of them?"

"I'm sorry, okay?" She stared down at her hands with their blackened nails, misery flitting across her perfect features. "I thought maybe you could help me."

I frowned. "Help you how?"

Eve lifted her head. No longer golden, her eyes had faded to the warm green of oak leaves on a sunny day. They brimmed with tears and a luminous plea. "You're a lawyer, aren't you?"

"Um, yes. I am." Despite myself, my heart went out to her. "Why do you ask?"

"Because I think I need one." Eve gulped, and the tears slipped down. "Miss Knight, I...I think I might have killed someone."

"Holy hell." Knees weak, I tottered back, reached for my shabby old desk chair, and sank onto it.

It all made sense now. The stains on her top, the dark crescents under her nails, and the dirty streaks in her hair weren't dirt at all.

They were dried blood.

"You did follow me, from the frat house. Didn't you?"

She nodded. "Please, will you help me? I can pay."

A paying client sounded like a novel idea. A sudden urge seized me to do whatever I could to help. Maybe this little waif of a demon who'd fallen into my arms also meant a lucrative opportunity. I could tell Ira to go fuck himself. I could go solo. The impulse to say yes almost overpowered me. But I set my jaw and reined it in.

That little twit had pulled a Presence on me. My human side couldn't resist her powers of emotional coercion, but my demon side took umbrage. So did my lawyer side, once it caught up. "Nice try, missy. I'm not that easy to bamboozle."

"I had to try." She drew her knees up to her chin, unrepentant. "I have money. Honest."

Well, that I very much doubted. "If you know who I am, you should also know I got fired from my last job. I could lose my license. And the court will appoint you an attorney to represent you if you're accused of a crime." I left out the conflict-of-interest problem. Telling her about my deal with Ira would only spook her.

It spooked me, too. What if this bedraggled little urchin had killed those men? It didn't seem possible. But I could already predict what Ira would think about it.

No, it didn't make sense. I could buy her losing control, but not the nasty blood business or the ritualistic implications of the feathers in the men's mouths.

"I don't care," Eve said. "I want you to do it."

"Why me?"

"Because you're the only lawyer I know who's a succubus, like me."

"Technically, I'm a cambion." But behind my glib words, cold seeped through my veins. She knew too much about me. "I'm only half-succubus."

"Whatever. You're still the only one who will understand what happened."

I kept my tone gentle. "I can't represent you, Eve."

"You mean you won't help me." She scowled.

"I'll help you if I can." Even if she had nothing to do with the deaths, she knew something, and for both our sakes, I needed to find out what. "Why don't you tell me what happened. Why were you at the frat house in the first place?"

Eve drew a deep, shaky breath. "I went there for a party. It wasn't the first time. I went there because, well. *You* know."

"You were hungry," I said softly. "I do know. There's no need to feel ashamed. You can't live without feeding." Funny how easy the words came to my lips for her, when I couldn't give myself the same forgiveness.

Ariel's remembered words echoed behind my own. *Is a cat evil because it kills a mouse? Of course not. It's only doing what is in its nature.*

Not everything in this world is as black and white as you think it is.

I didn't trust myself with the shades in between. The gray area seemed more like a slippery slope from where I stood, with blood on my hands and Ariel's death on my heart.

But this young succubus before me had real blood on her hands, didn't she?

"I didn't think it would be like that." Eve swung her bare feet down to rest on the floor, but she didn't try to rise. She sat with her head bowed, staring at her broken, bloodied nails.

Mother of monsters, had no one taught her the facts of cubine life? I chose my words carefully. "It would be better to hunt among humans your own age. Why visit the university? What about your classmates at school?"

"I don't go to school." She scoffed. "Besides, high school boys are boring. I thought college guys would be more fun. But I think there was something wrong with these ones."

"Tainted kether," I said.

"What?"

"They're adults, and you're a kid. If they were interested in someone your age, there's something twisted about them. Drawing from a tainted source is seriously dangerous. It can make you really sick, like drinking poison."

"I didn't know that," Eve said. "Can it make you black out?"

"Yes. It might make you dizzy or faint, or you might throw up. It's a lot like what humans suffer when they drink too much booze. But it can affect you for a long time, if it's really bad and you don't find a cleaner source."

"Oh." Eve studied her bare feet, black and dusty from the roof and who knew where else. Why didn't she have any shoes? Had she left them somewhere, at the crime scene, maybe?

Someone had walked, barefoot and bloody, through that house earlier tonight. Had those footprints belonged to Eve? If so, she was in more trouble than she knew.

"Is that what happened?" My stomach sank, but my lawyer's training kicked in and my voice stayed even. "Did you black out, Eve?"

"I don't remember. I partied with them. We went upstairs. And then—" She broke off, biting her lip.

I waited. Sometimes asking more questions at the wrong time made a witness clam up. Sometimes I had to give them a minute to work through it and they'd offer me more without prompting.

"Then I woke up." Her soot-streaked hands plucked at the multicolored blanket that covered the seat, a handmade gift from Danny's mom. "It was dark when I woke up, and so quiet. I didn't feel good. I was sick. I thought he was asleep. But—" She choked and fell silent.

"It's ok," I said. "Take all the time you need."

The silence stretched, her face twisted, her throat working as she tried to fit words around the awful truth. When they finally came, they spilled from her in a rush. "I touched him. He was cold. I tried to wake him, but I couldn't. He had no kether, no desiderata, nothing. He was dead."

"What happened then?"

She swallowed again, a convulsive gulp. "I couldn't do anything for him. I called 911 from his phone, and then I—I left. I felt so weak. I couldn't fly very far, so I hid. The cops came. And then you came." Her lip trembled, and she lifted her head. "I recognized you. And I didn't know where else to go, so I followed you home."

"Oh, honey." A lump rose in my own throat. "You've been through a lot."

She didn't seem to hear me. "It was me, wasn't it?" Her voice had gone dull and toneless. "I killed him. I must have. I didn't mean to. Does it matter that I didn't mean to?" Another tear streaked down her dusty face.

"First of all," I said, "we don't know you did anything. So don't go confessing to anything you don't remember doing. Not to me, and definitely not to any cops." And definitely not to Ira. "Got it?"

"Okay."

"Second of all, I saw that crime scene. I don't think you could have done whatever was done to those guys. Not in your state."

Eve's forehead creased. "How do you know that?"

"Just trust me on this." I hoped I was right. "Third, *if* you had something to do with it, it would matter that you didn't mean to. Accidents happen. It matters in the eyes of the law whether you did it on purpose or not. It matters to me. And it should matter to you, too. Okay?"

She swiped at her cheek with the back of her hand. "Okay."

"I do have one more question," I said, when she didn't offer anything more. "You mentioned you recognized me. How did you know who I was?"

Eve's eyes widened. "I've always known who you were. Well, for a long time, at least. My father showed me pictures. He used to talk about you all the time. He said you were the only succubus lawyer in the country."

"Your *father* talked about me?" A slow, cold, serpentine weight uncoiled at my core.

"He said you were a friend," Eve said. "His student. He said you were good at your job. He showed me your picture and said if I ever needed help, I should find you. He wouldn't say a thing like that if it weren't true."

The chill twined up my spine and twisted itself into a hard, painful knot in my chest. I jumped up from my chair, my legs a little steadier now that my natural human life force had started to refill.

"Eve." My heart thudded in my ears. "This is important. Who is your father? Is he a demon, too?"

"Of course," she said. "He's an incubus. His name is Ariel. You must know him, don't you?"

The clot of dread under my breastbone exploded into hot and cold running adrenaline. It burned through my veins like a shot of kether, only worse in every conceivable way. "Ariel." My voice came out flat and hard. "Ariel was...is your father?"

"That's what I just said." Eve gave me a funny look. "Are you okay?"

"What? Oh." I rubbed my temples. "Yeah, sure. I'm fine." *Fanfuckingtastic.* This girl was *Ariel's daughter.* He'd told her about me. She'd come looking for me, followed me home from a murder scene with blood under her nails to stalk me from my rooftop.

"You don't look fine," Eve said. "You kind of look like you're going to barf. And your energy just went all squirmy."

Smartass kid, but she was right. My stomach was doing Olympic-worthy flips. "It's not polite to comment on other people's energy. Didn't your father ever teach you that?"

"No, he didn't. I think you just made that up."

Not good. She could run circles around me at this point, just like her father used to do. Or maybe my head was just spinning.

"*Ariel* is your father," I said again. It sounded strange in my head and even stranger out loud.

"Uh, yeah." Eve side-eyed me, as well she might at an adult she'd come to for help who seemed to be having a stroke. "I don't understand why you keep saying that."

I tried to pull myself together. "I didn't know he had any family." I'd been his family, once, or so I thought. Until he came after me, and everything I thought I knew came crashing down.

And now this. Ariel had a daughter. Ariel's daughter was called Eve, because of course she was. Eve, the under-dressed, soot-streaked fallen angel currently seated with her colt-like legs pulled up under her on my window seat, wrapped up in Mrs. Rios' homemade blanket, looking bruised, peaky, and very, very young.

But not that young. If I had my math right and she hadn't lied about her age, I met Ariel after her birth, and he had never breathed a word. For my part, I didn't bother to ask if he had family somewhere. Did full-blooded demons even have families to speak of besides wild seeds like me?

What did I know of my own father's people? I didn't know how they lived, what they did when not courting humans for sustenance, what their family structures were like, how they loved each other, if they even did. I didn't know anything about them at all, except this.

Ariel had a daughter, and Ariel was dead.

Ariel was dead because I killed him. And now his daughter needed me.

Doubt brushed frozen fingers across the back of my neck. I'd driven the stake through his chest. I watched him die. I remembered the way the silver in my hand vibrated through my stained satin opera gloves as the metal tore through muscle and bone into his heart.

But cubines didn't die easily. I knew that, too.

"Have you...seen your father lately?" I struggled to maintain my casual tone.

"Not lately." Her face fell. "I used to live with him. But he left. He said he had things to take care of. They must have been big, important things, because he didn't come back. Eventually, I got tired of waiting for him, so I came to find him out here."

Oh yes, big things all right. Like shuffling off this mortal coil courtesy of yours truly. I collapsed back into the chair, exhaling. Killing Ariel had been bad enough. I didn't want to think about what would happen to me and everyone I cared about if it didn't stick.

But his daughter had come looking for him. He hadn't come home to her because of me. I made her an orphan, and she didn't even know it.

She watched me narrowly from the window seat and for a moment, the facade of the naïf she wore so naturally slipped, laying bare the workings of a shrewd mind like her father's. She was putting the pieces together. "You knew him really well, didn't you?"

What a question. I had to tread carefully, or she'd ferret out the truth before I could decide what to tell her. "Yes. I knew him. How well, I'm not so sure. We were close for a while when I was younger."

I scrubbed my hands over my gritty eyes. A highlight reel of better days flashed through my mind. Ariel, laughing at me, his face alight. Ariel teaching me to shape a glamour from a breath of kether and a human quarry's unique set of desires. Ariel's arm wrapped tight around my waist, his weight against me, warm and solid. Ariel kissing me firmly until my pain melted away.

Ariel's jet-black wings hunched around his shoulders like a hunting hawk, perched in the darkness outside Sebastian's bedroom window, goading me to follow him. Ariel's face twisted with rage as he lunged at me with cold silver aimed at my heart.

"You have a lot of feelings about him," Eve said. "Complicated feelings."

Shit. She was reading me. With an effort, I flattened my energy and conjured up a shaky laugh. "That's one way to put it."

Eve said nothing for a minute. Her gaze drifted away from me, out the window at the dark. Maybe she was remembering him, too. Pain sharpened in my chest, like a splinter working its way toward my heart. I focused on forcing my breath to come slow and even so she wouldn't sense my fear.

"So, what do we do now?" Ariel's daughter said finally.

"Right now?" The alarm clock by my bed read almost 2 a.m. Good thing I didn't have to wake up for work tomorrow morning. Finally, a silver lining to unemployment: I could run an after-midnight legal clinic for succubi on the lam. "Right now, we should probably try to sleep."

"Are you going to kick me out?"

I thought about that as I stretched my arms over my head and winced. My muscles screamed at the late hour and the lack of kether that would have loosened the grip of fatigue. Maybe I should tell her to go. But it didn't seem right to turn her back out onto the street, or the roof, for the rest of the night.

"No." Besides, we were practically family. "You can crash on the couch downstairs for tonight."

"Your friends won't mind?"

Had I mentioned my friends? My skin prickled at her ease with the details of my life. But I had made my decision. "As long as you don't steal anything, break anything, or get into their liquor cabinet, I'm sure they won't have a problem with it." I hoped. "Tomorrow, I'll make some calls and find you a place to stay."

That sparked an idea that pinwheeled around my tired brain. Maybe Rae McGuire could help me place Eve. Safe Haven funded housing for survivors of gender-related violence, and though I couldn't swear that Eve had experienced assault at the frat house, I had a bad feeling she might have. At minimum, Rae would likely know who to call to place an at-risk teenager in legal jeopardy.

"All right," Eve said, though she sounded wary.

"Come on." I stood. "I'll make up the couch. How are you feeling? Can you walk okay?"

"I think so." She demonstrated, swaying only slightly. I offered a hand, but she ignored it, her mouth set in a stubborn line. "I'm fine."

Damned if she didn't sound like me. "If you say so. Just don't fall down the stairs. The responsible adults in the house are trying to sleep."

Eve scoffed and cast her eyes heavenward but deigned to hang onto the banister as we descended. In the garage, I stopped by the dryer to grab her shorts and a t-shirt to sleep in out of my clean laundry basket. I tossed them to her, and she caught them, examining them with a vaguely disdainful air.

"I'm not commenting on your fashion choices," I said, "so don't you start on mine."

She made a face, but no further objection. With a shrug, I escorted her to the family room and pulled out blankets and pillows for the sofa. She hung back, motionless amid my housemates' shabby, homey furniture, clutching the borrowed clothes to her chest.

"You sure you're okay?" I asked.

After a moment's pause, she roused herself with a shake of her head. "What? Yeah."

"All right. I'm upstairs if you need me. Bathroom is down the hallway on the right." I headed for the hall, aching for sleep. "See you in the morning, Eve."

A small voice behind me said, "Lily?"

"Yeah?" I turned in the doorway.

"This is great," she said. "You've been great. Thank you."

Would wonders never cease? The teenager said thank you. An unfamiliar warmth flooded my chest.

"It's the least I could do." I meant it. I had orphaned her, after all, even if she didn't know it. She came here because of what I'd done. If not for me, she wouldn't have gotten herself messed up in...whatever the mess at the frat house turned out to be.

She was only a kid. She needed an adult, and she trusted me.

Did it matter, then, who her father had been to me? Did it matter what he'd done?

Did it matter at all that I didn't trust her in return?

PART II.

BLOOD OF EDEN

7

MY SISTER'S KEEPER

I woke the next morning with a start, my heart thundering like the beat of giant wings. Scraps of a nightmare haunted my mind, something about a courtroom where I stood accused before a judge with Ariel's smirk, where a wet warmth slicked my hands and dripped from my fingers to fall in scarlet pools at my feet.

It was only a dream. I sat up, squinting in the morning sunlight that streamed in through the gable window. A delicious aroma of grease and carbohydrates wafted from somewhere nearby, along with the muffled sound of women's voices and dishes clattering. The rest of the household had risen before me, and that meant—

"Oh, hell." I should have gone down before my housemates woke up and...what, spirited the delinquent succubus I'd invited to stay back up to the garret? Come up with a cover story?

Well, it was too late now. I pulled on my jeans, twisted my hair into a messy half-bun, and slouched downstairs to find out how much trouble I had gotten myself into.

In the empty kitchen, a pan half-full of scrambled eggs and a cooling griddle beckoned me from the stove. My stomach growled, informing me that I had used up my energy stores last night and should have really eaten the expensive dinner the government had comped for me.

I heaped the rest of the eggs onto a plate and wandered out to the dining room, doing my best to act casual. But in the doorway, I stopped, transfixed by the domestic tableau that greeted me.

Still dressed in my old t-shirt and shorts, Eve chattered away with Berry, shoveling forkfuls of potato latke into her mouth between animated gestures of her fork. My guest had combed her hair and washed her face. She looked almost presentable. Berry grinned and slid more latkes onto the girl's plate when space appeared, while Danny watched them both with an expression that walked the line between affection and alarm.

Their conversation broke off at my entrance and they all looked up at me, Danny curious, Berry delighted, and Eve with mixed chagrin, self-satisfaction, and defiance.

"Oh, hey," Danny said. "Sleeping Beauty awakens."

"Good morning." I slid into the remaining chair with a wary sideways glance at the interloper. What had she told them? What was she playing at here?

"Lily, I didn't know your sister was visiting." Berry answered my unvoiced question.

I raised my eyebrows at Eve, who lifted one shoulder in a fractional half-shrug. "I didn't either," I said. "Sorry about that."

"It's no problem, but if you told me, I would have set up the guest room. You're basically family at this point, which means Evie is too. She can stay as long as she likes."

My cheeks heated at Berry's easy generosity. I didn't deserve it after essentially lying to her face. She didn't know that her house harbored a demon. She saw me as no more or less than Danny's best friend, down on my luck through no fault of my own.

"Thanks." I mustered a tight smile. "Don't worry. She won't be staying long."

"That's what you think." Eve shot me a horrible grin.

Danny laughed. "You know, I never would have guessed you two were sisters."

"We're half-sisters, really," Eve said, tone lofty. "And I got all the good looks in the family."

"Watch it." I glared at her. I'd always wanted a sister, but if this was anything like the real thing, I might have to reconsider.

"That was sarcasm, Eve, honey." Danny rose, gathering a stack of used dishes. "You may not look much alike, but the attitude matches. Lily, I'm making more French toast. Come give me a hand, will you?"

"Um, sure." I followed her back to the kitchen, frowning. "You made French toast? Don't you have work today?"

"People were hungry. I just felt like making a big breakfast."

"And Berry made her famous latkes three months after Hannukah. Any of those left, by the way?"

"Sorry, nope. Your little sister ate her weight in them, and we're fresh out of potatoes."

I rolled my eyes. "Of course she did."

Danny deposited her stack of dirty dishes in the sink and turned, leaning her hips against the counter, arms crossed. "All right, Sugarbean. Time to fess up."

I busied myself rinsing bits of egg off the plates. "Fess up what?"

"Yeah, nope. Not buying your bullshit today."

"Do you ever?"

She ignored my attempt at deflection. "That kid out there isn't really your sister, is she? You better tell me what's really going on here."

"What makes you think she's not?"

Danny sighed. "You told me you were an only child."

"Ok, fine." I dried my hands and faced her. "She's not technically my sibling. But she is an, um, cousin. If you know what I mean."

"Your..." Danny's eyes widened. "*Mierda*. She's a *succubus*? Where on earth did you find her?"

A laugh bubbled up out of me. "On the roof."

"The *roof*? What, like a stray kitten?"

"Pretty much exactly like that. She followed me home."

"And you decided to adopt her." Danny grabbed a bowl and broke eggs into it with more force than strictly necessary. "Hey, you better help, or they'll get antsy and come in here. And I really want to hear you explain this."

I joined her at the counter and started slicing up the rest of a crusty sourdough loaf she slid my way. "I'm not adopting her. But she's in a tough spot. She needed my help."

"Well, she definitely looks like she hasn't had a good meal in a minute. She's skinny as a rail." Danny beat the eggs briskly. Then her hand paused mid-whisk. "*Oh.* Oh, my God."

"What?" I stared at her. "What's wrong?"

Danny shook the whisk at me, oblivious to the egg yolk dripping onto the counter. "Two things. First, listen to me. I sound like my mom. I knew I'd turn into her carbon copy eventually, but thirty-two is way too soon. Second...why *are* we making so much breakfast?"

"Because you're turning into your mom?"

"Don't you start," Danny said. "Your stray was hungry. We got the overwhelming urge to cook. Lil, she succubused us into feeding her."

I almost dropped the bread knife. "That little brat." She'd tried charming me with her Presence last night and failed, but the humans in the house didn't have my natural resistance to her powers. No wonder Berry hadn't blinked at an unannounced teenager showing up on her couch. "Shit. I'm sorry, Danny. I knew things seemed weird this morning."

"I mean, it's harmless, I guess. It's just breakfast. But—should I be worried? Is she dangerous?"

"I don't think so." I hoped not. "I'll talk to her about it. Are we still making this French toast, though?"

"Fuck yeah, we're still making this French toast." Danny retrieved the cutting board full of sliced sourdough from my lax hands. "You haven't had any and you never eat enough."

"If you say so, Mrs. Rios."

"*Tu puta madre.*"

"Too true." I grinned. If she cussed at me in Spanish, it meant she wasn't that pissed off about Eve.

We stacked a platter with syrupy bread hot off the griddle, and Danny waited until I sat back down at the dining room table and refilled my plate before she took her vengeance for my Mrs. Rios comment.

"So, Lily. Have you decided if you're going to Sebastian's thing tonight?"

"It sounds fun." Berry chimed in. "And if it's not, at least there'll be wine, right?"

"Yeah. Fun." I buttered my French toast with ferocious strokes.

"Who's Sebastian?" Eve looked from one to another of us, alert and interested.

"He's Lily's not-boyfriend," Danny said.

I groaned. "He wants me to go to his father's fundraiser tonight as his date. I'm not going."

"It's just a party," Berry said. "Why not go?"

"Because." Hunger fading at last, I set my fork down. "He wants to slot me into his life like the missing piece, and I don't fit. Besides, I don't love his dad's politics and I might not have the willpower to stop myself from telling him to his face. Also, I hate parties."

"I love parties," Eve said. "I'll go."

"No." I fixed her with my sternest look. "You will not."

"I get the politics part, I truly do," Danny said. "But I don't know that it's a bad thing, him wanting you to play a bigger part in his world. It means something to him."

I grimaced at her. "You're supposed to be on my side."

"I am on your side," she said. "I just want my best friend to let herself be happy. That's all."

"So, Eve." Berry shot a reproving glance at her fiancée. "Is Lily going to show you the city while you're here?"

"I don't know." Eve turned to me, dialing the wide-eyed innocence up to eleven. "Are you?"

"Sure, why not?" Despite the transparency of their efforts, I welcomed the change of subject. "I have some time today. Not like I have *work* to do." Like figuring out how much trouble my "sister" had gotten herself into.

"I believe that's my cue," Danny said. "I have to get to work. It's been a wild week in the Land of the Dead." She rose and dropped a kiss on the top of Berry's head. "Love you, Gooseberry. Eve, nice meeting you. Lily, I better not catch you moping around the house tonight."

"Love you too," I grumbled. She waved at me cheerfully and went out.

Eve stood up too. "I'm going to shower," she announced.

"You should ask Berry if that's okay," I said. "It is her house, after all."

"Fine." Eve heaved a dramatic sigh. "May I shower, please?"

"I already told her she should feel free." Berry smiled at her, and Eve flounced off. The room instantly seemed quieter.

"Sorry about her manners," I said. Knowing her father, he probably never taught her any. But I didn't say that out loud.

"She's a teenager." Berry began clearing the remaining plates.

"I've got the clean-up," I said. "You fed us, and I don't have anywhere to be this morning."

"Thanks, Lily. I'll leave 'em in the sink for you." She winked at me and backed through the kitchen door, arms full. "Get your sister to help you. It'll be good for her."

I snorted. Funny how easy it was to think of Eve as a wayward kid sister. "No chance. I don't think she's ever washed a dish in her life."

"Never too late for home training." Berry grinned and let the door swing closed. I sat back in my chair, staring after Eve.

What *had* Ariel taught the girl about her powers, about demonkind, about right and wrong? I cursed him internally for leaving this job to me. I didn't have it in me to play foster parent to his wild child. Besides, given my own history with Ariel's treacherous guidance and my human parents' less than stellar example, I doubted my qualifications to care for any child, let alone a demon one.

But if I didn't do it, then nobody would. And she'd already gotten herself in trouble on her own. She had the police and probably the feds on her trail, and no one in her corner but me.

I had to help her. If I didn't, I'd blame myself when she got arrested, or hurt someone, or worse.

I sighed and dragged myself into the kitchen to tackle the sink of dirty breakfast dishes. But no amount of soapy water could leave my hands feeling clean.

With Berry gone and the dishes put away, the house sank into a state of suspicious silence. The shower switched off, but Eve didn't reappear. I waited twenty minutes and then checked the bathroom, where I found steamed mirrors, puddles of water on the floor, and a conspicuous absence of teenager.

My heart sank. Had she made a run for it? But a soft sound from Danny and Berry's room suggested otherwise. I stuck my head around the half-open door. Eve stood with her back to me, wrapped in a large, fluffy blue towel, rifling through their closet.

"These clothes suck," she said, without turning around.

"Those don't belong to you."

"Thank *God*." She yanked a plaid flannel button-down from Danny's side and held it up against her tiny frame. "This one might be okay."

"Put that back," I said. "You can't just go through people's things, Eve. They've been nothing but kind to you."

She didn't move. "But I don't have anything to wear!"

"That doesn't entitle you to someone else's wardrobe." I stalked over, snatched the shirt from her, and hung it back up. Then I grabbed her by the arm and steered her out of the room.

"Hey!" She dragged her feet as I goose-walked her through the kitchen and out to the garage. "I just wanted to borrow something. I wasn't stealing it or anything."

"If you borrow something without permission, that *is* stealing."

"Who says?"

"I do." I pushed her through the door to the attic stairwell. "Up you go. You can borrow my clothes."

"Gross." But she slouched up the steps ahead of me. The sharp blades of her shoulders sent a pang through me. She did look underfed, and her hair hung in wet, uneven curls, like she'd cut it herself.

"Damn you, Ariel," I muttered under my breath.

Eve turned at the landing. "What?"

"Nothing," I said. "While we're talking about ethics and morals, I know you used a Presence on Danny and Berry this morning. It's not cool to mess with my friends like that."

"Why not?" Eve flung open my closet and surveyed the contents with a theatrical grimace. "They were happy, and we all had a delicious breakfast."

I sank down on the bed, massaging my temples. "It's not okay to take people's choice away." But of course, Ariel's daughter had no solid concept of consent or other people's agency. "When you used your powers to make them like you, you took away their right to decide how they felt about you for themselves. That's wrong."

"I don't get it."

"You don't see why it's wrong to deprive someone of free will?"

"Not if it doesn't hurt them." Eve pulled out one of my skirt suits and scowled at it. "Ew. You really wear this? It's, like, *terminal* frump."

Ouch. I tried a different tack. "Imagine I'm tired of you ripping on my style. I use a Presence on you and now you only want to wear timeless, affordable separates. Is that okay?"

She checked the tags. "Oh my God. This is mall label stuff. Designer lite. I'd never wear this."

"Oh, come on. That brand is classic." Damn it, I couldn't take her bait like that. "Never mind. My point is, what if you didn't have a choice? I could take away your personal opinion and substitute one that satisfied my own ends, like salvaging my shredded self-image. How would that make you feel?"

She glanced from the suit to me, brow furrowed. "So, making your house-mates happy to see me was like if you took my fashion sense away?"

"Pretty much." Maybe I could get through to her, after all.

Her expression turned crafty. "But if you did that, I wouldn't know this was a mall brand. I wouldn't care. What I don't know doesn't hurt me, right? So how is it wrong?"

"But it does harm you," I said. "If one of your skills is understanding what's on trend, and I take that away, you're less yourself. You lost a skill. And if you care about looking stylish and I manipulate you until you turn into a walking fashion disaster like I apparently am, it's not just unethical. It's straight-up cruel."

"Good. Because I don't like any of these."

"You don't have to like them." I joined her at the closet, where I selected a pair of navy slacks, a white dress shirt, and a tan blazer. "You'll just have to live with the pain of terminal frump."

"Ooookay," she said, but she accepted the armful of clothes without further complaint. Then she stood still, chewing on her lower lip.

I eyed her. "What is it?"

"Does that mean you're going to help me?"

"Yes and no." I sighed. "I can't be your lawyer, but I'll do what I can."

Her face lit up. "You're the best!" She dumped the clothes on the bed, bounded forward, and threw her arms around me in an enthusiastic, slightly damp embrace. "I'll pay you today, like I promised. Maybe we could go shopping. I could help you, too!"

"I can't take your money." I extracted myself from her grasp. She hadn't tried to pull kether, but I wasn't taking any chances. "I'm not doing this for money. I'm doing it because it's the right thing to do."

"Because you knew Father."

"Yes." Because I killed him. Because I owed her. Because I knew what it felt like to have no one in this world I could count on. Because if I didn't look out for her, no one else would.

Eve looked solemn. "Lily...can I ask you something else?"

"What's that?"

"Do you think maybe you could help me find him?"

Cold sifted through me, like the night wind on the high desert, like dust from my fingers as I stood in the depths of Tonepah where Ariel had fallen. I forced myself to look at her and swallowed my misgivings down so she wouldn't taste them on the air.

"Let's get you out of trouble first." I faked a light tone. "I know someone who might be able to find you a safe place to stay while I straighten things out with the authorities."

"Who?"

"Her name is Rae. She helps people who have survived terrible things. She's a friend." It wasn't strictly true, that last part, but I wanted it to be.

"Okay!" She almost skipped into the bathroom with her set of borrowed clothes. The door slammed shut, and I leaned against the wall, closing my eyes.

What had I done?

Her appearance complicated everything. I couldn't tell Ira about her. He'd jump to conclusions and assume she murdered those men. I would have to figure out some way to protect her, keep her existence secret until I could find the real killer.

As for Eve herself, she loved Ariel. She didn't know him the way I did. She could never know the truth. It would devastate her. Not to mention that she might decide to take up his legacy and try to kill me, to exact justice for my crime.

And I couldn't even blame her if she did.

8

The Sins of Eve

When I called the clinic and asked for her, the staff person on the desk told me Rae didn't work weekends. But a little while later, a text with an address in the west side of the city summoned us out to her home for a meeting.

"I don't understand why you don't have a car," Eve griped, following me up the steps from the BART station. "If we have to talk to your friend in person, it would be so much faster to drive."

I didn't have a car because I hated driving in the city, because I didn't have a designated parking spot at my old apartment, and now because I couldn't afford it. "Faster, maybe. Less annoying, definitely not. Especially with you in the passenger seat."

She ignored this. "We could have just flown."

"I couldn't," I said, "and you really shouldn't fly at all during the day. People might see you."

"No, they wouldn't. Don't you even know how to do a no-see-um?"

"I do. But it's different for me." Maybe I could use my powers of Presence to disguise myself from human eyes, but what if I screwed it up? The media would have a field day. Besides, I needed a power-up to manifest my wings for more than the brief downbeat I'd managed last night, and I wouldn't have time to see Sebastian until tonight. *If* I decided to go tonight, which I definitely hadn't, since I still had nothing to wear.

Eve shot me a curious look. "Because you're half-human."

"Sure." I checked the directions on my phone again and set off up the hill. Rae apparently lived at the very top of one. "But also, because I'm not a fool. It's an unnecessary risk."

"You're scared of them, aren't you?" Eve took long steps to match my stride. "Humans can't hurt us, Lily. Not if we don't let them. We're stronger and faster. They're weak and mortal."

"Keep your voice down." I slowed and let her catch up, frowning at her. "Is that what your father taught you? That we're better than them?"

"He taught me that we have to hide what we are because they can't stand to know they're inferior." She lifted her chin, jaw set. "He says humans always try to kill their gods. He says I should never let them see if I'm afraid."

A hollow ache burgeoned in my chest, and I avoided her gaze. "That sounds like him, all right." He tried to convince me of the same, right before I drove silver into his heart and proved that a half-human could still defeat him.

We walked on without speaking for a minute or so. Then Eve said, "It seems like you don't like my father much."

"It's not that." I laughed to cover my unease. "I liked...like him very much, in fact. But it was a complicated relationship."

"You were together." She said it like an accusation, wrinkling her nose.

"Not that it's any of your business, but yes. For a while, when I was a lot younger." And once much more recently, when he drained my kether reserves dry and deposited me in Sebastian's bed like a gift—the kind that woke up rabid and hungry for a man's immortal soul.

Sebastian probably should have run for the hills after that, but he hadn't. I still couldn't explain why not.

"But you're not together anymore." Eve's tone was thoughtful.

"No. Not anymore."

She went quiet again, chewing over that, as we climbed a sloping street lined with boxy, two-story houses and small apartment buildings, older and shabbier than the homes in Danny's neighborhood. At the top, in a small stand of cypress trees, an undeveloped rocky outcropping loomed over the city. A fierce west wind whipped the long grass around it.

"Look." Eve clambered up the rocks, pointing outward. "You can see the ocean from here." Her long gold hair blew around her and caught the sun. It enveloped her in a cloud of light, her face transformed by childlike joy.

"Rae lives right there." I pointed at a tall redwood fence on the other side of the street. A path led uphill through a wild garden to the front door.

Eve sighed and leaped from the rocks. She crossed the fifteen feet or so between us in one single, fluid, inhuman movement and landed beside me with a cat's precision, one hand braced on the pavement. Her sudden jump startled a flock of crows out of the cypresses. They rose from the trees with raucous cries of alarm, flying in wide circles out from the peak of the hill.

I glared at her. "Don't do that."

"I know, I know. Someone might see." She trotted after me up the path. "But it was fun."

"It was foolish," I said. The path wound through lavender and rosemary humming with bees. A wrought metal symbol hung over the door, an intricate, angular knot. Its reddish tint suggested rusting iron, not silver.

"Can we go to the beach after this?" Eve rolled her eyes at my hesitation and pressed the doorbell. "You said you'd show me the city."

I snorted. "Oh, like you haven't been bumming around here on your own before you found me. How long has it been, anyway?"

Eve's brow furrowed. "A few weeks, maybe."

"And you haven't gone to the beach?"

"I was busy." She stuck out her tongue at me. "Some sister you turned out to be."

"I never signed up for that job." But I broke off as the inner door swung open.

"Are you here to see Rae?" A young man stood on the other side of the screen door. Barely older than Eve, he wore jeans and a black t-shirt, and loose brown curls tumbled over his tanned forehead. Tattoos coiled around his wrists and up his bare arms in knots and whorls that echoed the symbol above the door. Eve looked him up and down, lips curving and eyes alight with appreciation.

"Lily Knight." I stepped forward. "She's expecting me."

He nodded, unlatching the screen and holding it for us. Eve smiled brilliantly as we passed by him, and I shot her a stern look.

"What?" she said.

"Behave yourself," I told her, under my breath.

She groaned but fixed her eyes straight ahead and composed her face. A smoky-sweet scent lay thick in the dim front room, juniper and amber mingled with sharp undertones of liquor. An altar draped in dark red cloth dominated the opposite wall, crowded with candles, chunks of black stone, and half-full shot glasses. Above it all hung a large sword, its engraved blade pointed downward—probably a Renaissance Fair replica, but deadly-looking, nonetheless.

The tattooed youth led us toward the back of the house, and I tore myself away from my examination of the altar. We followed him down a darkened hallway and out into an asymmetrical sunroom with windows on three sides, their curtains half-drawn. Rae McGuire sat curled in a wicker chair in a shady corner, clutching a large mug, her pale skin pastier than normal and dark circles shadowing her eyes.

"Hi, Lily." Her husky voice lacked its usual rich timbre, leaving it hoarse and almost harsh. "Thanks, Cormac. Door shut, please."

The young man dipped his head, and the door clicked softly shut behind him.

"Are you all right?" I asked Rae. Maybe we shouldn't have bothered her. She hadn't had those dark circles yesterday, but now she looked truly ill.

"Just a migraine." She waved away my concern. "Is this her?"

"This is Eve." I blinked. Where had my charge gone?

"Behind you." Rae grinned, then winced.

Eve, doing her level best to blend into the wallpaper, looked back at me with wide, wary eyes.

"It's all right." I waved the girl forward, frowning. But I had to admit that Rae did seem intimidating on first meeting, even barefoot with pain written clear on her face. Her energy hurt to look at, draped around her in a murky shroud shot through with stark flashes of white and red lightning.

"Don't worry, Eve," Rae said. "I don't bite."

"She had a very scary experience last night." I filled in for Eve when the girl still seemed at a loss for words. "She needs a safe place to stay for a while."

"That could be tough." Rae shifted her intense focus back to me. "Safe Haven's grants don't cover runaways."

Eve bristled. "I came here to look for my father, not run away from him."

"She qualifies for services," I said. "She went to a party last night with some college men and ended up blacked out in one of their beds."

Rae's expression darkened. "Roofies? Did you have anything to drink, Eve?"

"I might have." Eve's tone was sullen. "I don't remember."

"The police are looking for her," I said. "They think she might be a witness to the men's murder. Eve's worried they might suspect her."

Rae sat up straight. "You're saying the men who did this to her are dead. She's a suspect?" Her desiderata shifted, making my ears pop, as though the pressure had dropped in the room. The scent of copper and ozone clogged my nostrils.

"I didn't do it." Eve shot me an alarmed look. "I didn't, right, Lily?"

"That's right." I would have to give Eve some more prep before the police got to her and she talked herself into murder charges. "Rae, you know the cops aren't good at telling victims from perpetrators. You said it yourself just yesterday."

"Did I?" Rae seemed to come back to herself. The storm in her desiderata subsided as abruptly as it had risen, like she'd pulled hurricane shutters closed around her. She rubbed her temples, blinking. "I'm sorry, but I need to lie down. I'll make some calls later and see if I can find a bed for Eve in one of our safe houses. We don't always have space, but I'll do what I can."

"Thank you." I turned to usher Eve out, but she'd already fled. Rae bowed her head. When I turned in the doorway, she had covered her face in her hands.

"I hope you feel better," I said softly, but she didn't seem to hear me. On the other side of the house, the front door banged.

I hurried out and caught up with Eve on the path outside. "What's the matter? Why did you take off like that?"

"I don't want to go with her." Eve kept walking, the lines of her thin back stiff with tension. "I want to stay with you."

"Eve, honey, I'm flattered, but you'd be safer in one of Rae's shelters. If the police decide to arrest you—"

"I don't care," Eve broke in. "I'm not going anywhere." In the street now, she rounded on me. Her eyes glistened with tears and her lip trembled. "Why are you trying to get rid of me?"

Oh. Now I got it. What made me believe I had the wherewithal to handle a teenager? One moment she acted standoffish, spoiled, and entitled, and the next she turned on the waterworks like a needy orphan who had never known real kindness before. Emotional whiplash didn't begin to cover it. "I'm not trying to get rid of you. I'm trying to protect you."

"No, you're not," she snapped. "You're just trying to protect yourself."

"Eve—"

"I *wanted* to go to the *beach.*" Eve threw this back at me over her shoulder, flouncing away from me down the steep slope of the street.

For a moment, I entertained the thought of letting her go. At seventeen—assuming she had told the truth about her age, of course—she could take care of herself. She had taken care of herself before she'd come to me. She was no defenseless human child, but a demon in full possession of her powers. She could find her way back to the house when she finished her tantrum. I could go home in peace.

But I didn't. "The beach is that way," I told her, when I found her at the corner with her arms crossed over her chest, waiting for the light to change.

"I don't want to go anymore," she muttered. "It's probably just foggy and rocky and...and disappointing. I don't understand why my father left New York for *this*." Her sullen glance included me in the disappointing features of the city.

I tried to keep my voice casual. "You were living in New York with him?"

"That's literally what I just said."

"Not *literally*," I said, cueing yet another eyeroll from her. "How long did you live there?" Ariel and I had lived in New York together for several years before I left him to come out here for law school ten years ago. Where and how had he hidden a child from me? It made no sense.

"I don't know. Four years, maybe. Since he came and got me from my other family." The light changed, and she marched across, heading back the way we'd come.

"Other family... Eve!" I hurried after her. "What other family?"

Eve turned at the curb. "My human family," she said, matter of fact. "That's how it works. Don't you know anything?"

"I guess not." My voice sounded faint in my own ears. How could Eve have a human family? She was a full cubine, not a cambion like me. "Please, enlighten me."

"Um, okay." She chewed her lip and started walking again, her small face set and determined. "Father said that cubines are like cuckoos."

"I don't know what that means." I matched my pace to hers.

"They're birds," Eve said with exaggerated patience.

"Yes, I know that, but how—"

"They lay their eggs in other birds' nests. Then the bird parents raise the cuckoo chicks like their own babies." Eve heaved a sigh. "When grown-up humans take care of us, it feeds us. Getting kether is different then, not like when we're older."

"Oh." Disturbing, but it made a twisted kind of sense. Naturally, demon children would need to feed somehow, and taking kether from parental nurture seemed less horrifying than the other alternatives. "Why did he come and get you, then?"

"I don't know." Her shoulders hunched. It made her look very small and very scared. "He said it was time for me to grow up and get my wings. He said it was better that way."

Get her wings? Did that mean what I thought it did? "And you were what, all of thirteen at the time?"

She nodded, her expression perfectly blank, as if the wrongness of it all didn't even register with her. Or maybe she couldn't afford to acknowledge it.

Ugh. If I thought I couldn't hate Ariel more before this, I was wrong. And despite my misgivings about her, I couldn't stop the way my heart went out to this kid.

Danny's description of her as a stray kitten hit right on the money. She woke a protective impulse in me, strong enough to frighten me, almost like the effect of a Presence. Did young cubines project some innate aura that encouraged adults to give them that vital energy and keep them safe?

A bitter taste flooded my mouth, and I swallowed hard. If so, it hadn't worked for me when my powers started to manifest, when I needed protection. When my father looked at me, he hadn't seen a child in need of love, but an abomination against God. My mother had seen nothing but her own guilt, the evidence of her betrayal.

But if I had someone to protect me when I was Eve's age, maybe Ariel wouldn't have gotten his hooks in me. Maybe I would have learned to trust myself instead of depending on a liar and a killer to teach me how the world worked.

"Come on, little sister." I put an arm around her thin shoulders, and she looked up quickly, a hopeful light kindling in her eyes that made my chest ache. "Let's go home."

Maybe it wasn't too late for Eve to have that sense of safety, even if I couldn't.

"Don't you have plans tonight with that rich guy?" Eve inquired as we trudged up the hill toward Danny's house. "Sebastian. That's his name, right?"

I ground my teeth. I'd forgotten all about the gala until she mentioned it. "I already said I'm not going. And even if I were, I wouldn't take you with me, if that's what you're angling for."

"You're lucky," Eve said. "I wish I had a real boyfriend. One who wanted to take *me* to parties."

She sounded genuinely wistful, and I softened despite myself. "You could if you wanted to. You just need to find someone nice and good-hearted, with healthy kether. Someone your own age, not like those fraternity jerks."

She pursed her lips. "Father told me not to get too close to any human. He said it's dangerous to think of them that way."

Of course he did. "I used to think like that too. But it's not true if you pick the right ones to get close to. Like my friend Danny. And Berry. They're good humans and good people."

"And Sebastian?"

"And Sebastian," I admitted.

"Then why don't you like him?"

"I do like him. It's just—it's not that simple."

"Nothing is with you, is it? You said the same thing about my father. *It's complicated.*" She spread her arms wide. "If you like him and he likes you, that seems pretty simple to me."

"You'd think that, wouldn't you?" I sighed. "Why are you so interested in my love life, anyway?"

"I want to meet him." Eve engaged her power of puppy dog eyes at full force. "You said I should make good choices. But how am I supposed to know what a good man is like if I've never met one before? You should introduce us."

"I'll think about it," I allowed. "But you better behave yourself. No taste tests. Got it?"

"Okay," she said at once, her expression angelic. When I eyed her, not trusting her sudden agreeableness, she added, "What?" Innocence dripped from the word.

"Nothing." I shook my head and headed up to the house, keys in hand. The afternoon had grown late, and spring sunlight gave way to quick-scudding clouds on a brisk, chilly wind, a bank of fog already building over the Pacific.

Eve didn't follow me up the steps. She stood stock still on the sidewalk, head tilted back, her expression undecipherable.

I frowned, stepping back from the porch to follow her gaze. "Eve, what's the matter?"

For answer, she pointed upward, and I drew a sharp breath. A flock of crows lined the roof, perched on the sharply angled peak and above the little gable window of my garret room. They sat still and silent except for the occasional flap of wings needed to balance them against the wind, and the darting of sharp, dark, watchful eyes.

Eve shivered and hunched her shoulders. "I hate those things."

"They're just birds." But goosebumps prickled my arms. I glanced up and down the street. None of the other colorful Victorians had similar rooftop occupants.

"It's a murder." Eve almost whispered it.

I did a double take. "What?"

She wrapped her arms around herself. "Someone told me that's what it is when they flock like that."

Rae had said the same thing yesterday, and it sent the same shiver down my spine now. I returned to her side, resting a hand lightly on her jacketed shoulder. "Come on. Let's get inside."

She moved without further protest, but without taking her eyes off the roof. Just as we stepped under the eaves, one of the birds gave a long, harsh cry. A rush of wings followed with a chorus of answering caws. Then the sound faded, the flock moving into the distance.

"Well," I said. "That was freaky."

Eve shuddered. "That was *not okay*."

"They're only birds," I said again, trying to convince myself. Then I frowned. The creepy birds had distracted me enough that I only now noticed the long, rectangular black-and-white box propped on the wall next to the door, wrapped with an elegant white ribbon. "What the hell?"

"Oh my God," Eve said, bird phobia instantly forgotten. "That's a Saks box."

"What's a sax box?"

"Seriously? *Saks*. You know, as in Fifth Avenue?"

"Oh. I knew that." I gave the box a healthy berth. If it started ticking, I could hardly like it less. But even an ignorant plebe like me had to admit Saks didn't usually deal in munitions.

This was probably something much worse.

Eve had no such qualms. She inspected the package and turned back to me, wide-eyed. "It's addressed to you."

I'd feared as much. "Fantastic."

"You're not excited? *God*, you're weird. You should be excited. *I'm* excited. Come on, open it!"

Clearly, I wouldn't have a moment's peace until I acceded to her demands. Retrieving the surprisingly heavy box from the porch, I carried it into the living room and laid it on the floor beside the couch.

It irritated me how my hands shook as I untied the smooth ribbon and lifted the lid. Beneath it, atop a package neatly encased in white and gold tissue paper, lay a folded note in perfect calligraphy.

Dear Lily,

I shouldn't have pushed you the other night. Please accept my apologies for my behavior, and this gift. It comes to you with no attached obligation to wear it to the gala tonight, although I hope to see you in it sometime soon.

Regards, Sebastian.

"Oh, Sebastian. You *jerk*." I dropped the paper back into the box. "You absolute bastard. What in seven hells did you do?"

"What *did* he do?" Eve craned her neck, hovering over my shoulder. "What did he send you? What are you *waiting* for? I'm dying here." She grabbed for the tissue paper.

"Hey! No touchy." I smacked her hands away. "Come on, give me some room to breathe."

She rolled her eyes and collapsed onto the couch with a gusty exhalation. "Why are you like this? You don't want it but if anyone else does, you're all 'it's mine! Back off!' I bet you're the same way with him. Your *not-boyfriend*."

I gritted my teeth and fixed her with a stern look. "That's not it. People don't belong to other people, Eve. Especially not Sebastian, and certainly not to me. And for the record, that's *not* what my voice sounds like."

"*For the record*," she mimicked in a high, whiny voice. "Blah blah I'm a fancy lawyer who likes to make up rules and ruin people's fun. Blah blah blah." But she trailed off at my glare. "Okay! I'll be good. Just open it already."

"I'm working on it." I willed my fingers not to tremble and peeled aside the delicate layers of tissue paper. The sheets whispered apart to reveal a long swathe of shimmering dark fabric almost as delicate as the paper itself.

My breath hitched and I sat back on my heels. "That's what I was afraid of."

"What is it what is it *whatisit*?" Eve flung herself half over the arm of the couch.

I lifted it from the box, my hands now refusing steadiness entirely.

"It's a dress," I said, with grim resignation.

9

FOOLS RUSH IN

Eve's mouth hung open. "Holy cannoli. That's not a dress. That's a ten thousand dollar fucking *Oscar*."

"Who the what now? You mean like the awards?"

"I mean like Oscar de la Renta, doofus. The fucking *designer*. Who designs dresses that fucking movie stars *wear* to the fucking Oscars."

"Do you kiss your mother with that mouth?" Beginning to regain my equilibrium, I kept my tone mild.

"I don't have a mother," Eve said in an airy tone, and I stared at her, appalled. "You're going to the party now, right?" she added, with exaggerated impatience.

"No, I'm not going—I'm sorry, did you say *ten thousand dollars*?"

"Um, yeah. At least. I saw it in a magazine."

I goggled at the iridescent fabric draped over my knees. "I—No. It's too much. I can't accept this. I have to send it back."

"Are you kidding me? You *have* to wear that sick-ass dress and you *have* to wear it to that sick-ass party."

"I don't have to do anything, sick-ass or otherwise." I waved the note at her. "He said it right here. 'It comes to you with no attached obligation.'" Then I frowned at the paper. "'Regards?' Who says 'regards' on a personal message? Who does he think he is, Fitzwilliam fucking Darcy?"

"Do you kiss your mother with that mouth?" Eve smirked.

"Not if I can help it."

"You could at least try it on," she suggested, slyly. "Maybe you'll hate it. Problem solved."

I picked up the gown again. The silk bodice shimmered under my hands, a deep indigo, almost indistinguishable from black. The tule of the skirt had tiny sequins woven into it in flowering spirals, like galaxies of miniature stars.

I doubted very much that I would hate it. But Eve was right. It seemed a shame not to try it on.

And that was why, when Danny came home half an hour later, she found me standing in the middle of the living room in a heartbreakingly beautiful evening gown, fighting back tears.

"Whoa there, Cinderella," she said. "Don't cry. Your fairy godmother is doing one hell of a job. Hello again, Eve."

"It's not her fairy godmother," Eve said, smug. "It's from Sebastian."

"*Damn.*" Danny walked around me, taking it in. "Well done, sir. Well done indeed."

"Tell her she has to go to the ball." Eve bounced up and down, our earlier tension apparently forgotten.

I sniffled. "I told you, it's not a ball. It's a terrible political fundraiser for his terrible political father."

Danny came back around to my front and regarded me, head tilted to the side, her desiderata warm as cinnamon sugar. "Is that really why you're upset?"

"No. Yes. I don't know."

"You don't have to do anything you don't want to do," Danny said. "No matter how many beautiful dresses he buys you."

"That's not the problem."

"Then what is it?"

"He knew my size, which is creepy," I said. "He picked out a dress that I can't help loving, which is unfair. He apologized when I was the one in the wrong and I feel like the worst person in the world." I sniffed again. "And I don't have anywhere near nice enough heels to wear with this."

"Ah, I see," Danny said. "He's a perfect gentleman and you don't have the right footwear. I can't do anything about the first problem, but I think that between all the ladies in this household we can probably do something about the shoes. Besides, Sugarbean, no one, and I mean *no one*, will be looking at your feet while you're wearing that dress."

"You say that like I'm going."

"Well, aren't you?"

I opened my mouth to tell her no. Then I closed it again.

"That's what I thought," Danny said, and Eve cackled with triumph.

"I hate all of you," I grumbled, and stomped upstairs to find the right shoes.

"Wow." I turned my head one way, then the other. "I almost look like I belong in this dress."

"Um, because you do." Eve leaned over my shoulder and laid her shining mass of golden curls alongside my dark ones. "I don't understand why you hide yourself the way you do, Lily. Don't you know we were born for this?"

"Sometimes you sound just like your father." I shifted away from her and put the finishing touches on my makeup. "I prefer people see me as more than just a pretty face."

Eve laughed. "What else is there?"

Before I could marshal an adequate answer about looking beyond appearances that would almost certainly be lost on my audience, the doorbell rang from below. I stiffened.

"Is that him?" Eve shrieked.

She flew out of the bathroom and thumped down the stairs. I followed at the slower pace required by my long skirts, pulling on the opera gloves I'd found tucked in the gift box beneath the dress. Made of black satin and trimmed with feathers, they seemed a bit much at first. But I couldn't argue with the reflection in the full-length mirror on the bathroom door. I looked the closest to my true self I could get without manifesting my wings.

How had he known to get a gown of stars? Or had he just made an absurdly lucky guess? A male voice rumbled something indistinct in the kitchen below, and my steps slowed midway down the stairs.

Eve flung open the door at the bottom. "You must be Sebastian. I'm Eve. It's nice to finally meet you."

"Hello, Eve." He shook her hand in the doorway, sounding bemused.

My heart stopped. He'd touched her skin. Had she—But then his eyes met mine over the top of her blonde head, and his smile lit his face.

"Hi," I said.

"Lily." He dropped Eve's hand and strode around her, toward me. "You look incredible."

Eve pressed her back against the wall to let him pass, eyes wide. She mouthed, "*What?!*"

I grinned despite myself. "I told you so," I mouthed back, as Sebastian reached me.

He folded my gloved hands in his and looked me up and down as if drinking me in. In his dinner jacket and black tie, he didn't look half-bad himself.

Who was I kidding? He looked good enough to eat. So to speak.

"Oh, good, it fits," he said. "And it suits you. God, does it ever suit you."

"You knew it would."

His smile quirked sideways. "I had an inkling. Do you like it?"

"It's amazing," I said. "Thank you. But you didn't have to—"

He held a finger over my lips but took care not to touch them. "It was my pleasure." His stern tone sparked a warm flash of hunger in my core, and his desiderata tugged at me, magnetic, singing in my ears. Or maybe that was just the roar of my own blood. "Ready?"

I nodded, not trusting myself to speak, and took his arm. He picked up my overnight bag and we swept through the kitchen toward the front door. Danny gave me two thumbs up as we passed, and I shot her a sheepish smile.

"Keep an eye on you-know-who for me, will you?" I hesitated on the threshold. Maybe I shouldn't leave. Who knew what Eve would get up to without me?

"Nothing easier," she said. "We've got this, Lily. Go have fun."

I didn't share her confidence, but it was too late to turn back now. My coach awaited me at the curb in the form of Sebastian's fanciest Batmobile, a black and chrome beast of a Maserati. He held the passenger door open for me, patient while I wrangled my voluminous skirts into the front seat.

"I'm glad you changed your mind about tonight." The car roared to life under his touch. "I really didn't want to go to this thing without a date."

"Oh, please." I scoffed. "I bet you can't turn around in this town without women lining up around the block to date you."

He shifted the Maserati into gear, and it leaped away from the curb with a companionable growl. "I didn't want to go with just any woman. I wanted to go with you."

"Oh." I flushed. I didn't have a smart comeback for that one.

"So that girl, Eve," he said, when I didn't say anything more. "She's like you, isn't she? A succubus, I mean?"

I turned in my seat to stare at him. "You could tell?"

"It's hard to miss once you know what to look for."

"But she didn't even pull from you." I swallowed. "Did she?"

"Her? Nah. She's cute, no doubt, but she's just a kid."

"Seriously? You didn't feel any pull at all?"

He shook his head. "Nothing. Who is she? Any relation?"

"No," I said. "But I knew her father." I didn't elaborate. I didn't want to lie to him, but I didn't want to tell him about Eve's parentage, either. I doubted his feelings on Ariel were as conflicted as mine.

We drove in silence for a few minutes. The moon hung huge and yellow over the Oakland hills, cresting the peak of Mt. Diablo as we sped north over the Golden Gate Bridge toward the Marin Headlands. Finally, I said, "Sebastian?"

"Yeah?"

"Can I ask you something?"

"Of course."

"That first day we ever spent together," I said. "When you made me breakfast. Why did you help me?"

He shot a glance at me I couldn't read. "It seemed like the right thing to do."

"I didn't...uh...*succubus* you into it?"

He gave one of his short, startled-sounding laughs. "I don't think so. But maybe." A slight frown creased the space between his eyebrows. "I don't know if you know what you were like in that state. You had this...pulse of gravity around you. An absence of light, but bright in a way. Blindingly so."

"What do you mean?"

"I'm not sure." He made a noise deep in his throat, considering. It sent shivers of heat down my spine. "It made me think of what a dying star might be like to see up close. Or a black hole. Beautiful and terrible, something that hurts to look at, but is impossible to look away from."

"Wow," I said, shaken. "I'm not sure that's a compliment."

"Neither am I. It's just the truth."

"But you didn't pity me. You weren't afraid of me."

"No," he said. "I wasn't afraid of you. I was afraid for you, and I was angry because someone had done that to you. I wanted to help you."

I should have left it at that, but I couldn't. "But you didn't even know me."

"It wasn't about that. It wasn't transactional, Lily. I know *he* taught you to think that way about what you do, but it's not how I do things."

"I know." I still didn't understand it. But when Sebastian said *he*, he meant Ariel, and his desiderata stung like salt in an open wound.

"You keep acting like you think I'm only interested in you for one thing." He seemed intent on prodding the wound despite its sting. "Has it occurred to you that I happen to value the pleasure of your company?"

"I'm not sure I'm such good company. At least not lately."

"I wouldn't say that."

"Really?" I couldn't keep the skepticism out of my voice.

"You're prickly at times, yes. It's not always easy. You have a wall built around you, and no one gets to see over. But I'm not looking for something easy, Lily. I want something real. And if there's anything that you are, it's real."

"Do you practice these speeches?" I demanded when I could speak again. "Because if you don't, it's really unfair how good you are at them."

"I'm glad you like them." His mouth quirked upward. "No, I don't practice. I'm just saying what I think is true. And I've given a lot of thought to this particular topic."

There he went again. My laugh came out breathless. "You're incorrigible."

"I try."

"And impossible, as in you're too good to be true." I rested my head back against the seat.

Sebastian laughed. "Now you're giving me too much credit again."

"No, I'm not." I let myself look at him, finally, but he stared out fixedly at the night. We'd left the bridge behind us. Now the car wound through the hills of the North Bay, descending toward a sea of stars nestled below, the city of San Rafael. "Sebastian, you're probably the best thing that's ever happened to me. You're the best thing that's ever going to happen."

His eyes flicked toward me and away. "I hear a 'but' coming."

"*But* you deserve someone who can live your kind of life with you. Someone who's as good of a human as you."

"Don't do that," he said. "Don't put me on a pedestal. I'm not perfect. I'm not even close. You're valuing your own capacity for goodness too low, and my humanity too high. Why don't you let me worry about what I deserve?"

"Because you deserve a partner who doesn't have to stop herself from eating your whole soul every time we get close." My voice rang out harsh and loud in the Maserati's small cabin.

Sebastian said nothing for a while. We climbed again until the Petaluma River delta's wide fields spread before us on either side and the flat dark expanse of San Pablo Bay opened to the East.

Finally, he cleared his throat. "I didn't know it was like that."

"Yeah, well." I wrapped my arms around my satin-clad midsection. "There's a reason I'd rather not talk about it."

"I was fine," he said. "I didn't die. I woke up still fully ensouled. You're overestimating the risk."

He had such faith in me, a faith I hadn't earned. In a sick way, Eve's inability to pull from him had proved that. My Claim on him strengthened every time we touched. It protected him from other demons, but it couldn't protect him from the one that mattered. It didn't protect him from me.

I shook my head, chest painfully tight. "You're underestimating it."

"Maybe I am." He spoke with quiet emphasis. "Maybe I don't care. Maybe it's worth the risk for me, to feel the way I feel when I'm with you."

The aching pressure in my chest intensified, and I dared a glance at him. In the dim cabin, the sharp line of his jaw stood out in silhouette, rimmed by his blacklight desiderata.

"You're willing to risk your soul for me?" A tremor crept into my teasing tone, despite my best efforts. "How very Faustian of you."

"I'd prefer it didn't come to that." His lips curved, and his light eyes glinted at me. His desiderata glowed, an ember hoping for a spark. "It may be a little tarnished, but it's the only one I've got. I like to think I can still get some use out of it."

I bit my tongue on the urge to tell him how wrong he was. His essence wasn't tarnished at all. It had the intoxicating burn of a pure distillation. I could have drawn from his wellspring day and night and still come back for more.

And therein lay my problem. His intense desires, coupled with his rock-solid commitment to my consent and well-being, made him nearly impossible to resist. Just as tainted kether could harm us, energy like his exerted a potent, heady hold over a demon like me.

I might quibble with his products, his privilege, and his *pater familias*, but having drunk deep from him, I couldn't deny the condition of his character. It hit dark, smooth, strong, and bittersweet, like eighty percent cacao or high-octane coffee.

Sebastian Ritter's kether was the vice I couldn't quit, even though he would probably be better off without me.

IO

DEVIL'S BARGAINS

Sebastian pulled up to the door of the gala venue as if he owned the place, which in fact, he—or at least his family—did. I craned my neck to get a better look. The house towered over us, a stone-and-stucco confection of California excess, complete with flying buttresses and ivy-covered facade. Its windows glowed golden and inviting, the interior bustling with activity.

"This is a castle." I extracted myself from the low seat of the Maserati with care not to rip my gown. There was so *much* of it. "Your wine country villa is a freaking castle."

"What, this old place?" Sebastian grinned and offered me his arm. "It's all right, I guess."

"Show-off." I gathered my skirts, letting him guide me up the gravel walk.

Faint jazz notes floated from somewhere nearby, along with laughter, the clink of glassware, and the hum of human desiderata. Inside, an elaborate chandelier lit the stone and dark wood of the gigantic foyer with a soft, yellow glow. We climbed wide, carpeted steps to the second-floor ballroom, arm in arm. I tugged at the sleeves of my gloves with nervous fingers, readying my only shield against skin to skin contact with random gala attendees.

At the top of the stairs, a wave of energetic white noise and chattering voices swept over me. I drew a sharp breath, my pace faltering, and leaned into Sebastian's side. His steady, focused energy anchored me against the greasy undertow of avarice and ambition eddying around us.

Ah, yes. I had a good reason for hating parties. Large gatherings could quickly overwhelm my senses with their clashing energies. Music and dancing helped mitigate it, but despite the live band set up on one side of the ballroom, no one here seemed inclined to take the floor. This event was all schmooze, no two-step.

Sebastian picked up on my hesitation, pulling me aside from the whirl of activity to an open table in a relatively quiet corner. "Are you okay?"

I nodded and gritted my teeth behind a tight-lipped smile. "You're helping."

"Good." His desiderata flashed with concern, and for a moment it drowned out all the other noise in the room. "You stay here. I'll get us drinks and see if I can track down my dad."

I didn't want him to leave me alone, but the thought of wading into the melee didn't appeal either. I peeled my fingers from his arm and let him go. My dress didn't lend itself to sitting, so I stood, distracting myself by admiring the slim lines of Sebastian's back in his impeccable dinner jacket.

"He does wear it well, doesn't he?" a woman's voice murmured.

I flushed and turned. "I'm sorry, what?"

"Sebastian, of course." The sharp-featured blond woman beside me wore a shimmering rose-gold mermaid-cut gown, her hair sweeping past her bare shoulder blades. She lifted a glass to me, half-full of champagne that matched her dress and her brilliant, dry smile. "The fortunate son." Her desiderata gleamed like the naked edge of a blade.

I gathered my scattered wits. "He does look good in a suit. There's no denying it." Did I know her? She certainly seemed to know me, or at least, she knew my date.

"You're new at this," she said. "How long have you two known each other? Three months? Six?"

A hit, a very palpable hit, and she meant that blade for me. "I don't think we've met. I'm Lily Knight."

"So, you're the one he's seeing now." She didn't offer her own name. "I didn't believe it when I heard, so I had to come see if the rumors were true." Her tone suggested she didn't think much of what she saw.

"Excuse me?"

"I hope you know what you're getting yourself into."

"I don't know what you mean." My cheeks prickled with heat. What was taking Sebastian so long at the bar? I scanned the crowd for him, but he seemed to have disappeared.

"He comes on smooth, doesn't he? Makes you feel good about yourself. Makes you feel like the only woman in the world." She tossed back the rest of her glass. "But you don't know him that well. It's all business to him. He knows an asset when he sees one, just like he knows a liability."

My fingers curled in their opera gloves. I clenched my jaw and forced myself to keep my cool. "You never told me your name."

The blond woman looked past me. "Hello, Seb. James."

Sebastian stepped between us, a glass of champagne in each hand and his lips pressed into a thin line as he faced the blond. "I didn't know you'd be here."

A half-step behind his son, Senator Ritter looked between the three of us, his brows arching and eyes wide. "What's going on here, kids?" His chuckle sounded nervous.

I accepted the glass from Sebastian and tucked my other hand behind my back to keep from grabbing his arm. Showing weakness in front of this woman seemed like a bad move. "Sebastian, maybe you could introduce us."

But she answered instead. "Helena Ritter." Her smile sharpened. "I'm his wife."

The breath rushed out of my lungs like she'd punched me right in the solar plexus. My heart dropped like a stone in freezing water, sending ripples of numbness rising through me. Speechless, I looked from her to my date.

His face had gone white to the lips except for two spots of color flaming in his cheeks, his aura flint-hard and tinged with saltpeter. He was furious and holding himself in check. "Dad, Helena, this is Lily Knight."

James Ritter offered me his hand, but his deer in headlights expression gave away his discomfort. "Ms. Knight, it's a pleasure."

"We've met," I said. "But likewise."

"Lovely to meet you, Lily," Helena said. "I've heard so little about you. Absolutely nothing, in fact. What do you do again?"

I *would* smile back, even if it killed me. "I'm an attorney."

"Helena, enough," Sebastian said. "What do you want?"

"Nothing from you." She scoffed, but her desiderata roared like a hurricane with the bitter, bone-deep ache of a reopened wound. "You want him, Lily Knight? He's yours."

She tossed her head and swept away, chin high. In the awkward silence left in her wake, Sebastian's father cleared his throat.

"As an attorney, Lily, you might find my new bill interesting. I'm introducing it in the next session. Do you follow national politics at all?"

I tore my attention from Helena Ritter's departing back (bare, thin, immaculate) and forced myself to focus on Senator Ritter, who at least had the kindness to try to change the subject. "I do my best. Tell me about your bill, Senator."

"It's called the Humans First Act." He puffed his chest out. "With all the reports of nonhuman entities in the news lately, it's an urgent matter of domestic security to protect people from these predators."

Well, he had my attention now. "What nonhuman entities?" I sipped my champagne, ignoring Sebastian, whose posture and desiderata betrayed increasing agitation. For all I cared, he could stew for a while and think about what he'd done.

"I'm surprised to hear that from you of all people," the senator said. "You were very involved with those demon murders last fall, if I recall correctly."

Great. He remembered me. "I was the prosecutor on the case. Yes. But demons? No, that was never confirmed. It was all over-sensationalized press rumors." I gave him my best poker face despite the heavy weight in my chest. At this rate all my organs would sink through the floor by the end of the evening. I hoped they would take me with them.

"That's the official line, of course. But you and I both know the truth." He lowered his voice to a conspiratorial tone. "That corpse wasn't human. And now it's happening again. Only now, the demons are going after *us*."

My smile made my cheeks ache. What a word, *us*. It assumed so much. "Where did you hear that?"

"I have my ways, Lily. But it's been all over cable news tonight, even though the mainstream media doesn't have the guts to call it a demon killing."

"Please." I smiled harder. "Enlighten me." Ira would blow a gasket when I told him about this. Perversely, I found myself looking forward to it.

"It's a terrible thing." The senator frowned, his energy clouded and shrinking. "Those Delta Alpha Mu boys are my brothers, you know. I have to do something."

"You're a Delta Alpha Mu alumnus?" That made for an interesting wrinkle. At least it explained his inside info.

He nodded. "A DAM man, that's me."

"And this bill—"

"Yes, yes. The bill. You see, you can't fight demons with regular law enforcement rules. This law will make it easier for our guys to protect citizens by waiving restrictions on searches, arrests, and confinement of any suspected demons in connection with a crime."

"You're proposing to define an entire group outside the class of legal persons for the purpose of constitutional protections. I guess history really does repeat itself, doesn't it?"

The words hung in the loaded silence that had fallen around us. Both the Ritter men looked deeply uncomfortable. I knocked back the rest of my champagne by way of girding my loins for battle and set my glass aside.

"Lily, you have to understand," the senator said at last. "The Constitution wasn't written with these extraordinary times in mind. It protects people, not demons. And this bill shows remarkably high bipartisan support in our internal polling. You don't see that very often in today's political environment."

"I understand the Constitution, sir," I said. "And universal background checks for firearms ownership are broadly popular too, but you're not working to curtail those rights, are you?"

"That's a very different thing. We're talking about *demons*, for God's sake. The security interests of this country—"

"Are not compelling enough to justify the complete denial of due process rights to an entire subset of U.S. citizens based on urban legend, rumor, and superstition."

"Come on, Lily." Sebastian squeezed my gloved hand. His internal discord jangled along my nerves. He craved his father's approval, and hated him a little for it, and wanted all of us to get along. "Let's not make this worse than it already is."

"You're right." I pulled away from him, shaken by the conflict in him. "I'm done. I hope you have a lovely evening, Mr. Ritter." I strode toward the exit. Only my precarious heels, trailing tule skirts, and the prospect of falling on my face in front of Northern California's rich and powerful stopped me from breaking into a run.

"Lily, wait!" Sebastian's agitation prickled along the back of my neck and followed me out the doors toward the stairs.

On the landing, I rounded on him, and he rocked back on his heels. "What the hell, Sebastian? Your *wife*?"

"I can explain." His energy shifted, the anger twisting back on itself.

"You better do a lot more than that." My voice rose, and people passing by on their way to the ballroom turned to stare. I gritted my teeth and continued at a lower volume. "You could have warned me!"

"I didn't expect her to be here! I didn't even know she was in town." He shot a glance over his shoulder and took my arm, steering me toward a side exit.

"Really? And where exactly have you been keeping her? Locked up in an attic somewhere?"

"More like Europe. Ibiza. Paris." He held the door open for me. Steps led down from the ballroom into a courtyard fragrant with jasmine and illuminated with tiny fairy lights like fireflies. "We've lived separate lives for years."

"I don't understand." I turned my face away from the beauty of the court-yard garden. The fake fireflies could go fuck themselves.

"We have a deal. I keep her in the lifestyle to which she's accustomed, and she doesn't take me for half my assets and then some." He grimaced. "We got married before the company went public. I was far too young and very idealistic. No prenup."

"That's a really bad deal," I said. "I could tell you that even if I wasn't a lawyer."

"Yeah, well." He bowed his head. "I've been meaning to sort it all out. But you saw how she is."

"She seems like a real piece of work."

"She wasn't always like that." He glanced over his shoulder, but no one had followed us out. Probably too busy gossiping about what had just gone down. "I wasn't a great husband, and if it weren't for her, I wouldn't be where I am. I own my part of that. She supported me through some tough times, and the marriage couldn't carry that weight."

"You're bankrolling her permanent European tour because you feel *guilty*?"

"I owe her a lot," he said, tone heavy. "She's earned the right to her bitter-ness."

"But you never even told me you were married!"

"That was wrong, and I'm sorry. But, Lily, you didn't have to take it out on my poor father."

"Your father—oh. You thought that was about *her*?"

"It wasn't?"

"No!" Exasperated, I blew out a noisy breath. "Your father's politics are atrocious. He's working as hard as he can to erase my legal existence."

"I think that's a stretch. You're still half-human."

"Half-*human*?" I shook my head, the weight of his ignorance leaden in my gut. "You think that will matter if they get their way? I live as a demon and I die as a demon, and if your father has his way, dying is exactly what I'll do. Eve too. She's just a child, but to him she's not even a person. How the hell are you okay with that?"

He flushed. "I'm not. But that's politics. He's playing to his voters. He has to, or he loses his job."

"Right," I said. "It's just politics to you. But it's personal for me."

"I see that." He didn't, though, not really. He couldn't. "So that's why you didn't want to attend tonight. It never occurred to me that it was about politics."

"It's not only about politics." The truth seared through me, sick and sharp as silver. "It's about the fact that you think you can just slot me into your life when and where it's convenient, like the last puzzle piece in your frame, with the lubrication of enough money."

"What? No, I—"

Ruthless, I overrode him. "I'm a cubine, but I'm not going to be your concubine. You can't buy me with dresses and fancy whiskey and pretty words. I'm a person with my own life, my own needs, my own desires, and you need to respect that." The shock of meeting Helena and my tirade in the ballroom had opened the floodgates of brutal honesty, and I couldn't shut them now.

His face changed and his energy darkened. It pulled back from me and shrank away. "My *concubine*? Lily, when have I ever given you a reason to think I saw you as anything less than my equal?"

"I don't know how you see me. But I do know this. We're not equals, and we never will be."

"I don't understand." He slumped, and his eyes sought mine, but I wouldn't meet them. "Sure, I have more money than you, but it's just money. It doesn't mean anything."

"Yes, it does," I said. "But I didn't mean that. I meant that I'm a demon. You're human. We're fundamentally unequal. I don't belong in your world, and you don't understand what it means to live in mine."

I hiked my skirts up around my ankles with one hand and descended the stairs into the courtyard, gripping the railing to keep my balance. I couldn't count on wings to save me now if I fell. The harsh scour of my anger had drained any buoyancy out of me, and I needed to put space between us.

"I'm sorry." He followed me. "I wanted this to be a fun evening, something to help you de-stress. Will you let me make it up to you?"

"I'm not sure how you can."

"Lily." He spoke my name like an invocation, a talisman to hold me in place. And for the moment, it worked. "Listen to me. That dress wasn't about buying you. And introducing you to my dad wasn't about making you fit into my life a certain way. None of this was. It's about giving you the kind of life you deserve. It's about being the kind of *man* you deserve."

Under the trees laced with their starry lights, I turned to face him once more. His desiderata reached out toward me, long dark tendrils of pain and yearning. He was desperate. He thought he was losing me.

Maybe he was right, even if neither of us wanted that.

My voice softened despite myself. "I don't know what that means."

"When Helena left me," he said, voice low and urgent, "I deserved it. I wasn't ready to be a good partner to her—to anyone. I didn't think I ever would be. For a long time, I didn't even want that."

Where was he going with this? "I'm still wondering why you didn't tell me about any of this before."

"Because I'm an idiot." He sighed. "Because I was scared. Because...frankly, Lily, I didn't think we were at a stage where you would care to know."

I had to give him that. After all, I still refused to call him my boyfriend. "So, this is about our relationship status after all."

"Maybe." He paced away down the garden path, then back again. "The problem is, when you came along, I wasn't prepared. I thought I had it all figured out and I was better off alone. Then we touched that night in the jail, and everything changed."

Of course it did, because that was the moment my succubus powers started establishing a claim on his soul, freshly available after the death of his previous demon lover. "What about Nepenthe?"

He stopped a few feet away from me, intense gaze seeking mine. "It wasn't the same with her. I cared for her, of course, but we both knew it was an arrangement of convenience. Neither of us was looking for more than that."

"You're saying you think I'm looking for more."

"No," he said. "I'm saying *I* am. I can't pretend to know what you want. But I was hoping maybe you would tell me."

"I..." What could I tell him? All the honesty this evening already left me raw and aching, inadequate to the moment that now presented itself. Sebastian stood before me showing more vulnerability than he ever had before, and I didn't know what to say.

I raised my gaze to meet his. His energy pulsed, but he waited in silence for my answer.

I cleared my throat. "I think I want to dance with you."

"What?"

"You bought me this extravagant dress. It seems a waste not to dance in it."

Surprise flashed across his face, but he took it in stride. "That would certainly make a stir among this crowd."

"I'm good with it." The idea of dancing with him in front of Helena did have a certain appeal after what she'd pulled. I mustered a smile for him. "And then I think I'd like to go to bed." If nothing else, if we were doomed, I wanted one more taste of him for the road.

His brows drew together. "To sleep? Or...?"

"That would also seem like a waste. Don't you agree?"

"I hope that means you're forgiving me for the evening so far." He laughed, but his energy wavered, uncertain.

"Don't push your luck, Mr. Ritter." I extended a gloved hand, my olive branch. For now. "Shall we?"

He took my hand. "Let's go make a spectacle of ourselves."

We went back up the steps together. But the truth I didn't have the heart to speak lodged in the back of my throat, acrid and ugly as tears.

He wanted something that a demon like me couldn't give him.

II

THE TEMPTATIONS OF LILITH

Several hours later, I leaned on the railing of the landing, a half-empty glass of stale champagne in my hand, waiting for Sebastian to complete his rounds of the ballroom.

The dancing had gone well. The unknown thousands of dollars per plate dinner went less so. I sat through speech after speech about Senator Ritter's many qualities and kept my expression as neutral as I could manage. But all I could think about was how, if he knew what I was, he wouldn't see me as a person.

Sebastian, for his part, did his level best to make things up to me, as promised. I tried to take it in the spirit in which he offered it—genuine, generous, gentlemanly—but rebellion gnawed at me. He could ply me with fancy dresses, expensive whiskey, and fairy-tale castles all he wanted, and it would still fall flat. It didn't change the problems between us. It didn't give me what I wanted.

I wanted something deeper, darker, crueler, harder. I wanted something that hurt more, the way I deserved it to, something that drained me dry. I wanted the other side of the Exchange. I wanted to stop holding back.

I wanted—

No. I couldn't possibly.

I'd killed Ariel. I couldn't miss him.

Nothing about that had been good for me. He'd raised me on lies and poison, fed me convenient half-truths, and kept me dependent on his expertise while teaching me nothing of the use about my powers or my father's people. He'd taken without asking and given without kindness.

Here I had a kind, good-hearted man who respected me, who cared for me, and I was so broken I couldn't even appreciate that.

He slipped his hands around my waist, his breath warm in my ear. "Would you like the tour of the castle, or shall we go up to bed?"

My skin tingled at his closeness, but I pulled away. "Sebastian…"

"Not to worry." He released me, letting out a short, rueful laugh. "There are plenty of rooms. You can have your own if you like."

"No." I had to pull myself together. I couldn't keep running hot and cold with him. "That's not necessary. I'm tired, that's all. Let's go up."

At the landing, he pointed me down a long, lush-carpeted corridor with enough rooms to pass for a luxury hotel to a set of double doors at its end. The bedroom suite that lay beyond the doors was predictably large and extravagant, with wide bay windows, another elegant chandelier, and a canopy bed. I swallowed a laugh.

"What is it?" Sebastian must have sensed my discomfort. "You don't like it."

I turned in the center of the room. "It's not that." These accommodations were fit for a queen, and what was I? A monster. "It's beautiful. This is all—it's too much. I don't deserve this."

"Stop that." He folded his arms, frowning at me. "You think too much about who deserves what. It's not healthy, Lily. You have to learn to enjoy things without worrying about whether you've earned them."

"And you'd know all about that, wouldn't you?" The bubble of frustration in my chest popped, and its bitterness boiled up and out of my mouth. "All those glowing media profiles of you say you're a self-made man, but you're not." How had Helena put it? "You're a fortunate son, your father's son. This place proves it."

His expression froze in place. "That's not fair."

"Isn't it?" My words tumbled out, ahead of my thoughts, unstoppable. "You claim to have all these dark desires, you pretend you're deep and mysterious, but you're not. All you really want to do is drive around in your fancy cars and show off your toys. You treat me like a collectible you want to display on your wall, and meanwhile you can't even get it together to file for divorce from your damn *wife*. You're not a man. You're just a boy who doesn't want to grow up—!" I clapped my hands over my mouth. Shit, I said it.

His desiderata dropped away to a background hum, leaving my demon senses struggling to read him. "Well, at least you're finally being honest. Is that what you really think of me?"

"I don't know," I whispered. "I'm sorry. I don't want—"

"No, you're right." He paced to the wide window, hands deep in his pockets, frowning out into the night. "I can't quibble with the bulk of your argument. Nothing you said tonight is really untrue."

"But that was cruel. I shouldn't have said it."

"Not even going to disavow it for the sake of my ego? That's cold."

"I—"

"It's fine. My ego doesn't need coddling. There is one thing you said that I want to dispute, though." He turned back to me, his face serious. "I've treated you with caution because you went through a lot of trauma last year. You don't seem to want to admit it, and I haven't wanted to push. Those desires you mentioned are still here, believe me. I'm just waiting for you to give me a signal that you want any of that with me."

"I know." That much I could read in him, along with his iron control. "But I don't want to be handled like I'm a princess made of glass. I'm not. I don't want gentleness, Sebastian."

He inclined his head, studying me. "If all of this is just your way of asking for some rough sex, all you have to do is ask. You don't have to goad me into it by insulting me first."

I opened my mouth, then closed it again as the import of his words caught up with me. Was that what I wanted? Conflicted heat swirled in my low belly. "I want..." I stammered.

He took a step toward me. The pitch of his energy intensified, and he looked me up and down, a slow, deliberate gesture. "You want me to treat me the way you think you deserve. Is that it?" His hands flexed at his sides as if itching to grab me.

My heart leaped and staggered. Sebastian couldn't hurt me unless I let him. I was stronger, faster, an apex predator at my deepest core, and his kind was my prey. I held all the power here, no matter what we pretended.

But I could pretend with the best of them, and maybe that would be enough.

"Yes," I whispered. "I want that."

He didn't waste a second. In a few quick strides he crossed the room and took me by the shoulders. His grip dug into my arms with a force that might have bruised me, if I bruised. A soft sound rose in my throat, and I yielded to him, letting him push me toward the bed.

"Is this what you want?" His desiderata swelled. It tugged at me, dark as gravity. "Answer me!"

"Yes. I already said yes!"

"You'll say it as many times as I ask you to." He shifted his hold to my wrists, still avoiding any exposed skin. "Damn it, and I didn't bring any restraints. We'll just have to make do." Releasing me, he stood back and with a sweeping motion tore the canopy from the bed.

"Sebastian! What are you doing?"

"It's my castle." Swift and methodical, he twisted the filmy fabric into a thick rope. "I can do what I want with it."

"You think that will hold me?" But the heavy innuendo layered in his words, his sure movements, and the triumph singing in his aura made me weak inside. Maybe I didn't have to pretend as much as I thought.

"It will hold enough." He pulled his improvised rope taut, testing its strength. "Take off your dress."

"What?"

"You heard me. Stop stalling."

"You're going to have to help me with that." It had taken a team effort to get me into the thing, after all.

"Fine, but it'll cost you. Turn around."

I obeyed, head bowed, conscious of his gaze on me. I'd asked for it, but this new flavor of Sebastian had caught me off guard, even though he'd never made a secret of his kinky side. When we had sex for the first and only time, before my big showdown with Ariel, I told him I wanted his control, and he'd obliged. But he certainly hadn't obliged me like this.

A heated wave of need built in me as he stepped closer. His hot breath washed over the bare skin of my back, and he gathered my hair in one hand, moving it aside. Shuddering, I bowed my head to expose my nape.

He pulled the zipper down slowly, careful not to touch me. I shrugged the dress off my shoulders and stepped out of it. It half-stood on its own, a beautiful shell no longer occupied, crumpled a little like a shed skin. In my cheap heels, wearing nothing but a strapless bra and panties, I turned to face him.

He inclined his head. "You can leave the shoes on. Lose the rest. Gloves, too."

"Yes, sir," I whispered, and bit my lip.

"Don't call me that." He grimaced.

"What should I call you, then?" I peeled my gloves off, one at a time. Unhooking my bra, I let it fall to the ground.

"My name will do."

I skinned my panties down my legs. "Yes, Sebastian."

"Wrists, please," he said, when I was naked before him.

I held them out, my cheeks hot. He looped the twisted fabric of the canopy around them, drawing the knot tight but not so tight it would cut off my circulation, and left two long ends on either side.

"You've done this before." The sensation of the binding shivered up my arms, and where his fingertips brushed my skin, little shocks of kether tingled through me.

"So have you, I take it." He gathered the working ends and used them as a lead, tugging me toward the head of the bed.

"A few times." I'd done this with Ariel, long ago. Another shiver coursed through me.

"Hm." His voice deepened, approaching a growl. "Get on the bed. On your hands and knees."

I obeyed. I might have whimpered. He lashed each end of the bindings to the bedposts of the headboard, leaving me just enough slack to shift my hands forward and back. The snap of latex as he gloved up made me jump, my whole body attuned to every movement behind me.

"What are you—"

"Quiet." Gloved fingers gripped my hips, cool and smooth instead of the warm skin I craved. I bucked into his hands, and he pushed back, holding me steady. "Tell me what you want."

How many times was he going to make me say it? "I want this." The words trembled, high and reedy, almost a whine.

He shifted his grip to my thighs, pulling my legs apart. His body heat warmed me, his desiderata licking at me like building flames, but he still didn't touch me with his bare skin. He was tormenting me with anticipation. I arched my back and craned my neck to look at him.

He knelt behind me, unbuckling his belt, his eyes dark with desire. Our gazes met, and a slight smile played around his mouth. The sound of his zipper echoed loud in the room.

"Is this what you want?"

I licked my lips, throat suddenly dry. "Yes."

"My eyes are up here. Say it to my face."

"Sebastian..." Frustration seared through me, and I tore my focus from his cock. "I want you to fuck me. I want you to do it hard." *Hurt me if you can.*

His expression changed, and his desiderata surged around us. His hands closed around my hips again and he yanked me back against him, pushing into me. Kether flowed where our skin met, but it burned harsher than normal, sharp and aching like the stretching sensation between my legs.

I moaned, opening to him. He slammed into me hard, his thrusts shaking me, tingling pleasure rising from the base of my spine to the top of my head every time he drove himself home. His energy burst through me like fireworks, and I cried out, high, wild, wordless sounds that tore my throat.

For a moment, I lost control. I lost myself. Falling, soaring, I took him deeper, taking everything he had.

All at once, a vivid, disorienting memory seized me. I wasn't with Sebastian anymore. I was in another time and place, with another pair of masculine hands holding me fast. Another's energy invaded my senses without foreplay or preamble, as my desire and frustration and anger mixed into a heady haze of instinct and compulsion.

The hands holding my hips steady gripped tighter. With a long, guttural groan, he stiffened and emptied himself into me.

"Ariel." My own voice startled me, a ragged prayer, a name I didn't mean to utter. A heavy weight lay atop me, pressing down on me. And my body rebelled.

My chest tightened and my heart thumped loud in my ears. I reared up, breaking the skin-to-skin contact, and the curtains holding my wrists gave way with a tearing sound. I half-turned, up on my knees now, and flung him away from me as hard as I could.

His body hit the far wall with a sickening crunch. And at the sound I came back to myself. I knelt naked on the bed, tattered streamers of fabric adorning my arms, my muscles rigid and my breath coming in swift sobbing gasps.

My heart leaden in my chest, I turned my head. Sebastian lay in a crumpled heap on the floor by the opposite wall, unmoving.

"No," I whispered. "Oh, no, no, *no...*"

What had I done? Why had I reacted like that? He hadn't done anything wrong, nothing I didn't ask him to—beg him for, even. But I had Ariel on my mind. And when I lost the last of my control, I flashed back to the moment on the balcony of the Ritz when the incubus had drained my kether with my consent but taken more than I bargained for.

Damn you, Ariel. Even dead, the incubus tainted everything I felt, everything I touched. I couldn't escape him, because a version of him lived on in my own mind, in my memory, and in my body.

I hadn't lashed out against Ariel when he hurt me, because I didn't have the power to fight back, not then. But Sebastian gave instead of took.

He gave me power. And I'd used it to break him.

12

POSSESSION

I tottered to Sebastian's side. My limbs floated light with kether, but a weight of dread dragged at my core.

He didn't stir, but his chest rose and fell in short, shallow breaths. A lump swelled on his temple where his head must have hit the wall and blood welled from a cut on his lip.

"Sebastian?" I knelt beside him. He still wore his shirt, half-unbuttoned. I took him by the shoulder and shook him gently, careful not to touch his skin. I didn't think I could pull kether from an unconscious partner, but I didn't want to test that theory.

He didn't respond. I drew back, hands pressed over my mouth. I'd hurt him. This was more than a kether-drain.

I'd broken him. But maybe I could fix him, too. Thanks to him, I had kether reserves to spare. I could use it to heal the damage I'd done.

With trembling fingers, I reached out to cradle his head and kiss him awake. My touch could stop the bleeding, knit any broken bones, repair the bruising on his temple. He would awaken and I could explain and maybe he would even forgive me.

A crash behind me made me nearly jump out of my skin.

The pressure in the room shifted with ear-popping force. The air crackled with invisible energy, like the charged atmosphere before a thunderstorm. My scalp prickled, and a cold draft swept through the room, lifting my hair and frizzing it with static. The light bulbs in the big chandelier overhead fizzed, flickered, and exploded in a flurry of sparking reports, leaving the room in darkness.

Adrenaline screamed through me. I released Sebastian, his head lolling back onto the floor. Straightening, I pivoted toward the other side of the room with a horrible sense of *déjà vu*.

The central windows had been closed when we came in. I was sure of it. But now they yawned open, thrown ajar by—

Not by the wind. A hooded figure crouched on the windowsill, silhouetted against the stars. It swallowed the scant light around it in a way that hurt to look at.

The gust that blew in behind it carried a thick scent of petrichor and ozone, with a coppery overtone that clogged my nostrils, sharp and wild. Thunder grumbled, a low roll echoing back and forth across the hills that surrounded the house, and the stars outside the window winked out one by one, obscured by fast moving clouds.

"Who's there?" My voice rang out too loud and too unsteady.

The figure stepped down from the sill. At its full height, it stood tall and menacing, human-shaped but inhuman in the sharp tilt of its head, fierce like a hunting bird.

"Lily Knight," the apparition said. "You are known to me." The harsh, low voice vibrated with power, but its timbre belonged to a woman. It wasn't Ariel, then, returned from dust to wreak vengeance on me for his death, but something else.

"What do you mean? Who are you?"

White light seared through the room for a split second. I flinched, but it was only lightning. The swift flash revealed a momentary glimpse of the figure's face, remote beauty under a floating cloud of hair the color of clotting blood. Dark paint smeared her cheeks and forehead from temple to temple in a thick stripe that obscured her features, a stark contrast to the pale skin beneath. Her eyes glinted pure black, without a hint of white sclera.

"I am many things to many people." Her smile sliced her face like a blade, visible now as my night vision adjusted slowly in the wake of the lightning. "I am Battle-Crow and Justice. I am Wrath and its guardian. I am Nightmare and Storm-Rider, Queen of the Phantoms. The one I ride now calls me Morrighu, but I have had many names and will have many more."

"That's a lot of fancy words but not a whole lot of information." I spat out strands of wind-whipped hair. I had no weapon, and I was naked but for my precarious heels and the torn curtains knotted around my wrists like tassels. Still, I shifted my weight to the balls of my feet, ready for a fight. "Why are you here?"

"I am here to deal justice at the end of a blade." She sprang at me, quick as any demon. Light blazed in her hand, a sword that flashed like her smile and then not like it. Its edge ran brilliant with the eerie blue phosphorescence of St. Elmo's Fire.

"Wait!" I fell back, hands raised, to stand over Sebastian, shielding his unconscious body with my own. "This man is injured. Let me help him, at least."

To my surprise, she did stop. "You should have fallen before my dread by now. But you resist." She examined me with her head to one side, her eerie black eyes glittering. "You're not human. What are you, that you can stand before me and tell justice to *wait*?"

I bared my teeth at her. "I'm a demon. What the hell are you?"

She smiled back, slow and razor-edged. "What do *you* think?"

"You're a demon, too."

"Not exactly. And yet, we are not so unlike, you and I." She advanced another step. "I thirst for the blood of the guilty, you for the taste of human lust. You might even say we both depend on humanity's sins to sustain us."

"It's not like that," I said hotly, shaken. "Not for me."

"Maybe. Maybe not." She shrugged. "It changes nothing. My charge is the same." With that, she raised her sword again.

"That sword won't kill me." It would probably hurt a lot, though. But I had to keep this entity, demon or phantom queen, whatever she really was, talking. "Not unless it's silver."

"Silver is a terrible material for a blade." Her mouth twisted with disdainful amusement. She had no desiderata, unless that painful darkness counted. "It is malleable and weak. This sword was forged of steel and light, wrought from the heart of a fallen star. It will do for my purposes."

She stepped forward again. Her advance pressed my back against the wall. The blade moved too fast to evade. Its arc stopped with its edge at my throat.

I swallowed, carefully, mindful of the cold steel tickling my windpipe. I might not die, but I could still bleed. Whatever power illuminated the blade crackled with stinging electricity over my skin, a warning and a promise. Maybe a magic sword would dispatch a demon just as well as silver.

"It's not justice if the accused doesn't have a chance to defend themselves." My voice sounded thready and desperate in my own ears. "It's just murder."

"Murder. Yes." She flipped the blade, its flat pressing into my neck, its edge forcing my chin up. "Have a care you answer true, for you cannot fool my power. You have the blood of one of your own kind on your hands, do you not?"

"You know," I breathed. "But how?"

"Answer!" The pressure of the blade increased.

"All right." I choked it out, my throat unaccountably clogged. "Yes, I killed him, all right? I killed him because he used me, and he killed other women like me, and then he shot my best friend. I had to do it, because no one else could, and if I hadn't, he never would have stopped coming after me." My voice rasped thick and hoarse over the last words, and I began to cough, a racking shudder. Something needle-sharp pricked the inside of my cheek. "Ow!"

"Hush." The woman—demon—whatever she was took my jaw in her hand. Her touch burned like dry ice, ketherless, hard as the steel at my throat. "Open."

I stared at her, uncomprehending, and she made an exasperated noise that almost sounded human. With inexorable strength, she pried my mouth open with her cold fingers. I gagged and she drew back, pulling a single white feather from my throat. Dark wet spots flecked it here and there, and they ran and smeared like blood.

"What in the hell?" I wrenched my head away from her.

She released me, lowering her blade. I leaned against the wall, panting, my esophagus raw and sore, my mouth stinging.

My visitor turned the feather in her hand, a meditative look on her face. In a quick, bizarre, predatory motion, she licked the white feather from quill to tip, and handed it back to me.

It trembled in my palm, catching the breeze gusting in through the open window, and I closed my hand over it. It wasn't slick with her saliva as I would have expected, but downy and dry. The blood smearing its barbs had disappeared.

Without another word, the woman turned away from me and strode toward the window, sweeping her black cloak around her. Its substance shifted, whispering. I drew a sharp breath. The cloak was made of feathers too, huge black pinions. They weren't ethereal like my own, but real, rustling and solid, dark as the night outside.

"Wait!" My own wings lifted me, and I launched myself at her. "Why did you come here? Who sent you? What does the white feather mean?"

She sprang away from me, perched for a moment on the sill. "The sword has spared you." Her voice roughened, a wild cry, a bird's cry, and she leaped from the window.

"No!" I leaped after her, meaning to catch her, stop her fall.

But she didn't fall. She transformed, flying from the window in a bird's form, a huge black crow beating its wings against the wind of the oncoming storm.

I leaned out the window. The bird wheeled on the air, soared upward, and vanished into darkness that even my kether-sharpened night vision couldn't penetrate. Quick-gathering clouds obscured the stars, and thunder grumbled, far off this time. My pulse hammered, but otherwise, silence reigned.

She was gone.

The bedside lamp flickered back on, the only light that had survived the strange power surge that had heralded my visitor. With shaking hands, I drew and fastened the shutters. The white feather tickled my damp palm, and I frowned down at it.

What did it mean? What the hell had just happened? I had hurled my human lover across the room after a flashback from hell, and then a self-styled Queen of Phantoms had blown into the room and passed judgment on me—

My heart contracted. Sebastian. I'd hurt Sebastian. I had to make sure I hadn't broken him. I willed my wings away and crossed the room again, crouching beside him.

Before I could rouse him, his eyes fluttered open. "Lily?"

"Shh. Let me." I reached for him, but he flinched away from me, and I closed my hand. "Are you all right? Where does it hurt?"

"My head is killing me." He groaned, pressed his fingers to his ribs, gingerly testing them. "Among other things. I feel like I got hit by a semi. What happened?"

I sat back on my heels. "You don't remember?"

"I remember we fought. You were angry with me." He furrowed his brow and winced. "Then you wanted sex, so I bound you—and then—"

"I lost control." I bowed my head. "I can help you, if you just…"

This time, he didn't pull away when I placed my palm over his forehead. But when I leaned down to place my mouth on his, his desiderata quailed from me, and a sick weight settled in the pit of my stomach.

Sebastian had never feared me before, but he did now. He didn't respond to my kiss. I lingered just long enough to complete a small kether push, until the swelling on his temple smoothed under my palm. Then I drew back.

I'd done this with a human once before—with Danny, after Ariel shot her. That time, I'd given everything I had to save her life. Now, I only gave Sebastian what he needed to make him whole again.

Sebastian's face changed, and he sat up. "What did you do?"

"Kether push." I turned away, slipped the torn curtains off my wrists, and started gathering my clothes.

"Lily…"

"Don't." I tucked the white feather into my formal clutch for safekeeping, between my ID and my cell phone, and fastened my bra with unsteady fingers. I was tired of talking. Did we ever do anything else? Slipping my panties back on, I eyed the lovely dress waiting for me on the floor.

Then, struck by a thought, I pulled out my phone and dashed off a quick text message to Ira: *You up?*

The reply came quicker than expected: *Yep, working late. Why?*

I think I just met your murderer, I typed. Out loud, I said, "Sebastian. I shouldn't have—"

"I'm not him, Lily."

Damn it. Just my luck that he remembered my little slip of the tongue. "I know. I had a flashback or something. For a moment, I was back there with him, and I was so afraid." My phone buzzed in my hand, Ira calling me, and I silenced it with a touch. "I don't want you to be like him. That's the last thing I want."

"You could have fooled me." Sebastian's voice was low, uneven, and his desiderata flared behind me, furious and bright.

Fingers clumsy and numb, I tapped out a text response to Ira: *I can't talk now. I'll come to you. I have something to show you.* "I messed up. I *am* messed up." I hunched my shoulders under the weight of that knowledge. "I'm so sorry I hurt you. Calling his name like that—it was fear in my voice, not passion. I hope you understand that."

"I do," he said, with a long, ragged exhalation. "And it's not all on you, either. I broke my own rules tonight. We were both angry, and we didn't negotiate things properly. I—" He broke off.

"What?" I wheeled around to find him leaning against the wall, arms folded, his expression shadowed and his energy subsiding into darkness. "Sebastian. What were you going to say?"

He raised his head, and the bleak winter in his eyes said it all before he put it into words that seared through me like cold silver. "Tell me you're one-hundred percent certain you didn't make me do that."

"You think I succubused you into it," I whispered. I couldn't move, but the sensation of vertigo gripped me, a long freefall into lightless depths.

I'd kept telling him it would happen, that I could manipulate him like this. Why did it hurt so much that he might finally believe me?

"I don't know. It all seems...cloudy." He looked down at his hands, then back at me. "You didn't answer the question."

I turned my gaze away. "I can't." My solar plexus ached, and my eyes burned with tears I refused to shed. With a shuddering breath, I stepped back into my dress. "Will you zip me up, please?"

"You don't have to get dressed." He approached, steady now despite the slow ebb of his desire. "I can fetch your overnight bag from the car if you want something more comfortable."

"Hang onto it for me." I stood, back to him, waiting. "Please, Sebastian. I have to go, now."

"Ah." And with that soft exhale, the occlusion of his energy became complete. But he drew the zipper up my back, careful as ever. His fingers didn't brush my skin. "Where are you going?"

"It's for work." Slowly, I turned to face him one last time.

"You never did tell me about your new job." Sebastian folded his arms, frowning.

"I can't really talk about it." What would I tell him, anyway—that I needed to see a man about a murder? That strange woman threatened to kill me and then turned into a bird? Sebastian had never doubted my supernatural powers, but this story stretched my own credulity, even if Ira hadn't put the fear of government secrets in me.

Sebastian let that stand. "Would you let me drive you? I feel fine now."

I allowed myself one long, last look at him, taking in his angular features and lean-muscled body. He'd rolled the shirt sleeves of his formal white shirt up to his elbows, the better to bind me with, and his blue eyes waited for me like deep, still pools I could sink into forever.

But I couldn't. If I lost control with him again, he might not survive it.

"Thank you." I steeled myself. "But no. I'll find my own way."

"Lily..."

My phone buzzed with Ira's text: *At the church.*

I typed out: *Give me an hour.* "I'm sorry," I said. "I have to do this alone."

I didn't give him a chance to argue with me. I fled the room, out into the long hall with its soft-pile carpet, and down the ornate staircase toward the echoing front hall.

This time, he let me go, and he didn't call me back. Only his silence followed me.

I told myself I expected that.

Outside, I glanced over my shoulder at the house behind me, its stone facade and Gothic-style towers. On the second floor, the single lighted window went dark. Sebastian must have switched off the lamp.

Between the driveway and the road, rows of grape vines curved downhill, their large flat leaves gleaming in the moonlight. The sky arched dark and cloudless above us, clustered with more stars than even the clearest San Francisco night could reveal. It showed no sign of the brief thunderstorm that had blown that strange woman into our room.

The stillness out here pressed around me, no rush and honk of cars on nearby cross streets, no shouts or partying hordes passing by, no heartbeat of human activity under the skin of the city. And something else was missing too: the constant whisper of thousands of people's desiderata, which even when I slept alone managed to seep in through the walls, wistful yearnings and visceral cravings that demanded satisfaction. Here, with most of the gala attendees departed, only a few snatches reached me now and then as the house's occupants, family and friends who had stayed the night, dreamed on.

And yet, it was still, but not quiet. Crickets chirped from the oak scrub on the slope above the estate. Somewhere close by, a bird called, a hoarse, warbling sound that reminded me too much of the night sounds of the remote desert ruins where I'd confronted Ariel.

I walked faster. I needed a spot out of sight of the house and open to the air. I didn't have Eve's confidence that I could keep humans from spotting me in flight.

I headed uphill into the scrub, climbing until I reached an open spot among the oaks. With a long exhalation, I drew myself up, pulled my shoulders back, and let my wings unfold.

It shifted something inside me, a subtle click as of a key turning in a lock. The wings unfurled above and behind me with a soft sigh that echoed my own, their half-transparent pinions mirroring the starry sky above. The use of my power had grown on me with practice, and now it almost felt like coming home.

The cool night breeze caressed my skin. I lifted my head and took to the sky, leaving Sebastian's castle behind me in the dark.

13

DEMON IN THE DETAILS

I circled the towers of Ira's church once. Thankfully, the low, blanketing fog that encased the city blotted out the light of the full moon. Still, I wrapped an extra glamour around myself to turn away prying human eyes.

A hint of fatigue crept in at the extra energy drain of the glamour, and I dropped to the roof of the nearest cupola. Crouched beside the big cross atop the belfry, one arm thrown around its base for balance, I took a breath to gather my remaining resources. A few vehicles with late-night travelers or Saturday partiers sped past on the street below, oblivious to my presence, and my lips curved at the irony of it all. What a pity they couldn't see me up here, draped over their religious symbol, putting the lie to the myth that the crucifix repelled demons.

Light shone in the curtained window of the tower opposite me. With a final leap and glide, I soared over the peaked roof between the cupolas and landed on the molding in a cloud of windswept tule. This ledge offered much more precarious footing, but I trusted my wings to catch me if I slipped. I still had a little kether left in reserves.

A gap in the curtains revealed the circular room where Ira and I had first spoken. In a chair facing the window, Ira sat with a large hardbound book open in his lap, his head tilted back, his eyes closed. He looked asleep, but irrational panic clawed at my throat for a moment. Then his chest rose and fell under his leather jacket, a soft snore reaching my kether-sharpened hearing.

If I had Theo's skill, I could step through the glass into the room. Without it, I could drop down to street level and call him, wait for him to come down and open the door for me. That was probably the smart, mature thing to do.

Instead, I rapped on the window lattice.

Ira started, then jerked upright. In a split second, he sprang to his feet, his stance combat ready. His hand dropped to his belt and flicked away the hem of the jacket to reveal a pistol grip.

Then his eyes fell on me. He frowned.

I waved. "Just me. Your friendly neighborhood half-demon."

He frowned harder, but he strode across the room, threw aside the sash, and opened the window. "Ms. Knight, what are you doing out there? And what on earth are you wearing?"

"Oscar de la Renta, I'm told." I brushed the skirts back into place and let my wings dissolve into the night. "Please don't shoot me. It probably wouldn't kill me, but I would fall down and then you might have to explain me to a lot of people."

"I have no intention of shooting you." He moved aside, leaving me room to slither inelegantly inside, hampered by my expanse of dress. "But you should be more careful. This is no time to go tap tapping at chamber doors. Or windows, for that matter."

"'Tis no Raven, but the fair Lenore," I quipped, and collapsed onto the chair he'd vacated. The soft seat brought a new wave of fatigue, my human and demon sides uniting to inform me that between healing Sebastian's injuries, flying sixty miles back to the city from Napa, and running a no-see-um glamour, I had pushed my limits tonight.

Ira snorted and shut the window. "That poem would have gone a lot differently if the narrator was packing."

"Speaking of ravens." I pulled my clutch from its snug spot in my bodice where I'd stuffed it for safekeeping, earning a raised eyebrow but no comment from Ira. "Are crow shapeshifters a thing?"

That earned me a second eyebrow. "Supernaturals who can shift form are rumored, but not well-documented. Why?"

Rubbing my temples, I relayed the whole story. Well, most of it. I left out my tryst with Sebastian and its disastrous consequences. That was none of Ira's business. But I told him everything else. He stopped me now and then to ask a clarifying question, but he didn't seem to doubt the basic facts of what I'd experienced. I owed him appreciation for that, however grudging.

"She pulled this out of my throat." I showed him the white feather, now bedraggled from my sweaty palm and tight-packed handbag. "Remind you of anything? The other victims were found with feathers in their throats."

"But black ones." Ira considered my offering. "And many more than one. You say she *licked* your blood off it?"

"Don't remind me." I groaned. "It was gross. Like she enjoyed it. Almost, dare I say it, sensual."

"And then she turned into a crow."

"There must be some very weird physics going on there. What I can't figure out is how she managed the sword. How the hell does that work?" Did her sword become part of her when she turned into the bird and flew away? Had it been an extension of her all along? It made absolutely zero sense.

"How do your wings work?" Ira inquired in a mild tone. "They are extraordinary, by the way. I've never seen them up close like that. I'd like to see them again sometime if you'd allow it."

I couldn't decide if I should take that as a compliment, a come-on, or a creepy statement of intent to study me like a specimen, so I elected to ignore it, along with the uncomfortable fact that I still couldn't read him. "I don't know how they work. They just do. Do you know how your liver works? Or your brain, for that matter?"

His lips quirked. "We know something about it, thanks to science."

Damn it, I probably made him think about dissecting us again. Or whatever an ex-priest, ex-Marine secret agent did when he wanted to understand how something worked. Nothing good, no doubt. "Yes, but do you *have* to? Or do they just do their thing? That's my point."

"It's well-taken, Ms. Knight." Ira sat down on the other chair, leaning forward with his elbows on his knees. "I guess the real question here is, *what* is she, this being you encountered? You don't seem to think that she is one of your kind."

"Your guess is as good as mine." With a sigh, I flopped back in my chair. "She claimed she isn't, for what that's worth. And she gave me a name. Well, she gave me several, but most of them sounded like titles. Except one. Morrighu."

"What did you say?"

I sat up straighter at Ira's sharp tone. "Uh, Morrighu, I think. Is that something?"

"I've heard that name. Or something similar." He rose and swooped down on the huge, old-looking leather-bound tome that he'd held in his lap earlier.

"*The New Daemonologie?*" I eyed it with distrust. It had sigils embossed along its spine and fancy script. "What is that, some kind of demon encyclopedia?"

"One of the foremost authorities in the field." Ira flipped through it, though he shot an apologetic glance at me. "Unfortunately, academic studies of the supernatural have stalled out for a few centuries."

I relaxed back into my seat as he paged through it, grumbling softly to himself. I would need to eat, sleep, or feed again soon. In retrospect, I probably should have let Sebastian drive me back from Napa and saved myself the kether. But I didn't want to spend the long drive talking, or not talking, about what had happened between us.

I chose not to think about that now, either. "Ira?"

"What?" He didn't look up from his perusal of *The New Daemonologie*.

"I keep wondering why you quit being a priest."

"I was a chaplain," he said, absently. "It's not quite the same thing."

"Okay, why did you quit being a chaplain?"

"Because..." Now he paused, one finger marking his spot on the page. "No faith can continue to exist under conditions of absolute reality."

"Huh?"

"Faith requires the existence of the unknowable. When I found proof that demons were real, that the supernatural was in fact a natural part of our world and always had been..." He sighed. "I don't know. Perhaps my faith wasn't strong enough."

"Mine wasn't either." I believed in something once, too. The father who raised me taught me a faith that forgave all sins except the one that lived inside my blood and bones, my nature. And after I lost that faith, I believed in Ariel.

He looked up at that, his interest captured. "What faith was that?"

"The human kind." I laughed. "This may come as a surprise, but demons don't believe in God. At least, none of the ones I've known do."

What did I believe in now? Nothing, perhaps. Myself, on a good day, which didn't include today.

"Ah." Ira turned the page, and his expression shifted. Or no, it hardened, went still. "Well, that may be about to change tonight."

"What? Why?"

He turned the book to face me, and I stiffened, the breath rushing out of my lungs.

The page had an illustrated plate, a lurid painting of a warlike female figure with a black stripe across her eyes, her pale hands drenched in blood, and a sword at her belt. A large black bird gripped her shoulder, wings half-outstretched and beak open in mid-cry. She wore a dark cloak over leather battle gear and stood with one booted foot upon a man's body, which was also dressed for battle in medieval armor. Her dark hair swirled free as if tossed by a stormy wind, and ominous clouds gathered overhead.

The inscription beneath it read, *The Dread Goddess Morrigan, Queen of Phantoms.*

"Look familiar?" Ira said.

"That's her, all right." My new nemesis was a goddess, and wasn't that just my luck? "Different face, different outfit, but yeah, same vibes."

Ira's expression turned skeptical. "Vibes?"

"You know, the aesthetic." I waved my hands. "Blood, sword, Furiosa make-up, big dominatrix energy. She even called herself that Queen title. And she mentioned her dread. Something about how I didn't fall before her like I should."

"Interesting." Ira flipped the book around to study the text on the opposite page. "This says she's an Irish or Celtic war deity, famed for her ruthless defense of her people. She wore many aspects and bore many names, and crows heralded her arrival. 'Often called a demon, her true nature remains unknown.' What do you think?"

"I told you. I don't know anything about gods or goddesses. Demons may have supernatural powers, but we're not privy to the secrets of the universe." My comfortable seat offered no comfort any longer, and I sprang up, pacing the room. "Whatever this thing is, it's more powerful than me, and a lot more dangerous."

"Yet you mentioned you had some immunity to her power."

"Some, yes. But she still bested me. She could have killed me if she wanted to." I raked my hands through my hair, once perfectly curled by Eve's expert hands, now a wind-wrecked mess that caught my fingers in chaotic tangles. "Tonight was a warning. She said she knows me. If she can find me at the winery, she can find me anywhere, anytime. How am I supposed to stop her? How do I defeat a goddess?"

"That I can't tell you." Ira closed the book, his expression grim. "But the U.S. government is paying you the big bucks to find out, Ms. Knight. And you better figure it out fast."

At his tone, I paused my restless motion. "Why? Ira, what aren't you telling me?"

"It's what I need to show you," he said. "And why I wasn't asleep when you sent your message tonight."

"I don't like the sound of that at all."

"You shouldn't." He went to the desk and opened the laptop sitting there. It showed a web browser window with a paused video, its frame dark. The headline above the video said, *Freak Attack at Frat House - What the Hell Is That?!* Ira pressed the play button and stood back.

The video wobbled, the telltale sign of a handheld device, and the dim lighting left the resolution fuzzy. Shouts and whoops from the background suggested a large party raging nearby. But the camera focused on a blond girl engaged in a long, sloppy kiss with a young white man with longish light hair and a football player's build.

Behind the camera, ribald comments and wolf whistles rose. The two in the frame had an audience. The girl turned to the camera, and my heart dropped.

It was undeniably Eve in the video, and something was obviously wrong with her. She swayed, eyes glazed and unfocused.

"It's working." The male speaker stood outside the frame.

"Your turn." The man in the frame pushed Eve toward the camera.

Hands reached out, grabbing for her, pulling at her clothes. And then all hell broke loose.

The video shook, steadied, focused on Eve. Her head snapped up. Her face contorted into a feral snarl, and her forehead bunched, leonine and traced with darkened veins. Her dilated pupils caught and held the dim light, glowing like a tiger's in the dark out of irises golden and wild.

The jeering voices fell silent. The ambient noise of the party filtered in for a moment, and then the men shouted all at once.

"Jesus *fuck*."

"What the hell *is* that?"

"Get away from her!"

Eve's body tensed. Then she sprang. Her inhuman speed rendered her movement nothing more than a flash across the screen. The shouts dissolved into inarticulate screams and curses. The camera fell to the floor. The screen went dark, and the men's cries faded into ominous silence.

In that silence, someone else picked up the device. The pale blur of a face showed for a split second before the video cut off.

Ira closed the laptop with a click. "You see the problem, I hope, Ms. Knight."

"Where did you get that?" I managed to keep my voice steady, but it came out flat and cold.

"It was released online tonight by an anonymous throwaway account and immediately went viral. Her name is Eve DeLeon, and she's the same girl whose ID was found at the scene. There's a manhunt underway for her now. Or," he paused, rethinking that, "a demon hunt, as it appears."

Seven hells. Poor Eve. "Torches and mobs," I murmured.

"What?"

"Nothing. But that's not her! It's not the goddess. This girl—whoever she is—she may be a demon, but she's just a kid. She didn't do it."

"That may not matter. It's like I told you. People want blood."

"Right." I paced to the window, staring out at the city lights. "And they don't care whether that blood is innocent or not."

"She's a demon to them, not an innocent, and she's wanted for murder. This video gives the cops probable cause. There's even a whatchamacallit. A hashtag."

"You're kidding me. What is it?"

"I told you, I don't kid. It's #EvilHasAFace."

"Fuck," I breathed. There was a hunt on for Eve, and she had no idea. Danny and Berry had no idea the danger they faced. "I have to go."

"And why is that?"

"I have to stop this." I gathered up my clutch purse and my skirts. "I have to find her before they do." I could do that part, at least.

"Ms. Knight." Ira's stern voice stopped me halfway to the door. "Innocent or not, this young woman—this demon—is a person of interest. At minimum, she's a witness. She could be the last one to see those men alive."

Icy fear filtered through me. It froze me from the inside out. "I know that."

"If you do happen to find her, call me immediately. And take her into custody if you can."

"Yes, sir." I hazarded a glance at him over my shoulder.

"You understand, then." He stood in the middle of the room in his customary pose, arms folded, expression severe. "It's for her own safety—and everyone else's."

"I understand," I said. But as I descended the stairwell, my heart grew heavier with every step.

I understood, all right. They would disappear Eve and ask questions later. Ira saw her as a threat, too—he just wasn't saying it.

Only two days on the job, and I already had a conflict of interest. And with the general public ginned up for a demon hunt, not to mention the political tide turning against our personhood, my life had suddenly become a lot more dangerous.

Rae McGuire better come through with that safehouse, and fast. I would call her in the morning.

For now, I needed to get home and warn my charge that as far as the authorities were concerned, she had just gone from victim to target.

14

YOU WANT IT DARKER

I pushed the door of the guest room open, careful not to make a sound. Danny and Berry slept in the room across the hall. Waking them in these wee hours seemed like the mark of a bad housemate.

In the guest bed, Eve's golden curls spread across the pillow, her breathing deep and even. Asleep, she looked like a perfect angel, nothing like the snarling girl-creature who had charged the camera in the video Ira showed me.

Doubt nagged at me. Had she lied to me about what happened at the frat house? She told me she partied with the men before blacking out. But the video told a vastly different story. Far from a sick succubus tainted with bad kether, her actions looked like those of a demon in full control of her powers, if a frightened one.

What had happened after the camera fell and the video ended? Who had picked up the device—probably a phone? The unfocused frame at the end didn't give much to go on, but it could have been Eve's face. It could have been anyone's.

Eve stirred and her eyes fluttered open. "Lily?"

Damn it. Had she sensed my thoughts? "Hey," I said softly, and came all the way into the room, closing the door behind me. "I didn't mean to wake you."

"I thought you were staying with Sebastian tonight."

"I came home early." I grimaced.

She sat up, blinking. "What happened?"

My relationship problems paled in comparison to her situation, but she didn't know that yet. I swept my skirts out of the way and sat at the end of the bed. "I think Sebastian and I might have broken up."

"Oh no! You can't! He's so gorgeous. I bet his *kether* tastes sweet, like dark chocolate mousse."

She would have won that bet. I frowned. "That's enough."

"Not that I would know." An affronted note entered her voice. "He barely even looked at me."

"That's because he's a good man, and you're far too young for him." And because I'd gotten there first. Was I giving him too much credit? Was my Claim the only reason he hadn't felt her Presence? "Anyway, that's not why I came home early. Eve, we need to talk."

"Now?" Her eyes widened. "But it's the middle of the night."

"Yes, now." I took out my phone and turned the volume down to its lowest level before playing the video. "This went public tonight."

She shrank into herself as she watched it, pulling her pajama-clad knees up to her chest. Then she raised her eyes to mine, liquid with tears and naked panic. "You think I did it."

"I don't know what to think. Maybe you should explain it to me."

"I can't," she whispered.

"Can't, or won't?"

She shook her head, her hair falling forward to screen her face, lips pressed stubbornly together.

"Kid, you've got to talk to me. There's a warrant out for your arrest. People are freaking out about this big time. This is serious. Eve—" I reached to grasp her shoulder, but she shied away from me.

"Don't touch me!" She sprang to her feet.

"Keep it down. People are sleeping."

"I don't care!" Her pitch rose, tinged with hysteria. "I'm dangerous, can't you see? I could kill you. Like I did those boys. I know that's what you're thinking. *Isn't it?*"

"I'm trying to help you. But I can't help if you don't tell me the truth."

"Yeah, well, your help sucks. I didn't want any of this. I want to find my dad and then I want to go home." Her voice cracked on the last word.

What did home mean to her? Some tony apartment on New York City's Upper West Side where she and Ariel had lived together like the setup for a twisted demon family sitcom? A sharp pang twisted in my chest, a loss I couldn't name.

"Lily, is that you?" Danny's soft voice floated from the hallway.

Shit. "Yep, just me and Eve."

Danny appeared in the doorway, squinting at us. She wore jeans and one of her indie band t-shirts. Maybe we hadn't woken her after all. "Why are you arguing in the dark?"

"No reason. Sister stuff," I said at the same time as Eve said, pouting, "Lily wants to turn me in to the police."

"*What?* Why?" Danny's energy sparked with surprise. "What's going on?"

"Eve, hush. I'm not—"

"Whatever." Eve scowled. "You're a liar, too. You're worse than me."

She pushed past Danny and stomped toward the bathroom. The sound of running water drifted back to us.

"Sorry, Dan." I rose from my seat on the guest bed. "I can explain—"

"You'd better." In the shadows of the unlit hallway, Danny's desiderata flattened and glinted, steel reflecting fire. "You knew the cops were looking for her, and you still let her stay here."

Now it was my turn to avoid her eyes. "She's innocent, Danny. She didn't do it. I just need to figure out how to prove it."

"Didn't do *what*?" Danny's energy flared around her, and I flinched back. "Lily. *What do they think she did?*"

"Um." I stared at the hem of my dress and the nasty blister swelling under the strap that crossed my right big toe. "Well, funny thing. You're still working the Delta Alpha Mu case, aren't you?"

Silence stretched in the space between us. Finally, I chanced a quick look up. She stood stock still, her expression blank and closed. But an incandescent storm raged around her in my demon-sight.

"Danny? Say something."

"The Delta Alpha Mu case." Her voice came out strange, flat and strangled. "God*damn*it. You know I'm on that case. You were there last night—Lily! What the *hell* were you doing at that crime scene?"

"No. I wasn't there because of her! I didn't even know she was involved, then." Mother of monsters, I had really fucked this whole thing up. "I told you, Dan. She followed me home."

"From a *fucking murder house!*" Danny didn't scream it, but she managed to give the impression of yelling while keeping her voice low. "You don't know she's innocent! You don't know her at all. God, what an unholy mess. What the fuck were you thinking?"

I closed my eyes and leaned my shoulder into the wall, welcoming the cool touch of plaster on my cheek. "I was thinking that she's Ariel's daughter."

Danny blinked at me, her mouth falling open. "Ariel's *what*?"

"I know," I said. "It surprised me, too."

"Ariel had a—No. I don't care why or how. What I want to know is how that makes anything about this better." Danny rubbed at her eyes with a long, shaky breath. Then she softened her tone, but her desiderata still crackled around us. "Ariel was a bad guy. Bad demon. Whatever. He hurt you. He hurt me. So why—"

"Because I owe her." The words fell dull and heavy from my lips. "She's all alone in this world. She has no one, Dan. And that's because of me."

"Lily..." But Danny broke off.

Something had blurred between us in the hallway, moving too fast for human or cambion eyes to follow. It left a soft sound behind it, the noise of a sharp inhalation or a stifled sob.

A second later, the side door slammed, and the house fell quiet again. It was a true quiet this time, with no running water in the bathroom and no gusty teenage sighs.

"Shit." Danny backpedaled, peering into the darkened bathroom. "She's not here. I think she must have heard us."

"You think?" I limped to the side door and threw it open. Outside, the night breathed cold, damp Pacific air. The fog had settled in just over the peaks of the street's Victorian roofs, and the streetlights bathed everything in a muted sepia glow.

The street lay still and empty, with no demon girls in sight. Only a faint scent of sandalwood lingered in my nostrils.

Ariel's daughter had flown the coop.

The late morning sun glittered off the Pacific Ocean, summoning crowds of beachgoers who swarmed over the sands. It made a perfect Sunday for them, but with my negligible sleep, too much worry, and multiple recent fuckups, the cheerful scenery added insult to injury. I pushed my shades up my nose to block some of the glare and ordered an extra shot in my artisanal latte. Then I headed out to the cafe's outdoor seating, where Rae McGuire waited for me at a sunny table in the corner of the patio.

"Thanks for meeting me." I slid into the open seat across from her. "Are you feeling better?"

"Oh, yes." Rae waved a dismissive hand. Her hazel eyes did look less bruised than the other day, her face less drawn and pale. Her loose, sleeveless top showed off her toned arms and extensive tattoos. "Migraines happen. It's a curse, but I'm used to it. If I don't sleep, my body forces the issue."

"Must be nice. I don't think I got more than a couple hours."

She made a sympathetic noise in her throat. "Rough night? What happened?"

What didn't happen? "I had a date with the guy I'm seeing. It ended badly."

Her posture changed from relaxed to alert. She leaned forward. "What do you mean, badly?"

I yelled at his only living family, accused him of keeping me as a concubine, and then called him a wanna-be. Oh yeah, and: "I found out he was married and forgot to tell me."

"He *forgot*?" She let out a harsh, barking laugh. "That's rich. Please don't tell me you believe that nonsense."

"Of course not." Hopefully my shades hid the way my gaze kept snagging on her body art, but in my defense, it was spectacular. Snakes coiled around her wrists and up her forearms, transforming into leafy vines that twined in intricate knots around her upper arms. A lifelike bird stared me down from her left bicep, clinging to the vines with knobby claws. The exquisite detail of its dark feathers had to have taken ages, and the artist had used negative space to suggest light glinting off a beady, watchful pupil.

It seemed I couldn't get away from creepy birds these days. I toyed with the idea of asking Rae if she'd ever heard of a crow goddess, but then dismissed it. She said she'd studied biology, not folklore. She'd probably just laugh at me again.

"This is why I swore off men." Rae leaned back again in her chair, shaking her head. "Dick is abundant and low value. Not worth the drama."

Well, I didn't know how to answer that one. I shook off the sense that her tattoo had its eye on me and waved a hand at the view that spread out before us, changing the subject. "You come out here a lot?"

"I like looking at the waves." She lifted a shoulder, and the bird on her skin seemed to shift and settle its pinions with the flex of her muscles. "It's peaceful. Don't get a lot of that at home. Too many people."

"I didn't realize you had so many housemates."

"The joys of San Francisco living. Couldn't afford a place without them." Deadpan, Rae sipped her coffee. Her eyes skated away from the sparkling sea to rest on me with a piercing, curious gaze. "Your text this morning was pretty vague. What's going on?"

I took my time to answer. "It's Eve. The girl I'm helping. She ran away."

Rae's eyebrow quirked. "I thought she protested too much when I called her a runaway."

"No," I said. "She was telling the truth. She didn't run away from her parents. She ran away from me, last night."

"I see." Rae tapped her fingers on the table, lips pursed. "And you want me to do what, exactly?"

"I was wondering if she came to you."

"Ah." Rae's brows rose further. "And if she had, you think I'd tell you? Just what is it that you suppose I do?"

I sighed. "You hide people who don't want to be found."

"And does your Eve want to be found by you?" Rae smiled, gentle, implacable, infuriating. "She knows where to find you, right?"

"Well, yes. But she's just a kid, Rae. She asked me to help her. I can't help her if she won't talk to me."

Rae picked up her cup, gazing into depths black as the bird etched into her arm. "Maybe she changed her mind."

"So, you do know where she is."

"Me?" Dark red strands of hair lifted and tangled in the brisk wind blowing off the Pacific. She blew them out of her mouth with an audible snort and shook her head. "I have no idea."

"Really?" But her desiderata gave nothing away, all seafoam and bright reflections that shifted with the ebb and flow of the horizon. I blinked. A slight headache throbbed in my temples, but if she lied, her energy didn't show it. "She's in a lot of trouble, and if I don't find her first, it could get worse."

"If I see her," Rae said, "I'll let her know." Her focus shifted away again, out over the sea.

Maybe I didn't like her as much as I thought I did. I bit my tongue and took another sip of coffee, swirling its bitter velvet darkness over my palate with the truth I had to face.

Rae didn't want to help me, and that made sense. We hadn't known each other that long, after all. And maybe Eve hadn't gone to her. But the young succubus didn't have many friends in the city. I pitched my voice low, put the weight of my power behind it. "I need you to tell me where she is, Rae. It's important."

But the Presence didn't have the expected effect. Rae's head snapped around, her brows drawing together, and slate-dark clouds billowed up in her desiderata. "I told you I didn't know. Why are you pushing this?"

I sat back in my seat. How had that failed? I frowned, tried again. "If I don't find her, she could be in a lot of danger out there."

"That sounds like a threat." Her hand lay on the table. Now it clenched into a fist, knuckles stark white against her lightly tanned skin.

"The danger isn't from me, and you know it." I kept my voice even with considerable effort, thrown off by her resistance and her aggressive response.

"Could have fooled me." The tension in her pose didn't lessen as she stared me down.

Damn, but the woman had the build of a trained martial artist. How had I missed that level of athleticism? But I hadn't hung out with her like this on a casual weekend before. She usually covered her arms in a nod to professionalism—never mind the piercings and the combat boots—and her goth rocker aesthetic had distracted me from the strength beneath. She could probably put up a good fight even against my cambion strength.

Especially if I let her desiderata distract me.

Shit, she had me going, not the other way around. Who was this woman, really? And why the hell did she not bat an eyelash at my powers of persuasion?

I took a long, steadying breath, and eased off on my Presence. "I didn't mean to upset you." I chose my words carefully, my power held in neutral. "I'm just worried about her. That's all."

"Right." But she didn't sound convinced. She rose, pulling on her jacket with abrupt movements.

"Wait."

"No," she said. "I'm not here to play games."

"Neither am I." I stood, too. "I don't think you understand. Eve is on the hook for multiple murders. She's innocent, but they'll charge her as an adult. They don't care that she's a minor. They're out for blood. We're talking about a young woman's life here."

That got through to her. She paused, hands shoved deep in her studded bomber's jacket, and her face twisted with conflict.

"Fine," she said at last. "If you want to help this girl, Lily, I suggest you do a little digging into the men of Delta Alpha Mu. Those are the ones they think she killed, right?"

I gaped at her. "What do you mean?"

She pulled a folded piece of copier paper from her pocket, turned it over in her fingers. The paper crumpled under the force of her grip and trembled just a little.

"I mean," she said, "that there are probably a lot of people out there who might have wanted those guys dead. And they might have deserved it."

I frowned at her, and she dropped the paper on the table. The wind seized at it, but I whipped my hand out and snagged it before it could blow away. The storm had risen in Rae's desiderata again, too. For a moment, the bright midday around us seemed to darken, as though a cloud had blown over the sun.

"Who wanted them dead?" I couldn't look directly at her. The roar of the storm in her aura occluded her. It made her a negative space, a bleeding slash in the world.

A few years back, when a solar eclipse transfixed the West Coast, I stared straight into the sun while it vanished. It wasn't safe, of course. But what was my fast-healing cambion's blood good for if I didn't get to break the rules now and again, especially if the only person harmed would be myself? I let the thin circle of light sear itself into my retinas, while around me the daylight faltered, the wind blew cold, and humans *ooh*ed and *ah*ed into their shadowboxes.

The afterimages lingered longer than expected. My eyes healed in a few hours, the thin white crescents fading from my field of vision, but the memory of the dark disk within them stayed with me.

That's how Rae looked in that moment, like a solar eclipse, a space where light should dwell, but did not. A brief vision of what the sky might become if the sun winked out.

And then her face cleared. The storm passed. "I didn't give you this." She folded her arms, expression remote. "It's all confidential. Do you understand?"

I nodded, tucking the paper away, groping for words. "Rae—"

"Don't," she snapped, and turned on her heel, striding away down the boardwalk.

When her tall figure had diminished among the crowds of tourists walking the beach, I drew out the paper she'd given me and unfolded it.

At first, the words on it made no sense. It was a page from an official investigation report with the university's seal on it. The investigation purported to determine whether the fraternity brothers at the Delta Alpha Mu house had sexually assaulted an unspecified number of women students over the course of several years. In the end, the dean of students had found no credible evidence to support the allegations, and considered the matter sealed and closed.

The men in question had experienced no consequences at all. That was, until they turned up dead.

I glanced upward, but the sky over the Peninsula was blue, for once, without a cloud anywhere.

15

SHAME THE DEVIL

I spent the afternoon walking the shoreline, scanning the weekend crowds for slender young women with golden hair and sullen expressions. Eve had told me she wanted to go to the beach, after all. But she didn't show.

I didn't harbor much more than a faint hope of finding her. Even if Rae's claim that she didn't have Eve in a safe house somewhere proved true, a teenager could disappear into anonymity in San Francisco all too easily. She could have gone a thousand places. She could have hopped on a plane back to New York City by now.

Or she could be lying in a ditch, slowly crumbling to dust.

No. I wouldn't believe it. Ariel's daughter had more resilience than that. She had street smarts, more than I had ever learned. She made it out here on her own. She'd survived for six months or more on nothing but her wits, her Presence, and whatever her father had set aside for her in human money.

Why didn't I ask her where she'd stayed before? Why didn't I find out if she had friends here?

I took the Muni back uptown, growing more morose with every stop. The incongruence of my encounter with Rae nagged at me. How had she resisted my Presence? That made two humans in my orbit lately who seemed immune to my powers, and the novelty was wearing off fast.

Only three possibilities occurred to me, none of which I liked much. But none of them struck me as exceptionally likely, either. I liked that even less.

The first possibility was that Rae herself was a demon. This seemed unlikely because she had a desiderata, and a strong one at that. Demons didn't have desideratas. To have one of those, you had to have a human soul, whatever that meant. Or at least, that's how I understood it.

Then again, Ariel had taught me most things I believed about our kind. Half a year later, with his body crumbled to dust and his Claim on me reversed, I was still discovering new lies he'd told. I put my demon Rae theory in the category of improbable but not out of the question.

The second possibility was that Rae, like me and like Tobias, was a cambion. Tobias had a desiderata, a nasty one that required more proximity to detect than your average human, but no more execrable than your average asshole. And Ariel had claimed I had one too. He certainly seemed able to read it.

I could only tell whether Rae had half-demon powers by touching her, and after today, I put low odds on that ever happening. And cambions were vanishingly rare. Or at least, that's what Ariel had led me to believe.

I slumped in the grubby Muni seat. Once again, I couldn't rule it out.

The third possibility was that Rae, like Sebastian, was fully human, but claimed by one of us, making her immune to the charms of other demons or cambions. I should have liked this option the best, but I didn't, not one bit.

She hadn't pulled a Presence—I would have recognized that—but the power in her desiderata had reacted in an unusual way. Hell, maybe I should have tried to touch her. Just an experiment, to test whether she pulled from me, or I from her.

My skin tingled, pulse thumping, and I closed my hand, digging nails into my palm. The faintly sour recycled air on the Muni bus clogged my throat, claustrophobic and rich with human stink.

She'd done a real number on me. Scared me, sure, but something drew me to her, too. She'd gotten into my head and now I couldn't get her out, like a song I couldn't stop humming even though I couldn't decide if I liked it.

I fingered the wrinkled sheet of paper in my pocket. She seemed upset about the investigation that had come to nothing, if "upset" was the right word for a desiderata like a solar storm. And Safe Haven did crisis work for sexual assault survivors. That would explain the secrecy. One of her clients must have given her that report.

One of her clients might have killed them. Damn it. I shouldn't have let her walk away like that.

I wasn't sure I could have stopped her.

The announcement of my stop crackled over the bus's PA system, making me jump. I checked my phone for texts from Danny: nothing. Eve must not have come back yet.

I climbed down from the Muni with slow, unwilling steps and trudged the three blocks uphill, brain still churning out increasingly outlandish possibilities.

But my carefully assembled logic crumbled when I stepped inside the house. Danny met me at the door, her face grim and determined, as if girding herself for a terrible task.

"Lily, come have a seat," she said. "We need to talk."

In the living room, I eased myself into the big, overstuffed chair in the corner, while Danny and Berry sat down on the couch next to each other, but on opposite ends. Berry stared down at her hands, saying nothing, looking at no one. Danny cast a sidelong glance at her, and her expression darkened further. Their desideratas swirled with a discordant buzz, out of sync with each other and agitated every time I moved.

A sharp pang tightened my chest. My housemates had fought, and they rarely fought. They hardly even argued. But the tension and icy temperatures in the space between them told me this one had been bad. The cold intensified when I entered the room, and it frosted over when I sat down.

No need to ask what they'd fought about, then.

"What's up?" I asked, when neither of them seemed inclined to break the tension.

"It's about Eve," Danny said.

I let out a breath. Was that all? "I can't find her. I looked everywhere I could think of. But she could be anywhere."

"No. It's not that." Danny spoke in a slow, deliberate cadence, like she'd rehearsed the words and wanted to make sure she got every one right. "You didn't tell me she was wanted in the Frat Row murder case."

"She wasn't! They hadn't filed charges. They still haven't. Not for that, at least."

"That's bull, Lil, and you know it. It's only a matter of time." Danny's frustration flickered around her in tongues of fire. "I'm on the Forensics team for that case. I signed off on two of the autopsy reports. But now I have a conflict, thanks to you, and if this cluster of a case goes to trial, they could impeach my testimony. Did you think about that?"

"No." I bowed my head. "I didn't."

Danny shook her head, her mouth twisting. Disgusted with me, or herself? The turmoil in her desiderata didn't give much of a hint. "I knew she looked familiar. But she fooled me, didn't she? She messed with my head and made me forget I'd seen her picture in the reports."

My mouth dropped open. "Danny. Don't."

"It's okay, Lily." Berry's Arctic tones told me it wasn't okay at all. "I know."

"We watched the news this morning," Danny said. "Everyone knows what she is."

"The video." I sat back in the chair, the breath knocked out of me. "The cops leaked it. Those bastards. How bad is it?"

"Viral bad." Danny grimaced. "It's gone national. And it's getting the twenty-four-hour three ring media circus treatment. They slap the still of her face up on the cable channels every ten minutes. Her real face."

"Damn it." I clenched my fists in my lap. "She shouldn't be out there. It's not safe."

"I know. It really, really sucks." Danny set her jaw. "But that's not what we wanted to talk to you about."

"Oh." Shit. "Okay. What is it?"

Danny reached out and took Berry's hand. Berry squeezed it, stealing a glance at her fiancée for the first time that afternoon.

"For us, it's not about her being a demon." Danny took a deep breath. "Even though I don't like it, I understand why she pulled those tricks on us. She was just trying to survive." She stopped, her gaze sliding away from mine and fixing on her hand, intertwined with Berry's.

"You're doing good, D," Berry said in her gentle voice. "Tell her what you said to me earlier. She needs to hear it from you."

"The problem that I have—that *we* have—" Danny swallowed audibly. "It's what you did that really bothers me, Lily. You lied to me. You lied to us, and you put us all in danger. It was a lie of omission, but it was still a lie."

Heat buzzed in my face and neck, and my gut twisted. "About Eve, you mean."

"The worst part about it is that you expected me to lie to Berry for you—and I did. That's not okay, either. I know we've been friends a long time, but..."

Cold sweat trickled down my spine. "I didn't ask you to lie."

"No." Danny sighed. "You didn't have to ask. That's part of the problem. I've kept your secrets for a long time. But Berry will be my wife soon. I owe it to her to be honest with her. Especially where it concerns her safety."

"What are you saying?" The words trembled from me, flat with panic. This wasn't about Eve at all anymore.

Danny shot another look at Berry, who frowned, her eyes darting between us. "She needs to know, Lil."

"It's not your secret to tell!" I balled my fists again, pulse thudding like the heavy beat of wings.

"I know," Danny said. "But it's her house. It's her *life*. And it's about to be our marriage. I don't want to screw it up with lies right out of the gate. If you won't tell her, I'll have to."

"Danny." Worry crackled in Berry's voice. "What are you talking about?"

My short laugh held no mirth. "She's going to think we had an affair, Dan."

"What?" Danny's eyes went wide. "Shit. Berry, it's not that. Nothing like that."

"No," I said, sardonic. "It's much, much worse."

"But it's not," Danny said. "It's not that big a deal. Or it is, but only because you're not being honest about it."

"Wanna bet?" I flung myself back into the chair, arms crossed. Berry looked thoroughly freaked now, and I hadn't even said the thing yet. Softening my tone, I met her eyes. "Berry, you're a really awesome person, you know that, right? I like you a lot. I'm glad you and Danny found each other. You're good for her, and you've always been nothing but good to me."

"Okay." Berry looked from me to Danny, her trepidation obvious.

Danny shifted on the couch. "Lily…"

I overrode her, ruthless now. "In case you decide to kick me out of the house, I just want you to know those things. And that I won't hold it against you." If Danny wanted to force this out of me, she didn't get to have regrets at this late juncture.

"Lily, stop being a jerk," Danny said.

"I'm trying." I could still get out of this. I could weave a glamour around this moment, cloud their minds with happy thoughts and more happy lies. Then they wouldn't think I was a jerk at all. I had that power.

I didn't use it. I inhaled, long and slow, and waited for Berry to meet my eyes.

"Yes," I said. "Eve is a demon. But the truth is, so am I."

"I don't understand." Berry stared at me, her mouth twitching like she wanted to laugh, like all this was just some joke to her.

I wished it was. "Yes, we exist. No, we're not just a tabloid rumor. We don't drink blood, and we can't be exorcised. I hope that helps."

"But you seem so—I don't know." She waved her hands in the air, as if she hoped to pluck the right words out of the air. "So *normal.*"

"Thanks, I think." I bared my teeth in a mirthless grin. "Are you going to tell me it's just a phase next? Ask me if I've tried *not* being a demon?"

Berry winced. "That's not what I meant."

"Lily, enough," Danny said. "Honey, she's making it sound worse than it is. She's half-human."

Her words washed over me like icy water, too close to Sebastian's from the night before. "What the *fuck*, Dan." I should have seen this coming. A keen ache seized my heart and roughened my voice. "Worse than it is? What if I were all demon? Would you still be my friend, or would it be a bridge too far?"

"You know I would," she said, eyes wide.

"Stop it, both of you." Berry's soft command carried an edge that silenced both of us. "I won't sugar-coat it for you, Lily. This is a lot to absorb. But Danny's right—it's not about what you are. I mean, I do have questions about that, too. But I'm going to leave that be. My real concern is the same as it would for any human."

I bit my lip and dropped my head, waiting on her judgment. "I'm listening."

"This is about trust," Berry said. "You've been keeping a lot of secrets and telling a lot of half-truths. Not just with me, but with Danny, too. And what we don't know can hurt us."

"I know." A lump rose in my throat. "It's not fair to either of you. So where does that leave us, then?"

Danny and Berry exchanged uncomfortable glances, and Danny cleared her throat. "We don't want to leave you without a place to stay."

"We'd give you thirty days' notice, of course," Berry said. "But for right now, maybe it would be best..."

Mother of monsters, this was really happening. They didn't want me here. "I get it." My acquiescence came out flat and dull, the numbness of defeat overtaking me. "It's fine. I'll figure something out."

Danny said, "Lily, I—"

"No." I stood up. "Berry's right. I crossed a line. A lot of lines. And I want you both to feel safe. I want you to *be* safe."

"I didn't want it to be like this." Danny had gone ashen beneath her tan, her eyes overbright, her desiderata awash with salt-sea tears she wouldn't shed in front of me.

"I know, Dan." I mustered a smile for her. "Neither did I. But it'll be okay. We're still friends, right?"

"Of course." But her answering smile didn't reach her eyes, and her energy sunk into a vortex of conflict.

I'd lied to Danny, and now she was lying to me. The hollow place inside my chest yawned, bottomless. In the last twenty-four hours I'd succubused Sebastian and hurt him badly. I'd lost the girl I'd promised to protect, and my living situation had dissolved. I couldn't stick around to watch my best friend slip away from me, too.

"I'll be out by tonight," I muttered, and fled for my garret room to pack.

16

VERTIGO

"What are you looking at?" I hissed.

In the twilight, the crow fluffing its feathers on the gate of Sebastian's driveway cocked its head, considering me with one shiny black bead of an eye. It seemed unfazed by my shooing gestures. I didn't have a problem with birds, but lately, they seemed to show up everywhere: preening themselves on the Muni sign a block from Danny and Berry's earlier, congregating on the grassy slope of Mission Dolores Park, swirling in a cloud around the big radio antenna atop Twin Peaks.

Not to mention the one tattooed on Rae McGuire's well-defined bicep.

I tapped Sebastian's code into the gate, and it swung open, a silent invitation. At the movement, the bird cawed twice and took flight, vanishing into the tall oaks that screened Sebastian's house from the street.

I slung my bag over my shoulder, hunched a bit against an imagined avian gaze, and trudged up the driveway toward the house.

I had a change of clothes and some essentials in my bag. After our talk, Danny had hovered around, silent and apologetic, while Berry disappeared into their shared bedroom, having had her fill of confrontation for the next year or so. I didn't have to leave immediately—they kept telling me that I could stop by anytime and Danny had promised to take good care of Delilah until I found a place to stay that allowed pets—but I didn't want to show my face there for a while.

With no job and no place to live, I had limited options. My text to Sebastian had elicited an unusually slow response, but eventually it came. Of course, I could stay as long as I liked.

He probably loved that I asked to stay, especially after our fight. But this meant becoming even more dependent on his largesse. And besides, there was that whole thing about him being *already married.*

At the top of the driveway, I stopped in the shadow of the huge cypresses that screened the property from the street. A sporty white convertible I didn't recognize sat in front of the big, sprawling, beautiful house with its modern lines and big bay windows, the yellow light from within spilling from behind filmy white curtains.

Right on cue, the front door opened, and voices echoed from within. I froze, drawing back under the trees.

A woman stepped out of Sebastian's house. She was tall, blonde, and dressed in effortless style. Her sparkling heeled sandals and white sundress set off her perfectly tanned and sculpted legs. My jeans, sweater, and running shoes made me look like a slob next to her.

She had her back to me, her voice pitched too low to make out, but her laughter carried across the expanse of the lawn. She reached a hand toward the door.

Sebastian stepped out, taking the hand she offered him. He looked down at the blonde woman with an unreadable expression. Even at this distance, a whisper of his desiderata reached me, complex and multi-faceted, deep and dark and rich. Then she dipped her head to the side with a smile, exposing her profile, and recognition punched me in the solar plexus.

It was Helena Ritter. I swallowed against the sharp ache in my throat. Did he still love her? Had our rift shifted something between them?

Only one way to find out. I stepped from the shadows, a desperate demon with not much left to lose.

"Sebastian?" My voice trembled, but I held my chin high.

What had Eve said? *Never let them see you're afraid.* A lesson from Ariel, maybe, but just because he was a bastard and a murderer didn't mean he wasn't right sometimes.

Sebastian's head snapped around at my voice, his energy fragmenting, taking flight like a flock of startled birds. "Lily? What are you doing here?"

"You said I could come over." I stopped at the bottom of the front steps. "You didn't warn me *she*'d be here."

Helena glanced between the two of us with an expression of open curiosity. "You didn't tell me she was coming." She addressed this to Sebastian, who looked flustered.

"I don't have to *stay*." I also addressed this to Sebastian, pointedly.

"No, no, it's fine." He flushed. "Helena was just leaving."

Helena favored him with a long look that made him flush deeper. I almost felt sorry for him in his discomfort. His desiderata flickered and darted, reaching for me, pulling back, tentatively flaring in Helena's direction. Poor man. But I still shrank inside at his conflict, at what it could mean for us.

Then Helena swept down the steps. She paused before me, giving me a slow once-over, her immaculate eyebrows raised. I met her assessing gaze and bit down hard on the temptation to send her running with my Presence.

"It's good to see you again, Mrs. Ritter." I elected to kill her with kindness, or at least courtesy.

Helena Ritter laughed. Her desiderata flashed around her, the first time I'd sensed it, bitter and harsh as sandpaper. "Mrs. Ritter? Hardly." She cast a sideways, narrow-eyed glance back up to where Sebastian stood on the porch.

"Helena, don't." In the shadows of the porch, Sebastian's expression had changed, remote now, lips pressed into a thin line, but his desiderata still churned.

Helena didn't say anything more. She favored me with a long, piercing look, her energy serrated and sharp as ever. Then she tossed her head and strode down the driveway to the white convertible parked there. The engine growled and she spun away in a squeal of tires toward the gate.

I sagged, suddenly exhausted. From the porch, Sebastian's sigh was audible. "I'm really sorry about that," he said.

"Well, I mean." I didn't come up the stairs. He would have to invite me. "She *is* your wife. I suppose she has the right to visit."

He didn't move, staring after her. Down the driveway, the gate clanged shut, and the convertible's engine roared away. "She certainly thinks she does."

"What was she doing here?"

"Nothing useful." His energy darkened, shrouding his essence from me.

One of us was going to have to break first, but it wasn't going to be me. "You two looked pretty friendly."

That seemed to reach him. He made a noise in his throat, something between a snort and a cough. "You're jealous." It seemed to lift his mood, a half-smile tugging his mouth up on one side. "Are you going to come up?"

Aha. "If you want me to." Victorious, I scaled the steps, but halted before I reached him.

After a beat, he went in ahead of me, holding open the door with a quirked brow that said he'd caught on to my games. "You didn't tell me what happened."

"Danny and Berry kicked me out." The words floated out before I could stop them. The finality of saying it out loud shook me. I blinked back tears.

He stared at me. "They *what*? Why?"

"They decided they didn't feel safe with me living there anymore." I couldn't look at him, so I stared at the scuffed toes of my running shoes. "Because I'm a demon. And because Eve...I lied to them about Eve."

"I see." Sebastian frowned, but he didn't say anything else. His desiderata offered me nothing but conflict. The exchange with Helena had upset him more than he wanted to admit.

"Thanks for taking me in." His beautiful home made for the nicest homeless shelter in the Peninsula for sure. "I literally had nowhere else to go, so..."

"Good to know I'm the haven of last resort." His energy shifted, sharper now, but aimed at himself, not me. "Why don't you make yourself comfortable? I need to make a phone call."

"Okay." Disappointment welled up, and I swallowed it back down. What had I expected, that he would sweep me off my feet the moment I stepped inside? We hadn't talked about what happened the night before. We hadn't really talked at all. And I had little to offer besides danger and my own self-doubt.

He disappeared upstairs. I dropped my bag in the hall and collapsed on the couch, which probably cost more than my law degree. It enveloped me, its upholstery soft and buttery. Now that I was finally alone, I couldn't hold back the tears.

What a week. I'd made a mess of everything I'd tried to do. I didn't get the job I wanted, I leaped at the opportunity to hunt my own kind, and I'd tried to help Eve but only made things worse.

Shit. I yelled at Sebastian's father. That happened. Right before I blew up my living situation, scared away the girl I wanted to save, and alienated the only other person who could possibly help me save her.

A memory of Rae's desiderata clung in the back of my throat, petrichor and ozone like an oncoming storm. The way she'd darkened out of my demon sight.

What did it mean? Did it mean anything? Ira, too, somehow evaded my senses, and Sebastian's desiderata sometimes obscured him too, like it had on the porch. And he was human, if still a mystery to me at the moment. So maybe it meant nothing at all.

Speaking of Sebastian, what was taking him so long? I crept down the hall to the foot of the stairs. His voice floated faint to my ears from above, tight with strain.

"Greg, she'll take me for everything I have. You don't know what she's capable of."

Greg? I knew his attorney, Greg Greyson, from my former job and from the time I almost indicted him for murder. But who were they discussing?

Sebastian's voice grew louder, than softer again, rhythmic footsteps punctuating his words as he paced. "No. Last night, with Lily—you don't understand. She's not stable. She could do a lot of damage."

I stiffened, the import sinking into me like icy claws, grasping for my core. He was talking about me, and he was right. I wasn't stable. I could do a lot of damage. I had hurt him, and now he feared me.

My vision swam. I groped for my bag and swung it over my shoulder, banging my way out the front door and down the winding driveway.

Behind me, the door opened, and hurried steps pursued me. "Lily, wait! Let me explain."

"Don't bother," I mumbled, and broke into a run.

I didn't need Sebastian. I didn't need Danny. I had a government expense account, and I knew how to use it.

I didn't need anyone.

In the end, I did the only thing that made sense, and what I probably should have done in the first place instead of running to Sebastian for help. I gave the rideshare driver the address of the Four Seasons Hotel downtown. What better way to use my expense account then get myself a pricey room where I could wallow comfortably in my self-pity?

I raided the minibar, pouring all the tiny bottles into a water glass and topping it off with a splash of Coke for the world's worst Long Island Iced Tea. Sebastian could have told me exactly how to mix one, but I made do without his expertise and downed half the drink in one swallow. It burned all the way down and settled in my stomach with the uneasy heat of bad choices and future regrets. *Perfect.*

Not ready to think about Sebastian just yet, I pulled the bedraggled white feather from my billfold and turned it over in my hands.

I am Battle-Crow and Justice, she'd said. *I am Wrath and its guardian. I am Nightmare and Storm-Rider, Queen of the Phantoms. The one I ride now calls me Morrighu...*

"The one you ride," I muttered. "What the hell does that mean?"

I'd never met anything like her, this alleged goddess who changed shape and flew away like a bird. She'd used some creepy magic trick to extract this single white feather from my throat, and then she let me live. And a few days ago, I'd stood in the doorway of a murder scene and watched Danny pull black feathers from a dead boy's mouth.

That couldn't be a coincidence.

She had something to do with the murders. She had to. The white feather meant she spared me. Black feathers meant something else. She'd found them guilty of something deserving death and executed them.

Flopped on the giant bed with its pristine white coverlet, I paged through the channels on the big screen TV until I found the classic movie channel. They had a Hitchcock marathon running, and I drifted off into sleep to the uneasy orchestration and familiar San Francisco set pieces of *Vertigo*.

Huge dark wings pursued me in my dreams, drumming like the pulse of a giant heart. I fled from them through a maze of high-ceilinged corridors and found myself somewhere familiar: the city courthouse.

The heavy doors swung open. The lawyers packed into the courtroom turned to stare at me, and my face flushed hot.

"All rise," snapped the bailiff, a tall woman with jet-black hair and piercing eyes. The murmurs fell silent.

The judge swanned into the room. His black robes billowed behind him like night-drenched pinions. His hair was tousled gold, his eyes glowed amber, and the beauty of his face would make angels weep.

"But you're supposed to be dead," I said into the silence.

"Am I?" A supercilious smile played around Ariel's full lips, and he took his seat in judgment with a flourish of sleeves.

"The court calls item number thirteen on page thirteen," the bailiff said in her harsh, ringing voice. "Defendant Knight, Lily. Please approach the bench."

I hadn't come here to represent a client. I was the one standing trial.

The aisle stretched before me for miles, and I marched for an eternity under the burning gazes of my peers. Finally, I stood at the podium and glanced back. Would any of them step forward and argue my case? But no one did.

"How do you plead, Lilith?" Ariel's eyes glinted, mocking me.

I opened my mouth to shape the words "Not guilty." But a fierce cry tore from my throat, no human speech but a bird's wild call. A wet warmth slicked my hands, dripping from my fingers to fall in scarlet pools at my feet. In the judge's aerie, a silver stake protruded from Ariel's chest, his face going slack and still, his head slumping down toward the desk.

The thunder of dark wings beat above me. I ducked, expecting a demon stooping over me with a bright sword of justice. But no: a giant crow swooped low, its eyes glowing red as the blood coating my hands.

It cawed again, harsh and wild, and its cry echoed my own. Its talons raked my face.

I ducked and ran, and the bird pursued me, flying low over the gallery behind me. In the judge's chair, a body slumped, bleeding wet and dark over its black gown. A sword pierced its breast, glowing with an ultraviolet light. The body had been Ariel's, before. But now the face looked just like mine.

With a strangled sob, I fled past the podium, flinging open the door to chambers—

And stepped through it into the breathless air and restless silence of Tonepah Basin's boundless desert night. The ruins of the old internment camp rose around me like standing stones.

I stumbled forward. Behind me, the crow called, and sudden light blazed all around, white and blinding, as if a spotlight fell over me. I squeezed my eyes shut against the glare. The force of an impact vibrated through my arms to my shoulders from the stake I gripped in both hands.

I hauled my eyes open and stared into Eve's pale, narrow face, into leaf-green eyes wide with shock and pain. Bright blood bubbled from her lips to run over my hands as I drove the silver through her heart. The thunderous wings of the crow bore down inexorably upon me, and I awoke to the insistent vibration of my phone on the nightstand.

On the TV, the movie had switched to the all-too topical *The Birds*. No wonder I'd had nightmares. I groaned and switched it off, rolling over to grab my phone. Sebastian's name showed on the caller ID.

What to do? What to say? If I answered, I would have to explain my quick exit last night and listen to his Perfectly Rational explanations for his tete-a-tete with his ex—no, *current* wife. He would want to have a Mature and Reasonable conversation about our relationship. But I didn't have Mature and Reasonable in me. I only had Angry, Exhausted, and Undercaffeinated, which didn't bode well for a continued relationship if I talked with him right now.

I dropped the phone on the bedside table with a clunk and lay back, massaging my temples. The buzzing stopped and a notification appeared indicating I had several missed calls from him, Danny, and Ira.

Shit. Ira. I needed to talk to Ira, keep him off Eve's trail until I found her first. I should get his take on the Delta Alpha Mu investigatory document Rae had given me.

The last line of the investigative document echoed in my mind. *In conclusion, the University has found no credible evidence to support the allegations. As such, the matter will remain sealed and closed, and will not be reflected in the students' academic records.* And under it, the dean's name and signature, Roger Jeffrey.

Who was it who said never to trust anyone with two first names? Roger seemed like a man who knew where the bodies were buried. Buried, like he'd buried this investigation. I wanted to talk to the accusers, and maybe he could point me in the right direction.

Maybe one of them had sent a bloodthirsty crow goddess after the men who assaulted them got off scot-free.

The Queen of the Phantoms, whatever she was, had come to judge me for a single crime: Ariel's death. But these men had escaped punishment for more than one violation. Did each feather represent an accusation for which she'd found them guilty?

I swallowed hard, throat tickling with the memory of the single feather working its way out of my esophagus. Had the frat boys choked to death on their crimes?

How many feathers? How many victims?

How many suspects with a damn good reason to seek revenge?

17

HELL TO PAY

A few hours, a long ramble through the shadier portions of the internet, and another significant hit on my expense account later, I stood outside an elegant Sea Cliff condominium, ringing the doorbell and waiting for Roger Jeffrey to make an appearance.

He didn't. Nothing stirred inside the house.

Another dead end. Why did I think this would work? He was probably out of town for the weekend, or just had no intention of answering the door.

I started to turn away but stopped short. Above me and to my left, the building had an overhanging balcony, and the French doors leading out to it hung ajar.

"Hello?" I called. "Anyone home?"

No one answered—no human, at least. From a tall cypress towering over the street, the croaking call of a bird floated down to me. The sound brought my dream back in vivid color, and I flinched, my spine tingling with foreboding.

"Hello? Mr. Jeffrey? Anyone home?"

No response. Even the birds stayed silent.

"Fuck," I muttered. I could leave, or call the police, but I didn't have a way to explain to them why I suspected something had gone very wrong inside the house.

I paced down the front walkway, then back again. My kether reserves had regenerated a little after the deficit I incurred by healing Sebastian's injuries and then flying sixty-odd miles back to town, but I didn't trust myself to make a jump up to the balcony right now. Besides, the balcony faced the street, so I would have to run a don't-notice-me Presence at the same time. Both would take something out of me, and given where things stood with Sebastian, I had no guarantee of a power-up any time soon.

Everything I did worked better when I didn't give my power away, even if I did so to fix my own fuckups.

I stared at the door. Ariel and Theo had the ability to phase *through* solid matter, as if their body, like their wings, had an ethereal quality—even though they felt solid enough when I touched them. Despite Theo's less-than-patient tutelage, it still seemed like a good way to break something, possibly my own bones. Or worse, succeed halfway and get stuck. But maybe if I could just reach in and unlock the door...

Closing my eyes, I pushed my fingertips against the painted wood. It yielded not at all. How in the hell did they do it?

It was a trick Ariel had never taught me, had never shown me until he used it against me. And Theo had dropped off the radar once I admitted the government was onto my secret identity. Once again, when it came to my demon abilities, I had no guidance and no teacher. I had no one but myself and my hobbled powers.

Sudden frustration boiled up from the pit of my stomach. So what if someone saw me breaking in? What did I have to lose at this point? Besides, if worse came to worse, I could probably persuade them that I belonged here.

Still, I took a quick, furtive glance around and turned up my Presence to deflect human attention. I'd kicked in doors before, but not in a neighborhood as nice as this one.

Satisfied that no joggers or stroller-pushing moms were looking my way, I reared back and drove my foot into the door, just under the lock.

At least I still had some of my demon strength. The frame splintered with a gratifying crash and the door swung askew on its hinges.

I slipped inside into a dim interior. A fast-paced beeping from the hallway told me I'd triggered a security system. I would have to move quickly, or the cops would get here before I learned anything useful.

I probably should have contacted Ira before I went about violating Mr. Jeffrey's Fourth Amendment rights. But no one shouted or came to confront me. The house lay still. Maybe Jeffrey was out of town, after all.

I picked my way inside the house around splinters of the wounded door. The first floor of the condo yielded little of interest until I got to the stairs, and my steps halted of their own accord.

There, in the stairwell, hung a graduation photo showing the dean in his mortar board and the sash of a USF class from twenty-odd years ago. And he stood with a laughing group of college men under the eaves of the Delta Alpha Mu house.

He wore their colors, red and black, in front of the same house where the men he'd shielded from consequences had met their ends decades later.

And now I understood why. He was a Delta Alpha Mu alum. The men who died had been his brothers. That was why he'd protected them.

Behind me, the security system's beeping sped up. It hastened my pace up the stairs in search of the room that led out onto the balcony I'd spotted from below.

I found it behind the first door on the left after I came up the stairs.

The alarm reached the end of its countdown as I stood frozen on the threshold. It shrieked its fury, echoing up the stairs and down the empty hall. The metallic smell of copper laced with ozone coated the roof of my mouth.

There was a bed in the room, and a figure lay sprawled there, skin bloodless and pale, eyes open, staring at the ceiling. His mouth was open too, and black feathers spilled out of it. They scattered across the bed's rumpled sheets, drifted over the floor, and eddied in the breeze that swept in from the wide-flung French windows.

Well, there went my best lead. I slumped against the wall and wished I felt more surprised.

Roger Jeffrey had not left town after all.

The SFU Dean of Students had left this world behind for good.

Standing in the doorway of Roger Jeffrey's master bedroom, the plainclothes officer frowned at me. "Tell me again how you came to discover the body, Ms. Knight."

She was only the fourth cop who had asked me that same question in the thirty-five minutes or so since the first responders had arrived, and I didn't recognize her. She looked young, about my age, with glowing skin and dark blond hair pulled back in a no-nonsense ponytail. Her menswear-style suit and white silk blouse that made me feel like a slob in my day-old jeans and sweater.

I craned my neck to look around her. "Where's Agent Delaney? I'm telling you, this is related to the Delta Alpha Mu murders. I need to talk to him about—"

"I'm in charge of this investigation." She folded her arms, expression forbidding. "Meghan North. Answer the question, please."

"Nice to meet you, Ms. North." I didn't offer her my hand, and she didn't appear inclined to shake on it, anyway. "I'm Lily Knight."

"*You're* Lily Knight—?" The officer's brows shot upward toward her hairline. "SFPD warned me about you."

"Warned you about what?"

"They said your methods are…um…unorthodox." She averted her gaze from mine, aimed it to the right of me, out the open French doors to where the forensics team went over the balcony inch by inch. When she spoke again, her tone was measured, careful, unruffled. "Regardless, I still need you to tell me what you were doing at Mr. Jeffrey's house."

I refocused on her. My vagueness and deflections didn't seem to affect her as much as expected. "I told the uniform already. I came here to talk to him about the SFU fraternity murders."

She fidgeted with her jacket sleeves, pulling them lower over her wrists. "You must be aware that your actions constitute breaking and entering, trespassing, and tampering with an active crime scene. Can you explain yourself?"

I couldn't, seeing as how I'd kicked down the door because I was sleep-deprived, kether-short, and didn't have a lot to lose. "I didn't *know* it was a crime scene."

"Then why did you feel it was urgent enough to break down the door?"

I squinted at her. "I heard something." Whatever she had heard about me—from Ira, maybe—must have really spooked her. I smoothed out my Presence, embodying a responsible citizen who acted out of concern, not criminal intent. "It made me think something might have happened to him, that he needed help. And he doesn't—didn't seem like the kind of man who would miss an appointment."

"You heard something," the detective repeated, her cadence skeptical. "Something like what? A scream? A shout?" Her glance flickered to my face, then away again.

I couldn't tell her I'd heard a crow caw and it made me think of a dream I'd had, let alone a murderous visitor of my own. I laid the Presence on thicker, a model of trustworthiness. And after all, I hadn't lied to her once. "A—well. I thought I heard someone cry out."

"You're saying he was alive when you got here?" Her desiderata seemed clouded and hard to read, but her tone didn't hide her intense skepticism.

"I don't know. All I know is that I had a bad feeling about him."

"You had a bad feeling." The way she repeated my words, with that heavy layer of sarcasm, made it clear I was getting nowhere. "What kind of feeling is bad enough to make you break down the door of a man who, if I'm not mistaken, you had never met before?"

Why didn't my Presence work on this woman? I dialed it up a notch, focusing harder on the influence I wanted to project. I was an upright member of society, an attorney with nothing to hide, scrupulously ethical. Or at least I was trying my best in a bad situation. *Damn it, that won't do. I have to own it.* "Are you accusing me of something, Officer North? Am I under arrest?"

She snorted. "If I were detaining you, I assure you that you'd know about it. I'm only trying to get to the bottom of things. You're just one of the strange factors in this very strange case, if you haven't noticed."

I glanced behind me at the body on the bed. "I did notice." Another detail nagged at the back of my mind, something I should have picked it up immediately, but then again, I had a lot on my mind today. "You said SFPD warned you about me. What division are you from again?"

For the first time, Meghan North smiled at me. She had a shockingly nice smile. Her eyes sparkled like she had a private joke on the tip of her tongue. "Oh, Miss Knight." She reached in her jacket's breast pocket. "Did I forget to tell you?" And she flipped her badge open to display the letters "FBI."

Shit. "You're with the feds, too?" My mind raced, and I took an involuntary step backwards into the room. "But Ira said this was still a local matter. Officially, at least."

But Eve had come here from New York. *How much did they know?*

"Ira Delaney doesn't know everything," North said, her tone icy. "And you need to come with me." She grabbed me by the forearm and pulled me out of the room into the hallway.

A sudden burning chill set in on the top of my hand. Half in shock, I let her drag me along. My limbs tingled, numb and heavy, and black spots swirled at the edges of my vision.

"Hey!" A familiar voice broke through the haze that had descended on me. "Where are you taking her?"

"Danny?" With difficulty, I broke away from North's iron grasp. My knees wobbled, and I braced myself against the wall. "What are you doing here?"

"This is my job, you dolt. I should ask you the same question." Danny's face swam into view, her brow lowered, her desiderata stormy. I winced, but her anger wasn't for me.

She gripped me by the shoulder, and I considered yanking away from her, too, but it seemed like it would take a lot of energy. I liked it here against the wall. It was a good wall. Solid, steady, and incorruptible, like my best friend, who now glared past me at Agent North.

"What the hell did you do to her?" Danny demanded.

"Me? I moved her away from an active crime scene." But North's voice resonated with smug satisfaction, like she'd scored a point. I raised my head—it took considerable effort—and found her regarding me with more than the expected level of interest.

"She's FBI," I managed to croak, but that didn't answer anything at all. Had she done something to me? It seemed obvious now that Danny had asked the question. Nausea twisted my insides, burning the back of my throat, and I choked it back down.

Agent North smiled again. Why had I thought I liked her smile? She held up one hand, then the other, and pulled her sleeves down with the air of a magic trick to expose the wide silver bands she wore on her wrists.

They looked like Wonder Woman's gauntlets, only evil. I flinched, and Danny swore. No wonder I couldn't read her desiderata.

"Something you'd like to tell me, Miss Knight?" North said.

"She's allergic, you *jerk.*" Danny thrust her head forward, shoulders squaring off, fierce and ready to fight for me. It sparked a tiny flame of warmth in my chest.

All the same...I dropped my head back against the wall with an audible thump. "I think she knows that, Dan. I think that's the whole point."

"Indeed," Meghan North said. "I know your little secret, Ms. Knight. Or at least, I suspected as much, and I came prepared." But she lowered her arms and clasped her hands behind her back.

With the silver out of sight, I relaxed a fraction and rubbed the back of my hand with my forearm to avoid touching the welt with my bare fingers. The knit fabric of my sweater scratched like sandpaper over my sore skin. The rapidly swelling blisters broke and wept at the pressure, and I dragged the sleeve down over my fingers to hide the ugly sore. "What do you want? Are you investigating me?" If so, why hadn't she arrested me yet?

"I didn't get called in on this case for you," Agent North said. "I'm here because of the girl. You're an unanticipated complication, but a very interesting one to me and my superiors."

Great. They *were* investigating me. My vision cleared enough for me to straighten up, though I kept my good hand ready to brace myself if another wave of dizziness came over me. My wrist hurt like hell. Since when did cops wear silver to repel my kind?

"Listen to me, Agent North." This was my chance to make my case before the feds screwed up Eve's life more than it already was. "Eve is innocent. She didn't kill those young men, and she didn't kill Roger Jeffrey."

Another suspicion wormed its way into my brain. Was silver-wearing why I couldn't read Ira? Or Rae? How many people around me knew my secret and shielded their true selves from my senses, stripping my only means of defense and camouflage away?

"What makes you so sure?" Agent North frowned at me.

"I'd like to know that myself," a new voice drawled from the stairs.

Speak of the devil, so to speak. "Ira!" I turned too fast for my silver-addled balance and had to brace myself against the wall again. White sparks flashed in my vision like my own private fireworks show.

"I apologize for my tardiness. I got here as soon as I could." Ira's gaze traveled between us, dispassionate and curious. "Agent North, this is my operative. Why have you damaged her?"

Meghan North's mouth flattened into a line. "She contaminated the scene and obstructed my investigation. Sir."

"I see." Ira raised an eyebrow at me. "Is this true, Knight?"

"I found the body," I said. "It's *my* investigation. Well, our investigation. Mine and Ira's." Ugh. My wooziness wasn't helping my coherence or my case.

"And you have a theory of why young Eve didn't do this," he prompted me.

"Right. My theory." I shifted myself around to face Agent North and lowered my voice so that no nosy cops would overhear. "I don't know how much you know about demons, but Eve is a succubus. Succubi don't drink blood. And they don't do that—feather thing."

"You're saying there is more than one kind of demon?" Agent North looked less skeptical and more interested now. "What kind of demon do you think did this?"

The kind that rode in on a thunderstorm with black eyes and a fiery sword. The kind that leaped from a second story window and turned into a crow. The kind that pulled feathers from one's mouth like an absolution.

Only absolution hadn't happened here. I took the signed page of the dean's report out of my pocket. "I think these men died for a reason. I think it has to do with this."

Agent North took the paper from me and frowned at it. "I don't see what this has to do with demons."

"It doesn't," I said. "It has to do with justice, and the lack thereof." My voice took on more resonance, easing into the cadence I used in the courtroom. I turned to Danny. "How many feathers did you find in the DAM boys' mouths? Five each? Ten?"

Her desiderata swirled like a murky and restless sea, protective anger mingled with distrust and confusion. "About that. I'll check back on my reports. Lily—"

I shook my head and hurried on before she could tell me to butt out. "Those feathers stand for crimes. One feather, one crime unpunished."

"And Roger Jeffrey?" Ira inquired. "What did he do?"

"He shielded those boys from the consequences of their actions. And they probably weren't the first." I glanced over my shoulder at the door to the room where Jeffrey had died. The feathers covered the floor in there, swirled like flurries of black snow. Some poor forensics grunt was sweeping them up into evidence bags. "I believe whoever did this held him responsible for every single time he dismissed a sexual assault complaint against one of his fraternity brothers."

"That's an interesting theory," Meghan North said. "But it's quite a logical leap. And I'm not seeing how it exonerates our suspect. She was a young woman who attended a party there. Maybe one of them assaulted her, and she decided to take revenge."

"Eve was never a student at the university," I argued. "She had no way of knowing about the investigations or their outcome. These complaints are from before she even arrived in California."

"May I?" Ira took the page of the report from North, a thoughtful line etched between his brows. After a swift perusal, he pocketed it. "I'd like to see the crime scene, too, if you would, Agent North."

"Of course. Right this way." Agent North gave me a thin, close-lipped smile this time. "We'll be in touch. Don't go on any unscheduled trips, Miss Knight. As of today, you're a person of interest in this investigation."

She stalked back into the bedroom, clearly dismissing me from her presence, and Ira followed her. I abandoned my facade of strength and bit back a groan as I sagged against the wall.

"Are you all right?" Now that we were alone, Danny got right up in my personal space. "What did he mean when he said you were his operative? Lily?"

Shit. That made another thing I hadn't told Danny. "Remember how I said I had a new job?"

"You didn't say you were working with the government on a serial murder case and putting yourself in harm's way." The air around us thickened with her worry and the conflict that still roiled beneath it. She grabbed my sleeve and turned my wrist over, eyes widening. "This looks awful."

"It'll heal." She was too close, too warm, too...everything. Despite her turmoil, her cinnamon and sea-salt desiderata wrapped around me like an embrace I could never accept. I closed my eyes and breathed through my mouth. This dangerous gap always lay between us, waiting to be crossed, and I—

After my brush with silver, I was kether-starved.

"Okay, but at least let me put some antiseptic on it. Or..." Her brown eyes softened, a question and an offer she wouldn't voice.

"No." I sidled along the wall, putting space between us. "Don't touch me. Stay away."

But she followed me. "You're still mad about yesterday, aren't you? Lily, I had to. You know Berry doesn't put her foot down often."

"I know. It's not that." I backpedaled, and in my pocket, my phone chimed, once, twice, three times. Eager for a reason not to hold her gaze, I took it out.

I had a series of text messages from an unknown number.

[Unknown]: *I need to talk to u asap*

[Unknown]: *meet me here plz*

The next text was just a link to an address downtown. I frowned at it. It wasn't far from my hotel.

[Unknown]: *apt 6403*

[Unknown]: *this is Eve btw*

[Unknown]: *come alone no cops!!!*

"What is it?" Danny took another step forward. She reached out as if to take my hand.

My body still weighed down by lethargy in the aftermath of the silver burn, I barely dodged out of range. "Nothing." I swayed and grabbed the banister of the landing for balance. "I have to go."

"Are you sure? You look like death warmed over."

I gritted my teeth and eased myself down the first few steps, leaning heavily on the railing. "I'll be fine."

"You always say that." But Danny let me go, her desiderata colorless as morning fog.

18

SNAKES IN THE GRASS

At the address Eve had sent me, a high-rise dominated the skyline between the Embarcadero and the Bay Bridge, a soaring citadel of blue-tinted glass and steel. It screamed of an in-your-face brand of ostentatious luxury and a brassy confidence that didn't care who knew it.

I did my best to absorb a fraction of that confidence. Striding into the lobby with its vaulted, airy ceiling and tinted glass, I nodded to the uniformed doorman and made a beeline for the elevator like I owned the place. He favored me with a skeptical once-over, but I pretended not to notice. If I acted like I belonged here, my wrinkled sweater and less-than-fresh appearance would mark me as someone who didn't give a fuck, not someone without a home who had slept in my clothes. And if I pulled it off, maybe one of us would believe it.

As my luck would have it, the elevators required a key card. I ignored the sensation of the doorman's eyes boring into the spot between my shoulder blades. It took me a moment to find the building's intercom, tucked in a nook beside the elevators and disguised as a vintage rotary telephone covered in ornate molded scrolling. A directory hung from its booth, and I scrolled through it for Apartment 6403.

When I found the listing, my breath hitched in my chest. Still woozy from the contact with North's silver bracelet, I gripped the side of the intercom booth to steady myself and leaned my forehead against the cool plaster.

The name beside the apartment number read "Ariel DeLeon."

Ariel had lived here? In a way, it made sense. This place fit his tastes to a T. He never did care for the understated. But it implied he had stayed in San Francisco even longer than I thought, hunting me, hunting the other succubi he'd killed. It also suggested that he might have intended to stay.

How on Earth could he have afforded a home away from home like this, while keeping his New York apartment that he'd lived in with Eve? None of the condos in this skyscraper could have sold for less than a million dollars, and I'd never known anyone less inclined toward an earned income than Ariel.

The sixty-fourth floor was near the top of the building, too. Of course, Ariel would pick the highest point in the middle of the city's throbbing heart for his aerie. Maybe he even used it as a point from which to travel the old-fashioned way, on the wing, when he could get away with it. And Ariel usually got away with things—or he had, until I put a stop to that.

My fingers trembling, I picked up the intercom receiver and dialed the unit code. The ringer buzzed. I fiddled with the stretchy cord of the antique phone and waited for an answer.

The ringing continued until it clicked over to an antiquated message machine beep. And then I froze as a ghost spoke in my ear, its timbre melodious, caressing, *seductive* even in recorded form.

"Hello," it said, and I almost dropped the phone. "You've reached the DeLeon residence. No one is available to pick up your call at the moment. So sorry to have missed you! Please leave a message after the tone and I promise I'll make it up to you."

The machine beeped again. I gulped for air and let it out on a long, shaky exhalation.

I'd forgotten what a beautiful voice he had. It was the kind of voice you never wanted to stop listening to, musical and ever so slightly accented. He could probably read the Federal Rules of Civil Procedure out loud from cover to cover and turn it into a sublimely sensual audio experience.

But no, he couldn't, because he was dead, and a murderous asshole to boot. Why was it so hard to remember that sometimes?

Besides, I couldn't think about Ariel now, or examine the chaotic emotions that clawed their way up to coalesce in the back of my throat, a lump I couldn't swallow away. I didn't have space to grieve a demon who didn't deserve my time or my tears. I had his daughter to worry about. Eve was all alone and probably scared out of her mind. She'd been scared enough to run from me before. Would she let me help her now, or would she try to kill me instead?

Coming here could prove my biggest mistake yet. Eve had learned Ariel's lessons of manipulation well. She showed me who she was when she succubused my friends and tried to glamour me.

But she couldn't help that, could she? She didn't know any better. She only knew what she'd been taught—what Ariel had taught her. Just like I had for so many years, and like I still did when I forgot to check myself.

She reminded me so much of the girl I once was, defiant, scrappy, desperate, and alone. I became an orphan in all the ways that mattered when my parents abandoned me at the remedial school where Ariel found me all those years ago. Now Eve had become a real orphan because of me.

I couldn't go back in time and show young Lily a different path, but if I believed myself capable of becoming more than what Ariel made me, I had to believe his daughter could make better choices with the right guidance.

"Hi, Eve." I clutched the receiver for dear life and hoped the tremor in my voice didn't translate over the wire. "It's, um, your sister, Lily. If you're there, please pick up. I'm glad you contacted me, and I came alone, like you said. Can I come up, please?"

A few seconds of silence stretched over the line. Then came a click and the dial tone sounded. I stared at the receiver, then slowly replaced it on its hook.

Behind me, the elevator dinged. The doors slid open, as if waiting for me. Knees weak, I wobbled over and slipped inside.

The doors closed, and the number 64 lit up on the floor display above them. I leaned against the back wall and forced my breathing to slow.

One epic elevator ride and one long, thick-carpeted corridor later, I knocked on the door marked 6403. "Eve? Are you there?"

No one answered, and I sighed. This was getting old. I didn't want to break into another home. I'd pressed my luck with the police more than enough for one day.

One more try. This time, I didn't hold back. I brought more of my strength to bear and hammered on the door as loud as I could.

"Eve! I know you're in there!" I didn't know that, technically, but the nice thing about yelling that was if they weren't there, they wouldn't have any way of knowing you were guessing.

"Lily?" a small voice said.

Scratch that. They wouldn't know you were guessing—unless they happened to be standing right behind you. "Mother of monsters," I groaned. "Do you have to sneak around like that?"

"I wasn't sneaking," Eve said. "I was just walking. Like a normal person."

"Uh huh." I turned, arms crossed, to glare at her. She wore the coat I'd lent her, though she'd acquired a pair of strappy high-heeled shoes that looked unfamiliar and expensive—much more expensive than anything I owned. Given the flexible attitude toward human conventions of ownership she'd displayed earlier, I decided to preserve my plausible deniability and not ask where she got them. "Where have you been, missy?"

"Oh, you know." She shrugged. "Around."

"I'm glad you're safe. But you didn't have to disappear like that."

She looked mulish. "I wanted to go home. I wasn't sure if you'd let me. And there were things I had to do."

"First of all," I said, "I would have been happy to take you home, if only to save myself two days of heartache. Second of all, what things?"

Her gaze shifted away from me, over my shoulder. "Just things. And I couldn't let Lucy go hungry."

"Lucy? Who's Lucy?"

She rolled her eyes at me, that same expression of *why are you so dumb* written all over her face. "Lucy's my snake," she said. "Well, technically Father's snake, but my snake until he comes back. Did you want to go inside, or would you rather talk out here with the neighbors watching?"

"Do you even have your keys?"

The mischievous grin Eve flashed me transformed her features. "Don't need 'em." She waved me aside with a blithe grin and stepped up to the door, angling her body so a casual observer wouldn't notice she was actually reaching her hand right through the solid wood. I heard a soft click as the door unlocked from the inside.

"Ugh," I said. "I will never get used to that."

She opened the door with an air of smug satisfaction. "You can't do it? It's so easy."

"I just don't like it. It's creepy."

"Oh, Lily," she said, sounding for all the world like the sister I'd never had. And, to no small degree, like her father. "You're such a prude. Come in. I want to show you my house."

I followed her inside, my heart beating an uneven rhythm. So, this was Ariel's home—no, *had been* Ariel's home. Despite the extravagance of the rest of the building, I hadn't expected a place so spacious, beautifully furnished, and drenched in light.

The front door opened into a kitchen with gold-flecked white quartz counter tops and brass fixtures. Beyond the open-plan dining area, a glass sliding door led out to a small terrace bright with ornamental plants and flowers. A large terrarium separated the dining area from the living room, where wall-to-ceiling windows displayed a stunning panorama: a sparkling blue-gray expanse of water girded by the long span of the Oakland Bay Bridge, its steel towers marching across the middle distance to the hazy eastern shore.

The whole place smelled strongly of cubine, the rich frankincense teasing my sinuses with the beginnings of a sneeze. Traces of its teenage occupant showed amid the elegance: fashion magazines strewn across the fancy glass coffee table, the chaos of a full makeup caddy spilling over onto the kitchen counter beside an open box of cereal, a staggering variety of shoes scattered by the couch or wherever else their owner had kicked them off.

I frowned. How long had Ariel lived here? And how long had Eve stayed here before she found me? The state of the apartment suggested she had occupied it for some time.

Eve tossed my coat over the back of a chair, adding to the general atmosphere of clutter. Approaching the terrarium, she cooed loving baby talk to its inhabitant, a bright green python of alarming size.

"That snake is big enough to eat you," I said.

Eve made kissy sounds at the snake, who lifted its head and uncoiled about three feet of its length, rearing up to follow her movements. "No way. He's a big boy, but he would never eat *me*. Would you, Lucy?"

"Lucy is a boy snake?"

She shot me another one of her patented looks of disgust. "Yes, he's a boy snake. Do you have a problem with that?"

I raised my hands. "No problem at all. The snake's gender identity is his own business. Obviously."

"*Obviously.*" She stalked to the kitchen and rummaged through the freezer. Pulling out a Tupperware container, she popped it open, revealing a selection of what looked like frozen rats sealed in plastic bags.

Oh. Snake food. *Obviously.* I shuddered and wandered away into the living room, staring out at the view without really seeing it. The rodent Popsicles troubled me less than the reality of Ariel's dual life. He'd been a father, pet owner, and luxury high-rise resident, but also a ruthless murderer of his own kind and a Machiavellian master of deception.

It wasn't that the two sides didn't add up. The sum of them bothered me more than the difference.

Not everything in this world is as black and white as you think it is.

I turned. Eve slid back a panel of the terrarium, reaching out her hand to Lucy. The snake twined his way up her arm and wrapped itself in a loose loop over her shoulders like a scaled stole. She stroked him with light fingertips, murmuring reassurance.

"What was it that you wanted to talk to me about?"

She busied herself with cleaning the bottom of the terrarium, her lips pursed in concentration. "Is it true?"

"Is what true?" But I knew what. She meant Ariel, what she'd overheard at Danny's house before she ran away.

She squared her jaw and faced me. "Danny said my father hurt her. And you. And you said..."

She has no one...And that's because of me. "Yes. It's true."

"You were the reason he disappeared." She drew a long, shaking breath, eyes glinting gold beneath their green. "He left because of you!"

Cold fear shot through me, knife-sharp and aimed at my heart. "Eve, you have to understand. He shot Danny. I had to defend her—and myself."

Her face worked, evidence of some internal struggle against tears or violence. I tensed, waiting for the one question I didn't know if I could answer. But it didn't come.

Instead, she dropped her gaze, coaxing the snake off her shoulders and back into the glass case. "I made a mistake," she muttered, the words so quiet I had to lean forward to catch them.

"What mistake?" At her silence, I gritted my teeth. "Eve, what did you do?"

"I didn't mean to!" Her head came up, her eyes wide and frantic. "Rae said—"

"Wait." I held up a hand. "*Rae* said? What does she have to do with any of this?"

"I thought she would help me," Eve said, pouting. "But she didn't. I don't like her very much. She's scary."

"She is intimidating, I'll give you that. Eve...did you tell her about me? About us?"

"About being demons? Of course not." Eve snorted, disdainfully. "What do you take me for? I just said that *someone* hurt me, and I didn't know what to do about it."

I clamped down on my guilt and my immediate instinct to apologize. She wanted me to, no doubt, and I didn't want to give her that. Not now. Not yet. Was she really so different than her father? Cold tendrils of fear wrapped around my heart and squeezed. "Tell me what Rae said. Her exact words if you can remember them. It's important."

"She said..." Eve's brow furrowed. "She said that sometimes, when your anger feels too big to hold inside and nothing seems fair, it's better to give the anger to the gods to hold. She said that's what gods are for. She said I would feel better." She hung her head.

A terrible suspicion grew under my breastbone like a poisonous seed. "What gods?"

Eve shrugged. "She had this altar set up. You saw it when we went there. She said you could ask for justice at the altar and the goddess will take care of it."

Lightheaded, I groped behind me for the back of the couch and leaned against it, closing my eyes, trying to think. The effect of the silver exposure still fogged my brain. My thoughts whirred, stuttered, and leaped forward, then stalled like Sebastian's vintage Camaro when he tried to teach me how to drive a stick a few months back.

Rae had a hand in this. Rae had told Eve to ask a goddess for justice. That same goddess had come into my bedchamber on wings of storm and fury, held a fiery sword to my throat, and demanded I account for my sins.

"When did you have this conversation with her?" My voice came out hoarse, my throat tight. It had happened just as I feared. Blood would out, and Eve had betrayed me as her father did before her.

She looked puzzled. "Sunday, I think? It was after I, um, ran away."

My breath hissed out of me, and I sank down onto the couch. Maybe it wasn't as bad as I thought. "You're sure?"

Eve nodded, wide-eyed, and I rubbed cold hands over my face. The timing didn't make sense. The goddess had come for me on Saturday night, pulled a white feather from my throat and let me live. Maybe Eve hadn't sold me out, after all.

But Roger Jeffrey had not lived. Roger Jeffrey, and his younger frat brothers before him, had died choking on a flood of black feathers.

Rae had given me that signed report. Rae knew what Roger Jeffrey had done. Rae had an altar in her living room for a justice-seeking goddess.

That's what gods are for…

"Mother of monsters." My childhood had given me enough experience of religion to last a lifetime, and the internal scars to prove it. I rejected it when my family rejected me.

I didn't believe in gods, not even the ones I swore by. *Ariel* didn't even believe in gods, and he claimed to be as old as humanity itself. But then again, Ariel had lied to me about so many things. Maybe he lied about theology too. I wouldn't put it past him.

"Lily?" Eve's voice, hesitant and worried, filtered through my confusion. "Are you all right? You look terrible."

"Thanks a lot, kid." Everyone was so complimentary today. I opened my eyes to find her peering up at me and way too close for comfort. "It's been a hell of a day. Nothing a little kether won't fix, though."

But I had no kether donor, now, since I'd squandered my good will with Sebastian by accusing him of being a man-child, almost killing him, and then running away, twice. Whatever relationship we had, I didn't put good odds on it coming back from that.

"You're hurt," she insisted. "I can smell it on you."

"Just had a little run-in with the feds." I flipped my wrist up to show her my oozing wound.

"Oh my god. That's a silver burn." She reached for me, and I edged away. "Let me do that thing you did for me. A push."

"No!" I pulled my sleeve back down.

She looked crestfallen. "But I can help."

"Don't worry, I'll heal. I just need time." Her father had used kether pushes to beguile and control me, bend me to his will. That was one mistake I wouldn't make again. Besides, though the exchange didn't require a sexual touch, it felt wrong to take energy from a child even if she freely offered it. "But I want you to understand the danger, Eve. They're getting wise to us. Now that there's a warrant out for your arrest, they'll come armed with silver bullets, and they won't hesitate to shoot."

"But I didn't do it. I didn't kill those guys!"

"That's what we have to convince them of." My head spun and I rested it back on the cushions. "They won't stop hunting you if we don't."

"So, what do we do?" Eve looked at me with those huge eyes of hers, luminous in her pale face.

Good question, kid. Despite the mess she'd embroiled us in, she was just an angry kid with no one in her corner to protect her. No one except me. And I'd be damned if I wasn't going to do my very best.

"Do you trust me?" Even though I knew her tricks by now, I still reached out with my good hand and squeezed her shoulder. "After, well, everything, do you still trust me to help you?"

For a long moment, she said nothing, and I tensed, waiting for an attack, either verbal or physical. But when she finally spoke, her voice was soft and slow, uncertain. "I know you're a good person. If helping me is the right thing to do, you'll do it. But..." Her lip trembled. "I'm not sure *I'm* a very good person, Lily. So maybe helping me isn't the right thing."

"Don't say that." I sounded more certain than I felt. I could only hope this *was* the right thing to do, and that I could talk her into going through with it. "Being a good person isn't something that you are or aren't inside, Eve. It's what you do that matters. And what you need to do now isn't going to be easy."

Her forehead creased at that, but she said, "Okay. What is it?"

I levered myself off the couch, my stance still unsteady. "You're going to have to talk to them."

She swallowed hard. "Them?"

It wasn't the time for pulling punches. "The police, Eve. You have to tell them the truth. If you tell them everything you know about Rae and everything that happened at that frat house, we might still get you out of this."

19

BROKEN THINGS

Eve paced—or rather, flounced—the length of the apartment's living space, from the terrace door to the kitchen and back again. "I don't understand why I have to turn myself in. How does that help anything?"

"Because, Eve, honey." My joints ached with a fierce, burning fire. I lowered myself onto the couch, marshaling my patience and my arguments. "It will be worse if you don't. For all of us."

"Ugh." Eve flopped on the couch with a heavy sigh. "I should just leave. Go back to New York. My whole reason for coming out here was to find my father, and he's…" She trailed off, swallowed. Maybe she didn't want to think about the end of that sentence any more than I did. "Gone."

"You can't escape the feds by going home, Eve. They'll follow you, and eventually they'll find you. And when they do, I won't be able to protect you."

"Have you ever been to New York?" She scowled. "It's big and bustling. It's easy to disappear there. Easier than here. And *you* couldn't even find me here."

"I have been to New York, in fact. I lived there once." Images of the stripped-down loft Ariel and I had shared in a stylish Manhattan brownstone sidled in, unbidden and unwanted.

I used to feed wild doves in the high unscreened window, in defiance of Ariel, who scoffed at them and called them glorified pigeons. We danced together in the tiny kitchen on late nights with the winter air blasting in, oblivious to the cold or hunger. After we came home from a hunt, Ariel would often go out again. I would lie awake on the bare mattress that took up most of the floor, my skin buzzing with the kether of strangers and the electric hum of the city's sleepless streets, waiting for him to come back.

Sometimes he left for days. Eventually, I would tire of wandering around the loft like an uneasy ghost and venture out to the clubs, toying with potential prey. But without my mentor, I didn't dare go home with anyone. I didn't have the control, or so he told me.

"All in good time. It takes years to learn real finesse, Lily fair. Don't get ahead of yourself." His dulcet tones etched themselves into my brain, and even now, I couldn't erase the mark they left.

That good time never came, and I got increasingly restless. I finished the last credits of my degree in stray stolen moments. I didn't tell him when I graduated. I didn't tell anyone, because I had no one else to tell.

Where had he hidden Eve during that time? She would have been young, seven or eight at most. Was that where he went when he left—to see his daughter?

Why had he never told me about her?

"You didn't like it there, did you?" Eve's question pulled me back to the present.

"No. I mean, that's not it. I had wonderful times there." This waif didn't need to know about my wild years with her father, and she probably didn't want to. "The point is, New York isn't a safe place any more than San Francisco is. And I took an oath to uphold the law. I can't aid or abet you in evading it."

She scoffed. "What, like you've never broken any laws?"

"I—" When she put it like that, what hadn't I broken? Laws, doors, promises, the man who professed to care for me, my own black and foolish heart. Some of those things I could fix. "I've put a lot on the line for you. I got kicked out of my house because I took you in, for one thing."

"You're kidding." Eve looked shocked. "Danny and Berry kicked you out?"

"They were within their rights to ask me to leave. But that's beside the point. I'm already on thin ice with the State Bar, and I can't advise you to go on the run."

"I bet you can't stop me, either."

I grimaced. Silver-burned and kether-starved, I couldn't run a decent mile, let alone catch a full-blooded succubus who didn't want to be caught. I did have a gun loaded with silver bullets in my backpack, but damned if I would shoot a teenager whose worst crime was not wanting to go to jail.

"No," I said. "I won't stop you. I told you what I think the right thing to do is, but I can't make you do it. You have to decide for yourself."

Her face stilled, and she seemed to contemplate this. "You're big on that, aren't you," she said finally. "People deciding for themselves."

I hadn't let Sebastian decide for himself. I had failed to control my hold over him. "I try to be."

"Can I think about it?"

"You can sleep on it." I headed for the door, my steps steadier now, but still weighed down by fatigue. Thank goodness my hotel wasn't too far. "You have until tomorrow morning at nine am."

Eve straightened out of her slumped posture. "You can stay here if you want." She said it quick and offhand, but when I turned back, her eyes pleaded with me.

"What?"

"You said Danny and Berry kicked you out. It was because of me, wasn't it?"

I opened my mouth to say yes, then closed it again. "No. It wasn't because of you. Not really. It was because of me. I lied to them, Eve. I didn't warn them of the danger. I didn't give them all the facts they needed to make their own informed choice. I failed them."

"But it's not fair. You didn't mean to!"

"It doesn't matter."

"How can you say that?" Her voice rose, fierce and indignant. "You told me that intent matters. Why does it matter for me and not for you?"

"Because." I let out a long breath. "I still intended to lie. *That* was the real harm."

She sat back against the arm of the couch, frowning. "I don't understand."

"I broke their trust. That's what matters."

"Oh." She considered this, head tilted, lips pursed. Then she shrugged, dismissing moral conundrums with a toss of her golden curls. "So, you'll be staying, then?"

I sighed and set down my bag. I had reservations about staying in the place Ariel had called home, even if for a brief time, even if he was dead. But this way I could keep an eye on Eve. It didn't have anything to do with the hopeful expression on her face.

Well, it didn't have *much* to do with it.

"I'm staying," I said.

The couch in Ariel's apartment was far more comfortable than a murderous incubus's couch had any right to be, but I still tossed and turned all night. I kept one ear peeled for Eve in case she decided to run again, even though I couldn't do a thing about it if she did. And every time my eyes cracked open, I couldn't stop myself from checking the window across from me for the silhouette of a vengeful goddess, blowing in to finish what she started.

Maybe Eve was right. Maybe, if she ran, I should let her go. Maybe it would be better for both of us.

I must have drifted off eventually, though, because I woke to early sunlight pouring in through the sliding glass door. A figure stood over me, a dark silhouette haloed in gold.

Heart in my throat, I scrambled away to the other side of the couch, pulling the throw blanket with me as an inadequate shield.

But it was only Eve. I blinked furiously, my eyes adjusting slowly to the bright light suffusing the room. She looked down at me with an odd expression.

"Eve? What are you doing?"

"Waiting for you to wake up."

"How long have you been watching me?"

She lifted one skinny shoulder and let it fall in a half-hearted shrug. She'd changed into a pair of skin-tight, stylishly faded, distressed jeans, a thin, loose gray tank top that hung nearly to her knees, and shiny rainbow-colored high-top chucks. "Did you know that you talk in your sleep?"

"I do not, and let's never speak of it again." I frowned at her. "Please tell me that's not what you're planning on wearing to talk to the feds today."

Eve folded her arms and bit her lip. "About that..." She looked away, her blond curls falling over her face.

My stomach sank. "You're not going, are you."

"I'm sorry." Her lip trembled, and her gaze slid toward me, then away again. "I came here to look for my dad. Now that I know he's not here, I just want to go home."

"I understand." With a sigh, I fumbled in my bag for my phone.

"You're not mad?"

I shook my head. "I told you it was your choice. I'm mostly surprised that you waited." My fingers met the cold metal of the gun I'd shoved in the bottom of my bag, and I pulled them away as if the bullets nestled inside could burn me. "I'll get you a ride to the airport. You'll be ok from there?"

"I flew here by myself," she said, a hint of affront creeping into her tone.

"You'll need to be gone before they issue the warrant." I stabbed at my rideshare app. "Get your things together. The car will be here in twelve minutes."

"Okay," she said, eyes wide, and headed for the master bedroom with startling speed. The thump of unorganized suitcase packing issued from within.

In the meantime, I grabbed my bag and headed for the bathroom, where I switched out my own jeans for slacks and a blouse that were only a little wrinkled. After a splash of cold water on my face, I assessed my reflection.

I looked like death warmed over. My eyes stared mossy and hollow from dark circles and bags, my cheeks pale and forehead pinched. I gathered my last shreds of kether to freshen my appearance, but the throb of my wrist made me wince, and I leaned on the sink for support.

Fabulous. Just fabulous. I entertained a brief fantasy of crawling back to the couch and napping for a week until my energy replenished. But then a ruckus of thumps and curses echoed from the other room. I sighed and turned away from the mirror. Ready or not, I had a teenage demon to wrangle.

No rest for the wicked. I crossed the hall to the master bedroom. Eve stood in the middle of the floor, engaged in a pitched battle with the zipper on her overflowing suitcase.

Throat tight, I watched her for a moment in silence. Things would get less complicated once she walked out of my life. I should have looked forward to the peace and quiet. But instead, a hollow space opened in my chest. It ached with the memory of another demon girl who had lost her family and gone it alone in the big city, trying to build a life without a foundation.

But I didn't go it alone. I had Ariel to guide me when I was that girl, for better or worse. Eve just had me, the woman who'd taken what family she once had away.

No wonder she'd decided to fly solo.

"Don't force it," I said. "You're too strong. It'll break."

"Everything fit when I got here." Eve abandoned her efforts and aimed a kick at the suitcase. It flew across the room and hit the wall with a thump, spilling clothes onto the floor.

I winced. It reminded me too much of how Sebastian—*no.* I couldn't think about that right now. I had to get through the next thing, and then the next, and then the next, and maybe somewhere in there I would figure out what to do about the not-boyfriend I couldn't bring myself to face.

Or maybe not. "Bring that here."

Eve made a face. She stomped to the suitcase, stuffed the fallen items inside, and dragged it over, where she dropped it on the floor in front of me. "Good luck. And *don't* say I have too many clothes."

"I wouldn't dare." I dropped into a crouch and opened the luggage. It held what looked like the entire contents of a large closet, dumped haphazardly into the small space. Not quite demon-swift, but as close as I could manage, I refolded several pairs of jeans, a NYU sweatshirt, and seven dresses in various stages of wrinkled and unwashed back into the suitcase.

Ironic that this came so easily when I couldn't seem to gather the motivation to fold my own laundry at home. But caring for Eve came naturally, even when caring for myself didn't.

Since I couldn't depend on my strength, I sat on the suitcase and used my body weight to force it closed enough to zip. "There. If you've got everything you need, we should go. The car's waiting."

"Okay," Eve said, but she didn't move.

I tipped the suitcase on its wheeled end, popped the handle, and pushed it into her unwilling hands. "Do you want to change your mind?"

She shook her head, blinking, and swallowed hard. Then, with a choked noise, she flung her arms around me.

I tensed. *I shouldn't have let my guard down, shouldn't have forgotten that she probably wants me dead, shouldn't have...* But she didn't press the attack. Instead, she leaned her head on my shoulder and let out a hiccupping little sob. "Oh, Lily. I'm going to miss you."

"What...? Oh." She wasn't trying to kill me. She was *hugging* me. Awkward and still tentative, I returned the embrace. Mother of monsters, but the girl was thin. The bones of her spine stood out under my hands. She was stronger than me right now, but I held her gently, afraid to squeeze her too hard. I couldn't handle breaking anything or anyone else.

She lacked such qualms. Her arms tightened around me, sinewy bands of steel, and I gasped for breath. "Ow."

"Sorry." She let go, backing away. "This doesn't mean that I've forgiven you for not telling me what happened with my dad," she added, and dashed the back of her hand across her face.

I swallowed the lump in my throat, which became a quiver of unease in my belly. I still hadn't told her the whole truth. How much had she already guessed? "Okay..."

"We aren't best friends, like I'd hoped. And we're not sisters. But...for a while this weekend, I had fun imagining we were."

"Me too," I said. "And I'm sorry too. About your father, about...everything. I did my best, but I failed you."

"You didn't fail," Eve said, fierce now. "You've been very kind to me. Kinder than..." She hesitated, like she'd changed her mind about what to say. "Well, anyone. Even though I make it hard sometimes. Even though you're still afraid of me. That has to count for something."

Her words stunned me into silence for a moment. "Well," I said. "I'm glad you think it does."

"And you'll take care of Lucy, right?" Her expression turned cunning. "That counts for something too, you know."

I laughed, and the hollow place in my chest echoed in the sound. "Yes, I'll feed your damn snake. Come on, we really better go now."

I threw my bag over my shoulder and led her out of the apartment, the wheels of her suitcase rattling across the tile behind me. We rode the elevators in silence, me counting down the floors, Eve chewing her lip and staring at her iridescent sneakers. Or so I assumed. She'd donned huge heart-shaped sunglasses that covered half of her small face, like something a Hollywood starlet would wear.

Outside, the honk and roar of Market Street flooded over us. On the sixty-fourth floor, sunlight had blazed in, but the building rose above the fog layer. At ground level, the frigid wind stole the breath from my lungs. *Damn kether deficit.* I pulled my reclaimed coat tighter to shield myself from the unfamiliar chill slicing through me and scanned the curb for Eve's ride. My app told me to expect a silver Prius, which didn't help much. At least three crawled through the right lane at the snail's pace of Monday morning traffic.

Behind me, someone screamed, and I spun toward the sound.

The men with guns came out of nowhere. They surrounded us, weapons pointed at our hearts. "Hands where we can see them! Down on the ground!"

A voice I recognized cut across the clamor, a clear alto that rang out like a church bell. "We're packing silver, Miss Knight," Agent North called. "I suggest you do what they say."

I froze, hands raised. I should have expected an ambush.

Just one more thing I'd gotten wrong.

20

RED GODDESS

"Lily?" Eve quavered. "What's happening?"

"Get behind me. Now." When she didn't move, I stepped in front of her, putting myself between her small body and the guns. Then I lifted my head and met Meghan North's eyes. She stood behind the ring of armed officers, head tilted to the side, waiting for my acquiescence.

The urge to fight fluttered in my throat like beating wings. If I went up against silver bullets, I wouldn't win. And if they all wore silver bracers like Agent North, then my powers of persuasion wouldn't work on them, either. I had my own gun stowed in my bag, but with my kether so low, I probably couldn't get it fast enough to matter.

That left me nothing but bravado and the hope that North would remember Ira considered me an asset. "If you want her, you're going to have to go through me."

"Oh, I see." She sneered. "You think I won't shoot you because you're Delaney's pet demon experiment. That's cute."

Well, there went that hope. The way she said word *experiment* went straight to the pit of my stomach and writhed there. I still had bravado, though. "If you were going to shoot me, you would have done it already."

In response, she raised her own gun and flicked the safety off, aiming right at my heart. "It would be my pleasure, Knight. Don't kid yourself. Now *step aside.*"

"Eve's innocent. Leave her alone." I bared my teeth at her, but Sebastian's rules of gun safety echoed in my head. *Never point a gun at anything you don't want to destroy.* This woman wanted to destroy me all right. She wanted to pull the trigger herself.

"It's all right, Lily," a small voice beside me said.

"Eve, no. I said get back!"

It was too late. Eve stepped around me, her hands in the air. "Don't shoot." Her voice wavered, but she held her chin high. "I'll come with you. I'll tell you everything I know."

Two of the armed men stepped forward. They grabbed Eve with gloved hands, yanking her arms behind her. Silver glinted, metal clinked, and the cuffs closed around her wrists. She screamed.

"No—!" I reached for her, but the barrels of their assault rifles swiveled toward me like empty, malevolent eyes.

"I said get down! Hands where I can see them!"

I raised my arms and dropped to my knees. Without my hands to catch me, sharp agony spread upward through my joints. I didn't have enough kether in me to cushion a blow like it normally would.

The nearest barrel swung down to point toward me. "On the ground, now!"

I eased myself forward onto the sidewalk, gritty, filthy concrete scraping my cheek. Eve sobbed somewhere nearby, the sound interspersed with quiet yelps of pain. I waited for the burn of the cuffs on my own wrists. It didn't come.

"Lily!" Eve's panicked scream made me crane my neck around. The officers dragged her backward, her iridescent sneakers beating a frantic tattoo on the pavement. She hung limp between them, only her fierce golden eyes alert and alive, blazing their feral rage at me, at the officers, at the world. "You said it would be okay," she shrieked. "You said if I told the truth, they wouldn't hurt me—"

A black unmarked car waited by the curb, and they pushed her inside. The door slammed shut. A pair of shiny black one-inch heels followed after them, tailored black hems swishing above them. They paused beside me.

I glared up at her, though I doubted it would faze her given my current position kissing the pavement. "Where are they taking her?"

"Somewhere safe." Her gaze flicked to the car. "You can get up now, Ms. Knight. But don't make any sudden moves."

I pushed myself up to a kneeling position again, ignoring the protest of my abused kneecaps. "Those cuffs will kill her. There's nothing safe about that!"

"Oh, I didn't mean safe for *her*." Her lips twisted in a mirthless smile. "I meant safe for the rest of us."

I drew a shaking breath. "That's monstrous." I spit bitter grit from the sidewalk at her feet, barely missing her shiny shoes. Too bad. "And I'm something of an expert on monsters. You know, being one and all."

"Call me what you want," she said. "But it's my job to keep people safe from harm and put monsters behind bars. Demons or otherwise."

She stepped fastidiously around the place I'd spat and strode toward the car without another word. One of the other agents held the door for her as she slid into the front passenger seat, then shut it behind her. The car peeled away from the curb. Honks and curses heralded its progress forward as the drivers who had stopped to stare at the scene unfolding on the sidewalk all turned their attention back to the road.

A heavy hand fell on my shoulder and hauled me to my feet with a painful, uncompromising grip. I wheeled, arm drawn back to strike out, but the snarl froze on my face, and I pulled my punch. "Ira?"

"I wouldn't if I were you, Knight." He lifted his jacket high enough to show me the pistol holstered at his hip. "Come with me. We need to have a talk."

"You're part of this," I breathed, but I let him steer me around the corner, where his SUV waited. "You let them take her!"

"I can't overrule the FBI." He paused with his hand on the SUV's door latch and looked me over, his expression closed. "I would have preferred a more discreet approach, but it wasn't my call."

"But you know she didn't do it!"

"I'm not sure what I know anymore." His soft, even drawl held a warning that chilled me. "The only thing I'm sure of right now is that you've been keeping things from me. You knew where the girl was all along, didn't you?"

"Not *all* along..."

"You didn't feel the need to share that information with me?"

"You don't understand. She's just a kid. She's alone. She has no family. I'm the closest thing she's got. I had to protect her—from people like *you*."

"And that seems to have worked out so well for both of you."

Asshole. I glared at him. "So, what are you going to do? Fire me?"

"I haven't decided yet. Is there anything else you haven't told me?"

I blew out a long breath. Guilt tugged at me, a sense of justice betrayed, but the sound of Eve's scream when they put the cuffs on her burrowed its way deep into my heart and festered there.

Somehow, I had to get her out of Meghan North's all-too-capable and Presence-immune hands. I had to save her from whatever fate awaited her there. A life in captivity as a government lab rat seemed like the best-case scenario, but I could think of a lot of worse ones. Life in solitary. Torture. Death by silver. Dissection.

I couldn't protect both her and Rae. I had to make a choice.

Time to come clean. But maybe, if I played my cards right, I could still walk the line between personal and professional obligation.

I folded my arms and met Ira's questioning gaze. "I have a lead on our murder goddess."

"Do you, now," Ira said. "Let's hear it, then."

"I'll tell you." I favored him with my coldest smile. "But first you have to let me see Eve. I need to make sure she'll be okay."

His eyebrows went up at that. "I'm not sure either of us have that kind of bargaining power."

"Then you're willing to let Morrighu, or whatever she is, kill again. And when she does, Agent North will have to admit that Eve's not the culprit."

"I wouldn't bet on it," he said. "But I'll do what I can."

"You'll have to do better than that." I pitched my voice low, but I didn't bother with a Presence. It probably wouldn't work on him, anyway. "I want to see her *now*."

He shook his head and held the SUV's door open for me, a strangely courteous move for a man who might decide to put a silver bullet in me at any given moment. "You have a lot of faith in me, Knight. I fear it may be misplaced."

"It's not faith," I said, grim, but I climbed into the seat. "It's realism. You need me, Ira. Who else is going to take this goddess out?"

He didn't respond, and I took that as a win. But the small victory gave me no satisfaction.

Ira and whoever he answered to might think I represented their best chance against a supernatural threat, but I had my doubts. My gut said this force was something I didn't understand and didn't know how to counter, something hungry for blood of the guilty, something that didn't care who it hurt in the process.

How could a half-demon hope to bring a deity to justice? How could I stop her, when I feared she and I had more in common than I wanted to admit?

I didn't have any moral high ground. I had killed without due process and enacted my own vengeance. I played Ariel's judge, jury, and executioner.

We are not so unlike, you and I.

She had spared me. But if I wanted to save Eve, I might not have the option to do the same for her.

"You have to stop this." I turned to Ira, wishing more than ever that my powers of persuasion worked on him. "She won't last long at this rate. That silver is going to kill her."

Seated under the harsh light in the interrogation room, Eve's face took on a gaunt cast, her closed eyes sunken and shadowed. In the harsh lighting, it reminded me a little too much of another succubus I tried to save, lying on a slab in Danny's morgue. She seemed smaller somehow, fragile. The silver worked fast.

No wonder Agent North had done her best to keep me from seeing her.

"Don't even think about releasing that prisoner." *Speak of the devil*. North's crisp tones cut through the air, and she rounded the corner, heels clicking on the worn linoleum. "She must remain restrained for everyone's protection, including her own. We don't know what she's capable of. If she were to escape and attack someone—"

"Then what?" I eyed her with growing dislike. "You'd kill her?"

"If necessary." Agent North's cold expression didn't falter. "The guards here have been issued silver bullets."

"Listen." I gritted my teeth and sunk my nails into my palms, the sharp pain keeping me civil—barely. Well, that and the threat of silver bullets. "She's having a reaction to those cuffs. She needs medical attention. You have to let me in there."

Ira stirred from where he leaned up against the cell block, his arms crossed, and eyes shadowed with an expression I couldn't quite read. "Agent North, despite Ms. Knight's divided loyalties, she does have a rapport with the girl. Maybe she can get her to talk."

"You're wrong about her," I said. "If she dies, her blood will be on your hands. As will the blood of anyone else who dies because you were too busy torturing a kid."

Silence stretched as Meghan North thought this over. "Fine," she said at last. "But it's your funeral. If she attacks you, we may not be able to help you in time." Her flat tone said they might not care to help me in time.

"I'll take my chances," I said acidly. "*I'm* not afraid of her."

She favored me with a long, dour look. "You should be." But she punched the unlock code into the door and stood back.

I walked through the door without sparing her another glance. The door closed behind me with a loud clunk and click, the sound of Agent North locking me in with the monster girl. Or maybe she figured she'd catch two demons for the price of one. Trust me to talk my way into a trap I didn't even see until I sprung it on myself.

But she hadn't tried to arrest me yet, so maybe my luck would hold.

Eve sat with her head bowed, her wrists and ankles shackled. She didn't open her eyes or acknowledge my presence.

"Oh, Eve. I'm so sorry." I touched her shoulder. "Are you all right?"

She lifted her head. Her unfocused eyes glowed cubine gold and shimmered with tears. An odd distortion rippled over her features, a shifting tremor like static on an old TV. The basic defensive glamour that humanized her features had started to fail. Her lips moved, almost soundless, shaping faint words, and I bent my head toward her to catch them.

"The crows," she muttered. "Their wings, like thunder. The red lady...she'll come for me." Her face scrunched, pain etching its signature across her demon features. "Father, help me. It's all so dark. Where are you? I can't see you..."

A sharp rap on the window made me turn. "No touching!" Meghan North glared at me from behind the glass, her warning muffled.

I shrugged, returning my attention to Eve. Her eyelids fluttered open, her gaze beneath dull and vacant. Her voice rasped, weak and strained. "Father?"

"It's just me. It's Lily."

"Lily..." She frowned, squinting at me. "Where am I?"

"You're in jail, honey."

She tried to reach for me but winced and stilled as the metal shifted against the skin of her wrists. A swollen band of angry red welts marred her forearms, blood and pus oozing from the wounds. "It hurts."

"I know." I suppressed a shudder. It wasn't my first time witnessing what silver could do to a demon's flesh. Pure, it could eat away at our skin like acid. After Ariel attacked Tobias last fall, Theo's hands had sustained deep burns after she'd grasped a stake to pull it from the other cambion's chest, the suppurating wounds on her palms bleeding like stigmata.

By contrast, Eve's skin had blistered, but the metal hadn't instantly eaten into her skin. The shackles couldn't be pure silver. But left long enough in contact with the kether-draining substance, she would continue to waste away.

"I feel sick." Eve panted, her words faint and labored. "Lily, the silver...am I dying? I think I'm dying."

"You're not dying." Not yet anyway. "You're having a panic attack. Take deep breaths. It's going to be okay."

"You don't know that." Eve pushed herself halfway upright, then fell back with a pained moan. "You don't know *anything*!"

"Hush." I leaned closer. "I'm trying to get you out of here, but I need your help. Tell me everything you remember about the night the boys got killed, even if it didn't seem important at the time. Did you see anything strange? Anyone who didn't belong?"

"Yes." Her focus drifted. "I saw the crows."

The crows. They had shadowed me all week, their croaking calls so frequent they faded into background noise. "What do you mean?"

"At the party house." Eve's expression had turned almost dreamy. "She said it was a murder."

Where had I heard that before? Eve had said it when we got back to the house on Friday afternoon. That seemed so long ago now. But before that, someone else had said it. Someone who spoke in a low, husky voice, like the crows' own calls given depth and softened. *It's called a murder.* "Who said that?"

"The red lady."

"What red lady? Why didn't you tell me about this before?"

"She tasted like a thunderstorm," Eve said. "Like blood in my mouth. Like a lightning strike." Her eyes drooped again, a shudder running through her thin frame.

How much weight could I put on the words of a delirious teenager? But if I did believe her, I knew of one person who tasted like lightning and copper, a person who might have wanted the men of Delta Alpha Mu dead for her own reasons.

"Eve." I leaned over her, speaking in a low, urgent tone. "Try to focus. Was Rae McGuire at the frat party that night?"

"Father." Eve's chin sunk closer to her chest, her voice a soft, slurred whine. "We should go to the desert. They can't hurt us there. Please, Father, they won't find us if we go tonight…"

The desert… I shivered. Did she mean Tonepah, site of Ariel's betrayal and his unrealized fantasies of demon supremacy? But she said nothing more, and I bowed my head, out of options. A kether push risked incapacitating me at my current level of depletion and Eve's body would quickly spend any energy trying and failing to heal her silver burns. And she might not have any more useful answers to give.

I couldn't put it off any longer. I needed to talk to Rae. I needed to ask her what she knew about the goddess, Eve's red lady. Maybe she had an alibi. But if she didn't…

My movements deliberate to hide the weakness in my limbs, I tapped on the door. North had stepped out of view of the window, and for a moment nothing happened. I held my breath, but then the seal buzzed open, and the handle turned. I stepped over the threshold, not a captive after all, at least for now.

Behind me, Eve slumped in her chair as she slipped deeper into delirium, undisturbed by the harsh sound of the prison, lost in a world where her father could still save her. If he ever could have or would have. I had my doubts, but my revelations about his dark side didn't seem to shake her faith in his love.

Like I told Ira, I didn't have faith like that. I didn't have faith in anything. Not anymore.

But faith or no faith, goddess or no goddess, I had to find Eve's Red Lady.

21

A MURDER OF CROWS

Safe Haven's service coordinator, Olivia Leung, adjusted her thick-rimmed glasses as she took in my question. "Rae? No, she's not here. She takes the week of May 1st off every year. It's some kind of religious holiday." She frowned at me. "You didn't know?"

"Oh, was that this week?" I subtly readjusted my Presence, reassuring her I had good intentions, that she could trust me. I didn't have much juice in me, but I had enough. "She had a case she wanted me to work on. It sounded urgent. Did she leave a contact number?" Guilt twisted in my stomach, but the image of Eve's wasted face and lesioned skin haunted me. I had to prove her innocence, or she might never make it out of detention alive.

"No. I think she's camping or something." Olivia looked doubtful. "She might have left the file for you in her office. You could check if you want."

"Thanks. I will." I headed toward the back offices, then paused as if something had just occurred to me. "You wouldn't happen to know what the holiday is, would you?"

Olivia scrunched up her nose. "Like a New Age festival. Beltane Eve, I think she said. She's into that kind of stuff."

"Ah. Do you know her pretty well, then?" I tried to sound casual, but I layered on more Presence, encouraging her to elaborate. *We should be friends. You can tell me anything.*

"I wouldn't say that. She usually doesn't tell me much. She's very private. But I've worked here nine years, since she founded the clinic. You get to know bits and pieces."

Turning back to her, I leaned on the counter and lowered my voice. "Have you noticed anything different about her recently? Has she been acting strange?"

"She *is* strange," Olivia said, frankly. "But...now that you say that, she has never been the same since she took that trip to Ireland last fall."

I stared at her, taken aback. "What trip? When was that?"

"About five, six months ago, I think. Around Halloween. When she came back, she got more serious, angrier. Like she had a new mission in life."

I shuddered. Rae's return from her trip coincided with the first murder in Ira's files. "You mean a new mission that wasn't Safe Haven."

Olivia shook her head. "She works as hard as ever. If anything, she's more driven. She's a fiercer advocate than ever. But she seems...haunted, somehow."

"Interesting." I straightened. "Thanks, Irene. Just one other thing. Do you know if Rae went to SFU?"

"She did, actually." Her energy shifted from surprise at the question to subtle wariness. "But she dropped out before she finished her degree. That was right before she founded Safe Haven. Why?"

"Just curious." I let my Presence wash over her, calming her suspicion with my idle curiosity. "Anyway, I won't take up anymore of your time. I should go look for that file."

I waved at her and hurried down the hall to Rae's office, where I shut the door without turning on the light and sank into her empty chair. My heart pounded an irregular rhythm in my ears.

It sounded like I was on the right track, and I hated where that track was leading me. I liked Rae. I didn't want to fight her. But the timing of her trip and return, the change Olivia had noticed, couldn't be a coincidence.

She had gone to Ireland and brought back—what? An ancient goddess, thirsty for blood? A sword that could tell innocence from guilt, perhaps?

I pulled out my phone and dialed Ira.

"I have that lead," I said, when he picked up. "And a suspect. Can you meet me? I have a house call to make, and I might need backup."

"Asking for backup?" A long whistle echoed over the phone line. "So, you can be taught after all."

"Don't start, Ira. I'm texting you the address now."

"I'll be there," he said. "Good work, Knight."

The praise silenced the smartass comeback I had cued up, and while I was still searching for an answer, he hung up. With a sigh, I leaned back in Rae's chair, staring into the dark.

Why did it keep coming down to this, to me squaring up against a murderer no one else could face? I was no hero. I was a whole damn mess.

I had gotten myself into this. I should never have taken this job, and now I had no choice but to see this through. If I didn't, Eve would suffer for my failures.

I might be a whole damn mess, but I was a whole damn mess on a mission.

"What exactly are we doing here again?" Ira's tone remained deceptively mild.

"I'm telling you. Rae McGuire knows something about those murders." I paced along the side of Rae's house, peering in the curtained windows to no avail. No one had answered my knock, and my boss didn't seem inclined to lend much credence to my theories anymore.

"We need evidence," Ira said. "So far, you haven't given me anything I can use."

"What about the timing? And that report I gave you—she handed it to me! She knew about them."

"That may be true, but it isn't enough for me to get a warrant for this place. And it looks like no one's home."

I turned. "You weren't so concerned about procedure at the Delta house."

"Yes, well." He stood on the stone walkway, hands shoved deep in his pockets, frowning at the house. "That was before the FBI got involved."

"What agency doesn't care about evidence in a case like this?" I didn't like the answers. It meant an agency that didn't intend to take its results to any court of law I could sway.

"One that doesn't exist." His lips twitched. "At least, not officially."

I folded my arms. The hum of bees filled the silence, along with the whisper of an afternoon breeze that promised a colder night to come. "Ira, can I ask you something?"

He raised his eyebrows. "Something else? You can ask."

I could ask, but he might not answer. Well, what else was new? "I noticed I can't read you at all. Do you wear silver like Agent North does?"

"What do you think?"

"It's either that, or you really aren't human."

"Ah." He held up one arm, rolling his sleeve back a fraction. Metal glinted in the slanting sunlight. "Regular mortal flesh, I'm afraid."

"Are those standard government issue these days?"

"That's classified." He said it like a reflex. "Don't look so offended, Knight. I'd be a fool to work with you unprotected. You can't tell me you wouldn't have used your powers to bend me to your will."

"I'd rather not."

"But you would if you had to."

"I'm going to check around back." Two could play at the not-answering-questions game. "You stay here and make sure no one makes a break for it."

"If she's as dangerous as you say, maybe I should call for more backup."

"I don't think she works like that." Leaving him to his post, I rounded the corner of the house, following a winding trail through the bee-laced herb gardens in search of a back door.

I found it right where I expected it, sliding glass leading into the sunroom where Eve and I had met with Rae last week. Closed vertical blinds hid the interior. Hoping for a lucky break, I tried it, but it was locked.

That tracked with my luck so far this week. And I didn't have the strength in me to break this door like I had the door of the university dean. I kicked at the concrete step, then swore under my breath as pain radiated up my foot.

That's it, then. Over my right shoulder, the nightly fog bank swelled upward, enveloping the sun. Time was running out. Ira wouldn't ask for a warrant, I couldn't break in, Eve would die of silver poisoning, and Rae, or whoever she was—whatever she was—would never answer for any of it.

If I had Eve with me, she could have unlocked the door with her uncanny phasing-through-solid matter skill, or maybe just stepped through it. I flexed my right hand, considering my fingers.

Theo said the phasing ability didn't use kether, not the way our other powers did. *We are masters of our matter.*

"Wouldn't that be nice," I muttered. My body had spent the last twenty-four hours reminding me it was mortal, achy, and ruled by all the natural laws that flesh was heir to, like gravity, entropy, and crushing guilt. Silver changed the rules for us. It disrupted our superhuman abilities and I knew all too well how it could eat away at our corporeal form until we crumbled into fine, sifting dust. I'd seen it happen six months ago with Penelope and her sister, Astrid.

Then again, if my flesh did resemble a crumbling shambles, maybe that made incorporeality easier. Maybe it was like a Presence, a trick of the mind, only *I'm not here,* not just *You can't see me.* Usually, our Presences affected the minds of others, of humans, but this time I needed to trick my own mind.

I pushed the tips of my fingers against the glass experimentally. It pushed back, as solid as expected. It obeyed the natural law that said for every action, there was an equal and opposing reaction. Or something like that. I'd never had much of a mind for physics.

If only I understood myself and my powers better. If only Ariel had taught me everything he knew, instead of what suited his purposes, keeping me ignorant of the full range of our powers. He hadn't even taught me about our wings, let alone this.

I drew a deep breath, swallowed down the heavy scald of rage that rose every time I thought of his false lessons and the trust I'd given in return. But in its wake, determination bubbled up from some hidden, dark spring, deep within the hollow place in the center of my chest where I felt Eve's losses, and through them, my own.

I had come a long way from that naive demon girl who trusted a trickster. He was dead now, and I had survived. I had beaten him. I could beat this.

"I don't need you," I whispered, and closed my eyes, fingertips pressed lightly against the cold, slick glass. "I never did."

I am the master of my matter. I was dust, held together by will and the force of my kether. I was air and darkness, like the mysterious stuff that shaped my wings out of the ether, passing through clothing without tearing but solid enough to lift me into the air. I was atoms and empty space, including the hollow place that ached and sometimes stretched out to consume me. I was nothing. I was an impossible thing, and the laws of nature had no hold over me. The glass was sand and dust fired by energy, just like me. We were the same.

My hand slipped forward. The glass didn't give way, exactly, and my hand didn't melt into an incorporeal state. They just occupied the same space. The glass slid over my skin, *through* it, slippery and cold, like sand at midnight.

Unwillingly, I opened my eyes. It didn't make sense to look at, my palm halfway through the door, my fingers reaching for the latch. I averted my gaze and flipped the lock up, then pulled back like I'd touched silver.

The glass didn't shatter. My right hand came back to me intact and by all appearances, unscathed. I prodded it gingerly with my other hand, finding it fleshly, unmarked, a bit chilled.

Then I opened the now unlocked door and stepped through the vertical blinds into the darkened room beyond. The blinds clacked together at my passage, and I paused, my pulse a swift tempo in my ears. But inside the house, nothing stirred except the slats behind me whispering against each other.

I let out a long breath and reached out with my demon senses, testing the air for the wayward song of human desiderata, half-expecting the copper tang of a lightning strike to clog the back of my throat. But I caught only faint snatches, far off and unremarkable. It was nothing more than the usual ambient background hum of humans in neighboring houses, packed close together and wanting things in a clamor of competing yearning, the music of the city's desire.

There were so many of them, but none of them were here in this house with me. None of them were the one I sought, whose will and wanting sang like a furious storm.

I crept through the dark hallway and out to the front room. There, I halted again before the altar that dominated the eastward wall, where Eve may or may not have petitioned a goddess for vengeance against me. And though the goddess had shown me mercy, that didn't convince me I deserved it.

My breath caught in my throat. The altar looked much the same as it had last week, except one thing. The sword that had hung above it had gone missing.

It shouldn't have surprised me as much as it did. I backed away from the altar and opened the front door.

"There's no one home," I told Ira. "The back door was unlocked." By me, but I didn't include that detail.

He came up the steps, frowning at me from the threshold. "Trespassing is no substitute for a warrant."

"You could come in and arrest me for trespassing. Hot pursuit exception."

"Trespassing isn't a federal crime, last I checked."

Ignoring this, I pointed at the bare wall. "See that spot there? That's where the murder weapon was stored. It's a sword, a really big one."

"A weapon that isn't there. I see." He squinted at the spot I indicated. "Also not grounds for a search, Knight."

"Fine," I said. "You stay there. I'll yell if I find anything interesting."

I headed for the back of the house, down the hallway, and stopped in front of the last door on the left. On my way out last time, I'd glanced over my shoulder in time to catch her slipping out of the sunroom. Our eyes had met, and her desiderata had pulsed with the pain of her migraine. Then she'd turned away, into the room behind this door, and shut it behind her.

What did I expect to find in here—a dead body, a smoking gun, a coffin instead of a bed? Or a signed confession? I still didn't know what Rae and the goddess had to do with each other. I was fairly sure Rae was human, and I was pretty sure the goddess wasn't. But all of this was a hunch and a prayer, and I had no evidence of anything.

I pushed the door open and froze, my heart lodged fluttering in my throat.

My wild speculations had nothing on the black silhouette of wings spread wide and leaping into flight or the beady black eye that glinted out at me. The giant mural of the crow on the opposite wall loomed out of the dim, rust-colored glow of the room, so lifelike that for a moment, I expected it to dive at me.

"What the *fuck*?"

"Knight, talk to me. What do you see?"

"Um. Let me get back to you on that." I took a cautious step inside. The light had a reddish cast in here because a dark red tapestry hung over the small window on the westward wall, not because everything was coated in blood. I flipped the light switch on the near wall, and a small antique wooden lamp on the desk beside me lit up.

Suddenly the room looked a touch more normal, or at least the kind of normal I would expect based on Rae's usual appearance: a little goth, a little crunchy, a little metal.

Except for that mural. Nothing was normal about that.

I saw the crows. Eve's words, but I had seen them too often myself in the last few days. There was Rae's tattoo, of course, eerily like this giant painting. There were the actual birds that seemed to haunt me, watching me with their bright black eyes, calling back and forth to one another. And of course, there was the one that the goddess became, leaping from my chamber window like a wilder, weirder interpretation of an Edgar Allen Poe poem.

Now this one lunged at me from Rae's wall, larger than life, its form painted with detailed, painstaking accuracy. Behind it, the lamplight revealed another kind of silhouette in the mural, a hazy, vaguely feminine figure shaped from shadow and mist. Her eyes burned out at me as if from under a hooded cloak, bright with the colors of fire and blood.

"Dear God." And at my muttered curse, Ariel's words whispered through my mind, an echo of a memory. *God has nothing to do with this...*

Not God, but a goddess.

Morrighu.

"One hell of a decorating scheme." Ira's voice from behind me made me jump out of my skin.

"Tell me about it." I leaned against the door frame, willing my heart to slow. I didn't want to turn my back to the thing on the wall. It reminded me of a creepy story I'd read once about an artist who painted portraits of monsters and devils in his basement studio. His admirers wondered how he managed to imagine horrors in such detail. But the twist, of course, was that he drew them all from life.

I didn't believe that paint could be haunted, but then again, I'd just put my hand through a glass door without leaving a mark on the glass or my hand. Besides, who was I to judge? Maybe those demons in the story were my own ancestors. Even demons needed pictures to send to their sweethearts back home, right?

Maybe this one was a relative, too.

I shuddered and put my back to it in deliberate defiance. The near wall, like the bed under the window with its pink and blue mandala coverlet, seemed more cheerful and pedestrian, with band posters and photographs tacked up above the desk—

Except they weren't just photographs.

"Holy...Ira, look. She has a hit list."

Ira followed my gaze and whistled softly.

The pictures were printouts from online profiles, stabbed through with silver thumbtacks. Some of them looked like they came from the fraternity's website, featuring distinguished alumni. I recognized them: the gourmet chef, the comedian, the news anchor, the doctor, the judge, and the university administrator, followed by five social media profiles, the young men from the murder house. Each one had an "X" slashed over their face in red permanent marker, except the last one.

I recognized him, too. "Oh my god. That's Senator Ritter! If she's targeting him—I need to call Sebastian."

"Wait. I'll handle the senator." Ira plucked another photo from the wall, one that had hung half-obscured by the hit list and held it out to me. "Is this her?"

Reluctantly, I slid my phone back into my pocket and took the glossy print Ira held out. It showed a group of people dressed in what looked like Renaissance Faire garb, posed proudly in front of a cluster of standing stones that resembled a mini-Stonehenge, if not for the familiar California chaparral surrounding them. The few men in the group wore long hair in braids, their faces and bare chests painted with intricate blue spirals. The women's hair flowed loose, their feet bare and faces painted with heavy dark stripes over their eyes, much like the goddess when she confronted me in Sebastian's vacation spot.

In the center of the group stood Rae McGuire, her bright red hair spilling over her shoulders and floating slightly as if blown by the wind. She wore a leather vest and a long black skirt, and a feral smile lit her face. Heavy black makeup obscured her eyes, dark lipstick making a curving slash of her lips that contrasted starkly with her pale skin, and a cloak of black feathers draped her shoulders

She held an unsheathed sword in her hand. Its blade caught and held the light, sharp and uncompromising, much like the woman who wielded it.

"I told you she had a sword." My voice shook more than I wanted it to, and I flipped over the photo. *Samhain, Mt. Diablo Stone City* was written on the back of it, with a date from fall of the previous year.

"Interesting," Ira said. "A pagan ritual, maybe. That sword looks real."

"Oh, it's real, all right." I sat down on the bed with a thump, mind racing.

Is this where Rae had gone? To Mount Diablo, to the standing stones, where she and her rag-tag band of hippie twenty-somethings had called down...what? Not the moon, but a goddess, or a demon.

I hazarded a glance at the mural, meeting the burning gaze of the entity painted there. Had Rae done this with her own hand? Or had something else guided her, ridden her, possessed her? Something that said, *the one I ride now calls me Morrighu...*

I had to find her before she, or whatever power she channeled, claimed another victim. And to do that, I had to follow her to Mount Diablo. Despite my deepening misgiving, a slight, sardonic smile tugged at my mouth.

The devil's mountain. How apropos.

22

WHERE ANGELS FEAR TO TREAD

I leaned my elbows on the railing of the Black Cat Club's upper level. My gaze swept over the churning crowd of dancers below, my muscles loose and my hand cupped around a half-full glass containing a toxic concoction of multiple liquors.

I'd asked the bartender for the most alcoholic drink available and watched him pick up five different bottles before topping the glass off with well bourbon and coke. It went down easier than it should and hit like a truck. Just what the demon ordered.

For the first time in a decade, I was on the hunt for a kether donor. And for the first time in my life, I hunted alone.

I had discovered at least one unexpected upside to the draining effects of a silver burn. It stripped away my demon invulnerability and made me weak, a fraction more human, but it turned out that fraction was just enough to allow me to get drunk.

That intoxication lowered my inhibitions enough that when my phone buzzed insistently against my hip, and I pulled it out to see Sebastian's name on my caller ID, I answered instead of sending him to voicemail like I had the last ten or fifteen times he'd tried to call me.

"Hello, stranger." I decided to play it cool.

"Lily. Finally." His voice vibrated with strain. "Thank God you're okay."

"Why wouldn't I be?"

"Oh, I don't know. Maybe because you walked out on me and then refused to answer my calls." Now he sounded mad.

Oh, right. I guess he had reason to worry, but what gave him the right? "I can take care of myself."

"I never questioned that." He paused, inhaled, and then continued, softening enough that I had to strain my ears to catch his next words. "I think I'm allowed to be glad you're not dead."

After I'd almost killed him, I didn't expect him to care. I didn't deserve it. "You don't give up easy, do you, Mr. Ritter?"

"I'm quite notably a stubborn bastard. I thought you read all my puff pieces. Surely one of them mentioned that."

"I'll check my scrapbook and get back to you." I tossed back another swallow of my drink. If he wanted another round of this dance, I might not get another chance to take him up on it. "What do you want? I'm kind of in the middle of something here."

"I wanted to apologize. I was too harsh the other night. I—"

"Too *harsh*?" My laugh raked my throat. "Seb. Sebastian. You damn fool of a man. You weren't harsh *enough*. I almost killed you. I lost control." I caught my breath, a ragged noise too close to a sob. "I don't understand you. I really don't."

Or maybe I understood too well. Maybe I held him in thrall, and that's the only reason he wouldn't quit me. No matter what he said and did, I couldn't shake the suspicion that my succubus charms had tricked him into liking me.

"I know you don't," he said, his tone resigned. "It would be easier to explain to you in person. Where are you? It sounds like you're out."

"I am out." My eyes narrowed, picking a likely-looking mark who hung back from the edge of the dancers, eyes bright with yearning, energy sharp with uncertainty. "Why do you ask? Can't you just track me with your creeper ware?" Sebastian's company invested heavily in security and surveillance tech, and I never missed an opportunity to poke him about it.

"You know very well that I only tracked your phone last year because you asked me to." His short tone told me I'd scored a hit, but he recovered quicker than I expected. "And I know you. You're being prickly because you're trying to drive me away. Because you're trying to protect me from yourself. Well, it won't work."

I didn't say anything. I couldn't, because he was right. And yet, if I told him to leave me alone, to never call me again, he would do it. The certainty of that knowledge beat at me like my own pulse, only steadier.

So why couldn't I just say it? Why couldn't I send him away for his own good? Set him free to live his own life, find a nice human woman who deserved the devotion he offered me despite every prickle and hurt I offered in return?

Was it possible that I was bound to him as surely as my power bound him to me? Theo had once told me that the Claim worked both ways. Was this how it got you, winding our souls together more tightly every time we touched?

Was that really what I feared, more than hurting him, more than my own power? I'd been soul bound once, by Ariel, and only his death freed me from his influence.

No. I had the power here. I had the responsibility. Sebastian was human, and this was different. Wasn't it?

"Lily, are you there?"

"What? Yeah." The guy I'd noticed at the edge of the dance floor melted back into the crowd around the bar. I sidled along the railing, keeping him in view.

I could tell Sebastian now that things were over. I could protect him from my power. I couldn't break our bond energetically without dying, the way I had with Danny, but I could keep him out of harm's way. All I had to do was tell him to go to hell.

I couldn't do it. "I have to go," I said, and ended the call.

I gathered my best Presence around myself as I swept down the stairway toward the club's ground floor. In my skin-tight black leggings, stiletto ankle boots, and the double-breasted Victorian-style tailcoat I'd dug out of the back of Ariel's closet, it didn't take much. With each deliberate step of my descent, I drew my captive audience's eyes and held them, magnets to my North Pole. The sense of power thrilled through me, delighting in the way their heads turned to follow me, their lips parted, their eyes dilated, all the force of their desire trained on me. Their gender didn't matter if their Kinsey score trended even a little in my direction.

I could have any one of them, anyone I wanted. I paused on the bottom step, and the room stilled with me despite the heavy electronic beat pulsing through the humid, electric air. My eyes searched the crowd for the man I'd spotted from above. He hung back against the bar, his gaze fixed on me, hungry and a little afraid. His broad chest, longish blond hair, and beard contrasted with his nervous energy and the sweat beading on his forehead.

His eyes widened when I strode toward him, pulling off my gloves as I went. The crowd on the dance floor parted for me, leaving a clear path between us.

A pang of *déjà vu* seized me. Six months ago, I watched a now-dead woman cut a swathe through this dance floor in the same way. Nepenthe had been the first succubus I had met in the flesh—the *living* flesh—and the ease with which she wielded her charm over humans gave me the first real glimpse of what I could become.

I had a taste of the power I could exert over a room full of humans a few days later when I danced here on the stage in an ill-fated gambit to draw out a killer who had hidden in plain sight at my side. But even that was nothing like this moment. My energy sharpened like a blade forged from the simplicity of the hunt and my singularity of purpose.

I stopped in front of my quarry, looking him over. He shivered under my gaze and sucked in a sharp breath. His desiderata didn't carry Sebastian's complexity, or his darkness.

That was good. I wanted this simplicity. I didn't have time for hidden intoxicants or any risk of tainted kether. And his size and strength meant he might withstand my worst instincts.

I took another step, into his personal space. "You'll do."

"Do I know you?" His brow crinkled under my scrutiny.

"Do you need to?" I had his desiderata dead to rights now. He wanted me, and I fit my movements to the rhythm of his want beating in my veins. I raised my hand to fit it along his square jaw, his beard scratchy-soft against my palm, my fingers seeking his skin beneath and the first whisper of kether-touch. Craving surged in me, and I pressed my hips against his. Our bodies fit together like they were made for each other.

"Let's dance," I said in his ear.

He shook his head. "I don't dance."

"You do now." I grabbed his hand and pulled him out onto the floor.

Caught in my rhythm, he didn't miss a beat. But he moved like a man in a dream, gaze fixed on me. I led, letting my hips grind against his, our bodies close enough that the hard ridge of his erection pressed into my leg through his jeans.

The energy of the club shifted around us. Beside us, another couple leaned into each other, mouths crashing together. The patterns on the dance floor seamlessly changed from small groups and single dancers to intensely synced pairings, threesomes, and even a few moresomes. Bodies closed the gaps that separated them moments before, their movements purposeful and aching.

The air seemed to thicken, honey-sweet and heavy. Even the music changed, the beat dropping like a skipped heartbeat as the DJ moved in a dreamlike trance to introduce a song with a slower tempo.

"What the hell?" The words slipped out under my breath, and realization chased close behind them. I still held them all in my Presence, and my Presence had told them all that it was time to bang. Any minute now, an orgy would break out on the dance floor.

My own partner's half-lidded eyes had glazed over, his lips parted, waiting for my next move. I grabbed his arm, the rolled sleeve of his shirt a thin barrier that stopped the kether pull I wanted more than anything in this world, but *not yet.* Not here.

"Let's go somewhere more private." I dialed back my Presence enough to ensure the whole club didn't follow us out and try to join in and turned to steer him outside.

A sudden jarring discordance nettled my skin, a key change that no one else could hear. It wasn't the music. It was the energy in the room, shifting again to something darker, deeper, more complex.

Then I saw him. Sebastian stood just inside the club entrance, his arms folded, staring straight at me. His desiderata cut across the sensual atmosphere I'd created in a sharp, painful descant that sliced through my own haze of desire and pierced my chest with ice.

His lips shaped my name, his eyes dark with a hurt deeper than any physical harm I'd done to him the other night. Then he spun on his heel and walked out.

"Sebastian, wait!" I dropped the other man's arm and rushed after my not-boyfriend.

His long-legged strides took the space of two of mine. I hadn't taken more than a few small sips of kether from chance touches yet, so I was panting by the time I caught up with him on the sidewalk outside.

"It's all right, Lily." He wouldn't look at me. "I shouldn't have come."

"How long were you watching me?"

"Not long. Long enough." He seemed about to say something else, but stopped, shook his head, and started walking again. But he slowed his pace enough that I could keep up without half-running.

"I'm sorry. I can explain."

"You don't need to explain." His aura flared, jagged and harsh, but the acid didn't direct itself at me. "You've made things pretty clear. I just didn't want to listen. I'll leave you be, Lily. I know that's what you want."

"But that's not what I want!"

He rounded on me, and the pain in him stabbed through me, tangible enough that I staggered. "Isn't it?"

"No! This isn't about us."

"Could have fooled me. What's it about, then?"

"It's about Eve," I said. "The feds arrested her. They put silver cuffs on her. She's dying, and I'm the only one who cares. I have to prove that she's innocent, but first I have to find the person who's really doing this. To do that, I need kether. I can't face down a monster without it."

"What monster?" He frowned. His energy swirled and shifted around us, pain and anger giving way to confusion.

"I don't know, exactly. Another demon. She says she's a goddess. She's scary as fuck, and she's out for blood. She doesn't care about collateral damage."

A muscle leaped in his temple, the shadows stark on his face under the monochrome illumination of the streetlight. "If you needed kether, you could have asked me."

"I couldn't." My heart contracted, but with his emotion or my own, I couldn't tell anymore. "After what I did to you, it's not fair to ask of you. I'm not sure it ever has been fair to ask of you."

"Well, it's your body." He set his jaw. "I don't have any right to tell you what to do with it or who to sleep with. We never said we were exclusive. I'd like to say I was beyond jealousy, but...was it fair to ask *him?*"

"No," I admitted, and raised my head so I could meet his eyes. "No, it wasn't fair. I just..." My voice faltered and I swallowed, pressing on. "I couldn't live with myself if I hurt you again."

His expression cleared, just a little. "You're worried that what happened in Napa will happen again."

"Aren't you? Sebastian, I'm a danger to you as it is. A danger to anyone. But if I were to have another flashback like that one—" My breath trembled out of me. "That's what scares me the most. The effect I have on you...it's too much."

"The effect you have?" Sebastian laughed, the short, sharp sound that had drawn me to him the first time we met. It always sounded startled, a momentary loss of control by a man who kept himself in check the way I couldn't. "You think it's because you're succubusing me."

"It must be that. Don't you think so? You did on Saturday night."

"Lily." He took me by the shoulders, his grip firm and warm through the leather, and I looked up in surprise. "Don't you see? That's what I came here to tell you. I realized something after you left that night. When my head was clear from whatever it was you did to heal me, I could finally see it. And when you came by and found me and Helena together—Lily, we were discussing the terms of our divorce."

"What?" My pulse skipped and sped up. It responded to his desiderata, which swelled in a rising chord and wrapped us in golden light, a sunrise too bright to stare directly into. And yet we stood on a dark street, with shadowy buildings towering on either side of us, while the last daylight faded behind a blanketing fog. The dual perceptions left me dizzy. I put out my hands to steady myself against his chest.

"It's true. And everything you said the other night was true, too. I've been avoiding the fallout from my failure with her. But now, I want to make it right. I want to be the kind of man you deserve."

"That's not—what are you saying?"

"The truth." His eyes shone blue as the morning sky. "Lily Knight, I think I'm falling in love with you."

The words didn't make sense. I stared at him, speechless, struggling to parse what he'd told me. Sebastian *loved* me? Me, the half-demon who used him as a kether battery and threw him against walls when she got spooked? No, I must have misheard. The alternative was too ludicrous to believe.

The heart-light enveloping us dimmed at the edges, laced through with shadowy fractures, and then it dawned on me. He couldn't lie, not to me. Not about this. His desiderata showed his vulnerability and the depth of his feelings, his fear that I would push him away yet again.

"Sebastian, I—" My words stuttered, failed. What did a demon woman like me know about love? What did I ever do to earn this man's devotion? Nothing but resist him and second-guess him, running hot and cold as a San Francisco summer. "I don't know what to say."

"You don't have to say anything." He gathered himself, bracing for a blow. "I didn't tell you that so you would say it back. I just needed you to know, before..."

He didn't finish the sentence, but we both knew how it ended. He expected me to break his heart to protect his soul.

I didn't have a good answer for him, but I found I wasn't ready to let go, either. Instead, I stepped into his arms and wrapped him in a fierce embrace. He froze for a moment, and then his arms went around me. His head bent to mine, but I turned my face aside, my lips beside his ear, almost touching.

"Take me home with you," I whispered, and with that, the truth came out. It wasn't the truth he wanted, but it came close enough, for now. "I need you. I've tried not to, but I can't help it. I'm sorry that I make everything so hard."

"Oh, you make it hard all right." His chuckle rumbled through me. "And I'm not sorry at all."

And at that, despite everything, despite myself, I couldn't help but laugh. I clung to him, giggling, even though my body cried out beneath my breathless gasps for a different kind of helpless paroxysm.

Finally, I released him and moved a half-step back, pulling on the gloves I'd stuffed in my pocket in the club.

Then I offered him my hand, and he took me home.

PART III.

BLOOD WILL OUT

23

Love Your Demons

Sebastian and I barely made it two steps into the house, unable to keep our hands off each other. As soon as the door shut, he turned to me with his desiderata aflame all around him and backed me up against the wall beside the door to his garage. I tipped my head back and opened my mouth to his.

For all the passion in his aura, he was gentle with me, but I wanted more and less than gentleness, my body restless for a firm touch and his weight pressing me down. I bit my lip to keep myself from voicing any inadvertent requests that he couldn't refuse and kissed him again.

His kether flooded my senses, heady and healing, the ache in my wrist subsiding as the last of the silver burn faded. It swept away my fatigue, healed my stiff joints and aching muscles, leaving me powerful and lithe.

I pulled back from the kiss, taking him by the shoulders to steady him. "Hold on. I want to try something."

"What?" His breath came fast, eyes half-lidded, his blue irises waning to a pale ring around the darkness of his arousal.

"A give and take. Not just a pull." I could hardly believe I was saying it. "It might make the aftermath easier on you. I've never done it before, but I think I know how. Is that okay?"

"You know it is."

I wouldn't have felt okay with it without his express consent. "Give me your hand," I said, and when he did, I took it between my two gloved palms, gently folding his fingers down one by one until only the index extended. Then I spun him around and switched places with him, his back to the wall for support in case I screwed this up. "Ready?"

He nodded, once, his desiderata blazing higher than before, and I tilted my head down and took his finger into my mouth.

A moan rose in his throat, and I hummed in answer, savoring the kether that exploded through his skin onto my tongue. He tasted rich and bittersweet, like dark chocolate and salted caramel.

He groaned, his hips bucking toward me. "Don't stop."

I didn't want to, but now came the test. I focused on the flow of kether and seized control, willed it to slow until something seemed to snap inside me. The polarity reversed. An unexpected rush of pleasure and weakness spread through my body as I pushed his energy back to him, suckling him lightly one more time before I released his finger and raised my head to look at him.

He moaned again, his head tipped back against the wall, his lips parted, his eyes closed. "Jesus, Lily."

"Are you all right?"

"Whatever you did, it feels amazing." His laugh startled out of him. "But if you think this will make things last longer, I have some news for you."

I glanced down. The taut line of his erection stretched the crotch of his jeans askew, and that gave me another brilliant idea. I reached for his belt. "May I?"

"May you what? Go down on me?" His eyes fluttered open, and a smile played around his mouth that lit a fire in the pit of my belly. "What a question. Yes, you may."

The two-way channel I opened with my reverse pull technique had changed things between us. Now, he seemed to exert a hold on me. His need washed over me with an urgency that almost matched a demon Presence. I dropped to my knees in front of him, fumbling with his zipper, and his breathless chuckle sent another wave of heat rolling through me.

"Oh, to hell with it." I stripped off my glove, the better to strip him, and finally got his pants down and his boxer briefs unfastened. His cock sprang free, straining toward me, and the tips of my bare fingers strayed across the silky-smooth skin.

We both gasped at the sudden contact. A shock of kether surged through me. I drew back, glancing up to find his gaze locked on me.

His eyes smoldered and his voice quivered somewhere between amusement and frustration. "Don't look so scared. It's not like you haven't seen it before."

"That's not what I'm worried about."

"I'm fine. This wall is very sturdy."

"I don't want to hurt you," I whispered, my lips inches from him.

"If I fall," he said, "you'll just have to catch me. Lily, we both know you're strong enough for that."

My heart contracted. He still trusted me, after everything. *Don't fuck it up this time.* My gloved left hand trembled slightly as I circled him with finger and thumb. The strangled sound he made at my touch spurred me forward.

I leaned forward and took him in my mouth, the hard hot length of him filling my senses and the strength of the kether rush almost more than I could handle. His hands tangled in my hair, tingles of kether electrifying my scalp. I closed my eyes and pushed the energy back toward him, taking him deeper, giving him all I could.

The head of his cock hit the back of my throat, and I had to come up for air before I choked. But the push and pull didn't leave me weak this time. The force of his energy flooding through me left me with more than I could direct back to him. I let it feed my endurance, moving faster, caressing him with lips and tongue.

He'd called it right. It didn't take long for him to lose his iron control, his hips bucking into me. It was my turn to moan, the beat of his kether thundering through me. At the sound, he wrapped my hair in his hand, tight enough to send a new wave of tingles down my spine. He pressed me closer, his girth swelling in my mouth. And then he stiffened, and shouted, and came hard, his sweet-sharp essence spilling over my tongue.

I almost lost control too until I noticed his legs buckling and belatedly pushed kether back to him. He stayed upright, though he still sagged against the wall. But that I could attribute to a normal human male reaction after a powerful orgasm.

"How do you feel?" I sat up and stretched, glorying in the warmth that suffused my body.

"Like I'm floating." His tone was dreamy, almost drugged. "Floating on a sea of stars."

I stared at him. "Why stars?"

His eyes blinked open, focusing on me a little slower than normal. "I have no idea," he said. "It's always what I picture when I think of you... What?"

"I want to show you something." I stood up, shedding my coat, and his eyes caressed me, hungry again already in defiance of his refractory period. His unbuttoned jeans barely hung on above his slender hips, doing nothing to conceal how hard he still was for me. It made me smile. "Not *that*. This."

I took a deep breath, remembering my dreams of flight, and stepped into the air.

Sebastian's jaw dropped. He gazed up at me with a stunned expression on his face, his energy a mixture of fear and reverence. "My God, Lily."

"Pretty cool, huh?" I flexed my ethereal wings, stars sparking in my peripheral vision. "What I want to know is how you knew. That dress you bought me matches them almost exactly."

"I feel like I've always known." He still looked flabbergasted. "Ever since I found you in my bed, since you drew from me the first time. That field of stars is like an afterimage in my mind when I look at you."

"That's strange." Humans weren't supposed to be able to see into us the way we could read them.

He waved it away. "What I want to know is whether you know what you are. What you look like."

Confused, I dropped back to earth on a downbeat. "I'm a demon, Seb," I said. "Or close enough not to matter."

"That's not it." He straightened up from the wall, disappointing me by fastening his jeans. His face was serious now, his voice slow and thoughtful. "How much do you know about where demons come from?"

"Not much. Why?"

"Because, Lily," he said. "You look like a goddamn angel."

"Thanks." I shifted my pinions into place with a snap of displaced air, uncomfortable with the implications. What was he getting at?

"Not what I meant, though don't get me wrong, you are stunning. No, I mean it literally. You look like you stepped out of the negative print of a Renaissance painting. No, out of Revelations. Beautiful and terrible. Is that what you really are? Are you an angel, Lil?"

Shock rolled over me and I stood stock still, letting my wings fade back into the light and shadow of the room.

Little Lilith, we were angels once...

I shivered at the echo of Ariel's words. I had only half-believed him them, and later convinced myself it was part of his megalomania. I couldn't trust anything he'd told me. But coming from Sebastian, it was different.

"No one really knows for sure." The origins of demons were shrouded in mystery. Ariel certainly hadn't given me much useful information about my father's people. "But I do know I'm not some divine celestial being."

"What makes you so sure of that?"

"Because I'm not that special." Still shaken, I sunk into a chair. "I don't have any mystical knowledge. Hell, I don't even know if there *is* a hell, or a God, or anything like that. I have some talents others don't have, but underneath it all, I'm just a person like anyone else."

"I never questioned that." His steps didn't waver, so my new method of keeping him safe from the drain had worked. He came to me and dropped to a crouch beside me, reaching to tuck a wayward strand of hair behind my ear.

I drew back from his touch. My mind swirled with the questions his words sparked, and I didn't trust myself to maintain the focus I needed to protect him. "I'm sorry," I said. "I didn't plan to come here tonight, and I'm running out of time. Eve's running out of time. I need to get out to Mount Diablo, before..."

Before someone else died.

"It's not all on you, Lily. You can't carry the weight of the whole world on your shoulders like this. I know you're strong, but that would crush anyone eventually."

"You don't understand." I shook my head. "She has nobody. No family. She's all alone. Helping her is the least I can do, considering...well."

"Considering what?"

I shut my eyes, the words balanced on the tip of my tongue. Hell, he wanted the truth from me, didn't he? May as well go for the gold. "Considering that I'm the reason she's alone."

He didn't say anything for a long moment. "What does that mean?" His tone sharpened. "Lily. What did you do?"

With a deep breath, I steeled myself. "Ariel was her father." The words thickened on my tongue, so that I had to force them out. "You wanted to know what happened that night. Well, here's the truth. I killed him." My voice broke and I covered my face in my hands. "I killed Ariel. I made that girl an orphan."

"Hey." Sebastian said. His fingers brushed over mine, closed around my wrist, and tugged my hands down. "Look at me."

I raised my head and met his clear blue eyes and steady gaze. His desiderata held nothing of shock and horror, only a gentle sadness that reached out across the space between us, caressing and accepting.

"Wait. You *knew*?"

"I suspected as much." He released me, returning his gaze forward. "You said you'd taken care of the problem. A round was missing from my gun. And you wouldn't say anything more about it."

"Then why—?" Why did he keep pushing me? Why make an issue of it? Why make me admit to it?

"I wanted to hear you say it. Because I wanted to tell you that it's okay."

"But it's not okay. I *killed* someone, Seb. Someone I knew. Someone I—" Swallowing, I changed tactics. "I could argue self-defense. He came after me first. But…it's not true. Not entirely. After he went down, I made sure he stayed down. I murdered him."

"He was evil," Sebastian said. "You did the right thing, Lily. Not an easy thing, but the hardest thing. You know he would have killed you, and he wouldn't have felt bad about it for a second. That was his plan all along."

"No, it wasn't." I set my jaw. "That's the worst part of the whole thing. He didn't want to kill me. He wanted me to join him. And you were part of it. He wanted me to pull from you all along, from the first time he brought me to you."

That shook him. "What? Why?"

"That was his whole strategy. Get me hooked on pure kether, come to me while I was drunk on power, and convince me to buy into his twisted fantasy of a world where demons rule supreme."

"But you didn't buy into it."

"No. I didn't." I flinched at the memory of his fury when I turned him down, his contorted face as he came at me. "I don't think it ever occurred to him that I would say no, or why I would say no. Even though Nepenthe did the same thing for the same reason. That's why she died, you know."

He frowned at Nepenthe's name. "What reason?"

Him. Sebastian. She did it for him. But I didn't say it. "She chose humanity over him, and he killed her for it."

"Jesus." Sebastian's desiderata rippled. I'd dropped a stone into his still waters with that one. Maybe I should have talked to him about this earlier, after all.

"Ariel was seriously screwed up," I said. "But that's not his daughter's fault. And now all she has is me."

"Does she know? About Ariel?"

I hung my head. "I didn't tell her. But she overheard me and Danny talking about him. That's why she ran. I *know*," I added, at the startled noise he made in his throat. "I should have told her the truth to begin with. I should have told everyone the truth."

He favored me with a lingering, unreadable glance. "So why didn't you?"

"Because it was selfish. I didn't want her to hate me. I wanted to..." What? Fix it? I couldn't bring Eve's father back. I wouldn't bring him back, even if I could. "I wanted to be there for her. But now it's all fucked up. I fucked it up, Sebastian. She'll never trust me now."

"Maybe not," Sebastian said. "But Ariel fucked it up first. You did what you had to do to stop him. It's not your fault he was the way he was, right?"

Reluctant to grant him the point, I chewed the inside of my cheek. "No. I don't know why or how he got so twisted, but it wasn't because of me."

"All right. Then why are you blaming yourself?"

I opened my mouth, closed it again. I had no answer for him because he was right, again. It had fallen to me to dispatch Ariel because nobody else could do it. I had to let him kiss me one last time, had to let him believe he won, before I could drive the stake into his heart and put him down. If I hadn't, if I'd let him kill again, I never would have forgiven myself.

Why couldn't I forgive myself now?

"I wish you could see what I see when I look at you," Sebastian said, into my silence.

"And what's that? An angel?" I scoffed, turning away. Whatever Sebastian said, whatever Ariel had claimed, I didn't have any evidence to believe it. Maybe my father's people had started that way, but my own experience told me I was no angel. How could I be? Human life force sustained me. It bound my flesh and bone together. Without it, I became a monster, feral and hungry.

With it...well, I was still a monster when I took kether. Just a monster who could think about what she'd done. It made me stronger, faster, sharper, more whole, and a predator if not a parasite, dependent on humans for sustenance.

"No." Sebastian had risen, and now he stepped behind me, his voice shivering up my spine. "I see a woman. A human woman."

"You know that's not true. I'm only half-human."

"Are you sure?" he said. "Science would say otherwise, Lily. Demons must share DNA with humans, otherwise they couldn't breed with us. You couldn't exist. So that would make you a subspecies of homo sapiens—or maybe an ancestor."

He'd clearly put some thought into this, his sharp engineer's mind worrying away at it while I worried about metaphysical problems like soul bonds and kether drains. Feeling exposed under his scrutiny, I wrapped my arms around myself. "I'm not sure genetics or science can explain us. We're supernatural creatures. Nature's laws don't apply."

"I doubt that very much. A more logical conclusion would be that we just don't know the laws that apply yet." His hands skimmed over my bare back, drawing another shudder from me. "In any case, I propose a different kind of scientific inquiry. I promise to be quite thorough and replicate my results as many times as necessary to prove my hypothesis."

I eyed him but took his hand with my gloved one and let him pull me back toward him. "And what hypothesis is that?"

He grinned at me and gestured to the stairs. "That the little trick you did means I have next to no refractory period. And that half-succubi can have an unlimited number of multiple orgasms, given the correct conditions."

"Oh. That's...*oh*."

"Oh, indeed."

"Sebastian, I don't think I have time for that."

"Call it proof of concept, then."

We didn't make it up the stairs, but their plush carpeting made them comfortable enough for our purposes. And our extended inquiry showed signs of bearing out Sebastian's hypothesis.

Too soon, I extricated myself and gathered my strewn clothes. "I have to go."

"I'll drive you," Sebastian said, but he didn't stir from his half-prone position on the landing midway down the staircase.

"You're in no shape to drive." I took a long look at him, fixing his image in my mind's eye. Leaning back on his elbows, naked, one long, slim-muscled leg outstretched and one pulled up to his chest, he could have modeled for a sculpture in the classical style. It wasn't the worst way to leave him for the last time if I didn't survive the night.

"Take the roadster, then. She's an automatic."

"You'd let me drive Betty?" The powder-blue coupe was one of his favorites.

"She's faster than public transit and she has driver assist. You'll be fine. The keys are in the cab."

"Okay." A frisson of anxiety ran through me. I didn't like driving in the most ideal of situations, and a late-night drive out of the city didn't sound like one. But I couldn't argue with his logic, and a flight across the bay would waste precious energy I might need for the fight that awaited me. "Thank you. And Sebastian?"

"Yes?" He raised an eyebrow, his smile slow and lazy. "You're stalling. Spit it out."

"About what you said earlier." I struggled for the right words. "I think...I think I could love you, too."

His eyes widened, surprise blooming in his desiderata. "You think you *could*?"

"I think I might," I corrected myself, all in a rush, and fled out the door to his vast garage before he could respond.

24

MORE IN HEAVEN OR EARTH

The signs at the trail head had warned that the park was closed at nightfall. No one was supposed to summit Mount Diablo after sunset, and yet here I was.

Before long, the last vestiges of twilight drained from the sky, and full night closed in around me. The wide fire road that led up from the trail head petered out into a steep climb up a narrow, rocky path. It wound through dark thickets of oak and along narrow ledges treacherous with mud from the previous week's rain. I thanked my lucky stars and my demon blood that I could see in the dark, but I still found myself questioning my life decisions.

Even with its constant looming presence on the eastern horizon, living in the city made it easy to forget Diablo was a *big* mountain. Not Sierra Nevada big, but it still promised a search at a few thousand feet of elevation in rough terrain for a group of young people with more imagination than sense. If worse came to worse, I could take to the air and hunt for signs of them that way. But for now, I preferred to save my energy for whatever showdown awaited me out here once I found them.

I crested the first of three ridges that rose ahead of me into the star-studded sky and paused. The wind gusting up the slope carried a faint sound of a drumbeat to my ears. The smoky scent of a campfire accompanied it, and then, for just a moment, the skin-prickling sensation of latent electricity.

They were close, but how close? I sucked in a long breath, irresolute. Then, on the exhalation, I took a running leap off the peak and flung myself into empty space.

I trusted my wings to bear me up, and they did. They manifested out of air and darkness, massive pinions that carried me over the shadow of the canyon below.

Ira's question about how my wings work floated to the surface of my thoughts. But I didn't have to think about them to use them. My body knew by instinct, used them to save me when my human body would have fallen. They worked like the faith I'd abandoned long ago. They shouldn't exist, they didn't make sense, and yet they still did their job. I didn't need to understand them.

An updraft caught me, buffeting me off track, and I fought for control with an undignified flap and muttered curse. In fact, the things worked better when I didn't think about them too hard. Sometimes, I had to let the demon in me take the wheel.

I followed the low rhythm of the drums, skimming the last of the peaks, and dipped into a shallow valley held like a cup in the mountain's hand. Firelight beckoned through the oak canopy ahead of me. I turned aside and circled, reconnoitering. Below me, a wide treeless space opened up. The fire burned in its center, its flames flickering around the base of standing stones.

The stones didn't live up to the pictures. Just one long slab laid atop two upright ones, they didn't qualify as a real henge, at least not what I thought of as a henge. But the tableau under the stones' auspices looked authentic enough.

Alighting outside the reach of the firelight, I folded my wings. They faded back into the night, insubstantial now as the smoke drifting from the bonfire. I crept closer, keeping to the edge of the trees.

I'd underestimated these people. I figured them for dabblers playing with forces they didn't understand. But now—

Maybe I was the one that didn't understand them.

The drums beat like a huge heart, steady, deep, and slow. The semicircle of humans gathered under the stones stood silent and intent. Two figures moved around them in a deliberate dance that paused at each cardinal direction.

Then, as if cued by an intangible signal, the people in the inner circle raised their arms to the heavens in unison and began to chant in rhythm with the drums.

I shivered, though the cold wind couldn't touch me with Sebastian's kether running hot in my veins. The desiderata of the singers rang out in unison with their words. The language didn't sound like English. It clanged like bells, both musical and harsh. And it stirred something in my blood that answered to it, something deep and dark, something old and demon-born.

Drawn inexorably by the music of their hearts and voices, I moved inward. Dry grass rustled at my passage, the ground uneven under my feet, but no one in the circle seemed to notice me even when I stumbled and phantom wings kept me from pitching forward into the dirt. The intensity of their invocation rose, their energy building with it.

I gathered a Presence around myself. I was unremarkable, unobtrusive, a part of this group, someone else's friend, someone they almost recognized. In my swooping tailcoat and boots, I could pass for one of them in the dark, at least to human eyes.

I stepped into the ring, took the place that opened for me, and raised my hands, copying the young man next to me. But an icy drip of foreboding trickled down the back of my spine.

Rae McGuire stood in the center of the circle. Stock still, with black feathers woven into her bright hair and a dark bar of paint obscuring her face around her hooded eyes, she waited with her head bowed. Her gown was scarlet and her feet were bare, but like me, she seemed impervious to the cold of a spring evening on the mountainside.

She held a tall spear in one hand and a sword unsheathed in the other. Blue flames flickered along its edge, a cold contrast to the light of the fire.

The crowd's chant peaked in a furious shout. As suddenly as it began, it ebbed into silence.

A single voice spoke, rich and singsong—Rae's voice, though she did not raise her head.

"On this Beltane eve, the gods of old first came from their ships on the misty seas to walk the land. As kings and queens, they lived and worked and loved alongside mortal men and women. They became flesh of our flesh and blood of our blood. By their power, the earth ran rich with milk and honey, and by their courage they defended their people against evil."

As luck would have it, I'd arrived just in time for the monologue. Rae stalked the circumference of the firelit circle, her sword arm extended from her shoulder, her voice settling into the rhythm of a much-recited story. "But evil came anyway, clothed in pious light. It drove the great ones into the shadows. It destroyed their indwellings and stole their legends away, and their spirits fell lost in the mists of time."

I stepped back into the shadows as she passed me, closing the circle. Her energy gave me the willies. It twisted and writhed, a fathomless darkness that rose from deep within her, shuddering with the unlight of an eclipse.

Now she stepped back to the center of the circle and raised her sword to the sky. "Today, that changes. Today we shall witness our great queen walk among us in the flesh, come again to fight for us as once she fought of old."

Rae's body shuddered. The polarity in the air shifted. The full voltage of the free-floating charge that sparked through the atmosphere around us crawled down her upraised blade and grounded itself in her. The taste of ozone and copper clotted on my tongue. The people in the circle shifted, murmuring in awe, saying her name.

"Morrighu…"

"It's her. The great queen walks among us."

"Hail, Morrighu."

The woman in the center of the circle lifted her head. The movement disquieted me, more avian than human. And something deep and dark and old looked out of her flat, black eyes straight at me.

"Come forth, little sister." She spoke with Rae's throat and Rae's tongue, but the tone rang harsh and wild, a crow's call like that which had haunted my dreams and waking hours of late. It held the resonance of command.

It did me no good to hide now. I stepped forward out of the circle and into the firelight. I let her see my face, my real face, the one I kept behind my human mask.

The crowd stirred behind me, muttered questions swelling like a whispering tide. But the thing that wore Rae's skin lifted the spear in its hand.

"Let her be heard," it—she—said. "Such is my law."

The others fell back, silent once more, but their desiderata lost its harmony. Waves of consternation lapped at my demon senses, a distraction I couldn't afford. I pushed the eddies of confusion and fear away and focused on my quarry.

Was she my quarry? Or was she hunting me?

We stalked around each other, two apex predators sizing one another up for battle. The wind picked up and whipped our hair around our faces. Above the standing stones, the stars winked out behind quick-mounting clouds. The scent of an oncoming storm washed over me, petrichor and ozone. Or was that just the raw power flaring out from the entity I faced?

Rae's people drew back further, huddling together under the trees as a few huge raindrops spattered down. Clearly this night hadn't gone as planned for them. Did they know about her? Did they understand that a real supernatural power had taken hold of their priestess? Or were they just innocent bystanders? Maybe I should have Ira arrest the whole cult and sort them out later—if I ever got off this mountain.

Rae lunged at me, and I jumped out of the way with a bare moment to spare. I couldn't think about her followers now. I had to stay focused on her.

"You told me you're not a demon." I countered her steps, watching her shoulders for the tell of an oncoming attack. She moved like a trained fighter, ready to feint. "But you're not a goddess either, whatever Rae might think. There's no such thing as gods."

"What is a god but a force that humanity does not understand?" She laughed, raucous as a murder. "There are more things in heaven and earth than you imagine, Lily Knight."

Great. The eldritch whatever-she-was quoted Shakespeare *and* she had delusions of metaphysical grandeur. I was way out of my depth here. "You didn't answer my question."

"As I said. We are alike in some ways, but not in others. While your kind chose to bind yourselves to mortal flesh and mingle with mortal souls, my kind stayed in the shadows, choosing our vessels only when the time was right."

"You mean you stole them. That body doesn't belong to you!"

"Perhaps. But I have its rightful owner's full consent." She smiled her blade-sharp smile. "She wanted my power, and she knew the price. Our interests are well-aligned. She'll have her flesh back when I am done, good as new. All part of the deal we made."

"That's not..." What, possible? Right? But we had passed far beyond the realm of logical possibility here, and this entity didn't seem like the type to have much use for mortal ethics. "You used her to kill people!"

"Did I?" Her keen black eyes glittered at me, a corvid's eyes in a woman's face. "She summoned me to deal out justice. And that, we did together. Can you say that they didn't deserve it?"

"That's not for you or me to say!"

"Isn't it?" Her gaze pierced my soul. "And yet you have done the same. You confessed as much to me."

This conversation was getting away from me. I dragged it back on track. "What are you doing here? The ones she called on you to judge are dead."

"Ah, yes. But my work is not yet done. Do you propose to stop me, little sister?"

"Yes." The wind howled, swirling around us. I raised my voice so all of them could hear me. "Because of you, an innocent girl is dying in a prison cell."

My adversary tilted her head. "And what has that to do with me?"

"They shackled her with poison chains because they think she murdered those boys."

"I know this foolish child." She tilted her head, a jerky, birdlike motion. "She resisted my dread, as you did. She tried to stop the sacrifice."

"She did see you," I breathed. "That's why you didn't take all their blood, isn't it? She interrupted the murders."

"She failed to stop me," the goddess spat. "I took enough, and I spared her. But I told her never to speak on what she saw, or she would face my fury."

"You threatened her?" No wonder Eve had looked so scared when she first met Rae. No wonder she pretended to know nothing about what had happened at that house.

"I did what I must." Her dispassionate tone irked me. "She is your child, then?"

"Not mine." The question caught me off guard, but in a way she was right. Eve was my responsibility now. "She's of my blood, not that it matters. She's innocent, and so I will defy you, whatever you claim to be. Queen or demon, goddess or nightmare. I don't care. It's not justice if a child pays the price."

Her smirk widened, and I caught my misstep a second after she did. "Surely, by that logic, you yourself hold just as much capability as I. Because of you, the child has no father. Did you not do what you had to do?"

"It's not the same!" Damn her, but she knew too much about me. "I didn't know she existed! You do. You know the cost and the consequences."

"And would you choose to act differently, knowing what you do now? Would you hold back the killing blow?"

"I—" Swallowing, I hesitated. Ariel's merciless, snarling face floated in my mind, splashed with Danny's blood. He'd shot her point blank and then used his influence to try to dominate me. If I hadn't driven the stake into his black and twisted heart, I would have never gotten free, and Danny would have died. "No. I had no choice."

"There is always a choice. Now stand aside, little sister." The sword in her hand flashed, cold and bright as her smile.

I held my ground, my gun with its silver bullets firm at the base of my spine. I dropped my hand to my side, reaching for it, but I didn't want to use it. Shooting her meant shooting Rae. And yet. "I can't."

"You've already been judged." She bared her teeth, more a snarl than a smile now. "This sword is not for you."

"Who is it for, then?"

"There is one more who has escaped my justice," she said. "By his blood I will be unleashed. The thirteenth sacrifice."

"This man?" I reached into my pocket and pulled out the newspaper clipping I'd plucked from Rae's bulletin board. "You were going after him that night, weren't you? You weren't at the villa for me at all. What are his crimes?"

"He knew of the others," she spat. "He has used his power unwisely, to hurt and harm and hold silent those who already have too little. He is complicit. They all are!"

"If you're going after Senator Ritter, I'm afraid I can't let you do that." I had no love for the senator, but his death would devastate Sebastian. And I had some questions about the proportionality of the punishment to the senator's crime. This goddess had to be stopped.

She sneered. "What is he to you?"

"It's complicated," I said, and lunged for her, drawing the gun at my back.

My wings ripped at the electric air for purchase, driving me forward. She moved with incredible speed, and lightning crackled around us. Her spear caught my wrist with a tingling blow. It knocked my gun aside and my shot went wide. The report echoed against the mountainside, and a roar of thunder answered it.

Distant shouts and screams of alarm floated to me on the still-rising wind. I'd forgotten about our audience when I unfurled my wings. I dipped back to the ground in dismay.

In that brief moment of distraction, my opponent came at me like a hurricane. Agonizing pain lanced through my chest, followed by a hard impact that shuddered along my spine. The world went white, then black.

Had lightning struck me? I gasped for breath and blinked.

I lay flat on the rocky ground, face up. The Queen of Phantoms stood over me, gripping the hilt of the sword piercing my heart.

It hurt like seven kinds of hell. I coughed, my mouth flooded with smoke and copper, thick and acrid as fear.

The entity inside of Rae bent over me. She placed her bare foot on my sternum, dipped her fingers in the blood that poured out around the sword's blade, and licked them clean like a cat savoring a drop of cream.

"You will not stop me," she said, with her razorblade smile, and went to pull out the blade.

Mother of monsters, her power flowed through that sword. I could feel it move inside me. It shivered through me in frigid rivulets as if seeking a way back to her, driven by that same ancient, inhuman intelligence and will that eclipsed Rae's desiderata.

If it linked the goddess to Rae somehow, I couldn't let her have it back. I grabbed it by the edge and held it fast. The movement pulled the steel deeper into my chest, and I screamed. But I hung on, forcing kether to my muscles instead of the torn flesh demanding healing.

Rae...Morrighu...whoever stood above me screeched in fury and recoiled, vanishing from my field of view. She screamed again, more distant now, and this time I could've sworn pain throbbed in that wild, eldritch howl.

Had I wounded her? I couldn't remember even touching her. Surely in a moment she would come back and finish what she started, pluck her sword from my weakening hand.

But she didn't come. Another gust of wind lashed at me, and this time I could feel the chill in it. My vision dimmed, shadows swelling. I gathered my last iota of strength and pulled the sword from my chest, my arm flopping out to the side. The sound of wingbeats rose around me like another thunderclap, and the air filled with the hoarse call of many crows.

My grip on the blade loosened and I fell back, breath rattling in my lungs. The fire exploded upward in a tower of sparks.

Then it went out, all at once as if snuffed. The croaking chorus faded away and left me bleeding in the dark, in silence, alone.

25

DEVIL'S MOUNTAIN

A low rumble brought me back to consciousness, and consciousness brought the return of pain in a strange, lightless world.

Had I gone blind? Was I dead? I stared up into the darkness of a starless sky for an unmarked amount of time.

Then I figured it out. I wasn't blind, but I was *night*-blind. I'd lost my demon sight. My eyes adjusted with almost-human sluggishness, and a little light crept in at the edges of my vision. The faint sodium-orange glow of the East Bay's lowland cities reflected off the cumulus clouds boiling above the mountain's ridge. In my periphery, the stark black shapes of the standing stones loomed against the horizon, silent strangers from a far-off land.

Another roll of thunder shook the air. I groaned and turned my head to the side. Dry stalks of grass scratched my cheek, and sharp stones dug into my spine. My kether-warmth had drained away, and the cold of the earth beneath me seeped into my bones. I shivered, teeth chattering, and lifted a hand to my chest. Sticky wetness soaked my coat.

I hadn't imagined it. She had stabbed me. But the blood had stopped flowing. I found the cut left by the blade and prodded the spot where the sword had pierced my chest. The skin beneath was tender but whole. Everything seemed to be in its right place.

The kether in my blood had spent itself on healing the wound. It had kept me alive, though it no longer protected from the elements or the headache that struck up a march in my temples.

The clouds above flickered with lightning—real lightning this time, not the power Rae had called upon for vengeance. A rumble of thunder followed it after too short of a pause for comfort.

The storm was close, and here I lay near the highest point for miles around. Of course, I'd survived a sword to the heart, and lightning strikes weren't a proven method of demon-killing. But as a lowly cambion who had used up her luck, her kether stores, and one of her nine lives already tonight, I didn't like my chances.

I pushed myself up on my elbows. The movement pulled something loose in my chest and sudden pain grated through me. The cough it spurred sounded bad, wet and productive, and I spat out a thick, coppery mouthful of spume onto the grass. *This is fine. That probably isn't a slice of my lung.*

Obviously, the kether hadn't finished repairing me. My labored breathing awakened pins and needles in my ribs, piercing me from the inside out, and I hadn't even tried to stand.

"Mother...of...monsters." My body was barely holding itself together. My kether-fueled healing factor must have triaged the worst of the damage, stopped me from bleeding out, and then taken an extended smoke break in the parking lot. So to speak.

Damn it, I was loopy too, patched up like a rag doll and coming up with stupid flights of fancy to personify my healing ability when what I really needed to do was get the hell out of this Night on Bald Mountain bullshit and find a real human doctor in a real human hospital to sew up my all-too-human parts. If I could find one that would take my crappy medical insurance.

That, or take another long, deep drink from Sebastian Ritter's well. But this would require more than the balanced dance of give and take we'd negotiated earlier in the evening. For this, I needed the real thing, skin to skin, nothing held back.

Hold yourself together, Knight.

I dragged myself further upright and bit back a cry of pain. It came out as a grunt through my teeth. On my knees, hands braced on the hard-packed earth to keep me steady, I swiveled my head and looked around.

I was alone. My gun lay near my knees, useless as usual, and I picked it up, grimacing. A few embers still glowed where the fire had roared. They gave off just enough light to reveal that Rae's followers—the demon goddess's followers—had disappeared. Either they'd hiked down the mountain and taken their priestess with them, or...

A chorus of raucous avian voices had echoed across the clearing as I lost consciousness. Could they have...? I shook my head, half in denial, half to clear it of its delirious notions. The rest of the ritual's participants had been human. I would have noticed, otherwise.

They couldn't have all turned into crows.

I crawled forward, patting the ground until I found my shoulder bag lying a few feet away, then felt inside for my phone. Relief washed through me until I hit the home button, and nothing happened.

Of course, my battery had died.

"Fuck!" I had no choice but to make the descent on foot. Either that or lie here waiting for lightning or a rescue. And I wouldn't bet my last dollar on which one was more likely to come first.

I pushed myself to my feet, but my left palm pressed down on something cold and sharp hidden in the grass, and I yelped, yanking my hand back. My palm oozed blood from a long shallow gash that reopened the deep half-healed wound I sustained when I grabbed the goddess's blade.

Great, just great. Like I had extra blood to spare. The new wound bled only sluggishly, but I wrapped my coattail around it and put pressure on the wound anyway. That's what Danny would tell me to do if she were here. But Danny didn't even know where I was, did she?

A pang rolled through me, or maybe it was just another twinge from my injuries. I set my jaw, and with considerably more caution, reached down with my other hand and drew the sword that had wounded me from the tall grass that concealed it.

Well, that was something, at least, a consolation prize of sorts. I should get that printed on a t-shirt: *I attended the summoning of an ancient blood-drinking goddess, and all I got was this flaming sword.* Wait, no. I shook my head again, which swam in protest. *And all I got was this bloody t-shirt?* No, that wasn't how the joke was supposed to work, either, but I couldn't get it to come out right in my head. The sword didn't seem inclined to flame, anyway. A pity, as I could use some light, but it seemed the cold, alien power that dwelled in it had no interest in acting as a demon's lantern.

Enough. I was losing it, and I had no more time, kether, or blood to waste. Rae hadn't taken the sword with her, after all. I could still hope my desperate, last-ditch attempt to separate her from her power had succeeded.

Now I just had to get down to business, or more to the point, down this blasted Devil's Mountain. I clenched my jaw even harder until it ached like the rest of me and leaned heavily on the sword. Using it as a cane to help me rise, I forced my legs to bear my weight.

They did, though not without protest and a slight watery consistency around the knees.

I sternly ordered them to keep their shit together and, sword in hand as a useful walking stick, began to drag myself, step by slow and shaky step, down the mountain toward the human world.

I didn't get very far before I almost tripped over something—no, someone, a woman's prone body near the edge of the meadow, at the roots of a huge live oak. Her hair spread around her pale face like a dark pool of blood in the grass, reddish even in this minimal light.

Rae stirred, groaning, and I drew back and raised the sword, pointing it at her. It weighed heavy in my weakened hand. "Stay where you are," I said.

"Lily? What are you doing here?" Her voice rasped in her throat.

I leaned against a nearby tree and focused on holding the sword steady. "You don't remember?"

She struggled upward on her elbows, her face a dim blur in the darkness. "I remember coming here. I remember the ritual. And you...Why do you have my sword?"

I brandished it at her. "I said stay down."

"All right, all right. I feel like hell anyway." She subsided, peering up at me, though I couldn't make out her expression in the dark, just the white blur of her face. "It's just me, Lily. It's Rae."

"I know what you are. And it's not just you. What about *her*?"

"Who?"

"You know who. *Morrighu*."

"Oh." She didn't say anything for a long moment. Then she sighed. "She's gone, for now. But I wouldn't say her name if I were you."

"Or what?" I poked her with the flat of the sword, experimentally, and drew a small grunt of pain from her. "Is she still in there, somewhere?"

"She's always with me," Rae said, her tone ravaged, resigned. "But she's...dormant, now. I think."

She didn't sound too sure, and I didn't like that one bit. "What do you mean, dormant? How do you know she's not off killing people without you?"

"She needed me to act as her vessel, and she wasn't finished yet." Rae stared up at the quick-scudding clouds. Rain pattered in the grass around us, dampening my hair and running down my neck like the stroke of chilly fingers. "Thirteen lives to bring her fully into this world. That was our deal. But whatever you did made her retreat."

"Whatever I did? I almost died."

"But you didn't." She raised her head again, squinting at my face in the darkness. "You're not all human either, are you?"

"I'm a cambion. A half-demon."

"Ah," Rae said, as if that explained everything.

Had that merciless, seeking force tried to take my life instead when it crawled through me out of the blade, then met some kind of fail state when I inconveniently survived? Or did the cambion's blood she licked from my wound have anti-goddess properties? "Tell me more about this deal," I said. "What did you get out of it?"

"It's complicated." Rae coughed. It didn't sound much better than mine. "What are you going to do? Are you going to just leave me here, or...?"

"That depends," I said. "Tell me what all this has to do with Delta Alpha Mu. This was personal, wasn't it?"

"It was, to begin with. I was a student at the university. And then one day, I went to one of their parties."

"Someone hurt you there."

"My life changed after that day," Rae said. "I lost something. I became consumed with justice. Then one day, I found *her*, and she saved me. She pulled me from a dark place, but she had a price."

"And the price was those men's lives?"

"No," she said. "It was *my* life. What was mine became hers."

"You're saying you don't control her."

"Control her?" Rae's laugh turned into another wracking cough. "She's a fucking goddess. Of course I don't control her."

I didn't buy it. She had that list of names on her wall, for one thing. But maybe I could hand her over to Ira and let him figure it out. I straightened from the tree that propped me up. "If you have a goddess inside you, I'm not sure why you need my help."

"I'm not even sure I can stand up," Rae said. "Hosting a deity is like riding the lightning. She uses everything you've got."

"Great, so getting off this mountain should be a walk in the park." If I had to fireman carry her down those cliffside trails in the rain with no kether to get my bounty, Ira definitely owed me hazard pay. I steeled myself and offered her my hand.

"If you think I'm a murderer, then why are you helping me?" Her skin was icy and her grip weak as I helped her sit up. No kether flowed between us. Sleeping or not, her goddess still had an exclusive claim on her, keeping her safe from my energy drain.

Good for her, bad for me. "I'm not helping you," I said with grim precision. "I'm taking you into custody. There's an innocent girl in chains because of you. Whether or not those men deserved to die, she doesn't deserve to pay the price."

"I see." She let me haul her to her feet, then staggered and leaned heavily on my shoulder, forcing me to use the sword as a counterbalance. "I'll come quietly on one condition."

"Oh, now you have conditions?" I took a step, prodding the uneven earth with my sword cane. "That's rich. I could just leave you here, you know."

"That's not a respectful way to use the Sword of Light," Rae muttered.

"I think the dignity of your magic sword is the least of your worries right now. What conditions?"

"You expose them all," she said. "The senator, too."

Unease churned in my stomach, or maybe that was just queasiness from all the blood I'd lost. How would Sebastian feel if I ruined his father's career?

How would I feel if I let them get away with it? "All right," I said.

"And you defend me."

I stumbled over a tree root and would have lost my balance if not for the alleged Sword of Light. "Oh, hell no. That's all kinds of conflicts of interest."

"I'll waive them. I can do that, right? I want you."

"Why?"

"A human lawyer wouldn't understand what it's like."

Eve had said practically the same thing. "I'll consider it—if I'm even still licensed by then, that is. But you have to tell me everything."

"I already told you."

"No, you didn't. Who are the gods of old from the ritual?"

"The Tuatha De. An Irish legend. They were demi-gods, heroes, a race of magical people, and the Morrigan was their warrior queen. They fought off the evil Fomorians and brought peace to the land—for a while."

"Were they demons?"

"Maybe. The myths don't call them that."

"But they bred with humans."

"So the stories go." Rae was quiet for a moment as we made our painstaking way down the trail. "You know," she said after a little while, "the wizard Merlin was a cambion."

I turned around to stare at her, even though I still couldn't see her well. "What, like in King Arthur and the Knights of the Round Table? You're fucking with me."

"No, I'm not. Look it up."

I would have to ask Ira, who would probably laugh at me. "Yeah, well," I said. "I'm no wizard, I'm no angel, and I'm no hero. I'm no Tuatha whatever the fuck it is, either. I'm just trying to make rent without totally hating myself."

This made her laugh, which made her cough again, and we continued our slow descent through the dark together in silence.

Several hours later, I came stumbling into the Mount Diablo State Park ranger station soaked from neck to waistband in my own blood, a sword of unknown power and pedigree clutched in my hot little hand as I leaned on it like an old lady's cane, and the mostly unconscious vessel of a goddess slung over my shoulder like a sack of potatoes. Rae had made it about halfway down the mountain before she started to fade. I'd earned my hazard pay and then some.

Despite my earlier protestations, I must have looked like some kind of avenging angel, or maybe a psycho fresh from a medieval killing spree. Before I could explain that the blood was all mine, the ranger on duty gaped at me and sprang to his feet, service weapon at the ready.

"Drop the sword and the, er, body, ma'am, and put your hands in the air!"

I sighed. "Yeah, yeah. I've got it." So many people had pointed various deadly implements at me lately that it was beginning to lose its novelty, much like the world was beginning to lose its sharp edges.

The sword slipped from my hand, and I staggered under the dead weight of the woman I carried. After the dark, dangerous hike down the mountain, the scuffed and worn carpet of the station office looked like a pretty comfy place for a forever nap. Someone else could clean up the rest of this mess.

In a slow, crumbling capitulation to gravity, I collapsed onto the obligingly firm floor and let Rae's unresponsive body slump in a heap beside me. Huh.

Natural forces did win in the end, after all. I had to remember to tell Sebastian he was right about me. That would probably do a lot to make up for my mistakes with him.

The ranger's expression transformed from fear to concern. "Ma'am, are you hurt?"

"Don't come any closer." My voice rasped in my throat. My hunter's instincts snarled behind it. He was young, handsome, full of vitality. I could use some of that right about now. "It's not safe. Stay back!"

"I'll call an ambulance."

"No." I pushed myself back up onto my elbows. "Call the San Francisco M.E.'s office. Please."

"But ma'am—" His eyes widened, and he looked me over, probably trying to decide if I was in fact a walking corpse. "You need medical care, not a coroner!"

"I need to see Daniela Rios. I need to tell her—" A long, racking cough stole the rest of my words. I didn't even know what they would have been. I needed to tell her what? That she was right too, that I was sorry, that she didn't deserve to be treated like I'd treated her. That I shouldn't have lied to her, ever. Too many things. "Just call her. And then call the FBI. Tell them...I found the suspect they wanted."

It occurred to me I still wasn't thinking clearly. It seemed to occur to the ranger too, because he frowned and got on his radio, calling for paramedics.

I groaned. I didn't need more innocent humans trying to handle me when I was half-kether starved and jonesing for a fix of their sweet, sweet mortal souls. Though loathe to abandon the imminent floor nap of my dreams, I hauled myself back to my feet.

By the time the ranger turned around, I had vanished back into the night, taking my allegedly flaming sword with me. Fortunately, it still didn't show any signs of lighting up and the shreds of Presence I managed to call up did enough to keep me out of sight. I dragged myself down the road toward the near-empty lot of a small winery nearby, where I'd parked Betty.

Poor Betty. Things didn't bode well for the state of her upholstery. Between the mud coating my legs and the blood covering the rest of me, I ached to think of Sebastian's expression when I brought her back. But mostly, I just ached.

A siren wailed, and I lifted my heavy head. By the flashing lights, at least two emergency vehicles screamed along the winding road that led toward the ranger station from the town below. I sidestepped off the road and crouched beside a hoary live oak until they tore past. Back at the station, the poor ranger would have to explain why the woman covered in blood had disappeared off his floor.

A few minutes more, and I would reach Betty. I stood and had to lean against the trunk of the oak for a long breath while my vision swam. I still had almost no dark vision, thanks to all the hard work my limited kether was doing to keep me upright and conscious. I stumbled on. A sudden flurry of shouts from behind me sped my steps somewhat, but I didn't have much more to give.

The roadster waited where I left her, her pale gleam absurdly fancy and out-of-place in this rural area, but such a welcome sight that I almost fell over. I found my keys after a prolonged fumble and fell into the driver's seat. As for the sword, I heaved it into the back seat before slamming the door shut.

I made it, and no one got hurt but me.

I sat still for a moment, and the adrenaline that had fueled my hike down the mountain drained away. A powerful lassitude crept over me. Maybe I could just close my eyes for a minute or so before I got out of here. It didn't seem wise to drive Sebastian's baby in my current state. I needed a rest.

Really, I needed kether. Right. Now I had a plan. I would close my eyes until my head stopped spinning. Then I would plug my phone into the charger, turn on the car, and call Sebastian to pick me up.

My lids drooped and I drowsed. Just for a moment...

I walked through a shallow sea of blood, dragging a heavy weight behind me. At first, I thought it was the sword, but when I turned around it was a body bag that glistened in the foam of the blood tide. Sick dread rose in my chest, and I knelt beside it, reaching to unzip it with a trembling hand.

Ariel, it had to be Ariel. What other corpse would I carry like this, baggage I couldn't seem to put down?

I unzipped the bag and my stomach flipped. The zipper's tines split apart to slowly reveal a pale face with dark hair that flopped over a wide forehead and light eyes that stared up at me, filmed-over, unseeing. Eyes that would never see again.

Sebastian's eyes.

"No." My heart pounded, loud as a hammer's blow, and I jerked awake, panting. A bright light shone in my eyes, and I flinched, squinting. The pounding went on.

But it wasn't my heart. Someone stood outside Betty's driver-side window and aimed a flashlight in my face. They tapped on the glass again, louder this time, and said something that sounded a lot like "Hey, Knight. Are you all right in there?"

I sighed, shielded my face with one hand to block out the light, and rolled down the window. "I'm fine, thank you. I was just leaving."

"You're not going anywhere," said the figure holding the flashlight, in a familiar voice. "Not until we debrief you. Besides, you're in no shape to drive."

I groaned and let my head fall back against Betty's patent leather seat. "Hi, Ira. You're late to the party. And it was a real banger, let me tell you."

"I wouldn't be so late if you'd told me where you planned on going," he pointed out. "And here I thought you'd learned your lesson about calling for backup."

"Don't need backup," I muttered. "Word on the street is that I'm a Tuatha thingy. Hero. I bagged your goddess for you. Look, I even have a magic sword. What more do you want from me?"

"I want you to slide over." He reached in and unlatched the door. "Come on, let's get you back to HQ. What's that about a magic sword, now?"

I dragged myself sideways and flopped into the passenger side, waving a hand at the back seat. "Sword of Light. I took it off her. It flames, I think, although not for me."

"Interesting." Ira raised an eyebrow, surveying me. "Knight, you're covered in blood. What happened out there?"

"Hazards of the job. Stopped a ritual sacrifice. Don't worry," I said, when he looked alarmed. "It's all mine."

26

BETTER ANGELS

I prepared myself for the worst, but when Ira led me to the jail infirmary room where Eve lay, I couldn't hold back my soft gasp.

The change that a few hours in silver shackles had wrought on her small body stole the breath from my lungs. Her delicate skull stood out under near-transparent skin, the last traces of baby fat melted away by the poison, and in her emaciated features, her demon characteristics stood out in stark relief. The heavy eyebrow ridge and slanting cheekbones revealed by the ravages of silver gave her a leonine, almost alien appearance, and her complexion had a blue cast traced with dark, swollen veins.

She tossed her head on the pillow, her once-glossy hair dull and greasy. Her lips moved, muttering words I couldn't make out, lost in silver-induced delirium.

I wheeled to face the guards. "Get these shackles off her and release her. *Now.*"

"She's still dangerous." Meghan North folded her arms, mouth tight with disapproval.

"The hell she is! Can't you see she's dying? Give me the keys."

To my surprise, North looked at Ira. He nodded. "Do it," he said.

I snatched the keys from North's reluctant fingers. With a curt gesture to the guards to follow her, she turned and stalked out of the room. Ira hesitated a moment later, but when I glared at him, he shrugged and went out after her.

The door slammed shut and the lockdown alarm buzzed. I ignored it, already at Eve's bedside. She didn't stir or open her eyes, already too far gone.

My gloves made me fumble the first try. I set my teeth and tried again. This time, the key turned, and the cuffs snapped open. I flung them from me.

They clattered against the far wall of the interrogation room, and I slipped an arm under Eve's spare shoulders, pulling her close. She sagged into my side, boneless and nearly weightless. Her cheeks had taken on a gray tinge.

Folding my arms around her, I pressed her temple against my collarbone, sending the barest push of kether across the barrier of our skin. It wasn't much. I didn't have much to spare.

"What are you doing?" Meghan North's harsh voice demanded over the intercom.

"I'm helping her, since you won't." I didn't glance up to the observation window. "She's ill, and she needs medical attention. Release her into my custody, and I'll make sure she stays out of trouble."

A pause, then the intercom crackled again. "If you're her legal guardian, we can release her to you," North said. "But she's still a material witness, and even with McGuire's confession, this is still an open investigation."

"The official guardianship is pending." I hadn't filed the paperwork, hadn't even considered it until this moment. But with Eve clinging to me, her color slowly returning, my statement held a ring of truth I didn't have to fake.

I released her and let her slump back into the bed. My kether push had done its job. The welts on her arms already looked less inflamed. A wave of exhaustion crested over me, the cost of my minuscule kether donation taxing the limits of my human ability to regenerate my energy.

"Oh, Eve." I sighed. "What am I going to do with you?"

Eve's eyes cracked open. The gold had ebbed a fraction, tinged with a more human shade of blue green, her powers of disguise returning with the strength of the kether I'd gifted her. I suppressed a shiver. Her father had favored that color too.

"I want to go home." Her weak voice cracked on the last word.

"Okay, kiddo." I sank back into the chair next to her and took her hand. "I'll take you home soon. I promise."

Her fingers curled around my gloved ones, her grip still frail but getting stronger. For a moment, the contact eased the pang in my heart.

But I couldn't let that stand. She trusted me now, but she deserved to know the truth about what happened to her father, what I'd done. And I had to face that truth, no matter how much I wanted to avoid the pain it brought me.

It ran deep, that pain, flowing fast and muddy as a river in a flood year. It hurt like that because I'd loved him, because I'd killed him. It hurt because he was the person who loved the worst parts of me. He loved the demon parts, the hungry parts, the ruthless parts that lied and killed and fed on human vitality to survive.

He didn't believe I was better than that or expect that from me. Even in the end, when I drove that silver into his heart, he understood why I had to do it. He saw me for what I was, a killer, a survivor.

We were the same.

That was the hardest thing, that no matter how messed up things got between me and Ariel, how cruelly he'd treated me, what he did to get to me, he still felt like home.

The truth will make you free. But right now, the truth was that I missed the lie. I missed the time when I didn't know what lay behind the mask, both his and mine.

"Lily, is everything ok? You're all bloody." Eve craned her neck to look up at me.

"It's fine. It will heal." I gently disentangled my fingers from hers and stood up, putting a small amount of space between us. I had to grip the back of the chair for balance. "Eve, I have something to tell you."

Her eyes widened. "Oh no. What is it?"

"It's about your father." The words weighed heavy and awkward in my mouth, like a language I couldn't remember how to speak. "I didn't tell you the whole story, and it's time you knew."

"You killed him," Eve said, her voice barely more than a whisper. "Didn't you?"

Taken aback, I stared at her. "How did you know?"

"I knew from the way you talked about him." She didn't meet my gaze, but fixed her attention on the ceiling, her expression blank, her tone dull. "It was in your energy when you said his name. All dark and twisty, full of grief and rage."

My knees threatened to give out, and I sank into the chair. "Why didn't you say anything?"

"Because," Eve said, "I could feel that you loved him, too."

Of course, my desiderata had given me away. "I didn't want to do it." The words sounded empty, meaningless. My intention didn't matter when I had done the deed anyway. "He left me no choice."

There is always a choice. That's what the goddess had said.

"Tell me everything," Eve said. "I want to know how it happened."

"Are you sure? It won't be easy to hear."

"Tell me," she insisted, her sunken eyes flaring with fierce light.

So, I told her. I told her how Nepenthe and Astarte died. I told her about the lies and threats. I told her how he shot Danny and what he wanted me to do to save her. How no one I loved would be safe as long as he needed leverage over me and my energy.

Eve listened in silence. When I finished, tears rolled down her gaunt cheeks and she closed her eyes, her breathing uneven.

I waited, my own eyelids drifting shut. Fucking hell, I was tired. Everything hurt. The crushing ache in my chest had a lot of competition. Or maybe that was just the half-healed wound where Rae had plunged her blade into my heart.

"I keep thinking about my mother." Eve's faint voice roused me from my half-stupor.

I blinked. "I thought you said you didn't have a mother."

"I don't. Not anymore."

"Did Ariel ever tell her who she was?"

Eve shook her head. "I'm not talking about my demon family. I'm talking about my human family."

"Oh. Right." I shifted, uneasy in my chair. The implications of Eve's odd upbringing still didn't sit right with me. Was it normal cubine practice for Ariel to leave his daughter with human foster parents, like a cuckoo in a songbird's nest? Yet another question I would never get answered. "What about them?"

"My mother—the woman who raised me—I had never seen her so afraid as she looked when he came to find me. But then he told her not to worry, and she just—stopped."

My heart dropped, heavy as a stone. "He made her trust him."

"I tried to go back and see them, afterward." She wrapped her bony arms around herself, shivering a little. "But they were gone. The house was empty. Later, Father told me they had died in an accident."

"Oh, no." What were the odds that he'd told her the truth?

"I always wondered," Eve said softly, "whether it really was an accident."

"Oh, *hell*." I scrubbed my hands over my face.

"So, you see, even though I don't—" A little hiccupping sob shook her, but she fought it back. "I don't want to believe my father did any of the things you said. But deep down, even though I loved him...I don't think he was a very good person, Lily."

That was an understatement, but I let her have it. "I know the feeling, kiddo." Still not trusting my legs, I scraped the chair over to her and took her hand again. "Hey. What do you say we get out of this place?"

She roused, looking around at me, and a trace of a watery smile quirked her chapped lips. "You don't look like you're ready for a jailbreak. You look more like you're about to pass out."

I eyed the cameras in the corner of the room. Even though no one had said anything for a while, I doubted they had gone anywhere. Ira was probably taking notes on demon family structure on the other side of the two-way glass.

"It would be a very slow-motion escape. But if I play this right, I think they'll let us go." At least, I hoped so.

I didn't have much fight left in me. I needed time to let my energy reserves recharge, but I couldn't leave Eve in here at the mercy of the government. If I did, I'd probably never see her again, and I didn't like that idea very much. Somehow, this orphaned waif had wormed her way into my heart.

We were family now, Ariel's two lost girls, and I'd be damned before I let anything else bad happen to her.

The overcast sky had begun to lighten by the time I negotiated our release from the FBI headquarters. I stumbled out into the lobby of the federal building, pushing Eve in a much-scuffed wheelchair before me, and found my best friend pacing the wide hall. Her booted steps echoed loud on the marble floor, her desiderata a chaotic vortex of worry and anger.

My stomach sank. She was still angry with me, and I deserved it. "Danny? What are you doing here?"

At my voice, she spun. Her energy changed in an instant, glowing with a rosy, warm dawn brighter than the gray light outside. "You put me as your emergency contact, you jerk," she said, but she at least had the grace to wait until we made it back to her car and packed Eve into the back seat before she started her own interrogation.

"What happened to you? Please don't tell me all of that is your blood."

"Okay. I won't." I slumped back into the seat of the Volkswagen. "I met a god. It didn't go well."

"Obviously not." She frowned at me. "Something's wrong. You're not healing right, are you? What did this god do, use silver on you?"

"Nothing like that. I just ran myself dry, that's all."

"You look terrible."

Her stunning flattery almost coaxed a smile out of me, but my exhaustion didn't allow much more than a twitch of the mouth. "Trust me," I muttered. "I look better than I did."

"I should take you to the hospital."

"No! No hospital." The last time I'd been in a hospital hadn't been pleasant. "Take me to Sebastian's. Please. I have something I need to do."

"Oh. For the, you know." She took her hands off the wheel to perform a gesture that involved squishing the air together suggestively. "Right?"

I made a face and twisted around in my seat to see if Eve was listening, but she'd curled into a small heap in the back seat. After a long moment, her side rose and fell in a slow, even breath, and I turned to face front. "Something like that."

Danny grinned and whistled something that sounded a lot like the chorus of "Sexual Healing."

I scowled. "It's not like that."

She just laughed and drummed the steering wheel. "And when I get that feeeeling..."

"Shut up, Dan."

"I'm sorry, I can't help it." She winked at me and hummed softly under her breath. "Makes me feel so fine..."

"Why are you like this?"

"Because you're so easy to tease, Sugarbean." She paused, then shot me a sideways glance. "And because I'm glad you're talking to me, even if you are being a fractious grump about it. Maybe because you are. Feels like things are normal again."

"Normal, huh." I stretched out my hands in front of me, flaking off the dried blood. It had an odd texture, granular rather than sticky now. Dusty, even. Hastily, I wiped my hands on my pants, though they didn't have much clean surface either. "What's normal about this?"

"You getting yourself into trouble and needing to bum a ride? Everything. But I meant this." She flapped a hand over the gearshift. "You and me. Being okay again. Bantering. You know."

I looked up, surprised. "You had every right to be mad at me."

"I'm not saying I didn't. But I still didn't like it. It's *us*, Lily."

"I wasn't sure there was an us, anymore." My eyes stung, and I blinked back the hot, prickling sensation.

"And I thought you'd never forgive me for backing Berry up instead of you."

I sniffed and dashed the back of my hand across my cheek. "More like I couldn't forgive myself. Danny—if anything had happened to you because of me—"

"Yeah," she said, her voice rougher than usual. "Well, it didn't. And I'm sorry. I judged you too fast."

"I'm sorry I didn't tell you the whole truth. It's a really bad habit I picked up."

"It's survival." Her tone softened. "And it's not like you had a great role model."

"Sometimes I think you give me way too much credit." I sighed. "It's easier to keep things to myself. It's easier to skip the judgment. But it hurts everyone, me included. I wish…" I trailed off, staring out at the monochrome dawn.

"What?"

"That it didn't have to be a secret. That I could just exist as I am, and not have to hide anything."

"Believe it or not," she said, "I get it."

"You do?"

"Sure do. I felt the same way at about sixteen, when I was in love with a girl and had no one I could tell about it. Not even my mama."

I remembered Danny telling me that her mother had taken some time to get used to the idea that her daughter would probably marry another woman, but she'd come around by the time Berry showed up. "You're talking about coming out."

"Isn't that what you're talking about?"

"Not really. No one had a good reason to be scared of *you*. I'm actually a monster."

She pressed her lips together, her tone stern. "Don't say that about my friend."

"Well, it's true. There was no justification for the prejudice you face."

"No. But it doesn't matter."

"I think it does."

"Justified or not, people will always be scared of the things they don't understand." She pulled the car up to the curb and came to a stop, and I looked around, startled. A few steps away, Sebastian's long driveway wound up away from the street. "I threatened my family's worldview. That feels just as existential to humans as their life force. Maybe more so." She offered me a lopsided grin. "We're not as good at assessing metaphysical danger as we are at defending our status quo."

"Still." I stayed in my seat. "I threaten both. How many people do you think could accept the reality of demons who walk the earth into their worldview?"

"Don't get me wrong. I'm not saying you should come out, Lil. It's not your obligation to tell the world everything you are." Her smile twisted, her desiderata taking on a salt-sea tinge. "I'm just saying not telling never gets easier."

"You're right, as usual." I swung the door open, fueled by a sudden rush of resolve. In the back seat, Eve didn't stir, sleeping peacefully on. I knew what I had to do. "Wait here."

"What? You expect us to wait while you—Lily!"

But I had already ducked out of the passenger side door and headed up toward Sebastian's house. In the gray-blue early morning light, all lay silent and still. Not even a single crow called from the trees in the yard. Thank God for that, at least. Or thank Goddess, I supposed.

Guilt pinched my stomach for coming by and waking him up as a thank you for the night we had together, but this couldn't wait. I couldn't let myself lose my nerve.

The motion-sensor lights went on as I climbed the steps to the front door. I paused on the porch and took a deep breath. I could do this. It was the right thing to do. I *had* to do this, no matter what it meant for me, for us.

I rang the doorbell, pressing it a few seconds longer than necessary.

Time stretched out. For a long moment, nothing happened.

Then the light switched on inside, and my heart stuttered in my chest.

Sebastian opened the door, his dark hair mussed into a fluffy bedhead that made me smile despite the adrenaline arcing through me. He wore a black t-shirt and flannel pajama pants, and his feet were bare.

It was a startlingly good look on him, all undone, so different than his normal well-put together and dapper appearance. It made me question myself all over again.

He squinted at me. "Lily? What—" His gaze swept over me, taking in my bedraggled and blood-smeared appearance. "You're hurt."

I found myself searching for words. "Only a little. It's fine."

"You should come in. I can help you with that."

"No, you can't." An ache tickled my throat, and I swallowed it down. "Not this time."

His desiderata, which had swelled, darkened into gray shadows like the dawn. "I don't know what that means."

"It means..." I faltered. "It means I love you."

And I shouldn't have said that, because at the words, he lit up like sunrise. "Lily—"

"Don't." *If you love someone, set them free.* I couldn't keep Sebastian. I couldn't let him believe he loved me if there was even a chance he wasn't feeling love at all, just the bonds I'd placed on him, the Claim I had started to place the first time he touched me. "Just kiss me, please."

His eyes questioned me, but he stepped forward and swept me into his arms.

For a moment, I let it all in. His sweet, heady energy enveloped me, and his mouth descended on mine with the fierceness of a declaration. I returned it in kind, learning his mouth, his taste, etching him into my memory. His kether rushed through me, and I'd lied to him, because the remaining stiffness and catch in my chest from the improperly healed wound eased. For one glorious moment, I was whole again.

Then I squeezed my eyes shut and reversed the polarity of the energy exchange as hard as I could. I gave him everything, every scrap of kether I had inside me. Every energetic drop I'd taken in, every incremental draw that had formed our bond, I pushed from my mouth to his.

He stiffened, jerked away from me. I swayed, eyes popping open as I groped for the door frame. Black motes swirled in my vision.

"What did you do?" he said, his own eyes wide. "Lily, what was that?"

I slid down the wall beside the door, a controlled collapse. I was really getting good at those lately. Somewhere, it seemed very distant, Danny called my name too. Feet pounded up the driveway.

"We're even now," I whispered, crumpling sideways, and let the darkness win.

27

MERCY OF THE FALLEN

The inner sanctum of Ira's deconsecrated church glowed with multicolored light. Mid-morning May sunshine streamed through the east-facing stained-glass windows above the nave. It illuminated the gallery, where a few black-clad workers were wrapping up paintings and replacing them, changing out the exhibition.

Migraine aura pulsed in my periphery, and I halted on the threshold, fumbling for the sunglasses I'd foolishly put away while I caught my breath. A week had passed since I gave Sebastian back his life force, but I still hadn't regained my full strength.

I'd convalesced in Ariel's condo with Eve as a nursemaid. When I could sit up with my laptop, a little research into public records had revealed that my mentor had owned the place outright and paid with cash. That made it legally Eve's property once we could sort out the convoluted probate issues. As her soon-to-be official legal guardian, the sorting would likely fall to me, and while we sorted, Eve and I would stay in the apartment together.

Whether I could handle that arrangement long-term remained up in the air. Living with a teenager in the house of the incubus I'd slain didn't sound like the life I'd dreamed of for myself. But Eve needed me, and there was no way I'd find a nicer place to live in the city, even with the financial breathing room Ira's agency bounty had granted me.

Soon after I woke up from my kether-drain, my erstwhile charge had a visit from Rae's young disciple Cormac that perked her up quickly. For my part, I gave her strict orders not to let any humans in, despite efforts from both Danny and Sebastian, until my own natural kether reserves had regenerated enough that I could trust myself around either one of them.

Between my recently healed wounds and my level of depletion, it would take some time for me to get anywhere close to normal.

The swirling spots at the edges of my vision subsided a bit, and I wandered deeper into the gallery. The incoming art was a series of vibrant and playful canvases. The nearest one arrested me with its depiction of a riotous cloud of floating and flying feathers in every hue of the rainbow, a brilliant storm. The placard labeled it as "Quetzalcoatl Transforming."

Could any of my kind have feathers like that? Eve's gold streaks suggested as much. Might other demons have a spectrum that was more than dark and light?

"Can I help you?" One of the workers spoke from behind me, making me jump.

"Oh! Yes. I'm looking for Ira."

"Who?"

"Ira Delaney. Big guy, ex-priest, DILF vibes, kind of looks like he should be commanding an army of kaiju-fighting mechas?"

The young woman looked confused. "No idea, sorry."

"Thanks anyway. I'll check upstairs." I put a touch of a Presence in the words, just enough so she wouldn't question my right to poke around.

But at the top of the belfry, Ira's tower office was empty. Not just empty of him, but empty of his books, computer, and the rest of his command center.

"Damn it."

"Something wrong, Knight?"

I spun and found him leaning in the doorway. His ability to move silently had caught me off guard again.

"You're leaving," I said.

"I didn't think you'd object."

The curtains in here were closed, so I took off my sunglasses, cautiously. "I came to thank you for what you did."

His expression shifted. "I didn't do anything."

"Like hell you didn't. I never should have won that hearing."

Ira had sat in the back of the State Bar Commission's hearing room during my testimony. He didn't say anything, but he must have put in a good word for me, because the commission rendered their verdict with only a few minutes of deliberation. I got to keep my law license for the low, low cost of an ethics refresher course and attending six months of psychotherapy. I didn't even have to use a Presence on them.

I almost did anyway because therapy sounded like a brand-new level of hell, but the better angels of my nature had their way this time and I decided to take my lumps. I had a sinking feeling both Sebastian and Danny would be disappointed in me if I didn't, and I didn't want to lie to either of them anymore.

I didn't know how I felt about Ira's involvement. I had looked for him after the hearing, to thank him, but he had already disappeared.

"Oh," he said. "That. You don't owe me thanks for holding up my end of our deal."

"Well, I did switch sides on you."

"Representing Ms. McGuire in a case you investigated is unorthodox. But if there is one thing I've learned about you, it's that you are not in the least orthodox."

"So, you're not mad about it?"

"You completed our contract. What you do afterwards is not my concern." He paused. "Unless, of course, more people get killed. Try to avoid that."

"I'll do my best." People seemed to die around me on a fairly regular basis these days, so I wasn't making any guarantees. "I'm surprised you haven't whisked Rae away for further study."

"We might have," he said, in a tone that hinted at wry. "But given your involvement, we deemed it wiser to leave well enough alone."

Did that mean he still considered me a threat—enough to shift his shadowy agency's responses? "What about the things she told me? About the Tuath De being similar to demons?"

"We're looking into it. There are some intriguing avenues of inquiry in that direction." He came into the room. "That reminds me. I have something for you."

"Oh?" I frowned at the leather case slung over his shoulder. "What is it?"

"Here." He shrugged it off and handed it to me.

Its weight surprised me. I unfastened the straps holding it closed and did a double take. "Ira! Don't you know it's illegal to carry a concealed blade in this state?"

"Perks of government work," he said. "I think you should have this. For safekeeping, as it were."

"Isn't it evidence in the McGuire case?"

"Technically, yes. But they've finished forensics around it, and I wasn't going to let a potential divine weapon float around where any law enforcement yahoo can get their hands on it. We don't want any more incidents of goddess possession."

I closed the case hastily. "I think the goddess is pretty safely bound to Rae."

"You don't know that. And it's clear the sword feeds into her power somehow. Besides, you might need it."

"You're not worried I'll give it back to her?"

"I'm trusting you not to make disappointingly unwise decisions, yes."

"Famous last words." I shouldered the case. "Have you met me?" Rae's magic sword was probably no more than just another deadly weapon I would stow under my bed and then fail to use properly the next time a supernatural bad guy tried to kill me, like Tobias's pistol.

"You're too hard on yourself, Knight. You're impulsive, yes, and you have a bad habit of holding back vital information, but you're smart." He cleared his throat, heading for the stairs. "Besides, where I'm going, it's probably better this artifact stays far away."

"What do you mean?" I hurried after him, clattering down the steps, my aches and pains forgotten for the moment. "Where are you going?"

He shook his head, a ghost of a grin on his face when he glanced up at me from the landing. "Mind your business," he said. "You don't work for me anymore, remember?"

"Ira—" I started to argue, then sighed, letting it go. He waved at me and disappeared down the winding stairs, probably out of my life for good.

I leaned against the curving banister, deflated. Maybe it was better this way. If he didn't think less of me after I agreed to take on Rae as a client, he certainly would after he found out what I planned to do next.

I settled the sword case more firmly on my shoulder. Yes, what I planned would probably make Ira's job harder. It would more than likely blow up my life again, right when I was just getting back on my feet. But I knew deep down in my dark little demon soul that it was the right thing to do.

Besides, my life would become pretty boring if I suddenly got it under control. I wouldn't want to get complacent. I wouldn't even know how to handle that.

"Lily Knight," Tobias said in his most self-important tone. "Thank you for agreeing to come on my show today."

I gave him my coldest fuck-you-too smile. "Thank you so much for having me."

"Before we get into it, you've been involved in a lot of controversies lately, haven't you? And those controversies seem to involve instances of the supernatural. For instance, you were the prosecutor last year when San Francisco's most eligible bachelor, Sebastian Ritter, was accused of murder. His victim turned out to be a demon, didn't she?"

"Careful, Mr. Kaine. Mr. Ritter was cleared of all charges."

"Ah, that's right. And you cleared him, isn't that right?"

"I'd rather not discuss cases that are the purview of the D.A.'s office."

"Of course. Because you no longer work there."

I gritted my teeth. "Yes, that's correct."

"And now you and Mr. Ritter have been seeing each other if Page Six is to be believed. He's going through quite the messy divorce of late, isn't he?"

"My personal life—and his—are our own private business. That's not what I came here to talk about today."

"I'll take that as a yes." Tobias grinned, clearly enjoying this. "Very well. Tell me about your latest case. You're on the other side now, defending Rae McGuire, who is accused of killing a dozen high-profile men over the course of the last six months under very mysterious—one might even say mystical—circumstances. Tell me, how do you live with yourself?"

"My client is innocent," I said, trying my best not to bristle. "The evidence at trial will show that she couldn't have committed those murders."

"And yet, multiple media outlets have reported that she confessed."

"I can't comment on rumors and uncorroborated leaks. That's not what I'm here to discuss either."

"Ah, yes. You did promise me an exclusive. What did you want to talk about, Ms. Knight, since you seem to want to get right to the point?"

I faced him, setting my jaw. "I came here to expose a cover-up that has involved some extremely prominent members of our community and damaged the lives of countless young women. It occurred over nearly a half-century of cover-ups, in a legacy of gendered violence that continues to this day on the campus and in the associated student organizations of San Francisco University."

I laid out the case of the Delta Alpha Mu cover-up for him in detail, leaving out Rae's name and the names of the men the goddess had killed.

"You're saying university administration and alumni knew about this?" Tobias leaned forward, eyes gleaming at the thought of all the views he would get for breaking this scandal, probably. "Aren't you going to name any names?"

"I can name one." I looked straight into the camera this time. "Senator James Ritter." *Sorry, Sebastian.* It was yet another thing I would have to ask him to forgive.

This knocked Tobias back in his chair, which gave me some cold satisfaction. He knew the senator—in fact, the two of them had allied to come after my job at the D.A.'s office, and ultimately succeeded. "That's quite a bombshell of an accusation. I hope you have proof to back it up."

Me, have proof? He was one to talk. "I'm prepared to release the documents I have regarding the activity of the fraternity and their communications with the university. I'd rather let the public decide for themselves."

"That's it?" He scowled. "That's all you have for me today?"

"No." I leaned forward, into the microphone. "I call on Senator Ritter and the rest of the fraternity's board of directors to resign from their posts and public offices immediately. Furthermore, I demand that the university initiate an independent investigation of the fraternity's activity and review all closed cases of assault against students for bias and political influence. I believe there are grounds for a class action lawsuit against the university's regents, and if that should go forward, I think a lot more damaging information will come out."

"That sounds like a threat."

"Consider it an explanation of the potential consequences. The ball is in their court. If they do the right thing now, they might be able to mitigate those consequences. If not..." I shrugged. "The real victims of Delta Alpha Mu might be entitled to a big payout. As far as I'm concerned, it's a win-win situation."

"So, you're in this for the money, then?"

"I'm in this for justice, Mr. Kaine." I shot him another thin smile. "Believe me, I would do this for free. What has happened at that university is absolutely heinous, and what's more heinous is that their inactions allowed abusive men and their enablers, like the senator, to go on and have long, influential careers."

"Some of those men have done a lot of good. You can't deny that."

"And you can't quantify the value of what their victims lost," I countered. "Some of them dropped out of school. At least two ended their own lives. All of them are living with sustained trauma. What about the good they could have done?"

Tobias shifted, his expression uncomfortable. For once, he seemed at a loss for words. "We had a deal, Ms. Knight," he said at last. "Did you forget?"

"I didn't forget," I said quietly. "Are you sure you want me to do this, Tobias?"

His eyes locked with mine over the interview desk. This affected him too, even though he wasn't ready to deal with the public knowing the truth about his own identity. But he was happy to make me the lightning rod. I'd argued this back and forth with him prior to the interview.

In the end, though, I agreed to his terms. This would change my life in ways I couldn't begin to imagine, but it also formed the basis of my case on behalf of Rae McGuire. I couldn't explain to a jury why she deserved to walk away from this if they didn't understand that demons—and other things, like bloodthirsty goddesses—were real, and that one had used Rae's flesh to enact her merciless justice.

There are more things in heaven and earth, little sister...

At Morrighu's remembered words, I shivered a little. Kether hummed under my skin, ready to burst forth. I stood up, backing away from the camera until the producer gave me the nod that said I stood fully in the frame.

"Well, Ms. Knight?" Tobias prompted me. His eyes blazed, eager for the moment of truth. "Did you have something to show us?"

I frowned, hesitating. What was in this for him? Clearly, he was willing to throw me to the wolves for his moment of national—possibly international-al—fame, but he had as much skin in the game as I did. Yet he wanted this revelation. Maybe he was tired of living in the shadows, too. My heart thumped and my stomach lurched as though I stood on a precipice over a bottomless gorge.

But I had no need for a fear of falling, because I could fly. I had wings.

"I do," I said, and unfurled them, stretching them out to their full span. My pinions brushed the edges of the stage lights, setting the shadows to swaying.

The crew gasped. Someone screamed. I dropped my glamours and stared the camera down. I let them see my true face, golden eyes, blue veins, the whole demon enchilada.

No more secrets. No more lies. No more hiding.

Ira was going to be so pissed. Eve would probably never forgive me. But in that moment, exposed for what I really was before the gaze of the whole human world, I had never felt so free.

"This is what I really look like," I said, my voice trembling but clear. "My mother was human, but my father was a demon. The truth is, we've always lived among you. We've shared human joys and endured human darkness. And now, it's time for us to come out of hiding and ask you to consider that we might be people, too."

A weight eased from my chest with the words. I'd carried that secret so long I stopped questioning its drag on my heart. I faced the cameras head-on, and I didn't let them see I was afraid.

Let them hate me if they wanted to. The people who loved me already knew who and what I was.

"My name is Lillian Knight, and I'm a cambion."

28

CUTS BOTH WAYS

A few weeks later, I rode the elevator up to the Ritter Security executive offices alone. No one stopped me, and the high-tech security system seemed to recognize my face. The ascent lasted an eternity. The urban canyon of gray concrete and smoked glass fell away into a panorama view of San Francisco, a slender strip of land barnacled with tight-clustered high-rises and surrounded on three sides by the smooth, bright glass of the ocean. It was morning out there, and the fog had begun to roll back in shreds and dissolve, letting in pale streaks of spring sunlight.

In his office, Sebastian stood by the floor-to-ceiling window, his white dress shirt half-untucked from his slacks, hands in his pockets with his sleeves rolled up to his elbows. His hair had the slightly mussed look it got when he ran his hands through it too many times.

The long, slim lines of his back held more tension than he usually betrayed, and when he turned at my step, his face looked drawn and tired. The divorce proceedings with Helena had only just started, and already the conflict had worn him down, left new shadows around the tight set of his mouth and in the aura only I could see and taste.

Soon, I might not have that privilege. The thought stopped me cold in my tracks and I just stood there for a long moment. I wanted to memorize him like this, shadows and all, the emotions that ran deep below his surface like a subterranean ocean.

If I didn't need him, would I still want him? Would he still want me?

"Lily! I didn't expect you."

"Um, hi." Awkwardness descended on me like a smothering cloud. "How is everything? Your father...?" Senator Ritter had resigned from office after my interview, citing the need to spend more time with his family. Apparently, he had no desire to sit across from me in a deposition.

Sebastian's energy flashed with sudden anger. "I have no idea. I told him I didn't want to speak to him. Not after what he did to silence those women. It's unacceptable."

"I'm really sorry," I said. "I didn't do that interview to hurt you."

"You have nothing to apologize for," he said, tone curt. "It was the right thing to do."

"I'm glad you think so." In the aftermath of my bombshell, I found myself caring a lot more about the fallout. The truth might have freed me, but it still hurt.

"Lily, if you wanted to ask me how I was doing, you could have just called." His desiderata stirred, gathering itself, preparing for the worst. "Is something wrong?"

Guilt stabbed at my core, and I tugged my gloves up, nervous, as I crossed the room to him. "I have something for you," I said, and thrust the box at him.

"What—" Then his whole manner changed, his energy sparking with the sudden brilliance of a roman candle. "This is a ring box."

"It's not a proposal," I said hastily. "Well—not that kind, anyway. Open it. I hope I got the right size."

He frowned, his eyes on me for an endless moment before he cracked open the little velvet box. "I don't understand."

"It's silver," I said. "It will protect you. If you wear it, I won't be able to draw energy from you." I wouldn't be able to sense him, either. But there was no other way to continue this in a way that didn't make me feel like the monster I was. Everything had its price.

He closed the box with a click. "No. I can't. It's too dangerous."

"If the silver brushed my skin, it wouldn't feel great, but it wouldn't kill me. Besides, you can wear a glove if you're that worried about it. It will be fine, I promise. Think about it? Please?"

"All right." He slipped the box into his breast pocket, his face still while his desiderata shuddered with conflict. "But I told you, I don't mind sharing my lifeforce or my life with you. When you gave it all back, I thought—"

"You thought I was trying to break up with you."

"Weren't you?"

"No." My voice cracked. The way he looked at me, his aura aching with the pain he wouldn't show, knocked the air from my lungs. "I want us to be equals, Sebastian. I don't want you bound to me by any supernatural power. I don't know if it's possible, but if you're willing to try it, then so am I."

"And what about your powers, your wings? Wouldn't this mean giving that up?"

"Well, that would be something else to negotiate." Adrenaline cramped my chest, and I drew a long, unsteady breath. "I can go elsewhere for my kether. If I don't return to the same source more than once, I won't be nurturing the same kind of energetic bond. I won't have to worry about—enslaving them or influencing them without thinking about it."

One dark brow arched upward. "I didn't consider myself to be enslaved by you, if that's what you're saying."

"You know what I mean." I bowed my head. "I won't seek kether from others if you're not comfortable with it. I've lived without it before. I can do it again."

"Lily," he said, a warm, rough rumble. He stepped close to me, reaching out as if to cup my chin and raise it, but his fingers halted a half inch away from my skin. His desiderata pulsed around us with the heat of a solar flare, and I lifted my eyes to his. "I don't care who else you sleep with. I don't own you, and you don't own me." A brief half-smile played around his mouth. "No matter what kind of power exchange we engage in, we are equals. We always have been, as far as I'm concerned."

"You really believe that?" I whispered. He had bent his head toward mine, but again, he held himself back, leaving that small gap of space between us. My skin tingled with the heat of his body so close to mine and the promise of his kether. All I had to do was lean forward and press my lips to his.

"And I'll keep saying it as many times as it takes for you to believe it with me."

If he had feared me after I hurt him at the villa, his desiderata showed none of that fear now. It was I who was afraid, of becoming everything Ariel had wanted for me, of taking part in the bond the incubus had tried to place on me. "You're too good to me."

"Stop that." His tone sharpened, plucking a chord of desire in me.

"Stop what?"

"You know what. You're the only person in your life who thinks you're not good enough to be loved."

Love. There was that word again. It lodged in my core with a sharp, sweet pang. "I think you should try that ring on," I mumbled. "See if it fits."

"Oh?" His gray-blue gaze searched my face. "And why is that?"

"Because I'd very much like you to kiss me now without worrying about what kind of damage I might do. I want to see what it's like."

His energy surged around us again in a dizzying wave, and I had to grip his shoulders to steady myself. His warmth singed my fingers through his button-down shirt as he looked down at me with that little quirk of a smile that never failed to disarm me.

"If you insist." He drew the box from his pocket again and took out the little circlet of silver.

Standing as I did in the golden haze of his desiderata, the effect was immediate and shocking. Was this what it was like to go suddenly blind? His energy winked out of my awareness, leaving me bereft.

But no, he hadn't gone anywhere. He was right there in front of me, frowning at me with a hint of concern.

"It's fine," I said. "Put it on."

He slipped it on his finger and closed his fist around it. After a moment's hesitation, he buried that hand in his pocket and stretched out the other to brush my cheek with his fingertips. The pad of his thumb skimmed over my lower lip, and I gasped.

Without the distraction of the kether flow between us, it felt like touching for the first time. The feather-light touch sent a strange tingling heat down my spine that settled in my core. I shuddered, mouth parting under his gentle thumb.

And then he covered my lips with his own, and his tongue swept over mine. That was entirely new too, an unfamiliar sensation, both less and more than what I was used to, hot and wet and overwhelming. I pressed my hips against his, moaning into the kiss, and he wrapped his hand in my hair and gripped the back of my head, holding me still as he explored my mouth with his characteristic intensity and attention to detail. That, at least, hadn't changed one bit.

Maybe I couldn't sense him in the same way, but I still knew him. I could do this. The demon-craving muttered in the back of my mind, restless and dissatisfied, but I pushed her back. She could let me have this one thing, this one man, without tainting our connection with need.

Finally, he pulled back. "Well, counsel? What's your verdict?"

I swallowed hard, mouth suddenly dry. "I think I'd like to review the full body of evidence before I make a case one way or another."

His eyes glittered, watching me. I couldn't tell what he was thinking, a frightening and exciting thought. "Perhaps," he said, "we should declare a recess."

"Sebastian, it's the middle of the day."

"So what?" His grin flashed sudden and brilliant. "They don't need me here. I'm an executive. I don't do anything useful anymore. Besides, it's about to be someone else's problem." He grabbed my hand and pulled me toward the elevator.

"Wait." I dug in my heels. "What do you mean, someone else's problem?"

"I'm selling," he said, as if it didn't mean a thing.

"You're selling the company?"

"That's what I just said. My part of it is inked and done. Now it's all over but the lawyers screaming. No offense."

I stood stock still and stared at him. "But why? You love this place. You built it!"

"Built it? Yes. Love it? No." He glanced around at the glass-lined room. "I'll miss the view, of course. But I won't miss the rest of it. My building phase here stopped a long time ago. And besides, I didn't really have a choice."

"The divorce," I said in a choked voice. "Helena's making you sell it."

He shrugged. "Technically, it's half hers anyway."

"Couldn't you buy out her share?"

"I *could*," he said. "I didn't want to." He came back to where I stood, horror-struck, and caught my hand again, interlacing his fingers with mine. He seemed to take great pleasure in the gesture, maybe because neither of us had to think about the consequences. "Come on, Lily. It's time for us to build something new."

I would have to relearn all his expressions at this rate. "If you're sure."

"I've never been more sure about anything."

I took his palm between my own, raised his knuckles to my lips, and kissed them, marking another new experience. Then we stepped into the elevator and began the long descent back to earth, together.

EPILOGUE

In a nameless fortress, deep underground, a tarnished cage held a monster trapped behind its silver bars.

The silver's touch burned the monster's hands and wrists. While fresh, the burns wept and scabbed over slowly. When they healed at last, they left scars behind, stripes of white and pink and purplish black.

A huge, gnarled scar discolored his chest, too. It lay directly over his heart.

They kept surveillance cameras trained on the cage at all hours, for security and for science. The monster didn't do much to interest them, though. Sometimes he paced the small space, head down, not bothering to hide his eyeshine or his inhuman nature. Sometimes he struck out at the bars, wounding his hands all over again.

Mostly he lay still, barely even breathing, until they came in and poked him with shock sticks to make sure he hadn't died. They drew straws for it. They spoke of it in lowered voices outside, while hunger sharpened his hearing. Whoever drew the short straw had to do the poking.

When roused, the monster would roar in frightening rage. They warned each other never to look in his eyes, and never, ever get close enough to touch him. They stopped up their ears when they entered and wore silver bands around their wrists so his glamours couldn't sway them.

But sometimes the monster had a visitor, and when that happened, they had orders to turn the cameras off.

When the reinforced outer door swung open, the monster stood despite his weakness and swung his head around. He knew her scent, now, the crisp clack of her heels on the floor. She was different from the others. She didn't fear him. She fed him, even though she hated him. Her hatred flowed through his veins like poison, but it was enough to keep him alive. He almost welcomed it now, the scalding scour of it, the way it overran the sick chill of the silver that surrounded him.

It sickened him too, her hatred, but when the sickness left him, his flesh still healed. He didn't know what to make of that, except that deep down, somewhere, some part of her must desire him. The hatred and desire came hand in hand. It was almost enough to make him smile.

The door closed behind her, and she stood looking at him. She still wore her silver armbands, so he couldn't read her, but his nostrils flared, drinking in her scent of gun oil and roses.

Finally, she drew a long breath. "It's been a while, hasn't it? You seem to be holding up better than expected." Her voice was sharp and smooth as a shard of glass.

He bared his teeth. No one had spoken directly to him in a long time. Not since her last visit. How long had it been? He had no idea. There were no clocks in the cage and no calendars. No daylight reached him in this place.

It took time to find a cogent response. The silver addled him. "I've...managed." The words rasped out, his tongue and vocal cords clumsy with disuse.

"Did you miss me?" She smiled, and the poison waited in her eyes for him.

"You know...I did." He lowered his head. She wanted his acquiescence, and he could give her what she wanted. For now.

A soft clink of metal reached his ears, a click as she released the hidden catches on her bracelets. She took them off, tucked them into her coat pocket. She had a gun, too, in a holster beneath the coat, loaded with silver slugs. He knew all this, and yet his entire being strained toward her.

She approached his cage, her steps measured and slow. She looked wary as always, moving with the trained, efficient grace of a combat-ready soldier. But with the silver away from her skin, he could sense her desiderata. It hung thick and heavy around her like the harsh, heady, bittersweet smoke of an opium den.

He forced himself to wait. It wouldn't do to go to her. Besides, he'd only hurt himself with the bars between them.

Instead of unlocking the cage door, she stopped in front of it, hands buried in her pockets. Her aura abruptly switched off as she fingered the bracelets inside. The loss of its siren song left him hollow inside, echoing and cavernous. He shuddered.

"I found out something interesting," she said.

"Did you, now?" He meant it to sound light, uncaring, but some hint of the emptiness within still made its way into the question.

"Indeed." When he said nothing more, she pressed her thumb to the biometric lock. The door slid open, and she stepped inside. He stiffened, every muscle on alert. The door closed behind her. Her aura flooded the small space between them, the heat of her flickering against the bare skin of his ruined chest.

He stepped toward her and the chain around his ankle pulled taut. He'd forgotten about the chain. He waited again with his head bowed. She did this on purpose. He could feel her satisfaction pulse around her. She got pleasure from breaking a monster like a wild stallion.

Well, he could work with that.

When she touched him, laying her hand upon the ugly scar over his heart, her energy hit him like a punch in the sternum. He staggered. She took his head between her palms and forced him to his knees, tilting his face up, forcing him to look into her eyes.

It was her first mistake, but in his bones, he knew it wouldn't be her last.

"Don't you want to know?" she said.

Her loathing seared through him, and he met her gaze, biding his time, gleaning strength from the sickness. "Do I have a choice?"

"No." She gave him a viper's smile, dripping with venom.

Someone once told him everyone had a choice. She'd said it right before she betrayed him. He held the memory of that betrayal close as he held himself in check. "Tell me, then."

She released him, a little late. When she stepped back, it was almost a stumble. "I know you have a daughter."

On his knees, her poison suffusing his awareness, he couldn't catch his breath. Of all the things she could have said, he never expected that. He whispered, "What?"

"She looks like you." Her laugh cut like a whip. "And what do you know? It turns out silver hurts her, too."

He lunged for her. She must have enjoyed her power over him too much, because she'd given him more than she meant to give. It would be her last mistake.

The chain snapped like twine, and he was faster than her now. He caught her by the throat. "*What did you do?*"

Her energy washed over him in waves, fear and hatred and desire blending into a powerful cocktail that he drank down thirstily. "I didn't...she's..." She grasped at his hands, scrabbling for purchase.

"Don't lie to me."

"I'm...not! Lily...Knight has her! I swear...it."

Lily. Of course, it was Lily, his traitor, his doom. He had what he needed, now. He tossed his tormenter away from him. Her body hit the bars of the cage and she slid to the floor, limp, her aura ebbing.

His head spun with the tainted kether he'd taken from her, but he'd built up tolerance to it over his months in captivity. He reached around her, found her gun, and slipped it out of its hidden holster. Then he grabbed her wrist and dragged her hand upward, pressing her thumb to the cage door to activate the lock.

When it opened, he stepped out over her still body. Turning, he kicked her back into the cell. The door slid shut.

Ariel smiled, a painful stretch of chapped lips that nevertheless felt as good as her poisonous essence simmering in his veins.

"Goodbye, Agent North," he said. "I hope you enjoyed this visit as much as I did."

Acknowledgements

To my editor, Heather McCorkle, thank you for believing in my writing. Your editorial insights took this book to the next level. I'm incredibly grateful for your patience, hard work, and ongoing support. And thank you to my fellow indie authors who have provided much needed pep talks, advice, community, and friendship. It's an honor to know all of you and get to read your amazing work!

To Ren Hutchings and the Chaos Bakery, I'm so lucky to count you all as friends and colleagues, and I can't wait to see what you all do next. Ren, you have grounded me through some tough times in the past year even while embarking on your own debut year journey—your generosity and positivity is a beacon for me. And to all the creative communities who nurtured me over the years: without you I would never have started down this path.

Big love to the Cool Kids Table, thanks for letting me sit with you! You're a light in the wilderness of the Internet and I wish every one of you all the celebratory octopuses for your brilliant talent. To my G-squad, thanks for sticking with me and standing up for me. And to my 2020 Pitch Wars crew and the devotees of Hellmo's Temple—S.A. Simon, Briana Una McGuckin, Rosalie Lin, Samantha Elden, and Sarah Codair, among others—thanks for helping me stay accountable, cheering me on, and sharing the highs and lows of this journey.

To my dear CP Mel, I still can't thank you enough for being my CP, always having my back, getting my humor, and loving on my work. To Keir Alekseii—you're a certified badass, a great listener, a fabulous hype woman, and a true friend. To Talhe, thank you for being the world's fastest and most generous beta—your thoughtful feedback is essential. And to all of my found family and friends, writing and otherwise, I appreciate you more than you know.

Finally, I want to thank my husband, Jake, for being my first reader, my best friend, my most loyal cheerleader, and my safe place. Favorite and best beloved Bear, you make me a better person every day. Thank you for loving my muchness in a way that gives me the strength and freedom to chase my dreams.

Coming soon...

Read on for a sneak preview of Cambion Book 3!

Lily Knight has faced demons, gods, and the monster inside her.

Her truth set her free...but the consequences might just damn her.

The future looks bright for Lily since she defeated alpha-hole incubus Ariel and went public as a half-succubus cambion. Despite her best efforts to avoid it, she's even started therapy.

It's risky enough negotiating the perils of newfound family, ancient fey powers, and romantic non-monogamy with human beau Sebastian, let alone not-so-platonic feelings for her engaged best friend. But the new normal becomes her worst nightmare when a selkie woman stirs painful memories for Lily. Plunged into a deadly chase across the city's piers and rooftops, Lily finds herself set up to take the fall.

Now, she must clear her name before she's trapped in a silver cage—or leave her life and loves behind, forever.

Cambion's Rise

Chapter 1 - Get Your Demon On

The Black Cat Club pulsed with the sweet promise of human desire laid over a hard industrial bass line, its deep rhythm fueling an urge in me to get my demon on. I rolled my shoulders to settle the electric hunger curling up my spine and handed my best friend her drink. The demon inside could wait, for now.

"Are you sure you're OK with this?" I slid into the upper-level booth next to Danny, leaning in close so she could hear me over the throbbing music and general clamor.

Danny cut a sparkling sideways glance at me over a long sip of her margarita. "Please, Lily. I've been bugging you to let me tag along for months."

Her brilliant smile sought to reassure me, but a discordant spike in her personal energy signature—her desiderata—snagged my succubus senses. My friend had something on her mind, whether or not she wanted to admit it.

"I don't need to do this tonight. We can just hang out instead." In fact, I preferred to hunt for kether—the human life energy my demon side craved—alone and unobserved, but the friendship 911 code she'd sent me via text earlier in the day meant DEFCON 1: *this is not a test, do not ignore, do not decline requests for a night out on the town.*

Thanks to the demands of my latest case—defending a woman possessed by a murderous goddess—and the stress of planning what Danny called her Big Fat Lesbian Wedding, we hadn't spent much time together lately. So tonight I'd made an exception to my normal procedure and invited Danny along to act as my wing woman, even though I hardly needed one.

I had my own wings, after all.

"I'm not here to cramp your style," she said. "Let me live vicariously for one night. That's all I want."

"If you say so."

She groaned. "Don't look at me in that tone of voice."

"Then talk to me." I sipped my own drink, whiskey and ginger, savoring the way it blended with the smoky cinnamon of Danny's desiderata. "That's what a best ma'am is for, you know."

Danny looked away, her energy swirling with a burnt caramel tang on the verge of an unfamiliar bitterness. "I'd rather help you find your next one-night stand."

I frowned at the edge in her words and the sudden heat flaring around her in my second sight. "Gotta say, you seem less than thrilled."

Was Danny *jealous*? Maybe she missed single life. She'd played the field with gusto before Berry came along, but threw herself into commitment with equal enthusiasm and no sign of regret—until now.

"Quit reading me." Danny's jaw tightened, her restless gaze scanning the dance floor. "It's not fair."

"I literally can't help it," I said, stung. "And I told you how to stop it if you really wanted to." If she wore silver, like the ring I'd gifted to my lover, Sebastian, she could hide her energy from me. So far, though, she'd resisted my advice to invest in protective jewelry with surprising vehemence.

On the other hand, I'd miss her aura if I couldn't read it anymore. I missed Sebastian's too at times, though his new unreadability had a certain sexiness to it that left me craving more of him whenever we parted.

"I'm sorry." Danny's warm brown eyes, dark and pleading, finally met mine. "I want to have fun tonight. No serious stuff. Like old times."

I laughed despite the sudden crackle of tension in her gaze. "What, all our old times clubbing together? Dan, that never happened!"

"I know." She chuckled, the current in the air between us dissipating as fast as it had gathered. "We were too damn busy studying."

Danny and I met when she advertised for a roommate and got a demon instead. With her in med school and me in law school, our all-nighters together involved a lot more caffeine than booze. Back then, nightlife reminded me too much of where I came from, my old life in New York with my fallen mentor Ariel whispering in my ear, guiding me into ever more boundary-pushing exploits with the partners he selected for me.

But things were different now. Ariel was out of the picture, I'd gotten my wings, and with Sebastian's blessing I could seek casual liaisons to explore my half-demon need for the energy of human emotion and pleasure. I couldn't protect any partner from the soul bond that sprang from my touch, but if I kept my encounters short, sweet, and singular, I could safely stay the one who got away.

So far, so good. I hadn't killed anyone yet, and I called that a win.

Hadn't killed anyone *else*, at least.

"Well, here's to fun." I raised my drink.

"I'll drink to that." Danny clinked her margarita against my copper mug, careful not to brush her fingers against mine. "Go on, tell me. Who do you have your eye on tonight, Sugarbean?"

"I've hardly looked." Other than Danny's warm aura close beside me, no one's desiderata had captured my attention. Indulging her, I let my senses widen into the space.

"What about him?" She nudged my elbow, pointing down at the dance floor.

My long-sleeved blouse shielded her skin from mine, but I tensed anyway, on guard against stray touches. "Who?"

"That tall boy on the dance floor, with the corset and the eyeliner."

"I'm probably not his type."

"Oh, please. Don't tell me your bi-dar is that bad." She smirked. Intoxication had slowed the turmoil in her aura to a lazy, heated swell.

"He *is* pretty," I conceded. "Hm. Sweet and insubstantial, like meringue, but he'd do in a pinch."

"Picky, picky."

"I'm trying to eat healthy."

She snorted with laughter, which I counted as a win. "Don't be crass."

"Pot, this is kettle. You're the one in the gutter."

"It's fun here. Join me." Danny knocked back the rest of her drink, eyes alight. "You know, for a succubus, you're kind of a prude."

"Hey, give me some credit. I'm the one on the make here."

"I'll give you that. You've come a long way." Her energy rippled around us, her voice softening. "I'm proud of you, Sugarbean."

"Thanks, I think." Sweet cinnamon haunted my tongue. Mouth suddenly dry, I took another hasty sip of my Irish Mule.

Maybe I'd made a mistake, bringing Danny here and buying her tequila with my hunger on the rise. We had a history of near-misses and stray touches, including one ill-advised kiss long ago that left us soul-bound without knowing it. I'd released the bond in the process of saving her life, almost a year ago now, but tonight that history seemed more present than past.

"I mean it," Danny said. Then, with a wink, she added, "How about that one?"

This time, I knew who she meant immediately. The girl had taken the dance floor as we talked, long dark braids swinging around her in time to her graceful, fluid movements. "Not bad," I admitted. "Much better, actually."

"I thought so." Danny pushed me out of the booth. "Go get her, tiger. I need another drink."

"Dan. Wait." I caught her upper arm, gloved hand over her jacket, but still she froze, eyes dark and wild as they met mine.

Her aura flared around us with the blue fire of ignited alcohol. "Yes, Lily?"

Damn, I made it worse. I dropped her arm as though the halo in my second sight had burned me. "Nothing. I wish you'd tell me what's going on with you."

"I'm sorry." The flame of her desiderata waned, ebbing to a faintly glowing ember. "I'm bringing the bad vibes. I should probably head home."

"No. Stay. Talk." I patted the seat. "And stop apologizing. I love your vibes, Danny Rios. Even when they're weird as hell."

"You're sweet, Sugarbean." She grimaced, then sighed. "Fine. But I really do need another drink for this."

"I've got you." I wasn't above using my supernatural powers to summon a bartender for a friend in need. I dragged her back to our table and re-supplied her before she could change her mind. "There. Now stop stalling and fess up. Is this about wedding stuff?"

Danny slumped into the corner of the booth, drawing one black jeans-clad knee up to her chest, the picture of resignation. "It's Berry's family again. They're having a fit over…well. It doesn't matter."

"Doesn't it?"

She made a face. "You're reading me again, aren't you?"

"It's who I am. What are they upset about this time?"

She swallowed a gulp of her fresh margarita, then gazed into its depths as if it offered a way out of the truth she didn't want to tell. "Her father is concerned about, um, the wedding party."

They'd decided to keep the party small, just me on Danny's side and Berry's sister on hers, with my teenage ward, Eve, handling the rings and flowers. "What, is he upset that you have a best ma'am and not a best man?"

"Something like that." Danny's tone turned fierce. "I told you, it doesn't matter. It's my goddamn wedding and I'm going to have you at my side."

"I could pull off a drag king look. Get Sebastian's tailor on it. Go all out—" I broke off at her expression, something between intrigue and panic. "Or not."

Her aura flickered brighter, then dimmed again. "Gender isn't the issue, Lily."

My gut twisted. "*Oh*. Shit. They saw the interview." The response to my public "coming out" as half-demon had surprised me—or rather, the non-response had. A few fundamentalist groups worked themselves into a righteous tizzy on the Internet, but the world at large talked it up for a day or so before giving a collective shrug. My earth-shaking revelation became a weird news item, and everyone else went on with life.

"Apparently her dad draws the line at having a demon *in* the wedding."

I hadn't expected to escape with no consequences at all, but I didn't think about how it might affect my friend's life. "When you put it that way, I can't exactly blame him."

"I can blame him plenty," Danny said, staunchly loyal but not entirely honest.

"I don't have to be in the wedding, Dan. I won't be offended."

"Well, I will," Danny said. "I don't care what else you are. You're my best friend, and I want you there."

"Then I'll do my best to wear him down with my preternatural charm." Ethically questionable, but I could justify using my powers in the name of familial harmony.

"That's..." Danny laughed. "Actually, not a bad idea. Maybe we can all have dinner together."

"I'll polish my halo for the occasion." I downed my drink. "There, that wasn't so hard, was it? Feeling better?"

"A little," Danny slurred. "Tipsy."

"You were tipsy before. Now you're tequila drunk." I slid out of the booth. "I'll get you some water. Stay here."

"Staying." Danny leaned her head back on the booth and shut her eyes. "Ooh. Spinnies."

Great. At this rate I would have to carry her home, which might end badly for both of us. Shaking my head, I headed for the bar, then halted mid-step. Prickles of ice crept along my spine and raised the small hairs on the back of my neck.

I scanned the dim, crowded recesses of the club's balcony, gripping the wood of the railing until it groaned and cracked. Alarmed, I let go and wiped my damp palms on the miniskirt barely covering my thighs. The railing didn't fall apart but looked somewhat the worse for wear.

Maybe I'd imagined it, but in my periphery, I could have sworn someone had leaned elbows on the railing across the open space that looked over the dance floor below, golden head turning to track me. I could have sworn that they had broad shoulders and a long coat that flared around them like dark wings, their absence of desiderata like a black hole in the club's shimmering human energy. And their face—I knew that face as well as I knew my own. It still haunted my dreams, the face of someone I'd loved and feared and murdered.

Someone impossible.

Water, I needed water for Danny and something stronger for myself. My pulse raced erratically in my ears, and I succubused my way to the front of the drink line, only half-aware of the humans who stepped aside to let me pass.

Clutching a neat whiskey and a water bottle icy as the adrenaline in my veins, I raced back to our booth. Danny was still there, slumped in the back corner with her eyes closed.

"Hey. You alive over there?" I scooted in. When she didn't answer immediately, I shook her shoulder hard in a sudden panic.

She jerked upright and relief bloomed in my chest. "I'm fine," she mumbled. "Just resting my eyes."

"Sure you are." I twisted open the water bottle, shoving it at her. "Drink this, or Berry will have my hide."

"Sweet Berry? Never." Danny swigged the water, then squinted at me. "What's wrong?"

"Nothing."

"Liar. You look spooked."

I swallowed half the contents of my glass. I couldn't get drunk so easily, but the whiskey burn blunted the chill rising within me. "I thought I saw someone I knew, that's all."

"You know people?" Danny guffawed, then hiccupped. "Damn it."

"That's what you get for being a jerk. Drink your water, lightweight."

"Lowered tolerance is a hazard of almost-married life. Would it be so bad, running into someone you know here?"

"It might be." Surreptitiously, I scanned the other balcony again, but no one stood watching me there. Probably no one had stood watching at all, except in my traitorous mind. "I'd rather avoid repeat customers. It keeps the soul-bonding to a minimum."

Danny set her half-finished water bottle on the table. "Lil, being bound by you isn't the huge burden you make it out to be." She paused. "Oops. Didn't mean to make that sound kinky."

Her aura blazed with notes of caramel and cinnamon that did more than the whiskey to distract me from my nightmarish imagination. I swallowed hard as she edged closer. "Danny, you're drunk."

"Yeah, I am. Super drunk." Her hand found mine, bare fingers with short-clipped nails interlacing with my gloved ones. "All I'm saying is, not everyone would mind it. Some might even—"

"Hush." Gently, I peeled her fingers from mine. "Come on. Let's get you home to your bed and your fiancée, shall we?"

"That's probably smart." She sank away from me into the corner of the bench, scrubbing her hands over her face. "I don't know what I—forgive me."

"There's nothing to forgive." I helped her out of the booth, steadying her with a hand on her upper arm. If she shivered at the touch, we both pretended to ignore it. "That's what friends are for."

"Hey, Lily," she said as I steered her toward the stairs. "Who did you think you saw back there?"

Between the whiskey, her eyes, and the sweet fire that had surged around us, I had almost managed to forget. "Nobody. It was nobody."

We made our slow way downstairs, Danny leaning heavily on me, but the unspoken truth hung leaden under my ribs.

Even now, after all I'd done to get away, some part of me still expected to see *him*. My mentor. The demon I'd killed. Some sick place in me still looked for that flash of gold, that preternatural grace, that cruel mouth in a beautiful face with its smirk sharp enough to shatter me. Something in me believed he would come back and come after me.

Something in me still waited for him to ruin me all over again.

About the Author

Erin Fulmer is a legal aid attorney by day, author of urban fantasy and science fiction by night. She lives in California's Central Valley with her husband and two spoiled cats named after famous dragons. When she's not writing or working, she enjoys soaking in nature, taking pictures of the sky, playing nerdy games, and napping like it's an Olympic sport.

Read more from Erin at her website where she occasionally blogs about writing, publishing, and mental health. She can also be found on Instagram, Threads, Tumblr, Facebook, or TikTok.